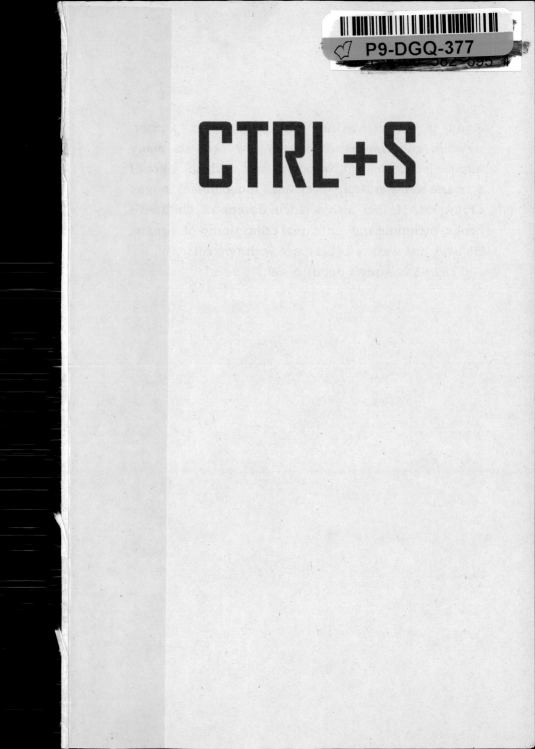

CTRL+S

Andy is a screenwriter, graphic novelist, author, traveller and conservationist. He's worked on many film projects, from Hollywood movies with the likes of Stan Lee to his critically acclaimed independent movie, *Crowhurst*. He has also written dozens of children's books, including the centennial reimagining of *Tarzan*. He lives just west of cyberspace with two cats.

CTRL+S is Andy's debut novel.

CTRL+S

ANDY BRIGGS

ORION

An Orion paperback

First published in Great Britain in 2019
by Orion Fiction,
This paperback edition published in 2019
by Orion Fiction,
an imprint of The Orion Publishing Group Ltd.,
Carmelite House, 50 Victoria Embankment
London EC4Y 0DZ

An Hachette UK Company

1 3 5 7 9 10 8 6 4 2

A CIP catalogue record for this book
is available from the British Library.

ISBN (Paperback) 978 1 4091 8465 2

Typeset by Deltatype Ltd, Birkenhead, Merseyside

Printed in Great Britain by Clays Ltd, Elcograf S.p.A.

www.orionbooks.co.uk

'All that we see or seem is but a dream within a dream.'
Edgar Allan Poe

Chapter One

The distinctive ammonia stench of approaching death told Theo everything he needed to know about today.

Thursdays were officially crap.

He gripped the stock of his BFG1138 assault rifle tighter. The carbon fibre felt smooth beneath his fingers, and refreshingly cool in the oppressive jungle humidity. Sucking in a sharp breath, he studied the lush crimson foliage that stretched upwards with such hunger it blotted the azure sky, allowing only thick spears of light to puncture the canopy.

A flock of reptilian parrots suddenly took flight with a warbling alarm call. Their silly circular wings frantically sliced through the air like paddle steamers as they detected an unseen threat. Theo's heart hammered in his chest. He flinched when Baxter bumped him from behind as the team clustered together back to back, facing the four avenues that stretched through the trees before them. Archways carved from the colossal trunks, each large enough to swallow a bus and dark enough to conceal death.

'You better pray you don't get out of this alive, Milton,'

Baxter growled at the towering barbarian next to him. He wobbled his machete for emphasis. Blue veins etched across the blade throbbed as if it were alive. 'Or this'll be going on a colonic adventure up your—' He did a double take. 'Where the hell's your rifle?'

'I d-dropped it,' stammered Milton.

He was the fool responsible for leading them down a mud chute that pitched them off the clifftop and into this hellhole of a crater. The six-foot-something barbarian cracked his knuckles, raising his fists and cycling them pathetically.

'But I'm ready.'

'You're a moron!'

'Boys? Oh, boys?' sang Clemmie in a voice at odds with the overlapping blood-red plate mail armour encompassing her mountainous body. Her helmet had a single shallow-angled V-shaped slit, hiding her face. 'We are on time crisis.'

She tapped a countdown on her wrist gauntlet; the basic red LEDs resembled an antique digital alarm clock face. It had already run over the ninety second mark.

'Bollocks!' exclaimed Theo. 'How did that happen?'

'I thought you were keeping an eye on it,' Baxter added, eyes darting nervously back to the tunnel in front of him.

'I don't know,' Clemmie growled, deliberately nudging her elbow into the armour protecting Baxter's kidneys. 'You lost track of time too.'

'Maybe it's broken?' said Milton hopefully. 'That last magic field might have crashed it. Nothing's working properly. This place is as buggy as hell,' he added, swatting at a fist-sized mosquito as it buzzed past him, its hypodermic syringe nose wagging threateningly.

Theo sensed all the effort they'd piled into this quest was about to unravel.

'Keep it together, guys. We manage to get through one of these tunnels alive and that's it.'

Salvation.

They couldn't afford to die now – but in less than one minute they would be ejected. And there was nothing worse than that. Well, almost nothing.

There was a sudden rush of movement from the tree in front of Baxter, accompanied by a strong waft of a bitter acid that made them all retch, as a screaming beast emerged. Standing twelve feet tall, the Tracyon was a combination of a ferocious dinosaur and a shark. The quadruped raced into the clearing at full pelt. A pair of laser cannons held by leather straps on its shoulder blades unleashed streams of green plasma that tore apart the dead wood around them. The monster unhinged its jaw and bellowed thick phlegm.

Theo tried not to inhale. The rank miasma was one of the Tracyon's basic defences. He retaliated with a war cry, and unleashed his assault rifle's fury.

'Come on! This is it!'

A well-placed shot from Clemmie blew one of the beast's cannons apart. The explosion ripped a chunk of the creature's shoulder off, forcing it to stumble sideways, narrowly missing crushing Milton, who had been attempting to sneak around it.

The Tracyon angled its body, flipping around a mighty tail barbed with a pair of jagged blades made from razor-sharp cartilage. They struck Milton in a powerful scissor motion.

'Christ!' Baxter yelled as Milton was cut in two.

Red mist sprayed the remaining three warriors as they scattered in different directions. There was no sense of co-ordination – just raw survival instinct powered them now.

Theo ignored the pounding of a laser weapon to his left. He presumed it was Clemmie; she was a pit bull and he hoped her brave actions would buy him enough time to circle around the monster and slip into the tunnel.

He panicked as he stumbled over Milton's still-twitching torso, slipping on the torrent of blood oozing out of his friend. His arms flailed as he caught his balance, but at the expense of his rifle.

Sod it. There was no time to retrieve it. A flicker of light in the tunnel revealed a glowing egg-shaped orb. The plasma on its surface rippled beguilingly.

The prize.

Everything they had been working towards this last week was almost within reach. He ignored a scream from behind him – that was Clemmie down – and raced for the orb. Then Baxter was suddenly beside him, racing for the prize. He shouldered Theo, propelling him towards the monster as bait. Theo's knee painfully cracked against the floor as he fell, the kneecap shattering on a jagged rock as it took his full weight.

A bass-heavy chime suddenly sounded and a voice reverberated inside his skull.

'Ejection protocol initiated. Prepare to sink.'

Distracted, Theo didn't notice the Tracyon catch up with him. Its expanding jaws, lined with six rows of serrated teeth, filled his vision. The last thing he felt was the powerful blow either side of his ribcage as the monster effortlessly chomped him in half.

The world around him rapidly dissolved into the familiar drabness of his living room. It took a few seconds for his senses to kick in. The stale smell of the flat assaulted him; scent was the first sense to go when ascending from The Real into the virtual, and the last to kick in when returning.

Rapid ejection from SPACE sometimes caused brief but intense nausea, and Theo's stomach was telling him it was his turn. He yanked his headset off and wiped the thin beads of sweat from his brow. He had to close his eyes moment-arily as the room swam around him and he fought to keep down the Marmite sandwich in his stomach.

He was alone; his friends were back in their respective homes, he hoped also throwing up on their bedroom fur-nishings. Feeling irritable, he filled a coffee-stained mug with lukewarm water from the tap and downed half in one continuous gulp, wincing at the chemical taste it left in his mouth. Being in SPACE for the maximum three hours had really taken it out of him. He gazed through the kitchen window, squinting against the bright sunlight reflecting off the carbon copy array of tower blocks. Somehow it didn't look quite as vibrant as the virtual world. Then again, he mused, that was the point of the mandatory time limit. To get people outside before their brains fried from being plugged into the system for too long.

He sighed. Where was the fun in that?

Chapter Two

The sizzle of meat made Theo's stomach twitch. He'd had a very different vision for his future than the reality thrust upon him: one where his dad was around; one in which he was having an awesome time in university, with more real-world sex than lectures. Life wasn't supposed to be like *this*. Where were all the opportunities? The flying cars? And what had happened to robots taking over jobs so he wouldn't have to toss burgers in a dump like this?

Whatever had happened to the dreaded singularity, when AI would turn the toaster into mankind's robot overlord? Yet another future prediction that was wildly askew from the facts, robbing his future of any possible thrills or adventures.

'Four cheese – extra cheese, no greens,' Wayne called from the counter.

Theo glanced at the customers, who looked almost as greasy as the synthetic meat patties he was preparing.

He had never envisioned working in such a menial job, especially in a place that prided itself on serving up burgers that have never seen a real animal – or vegetable – but had been grown in Petri dishes, then printed into burger-shaped patties straight on the griddle. Despite that, *Synger* was London's trendiest synthetic eatery, and since leaving college it was the only job he was able to get. All dreams of being an engineer were stomped on the moment his mother had announced she was struggling to pay the bills. And since it was just the two of them, what choice did he have?

He watched the genetically engineered proteins turn the burgers a perfect shade of brown in a minute. On autopilot, he dropped slices of substitute cheese – which had no direct genetic bovine link – on them before sliding them onto the waiting wheat-free buns. Kerry, the girl next in the chain, wrapped them in neat paper bundles and added the fries; they at least were real. The entire operation from order to delivery took sixty seconds. The very definition of fast food.

He glanced through the serving hatch as three familiar figures entered and headed for a corner table that had just become vacant. Theo took off his apron and tossed it to Kerry.

'I'm going on my break.'

He hurried from the kitchen before she could object.

'Hey! Morons!' Theo said, extending his arms in welcome to the newcomers.

Milton and Clemmie treated him to a subtle nod of the head in reciprocation.

Baxter glanced at his wrist, where his never-worn smartwatch would have been.

'Twenty seconds and the insults are already flying. What kind of welcome is this for your mates?'

Theo sat on the thin wedge of exposed bench Clemmie

had left vacant, and tried to ignore the warmth of her thigh.

'Mates who are only here to eat using my free vouchers – of which I have none left, by the way.'

Baxter slapped his palms on the table.

'Then that's me out. I'm not paying to eat this rubbish.'

Theo ignored him. 'That was such a dick move you pulled in the game.'

He shoved Baxter's arm off the table. Unlike their avatars in the game they were the same height, but Theo's slight frame was far less intimidating. Still, they'd known each other since primary school – seen one another grow, jump at shadows and vomit in sandpits – so there was zero Baxter could do to intimidate him.

Baxter caught Milton's eye and automatically targeted him instead. His shapeless mass of auburn hair, gangly build and nervous reflexes marked him as the card-carrying nerd he was.

Baxter stabbed a finger in Milton's direction.

'Because that wanker led us into the crater, and he even lost his weapon. What the hell are you good for, mate?'

'I meant all of you!' snapped Theo.

He looked between the scowling boys. Only Clemmie was uninterested, toying with her olive-green military satchel bedecked with characters copied from popular games and movies. She had a passion for the antique classics: Donkey Kong, Pac-Man, Space Invaders ...

'You all ditched me!'

Clemmie gave a loud, deliberate snort. 'You were going to die anyway, rushing in like that. And we were seconds away from ejection.'

She slid her rig from the satchel and put it on. Wearing headsets in public was as ubiquitous as glasses or shades, so nobody would give her a second glance. The device instantly activated in AR – augmented reality – mode, allowing her to see the world around her as high-definition lasers projected social media feeds on to the transparent curved glass visor, seamlessly blending them with reality.

AR was considered safe, so wasn't subject to the same time constrains that SPACE immersion was. Without the emotional link, the psychological and physical toll couldn't mess you up, but its scope was limited to real-world inter-action. Even so, Clemmie's attention was already lost online.

Theo looked obliquely at her, willing his temper to main-tain boiling point, but instead it evaporated. The fringe of Clemmie's bobbed black hair clung to her sweaty brow, framing her perfectly fused Pakistani and Middle Eastern ancestry. Her dark, almond-shaped eyes flickered across the images reflected on the visor.

'Face facts, we all cocked up,' she sighed in a distracted tone.

Theo held up his finger and thumb a fraction apart.

'I was *this* close to the orb.' He shot a look at Baxter. 'Until this dickhead tripped me.'

'What does that matter?' Milton shrugged. 'We died, which means we go back to the beginning, folks. We failed level one. Level *one* – do you know how sad that is for some-body like me?'

Nobody wanted to admit it, but he was right. They had been playing the new *Avasta* module for months as a team – or, as Milton often commented, as a collection of individuals who happened to be heading to the same place.

The early part of the level had many save points so players could enjoy a feeling of rapid progress, but as the game continued such safety anchors grew steadily further apart, providing just enough content for players to stretch the statutory daily limit.

'How did we eat up all that time?' Theo asked, in a deliberate move to assuage everybody's irritation. With the group's limited attention spans, it was an easy task to accomplish.

Milton counted on his fingers. 'We played past midnight last night. That was over an hour. Then this morning *Captain Can't Wait* –' he jerked his head towards Theo – 'said we should make a push for the orb so we ended up in that jungle hellhole.'

It all totalled up to ensure none of them could enter SPACE again for another twenty-four hours.

'You guys want to reconvene at mine tomorrow night?' said Theo, hoping that Clemmie at least would agree. 'I've got another shift here and Baxter's got his ... thing.'

'Yours? I dunno, mate. I'm allergic to the smell of your mum's vape and booze,' Baxter sneered.

Theo pulled a face, but couldn't summon up the enthusiasm to defend something so deeply rooted in fact.

'Clem?'

Clemmie gave a shrug. 'Maybe. But forget *Avasta*? I'd rather just hang in SPACE.'

Milton shrugged. 'I've got nothing better to do.'

Like Clemmie and Baxter, Milton was on summer break from uni, the only time the four of them were able to enjoy time together in the flesh. But the reality was they had all drifted apart since leaving college and these days tended to see more of each other virtually than in the flesh.

Theo nodded, glancing around the increasingly busy restaurant. It was easy to see why SPACE was a lure to avoid reality. He often fantasised about staying in the virtual world to live out the rest of his life in hedonistic escapism. Who would want reality when it looked like this?

Chapter Three

Theo rolled his thumb in a small circle between his eyebrows, attempting to knead the growing pain away. After his shift in *Synger* his migraine had crept back and wasn't helped by the thrashing rock music blaring from the living room, which punched his ears the moment he opened the front door.

'Christ ... Mum?' he called out. 'Mum?'

The living room door was closed and he wanted nothing more than to go straight to bed. He stepped into his bedroom and tossed his bag into the corner. He took off his rig and rubbed his eyes with the back of his hand as he debated whether to try to ride out the noise. He glanced at the peeling posters covering every inch of wall space: his favourite films and bands, many of which had been up for a decade, from the original *Avasta* to *Star Trek: The Final Generation*.

It was time for a change of taste, he thought, rather than cling on to his youth. Maybe Clemmie was right about the game. Was twenty too old? Why did reality have a way of sharpening its claws on your aspirations and pleasures? He took a deep breath and closed his eyes, as pain ping-ponged between his temples.

Like most kids, when he'd first experienced SPACE Theo had pushed the boundaries, and in those days automatic ejection hadn't yet been implemented. He had developed persistent migraines, one of the small percentage of Spacers who experienced prolonged side effects. He blamed his mum, of course. She was irresponsible and he shouldn't have been left alone at such a delicate age, but he supposed she had to work to support them both. He reasoned that head pain was better than suffering the other side effects of prolonged exposure: a crippling cerebral haemorrhage accompanied by a painful death, or – best case – permanent, crippling nerve damage known colloquially as *Lag*.

Lag was particularly unpleasant. A weird drunken feeling of wanting to move while your virtual body refused to, only for it to unexpectedly do so moments later when you'd already given up on the action, resulting in zero co-ordination and painful conflicting signals fizzling the brain's neural pathways. Worse, it was caused by the wetware interface between the machine and the mind effectively filing down the motor neurons controlling movement, so that the lag sensation was replicated in the real world and often led to paralysis.

'Ella!' Theo yelled over the music, the sound of his own voice rattling further shocks of pain around his skull. 'Can you turn it down? I need to sleep!' There was no response. 'For Christ's sake, Mum! Turn it down!'

He gently scratched the etched metallic silver winking emoji on his rig's stem, tracing its comical lolling tongue. It was the logo for Emotive, the megacorporation that had, with the help of international governments, created SPACE.

They had pioneered the interface that finally bridged the gap between the virtual and the emotional: Emo-tech.

James Lewinsky, the genius behind Emotive, pioneered affective computing from beyond the usual artificial emotions and machine learning to generating genuine *artificial emotions* and feeding them back to users: *SPecially Adaptive Chemical Emotions*.

That had started the SPACE revolution.

Even with photorealistic graphics, projected directly on to the retina by high-def lasers, there was still an uncanny valley between the physical and virtual worlds. Lewinsky had realised that the emotional connection the virtual world lacked had been hiding in plain sight for decades.

Emoticons.

Tagged at the end of messages to perk up dry text and convey an extra layer of meaning, emoji evolved from faces to items – cake, clapperboards, pizza, intimidatingly large aubergines – anything that would generate an emotional response from the reader. Within a few years, it had become the fastest growing language in history. Then emoji development had stalled – animation, audio, each a step in the wrong direction, nothing more than baubles to a fledgling language.

Emoji had to evolve to survive, and Lewinsky had done it with his revolutionary mobile phones. The early bio-interfaces were small touchpads on the handset that went beyond boring haptics and transferred people's emotions by stimulating chemical reactions in the end user's amygdala. Now text messages could be sent, read, and *felt*. It was an exciting new experience. In a text declaring undying love, you could *feel* it. The sorrow of bad news, the elation of a newborn baby – the emotions were muted, but you could sense them all.

Lewinsky knew that to deliver the mother lode he would have to plug straight into the brain. That's when the headset's wetware interface came into its own. Lewinsky soon realised that if the brain could be stimulated with emotions, the same techniques could trick the brain into *feeling* objects that were not there. Out went cumbersome haptic bodysuits and tactile gloves. Now skin could be made to sense textures and heat. Even smells could be simulated.

Creators became ever more inventive. A virtual BASE jump from a skyscraper was now accompanied by the full emotional package, shortened by the impatient to *pax*: trepidation; the zero-*g* stomach roll during free fall; the wind against the face; the fear of the chute not opening; the sudden physical wrench as it did and the bone-jarring impact of a high-speed landing. With flawless graphics, the experience could then be ramped up to a *space dive* from a suborbital platform, tearing apart Baumgartner's and Eustace's records.

Thus, SPACE was born and Jean Baudrillard's *hyperreality* became true. *More real than real*, as Emotive's motto bragged.

Of course, in the early days, the system was abused. People would spend days – sometimes weeks – in SPACE, which led to psychosis. Deaths followed. The global economy began to suffer. Just as mankind was finally gaining control of the environmental nightmare crippling the planet, people once again turned their backs on it.

Ever the visionary, James Lewinsky ensured that while SPACE was free, it was also regulated. The amount of pain a user could experience virtually was limited by the System, instantly slashing cybersuicide numbers that had plagued early versions and led human rights groups to try to boycott all virtual reality.

The compulsory time limit was implemented to prevent permanent brain and nerve damage. Now people had a reason to go back outside, exercise and ensure the real world functioned. It was a small price to pay for fragments of total escapism every day.

Theo carefully tossed his rig onto his bed. The Sony device was durable enough to take knocks and spills – even designed to be thrown against the wall in frustration – but he couldn't afford a replacement just in case something did happen.

'For God's sake!'

He strode down the narrow corridor that was the nexus of his flat, all white plastic walls cast in shadows by several blown light bulbs they had been unable to replace.

He heaved the living room door open. The room beyond was bathed in darkness. Theo considered shouting again but the music would just drown him out. Increasingly pissed off with each stride, he was about to shove the door open when something caught his attention – a noise barely audible below the music. Sobbing, maybe?

He hesitated for a moment. He knew how volatile his mum could be, and if his migraine wasn't slam-dancing through his cranium then he would have turned around and left her to it rather than waste time arguing in person. He sucked in a deep breath then gently shoved the door wide open, allowing the light from the corridor in.

The small living room was decorated, if that was the right word, with a wooden table they had found in a second-hand shop and which his mother had attempted to paint with vivid colours and all the skill of a six-year-old. The two mismatched threadbare sofas had been inherited third-hand from cousins. A potted yucca sat in the corner, its leaves brittle and brown – a sure-fire candidate for cruelty against plants. A rusting radiator half-hung from a wall, with an ancient 4K television above it, the casing cracked and the display washed out after being forced to stream TV shows years beyond its operable shelf life.

Ella sat on the floor, leaning against the arm of a couch, almost hidden in a veil of vape smoke. Her legs were splayed out before her in too-tight tracksuit bottoms, and her crop top revealed a small tiger paw print tattoo peeking just above her waistband. Her long black hair was pulled up into a ponytail, but wayward strands hung in front of her bloodshot eyes. A half-empty gin bottle had toppled over next to her bare foot, the clear liquid still dribbling onto the threadbare carpet.

'Mum . . .'

He wanted to stay angry, to make a point that he shouldn't be the adult in this scenario, but as her body shook with each deep sob his anger at her transformed to pity. He snapped at the hub entertainment system embedded in the wall.

'Freya, shut the bloody music off!'

Ella's head snapped up as the music stopped, and she

wiped her eyes with the backs of her hands as if pretending all was fine.

'Theo? I was workin'. What did I tell you about not comin' in here when I'm workin'?'

Despite over two decades in London, her West Country lilt still infused every word. Through the smoke she regarded him with bloodshot eyes.

Theo stared at her battered rig cast aside on the floor. He carefully placed it on the table before sitting on the sofa. He avoided her gaze as she clambered unsteadily to her feet, before losing her balance and flopping down next to him.

'I was the one working.' He indicated to the gin bottle. 'Unless you're getting hammered at work again?'

The instant the words were out he regretted them. He wasn't in the mood for an argument. His eyes fell to the lone personal item she hadn't sold over the years, a framed certificate on the wall. Time had faded the paper behind the grubby glass, but the words EMIV Diploma – Level 2, were still visible. A testament that even she had once had ambitions, whatever they were.

With a trembling hand, Ella took a drag on her e-cigarette. Theo wafted the smoke away.

'Do you really have to do that in here?'

'You're like your father – such a killjoy,' Ella said with a sniff, but she switched the device off and they lapsed into an uncomfortable silence.

Theo felt awkward talking to his mother about anything that slewed towards the personal. It wasn't something they had really done over the years; it wasn't natural.

She'd had him when she was only fifteen, so he figured

he'd inherited her emotional immaturity. He knew he was overly harsh on her, expecting too much. On the rare times she had turned up to parents' evening when he was in school, Theo had had the ignominy of watching various members of staff flirt with her; even fellow pupils assumed she was his older sister. On the plus side, it often meant they gave him better grades than his abilities bore out.

Despite his grievances, Ella *had* done everything she could to ensure they had a roof over their heads, food in the cupboards, and enough money to keep them in SPACE tech, so they could at least function like normal people. Access to SPACE might now be considered a fundamental human right by most nations, but having the required equipment certainly wasn't. Once you stepped outside the tech bubble, you ended up in a stratum of society that was sliding backwards. Being unable to afford to ascend into SPACE meant that entire sections of privilege would be forever beyond your reach.

Theo massaged the bridge of his nose and lowered his voice.

'Why are you crying, Mum?'

'Just a bad day, love.' She didn't want to meet his questioning look. Her lips pursed as she considered saying something more, but she decided against it. 'I got kicked off the Conservation.'

Theo fought back the urge to shout. The last thing she needed right now was him being a prick.

The Conservations were huge rooftop parks, linked together by a colossal network of motorway-sized bridges of nothing but wild countryside. Entire forests were suspended hundreds of feet over the city, connecting the more tradition-al earthbound parks together, cladding London in a green leafy shield. The Parkways provided not only a giant carbon dioxide sponge, but fertile soil to grow crops and flowering meadows that had bolstered the declining populations of pollinating insects. They spanned for miles, providing refuge for badgers, hedgehogs, foxes and deer that had become per-manent inner-city high wire residents.

The last time he'd paid attention, his mother was working in an apiary and he couldn't imagine how it was possible to get sacked from that. It was best not to ask.

Ella stood up, swayed unsteadily, and swept a disapprov-ing gaze around the flat.

'And Christ knows we need the cash.' Her chest heaved in a sharp double-breath, an aftershock from her weeping marathon. She looked sadly at the now empty bottle. 'I should sleep. We can always restart life again tomorrow.'

Theo had heard that before; it had become her life's motto.

She flicked her index finger under his chin, a relic from his childhood that had once made him giggle but now just annoyed him.

'Maybe I should go back to the Conservation. Get myself reinstated, if I beg.' She looked wistful. 'I loved that place. So quiet. Peaceful. I found a new me there. Somebody I really liked.'

Theo forced a smile. 'I think that's a good idea.' She huf-fed in disagreement, but didn't argue back. 'You go to bed. I'll tidy up here.'

She bent over and kissed the top of his head, mussing the side of his hair with her knuckles.

'How would I ever cope without you?'

'Night, Mum.'

Theo forced a smile. He'd long wondered if he'd ever escape the torment of living at home and pined for the independence his friends enjoyed at university.

She wagged a finger, but said nothing as she stumbled to her bedroom. Theo waited until she had left before he slumped back in the chair, the springs creaking. With a deep sigh he looked at the mess Ella had left and wondered when *he* had become the responsible one.

Chapter Four

'I said already, it's a waste of time,' Clemmie said breezily, waving her hand dismissively to emphasise her point.

'A waste of time?' Theo stopped in his tracks, unsure if he'd heard her correctly. 'It's *Avasta*!'

'I've already given it a two-finger review,' said Milton dismissively.

Theo regarded him with consternation. Milton had built up a successful games review channel streamed out of SPACE, with over three million subscribers and growing; he had already started to rake in some serious cash. He hosted it under the guise of Kaiju Killer, his old gaming handle. The avatar was designed to look cool by somebody who clearly wasn't. Mirrored shades, garishly bright retro jackets with angular shoulder pads that could take an eye out, and a larger-than-life personality – nobody outside his inner circle knew Kaiju Killer's real identity. His fans adored his alter ego's exuberant and blunt style and, to the disbelief of those who knew him, his opinions mattered to a *lot* of people.

'And it's the summer,' Clemmie said. 'We could be doing other things.'

The words tumbled from Theo's mouth before he realised how cringeworthy they sounded.

'Like what?'

Baxter irritably stabbed the spiked litter picker into three bioplastic bottles scattered around his feet.

'Like not doing bloody community service.'

He glanced disapprovingly at the dozen other fellow offenders, in their late teens to mid-twenties, all with their heads bowed, listening to music from their earbuds as they cleaned the grounds of St Dunstan in the East. The pretty ivy-clad grounds of the derelict church had become a vortex for discarded rubbish in the East End.

'Look at all this crap.'

The advent of biodegradable plastics had had the reverse effect on the environment than was anticipated. Knowing the plastics would dissolve within two years, people now recklessly tossed their litter in the streets, no longer burdened with social conscience. As a result, big cities suffered from wind-herded collections of trash that clogged the pavements and roads. Only months earlier, Westminster had been hit by a litter storm – rubbish whipped in from the suburbs and channelled into tornados between skyscrapers. In places, such as the enclosed ruins they were in, the waste had reached knee height. Two homeless people had even died, struck by turbulent debris.

Baxter scowled as he slid the bottles into a plastic sack clipped to his belt. Then he sneezed – several uncontrollable bursts that made his eyes water and forced him to wipe his dribbling nose on his sleeve.

'I don't want plague,' Milton quipped with an element of condescension.

'It's hay fever, you knob.' Baxter wiped his nose again as he eyed the plants clinging to the walls. 'Should've chose river duty instead,' he muttered, keeping one eye on the surly man dressed in grey who was overseeing the other eleven litter pickers. The words 'London Community Service Dept' were emblazoned on his back.

Theo tried to press his point. 'I know, but I was thinking about it all last night—'

Clemmie raised an eyebrow. 'You were up all night thinking about playing a stupid game? Don't you have anything better to do? Hobbies? Movies? Watching porn?'

When his pals had left London, Theo had sought companionship in games. In those precious three hours of his life he could escape, and that had resulted in him having little time for any other pursuits. His thoughts had vacillated between his own depressing plight and how being with Clemmie could make his life a whole lot better – but he didn't think now was the time to raise that issue.

Theo sighed. 'Look, we spent the whole week working out how to get to the end of the level. If we stick together it'll be a doddle slaying that Tracyon.'

Milton lagged behind the group, only half-listening.

'Theo, it's not like this *Avasta* mod is any different from the others. Just more of the same. Who can be arsed traipsing through alien jungles any more?'

'You're not serious?'

Theo looked between them, silently demanding an answer.

Baxter shrugged as he impaled a pair of beer cans and three plastic wrappers in quick succession. Clemmie and Milton seemed not to hear him. They had their rigs in full augmented mode and were hopping across their various social media streams.

Like generations before her, Clemmie had built a large social network of like-minded friends she had no desire ever to meet in the flesh. In college, they had all learned that people liked things to be uniform and regular and, with her bobbed hair dyed purple at the tips and a cute-as-a-button (or so Theo thought) nose piercing, combined with a fierce personality that people referred to as *bitch mode*, most fellow students hadn't warmed to her.

Theo wondered how she was faring now. Baxter was the only one who went to her university, and Theo had wanted to prise answers from him but hadn't yet got the chance. He looked expectantly at Baxter.

'Back me up on this.'

Baxter shook his head. 'I've wasted way too much ascension fighting stupid monsters. If you're up for just cruising around SPACE, count me in.'

Theo was about to reply when Clemmie gave a low chuckle that he was certain was definitely in the flirting frequency. He squinted at her visor, trying to make out any details on the tiny reversed AR feed projected on her rig's clear lens. He considered moving closer, but that would bring them nose to nose and that was definitely entering the creepy stalker realm.

'Okay, Clem, wanna SPACE out tonight instead?'

'Maybe ...' was her vague reply.

'Why? Got something better to do?' Baxter sniggered.

'How about we go to Eye of the Storm? We can ascend at my place? It's the nearest geo-lock, after all ...'

Theo had spent a lot of time cleaning up the previous day so only felt marginally embarrassed about his home. Plus, he hadn't seen his mother when he left that morning and hoped she could prolong her absence into the evening.

'I'm up for that,' Milton chimed in.

'Will your mum be there?' Baxter asked, smirking at Theo as he stopped to lean on his litter picker.

'I don't know. Why?'

'No reason.' After a long pause he added, 'Has she still got that tattoo? Flavoured ink, isn't it?'

'You're such a perv, Bax,' Clemmie said.

'I'm just saying ...'

Baxter spun around and yanked Clemmie's rig off, pressing it to his own face to view her social media feed.

'Roger Huntington-Stanley? You cyberstalking hypocrite!'

Theo's heart skipped a beat. Huntington-Stanley had been at school with them, transforming from a toothy whelk to the drama group's leading man. Sharp jaw, winning smile, and – this was the worst of it – a genuinely nice guy. He was the sort of person who had his future mapped out before him and it was all sunshine and rainbows. Theo had no idea he'd ended up at the same uni as Clemmie.

What an *absolute* bastard.

With a feral growl, Clemmie snatched her visor back with one hand, her other snaking across to grab Baxter's T-shirt. She pulled him closer, her voice dropping to a hiss.

'Touch my shit again and I'll tear out your trachea.'

Baxter raised his hands apologetically, but couldn't keep the sly smile from his face.

'Hey, I don't even have a *trachea*. Chill. I'm just concerned about you, Clem. You can do better than Huntington-Stanley is all. What about someone like Milton?'

They both glanced at Milton as he dragged the back of his hand across his nose, accompanied by a wet sniffle as he surfed his streams.

Clemmie thrust her middle finger up at Baxter and sat back down, pulling her rig on firmly. Baxter chuckled, then flinched when the grim-faced uniformed supervisor barked at him.

'Edwin Baxter! This isn't a social gathering. Back to work. And unless your mates are joining the line I'll be doubling your quota if you keep chatting.'

Baxter swore under his breath as he turned to the next patch of litter and impaled it with serial killer precision.

'You lot bugger off. I've got two weeks of community service left. I don't want you messing it up.'

Theo's mood failed to improve as the day crawled by. His migraine came back the moment he started his shift at *Synger* and refused to fade until he was back home.

His flat was on the thirty-third floor of a tower that had been copied and pasted for a dozen blocks, complete with a subtle artichoke leaf roof, courtesy of the Chinese construction company who now owned vast swathes of London. Large-scale 3-D printing had been a cheap solution to the housing crisis, resulting in dwellings of a standard that had previously been considered impossible. The dirt- and graffiti- resistant façades meant that, no matter how hard chavs tried to tag them, the communities remained pristine and graffiti artists had to migrate to the older, trendier areas of town.

'Hey, Mum. I'm back.'

Theo slammed the door, hoping it would get his mother's attention. He had no desire to walk in on her amid another bout of tears or something worse, like the time he had come home with Milton and caught her in the throes of a cybersex session. It had required a *lot* of blackmail to shut Milton up, which had included writing a dozen coursework assignments for him while he was up in SPACE working on his channel.

The living room looked just as neat as he had left it in the morning. Ella's rig was still on the table.

'Mum?'

The kitchen revealed a single used coffee cup; a lip-stick stain on the rim indicated she had left in a hurry. He double-checked her bedroom. That was the same bomb site it always was.

He ambled back into the kitchen and rummaged through the cupboard for something to eat.

'Hey, Freya, play some music.'

'No problem, Theo,' the automated AI system replied.

Plumbed through the flat, the shoddy speakers gave the voice a slight rasp, a permanent reminder that Freya was now nothing more than a piece of retro-tech. Able to tell what sort of mood Theo was in just by the intonation of his voice, the hub played mellow, soul-sucking, blues-fuelled depresso-rock, presumably designed to prolong his melancholy.

With a grumbling stomach, Theo found little to eat with the exception of a box of red wine and a single tin of sardines, something neither he nor his mother ate. Not even a packet of instant noodles was left, which meant he'd have to trudge down to the food bank again. Further exploration uncovered the dregs of a dubiously antique packet of cereal he could smother in dairy-free milk.

Theo slouched on the sofa, pulled his rig from his bag and placed it on the table next to his mother's. Why had she left it here? Even if she had exhausted her daily ascension limit, few people would consider leaving their rig at home – the combined phone and AR features were vital in a cashless society. Ella had always stressed never to leave his rig at home. Even the keys to the flat were programmed into them.

He studied it as he chewed the flavoured sugar rings and was already regretting inviting his friends over. He was experiencing a rare overwhelming desire to be alone. He knew he had to shake off this funk. Was it because of his mother's general wear and tear on his patience, or the news that Clemmie was flirting with the Hollywood Adonis?

After several mouthfuls, he put the cereal bowl down, his appetite not quite slaked, but his taste buds had been tormented enough. He slipped on his visor and activated the AR. He wondered what time the others would be arriving but decided against calling them. There was no rush. Instead he checked to see if Ella had left any emails for him. Nothing, just the regular spam that automatically played in his inbox, creating a maelstrom of vid-clips and punchy sound bites clamouring for his attention.

He looked around the apartment in case she had left any air-graffiti – a message, emoji or drawing that could only be seen in AR. That was where she usually left shopping lists or brief notes to him. It was harder to miss four-foot kaleidoscopic letters hovering in the middle of the lounge informing him she was pulling a double shift than it was to overlook an email.

He lay back on the sofa and cycled through several social media boards, and found himself on Milton's channel. Kaiju Killer, dressed in a neon-purple jacket, gurned at the camera as he reviewed Avasta. His voice was slightly pitch-shifted, giving him more of an American nasal tone, and his body language was loud and brash, the complete opposite of Milton.

'Been there, done that! And choked on repetitive boredom. Avoid this mod at all costs! I give it a two-finger salute.'

Kaiju Killer then raised two fingers at the camera and furiously – and repeatedly – flipped them like some ADHD kid on a caffeine high. He did it with such gusto that his tongue poked from the side of his mouth in a facsimile of the Emotive logo. He grunted with each oscillation – no doubt something that would cause millions of kids around the globe to howl with glee.

'Moron.'

Theo chuckled despite himself, then checked his own social streams. Despite several witty posts he had conjured up throughout the day, nobody had engaged. Clemmie had posted a new batch of selfies, taken at various flattering angles as she feigned interest at something off screen that only she could see.

He lingered on the photos, noting that she had deliberately disabled the emotional feedback, which was always a telltale sign the poses were not natural. Insecurity was not a good vibe to pass on when you were trying to impress somebody.

With a soft ping, a small window suddenly slid into view from the left, displaying a map showing Milton's location. The Echo was a discreet way for people to alert friends that they were en route. It saved brief phone calls or annoying texts. Seconds later, Baxter and Clemmie both responded with theirs.

Theo figured he could cram in thirty minutes of self-loathing before they arrived, if he switched back to Clemmie's feed. Or maybe he should jump into a quick level of *Surf Storm*, a massively popular immersive SPACE game that had him riding colossal waves on impossible seas. The adrenaline rush always perked him up and, despite never having seen the ocean in real life before, he was a natural.

His lungs were aching to burst, but in doing so Theo would surely drown. His head dipped beneath the cold, turbulent water once again. Salt water stung his nostrils as he fought to maintain his balance on the board.

Intellectually he knew he couldn't drown in the game, but his emotions had different opinions and were overruling common sense. He forced down his panic and focused on keeping the board straight. His arms and abs ached from countless micromovements, but just then he suddenly felt the board plateau out and his head broke the surface, allowing him to breathe deeply.

He'd only been playing *Surf Storm* for twenty minutes, but already he had inched his ranking a peg closer to the coveted 'gnarly' status, and had advanced to a hitherto unexplored 'extreme' level.

With a grunt, he hopped his trailing feet onto the board and raised himself into an arched position, giving himself enough stability to glance behind. The towering wave powering him along was some hundred feet tall and rising like a cobra against the inky turmoiled sky of an advancing hurricane. Lightning stabbed overhead, highlighting the growing whitecaps. He switched his gaze away and focused on his distant target, a red glow through the driving rain. He was perfectly aligned to catch it.

The frigid driving rain made the hairs on his arms stand on end and he shivered, such was the level of detail in the game. He shifted his weight to the left to nudge the board perpendicular to the wave, then jumped to his feet in a classic surfing pose.

'All right!' he yelled as spume slapped him across his face.

He had chosen to ignore the tutorials that came with the game and instead had watched online surf instruction videos, so was feeling pretty confident he was doing the right thing. He tried to ignore the fins slicing through the water ahead of him as a shoal of sharks gathered for a potential feast. The last time he had fallen in he'd been torn apart before respawning at the start of the course. It was a painful lesson he had no wish to repeat.

Ahead, further dramatic lightning revealed a narrow

channel between jagged islands, bathed in plumes of crimson lava sliding down the flanks of a pair of boiling volcanos. The flows hissed into the ocean, creating terrific plumes of white steam. Theo leaned forward, compensating as the wave began to tug him backwards with increasing ferocity. He knew there was little room for error in threading between the volcanic mounds.

The rumble of the tsunami made his ribs shake as the board was pulled upwards and backwards. Theo immediately banked a hard right, once again drawing himself parallel to the wall of water. His board's built-in engine revved to life and he climbed higher to the perfect spot, stopping short of the frothing caps, spitting spray that stung his eyes.

Still he pressed on. The moment he caught the wave the engine automatically stopped. He felt the power of the water surge him faster and revelled in the thrill of the surf.

With the islands drawing nearer, Theo sliced back down the flank to the roar of an unseen crowd of spectators, barely audible over the bellowing wind. His legs trembled from the effort but his balance remained true. A few quick jigs, first to the left, then to the right to avoid the great whites who had also caught the wave, and Theo was now on course to coast perfectly between the lava trap. The escalating ping of points sounded above another lightning flash.

This was it. He was going to complete the extreme course and finally advance a level.

The wave began to arch over him, forming a tube of ocean. His adrenaline spiked and he felt a euphoria no other game had managed to offer him.

· *More real than real*, he reminded himself.

33

Then a fork of lightning backlit the surf – highlighting the largest shark he had yet seen. The beast was zeroing in from the side. But that wasn't what alarmed him. The exit from the tunnel ahead, that would pitch him between the lava flows, was now blocked by a second wave rushing in perpendicular to the first. It was an impossible double wave. He didn't have time to curse the programmers who had dreamed it up before the second wave struck him face on.

It was as if he had raced into a brick wall. Pain racked his entire body as he was flung from the board into the maelstrom. Water forced itself into his lungs, causing him to gag. He flailed wildly and felt the board crack his skull. Through stinging eyes he saw a plume of blood spurt from his head, highlighted by another convenient burst of lightning – which also revealed the monstrous shark twisting towards him as it caught the scent.

Theo thrashed to distance himself, not wishing to be bitten in half twice in as many days. Before the shark could reach him, both were thrown into a stream of lava that was already cracking and hissing as it struck the water.

He felt his back melt from the searing heat as he burned to death.

Baxter pulled a pair of four-packs from his bag and handed one to Milton. Theo refused the offer; he was still trembling from the after-effects of *Surf Storm* and wasn't in much of a mood to discuss the details of his demise to an eager Milton.

Despite that, there was a collective sense that it was going to be a good evening simply hanging in SPACE. They sagged into the sofas and together ascended into SPACE. VR required a fidelity the AR rig's glass visor couldn't handle, so a loom of lasers projected threads straight on to their retinas, slowly superimposing the digitally rendered world with increasing intensity. The wetware interface, meanwhile, bonded with the brain's emotional centres, effectively tricking the brain into thinking everything visible was also real. James Lewinsky had even added a final flourish. A small feel-good vibe was built into the ascension processes so that, no matter how pissed off you felt going in, you'd arrive in SPACE with a smile.

During the six-second ascension other denizens of the virtual saw ghostly figures materialise, but were unable to interact with them until the incomers were fully uploaded. The whole process was calibrated so that people wouldn't suddenly upload themselves into a person, building, or oncoming traffic – or even a mile up in the sky above the Earth. After all, the last thing you wanted was a stranger materialising *inside* you.

Theo looked around the familiar park that was geo locked to his block of flats. He inhaled deeply, savouring the petrichor scent that filled his nostrils. The impressive London skyline lay beyond, but it was unrecognisable as the historical city. This was Nu London.

Across the park's beautifully sculpted rolling hills and dazzling trees, whose leaves shimmered with deep blue veins when the breeze caught them, stood neon skyscrapers twisted into impossible architecture and dwarfing anything in The Real. Many were clad with brightly illuminated holographic commercials that played different targeted content, depending on who was looking at it. Drones and disc-shaped police cruisers peppered the skyways – public aerial traffic had been deemed too hazardous even in SPACE, and essentially useless when ground-based traffic systems were flawless and avatars could ping themselves between cities in moments.

The ascension had soothed Theo's frayed nerves. He was surprised just how much better he felt by simply being in SPACE. It felt more like home than the flat; here possibilities were limitless. He had often wished he lived closer to Nu London's city centre, just to gain an extra five minutes in the virtual, but that was impossible. There were only a finite number of geo-locked locations that *precisely* matched The Real. The Thames, for one, was an accurate match. Camden High Street, Covent Garden and Leicester Square were others, although the reasons behind this were hazy. The same rules applied around the globe.

One of the topological quirks meant that even if two points were geo-locked, the distance between them wasn't necessarily the same as in The Real. A five-minute walk between Leicester Square and Covent Garden in the real world could stretch for two miles in Nu London.

Theo checked the others had all ascended. Here, they looked exactly as they did in The Real. Every blemish, mole and even haircut and colour transferred over, with the intention of helping combat crime, but all it did was fuel an illegal trade in second-skins that could completely change the look and build of your avatar. A devious tactic used by both criminals and online daters. Skins were regularly used in enclosed gaming bubbles where the rules were different, but hackers had been able to port them out of the games to be used illegally – for a hefty price, of course.

'Right, let's go!' said Clemmie.

She was already impatiently striding towards the distant buildings.

They quickly crossed the virtual gardens. The serenity of the park was shattered as they entered a huge plaza that marked the start of the digital urbanisation. Avatars of all kinds bustled about with a sense of urgency.

At any hour the city was populated by millions of citizens, some with their earthbound human doppelgängers slumped at home or in the office, while others were self-aware artificial lifeforms, Slifs, going about their business.

Ascension in SPΛCE was geographically locked to The Real to prevent millions of users appearing in exactly the same location at the same time and crashing the system. In the past, hackers had sent tens of thousands of people converging on the same few square feet of ground, triggering Denial of Service flash mobs – or DoS Mobbing – that crashed the system, but with tighter regulations that hadn't happened for a while. Ensuring people ascended in rough approximations to their real-world locations meant avatars were evenly spread across the virtual.

The only exception to the rule were the vPolice, SPACE's very own law enforcement, who could ascend in any outdoor location across their jurisdiction, instantly. They possessed the same powers of arrest as their real-world counterparts, and all wore identical deep blue uniforms: jackbooted giant muscular second-skins, their heads covered by angular helmets designed to intimidate.

With both the three-hour limit and geo-lock, Theo was conscious of the time wasted crossing the park to reach Eye of the Storm. Theo may have lived in a crummy neighbourhood, but at least he was the closest of his friends to the virtual fun centre. The club had once been their place of choice during their formative years, filled with fond memories. But with everybody spread across the country in university, it had been relegated to the past; too time-consuming to ascend then travel to the capital. And in SPACE, time was at a premium.

Around them, couples strolled in deep conversation; others air-skated eight feet above the ground, weaving through the trees at high speeds. Some walked exotic pets. One creature, resembling a two-foot long furry millipede, growled at a giant winged cat that strained at its leash, hissing furiously. He saw Milton watching with fascination. Deprived of a pet at home, he had always talked about having one in SPACE, especially as designing custom pets was becoming a huge business here. There were even a few Slifs around who kept to the park fringes, resembling nothing more than lanky stick figures in the distance.

Clemmie led the way, sometimes shouldering past slower people in her haste. She glanced over her shoulder as the others trailed behind.

'Will you hurry up? Tick-tock!'

Even having been here thousands of times, Theo couldn't help but marvel at the city around them. Every time he ascended something had changed. The virtual landscape bore no resemblance to earthly locations – what would be the point in that? Even so, the System did mirror the same time of day, so night was just falling to prevent immersion lag, which was a particularly unpleasant form of jet lag. Authorities had gone out of their way to make their cities truly impressive to lure visitors. Everything was bigger, brighter, bolder and not at the mercy of the pesky laws of physics. Nu London, being the birthplace of SPACE, was one of the grandest and had once again become a global powerhouse.

'There it is.' Baxter gestured at Eye of the Storm with a grin.

The building was a multi-domed structure that hung twenty feet above the ground and slowly rotated, giving the impression of a gigantic planet. The effect was further enhanced by a shifting pattern of red clouds and swirling celestial storms that moved across the surface. The single entrance was a gaping portal at the bottom of the lowest sphere. Baxter never failed to point out its resemblance to an anus, and today was no different.

Pounding techno-music from Eye of the Storm grew in volume as they approached. Being Friday night, it was heaving with life. Streams of people were coming and going by either floating up to, or down from, the entrance. There were no bouncers, no security – all were welcome.

As Theo drew nearer he felt the tug of gravity shifting him towards the entrance above, like a strong current in a river. Milton was already several steps ahead and rising into the building. Theo was about to follow but a noise caught his attention – an incoming call. But not from his rig, so he couldn't answer.

'Wait a sec.'

He held up his hand to stop the others, but Baxter was already following Milton into the club. He waved to Theo.

'Come on, Theo, fun clock's ticking!'

The others evidently couldn't hear the call; their rigs were overriding their senses. Theo always activated the awareness option on his set to keep him alert to what was happening in the real world, just in case there was an emergency. He had heard cases of people burning to death in apartment fires while completely immersed in SPACE; others had been stabbed or shot during home intrusions, completely unaware of what was happening in The Real.

'Ella's getting a call.'

Clemmie gave him an odd look. 'So?'

'I better take it . . .' He didn't want to explain that it was unlike her to leave her rig at home. It wouldn't look good if she missed a call while job hunting. 'I'll catch you in there in a minute.'

He didn't hear Clemmie's response as she shook her head, then stomped the ground in her new Nike Airs, activating their anti-gravs that gently levitated her into the dome.

Theo deactivated his headset and his senses sank back to reality. Eye of the Storm dissolved, music fading out as the vibrant world was replaced by his grim apartment.

He tugged his rig off, and replaced it with Ella's from the table. It was adjusted to her head, and pressed tightly against his ears. He'd already answered before it struck him that there was no icon to identify the caller. Which was odd, because even telemarketing callers had to identify themselves by law these days.

He opened his mouth to say 'hello', but was beaten to it

by an impatient voice on the other end of the line. Again, it was unusual not to have a video link – very few people ever resorted to mere voice calls.

'Ella, Ella, Ella ... what *were* you thinking, my darling?' The softness of the East End voice amplified its menace, even without the emo-tech running. It was enough to make Theo freeze and not divulge his identity. 'We graciously give you two days' extension and you still fail to deliver. Dom knows what you've done and, well, saying he's displeased is an understatement. In fact, I dare say he's immune to your ample charms. How the 'ell did you think this was gonna play out?'

The speaker paused. Theo couldn't tell whether it was for effect or if the caller expected an answer. He decided the best course was silence and waited for the caller to continue.

'It's most grievous, but we're not all savages in this game. Mirri says she understands and is givin' you a chance to return everythin' you took. But if we don't get it all tomorrow that streak of piss you call your son ... Well, we'll start with his kneecaps. And then we'll work our way inch by inch up that lanky bastard for every hour you stall. Don't worry, we'll keep him awake as his balls are slit open.' He gave a genial chuckle. 'A little vivisection to while away the hours until there is nothin' left of 'im other than a puddle of your shared DNA.'

The call disconnected with a melodious pop.

Theo felt a chill run through him. Hearing a death threat calmly delivered with such descriptive relish left him in no doubt that the man meant every word.

And if they would do that to him, what the hell would they do to his mother?

Chapter Five

With his heart hammering in his ribcage and bile burning in his throat, Theo collapsed on the sofa next to an immobile Clemmie. His mother's rig slipped from his hand and rolled to a halt against the coffee table.

'It's got to be a wind-up,' he said aloud, aware the others around him were oblivious.

Not that he really believed it was a prank call; outside the three people in the room he didn't have any friends remotely close enough to wind him up, and the man's callous inflection left little room for doubt. Had his mother left her rig behind so she could avoid these calls? That didn't make much sense to him but, still, the timing of it all made him uncomfortable. He held up his hand, fingers trembling from the rush of adrenaline.

'Shit,' he muttered, pressing his hand firmly against his knee to stop it twitching.

'Police,' he said out loud again.

Yes, he'd simply call the police. They could sort everything out. But the threat was targeted at his mum, so obviously they hadn't got to her. Yet.

Yeah, he was reacting too wildly. The threat to her life indicated Ella was a step ahead of the thug, so not currently in danger. Hadn't he been told she had until tomorrow? All he had to do is warn her. Wherever she was.

Maybe that's why she didn't take her rig. She didn't want anybody to track her down. Whatever mess she had bumbled into this time, maybe she was finally being responsible and trying to sort it all out.

That must be it.

Theo sucked in a shuddering breath, suddenly aware he had been much tenser than he thought. He glanced at his friends slumped on the sofas, as awkward and unmoving as if they'd been shot, betrayed by the steady rise and fall of their chests. In Baxter's case he was panting hard, no doubt enjoying some simulated physical thrill.

Should he join them? Tell them about the call? He couldn't think of a single useful thing they could do – especially not while locked in virtual limbo. Besides, Baxter would be disparaging – he always found a way to be – and the idea of panicking in front of Clemmie was even less appealing. He should join them, put it out of his mind, and when his mum returned his awareness alert would drift him back to The Real and he could get to the bottom of the matter.

That's what he should do.

Yet the calm use of *vivisection* had rattled him. This wasn't an irate thug demanding money. This was somebody who cultured threats to achieve results. A brash hard man the police could easily deal with; but a sophisticate who had the tech-wizardry to mask their user ID carried the threat of something bigger – something more organised. And implicating his mother in criminal activity was the last thing they needed.

Well, second to last, he corrected himself. Not being killed topped that list.

In a passing moment of paranoia, Theo switched seats so he could see straight down the corridor should somebody enter the apartment. He took the last beer, clutching the can in both hands to steady it as he sipped. His gaze kept shifting between the door and his mum's rig, Emotive's smiley emoji taunting him.

Still nothing happened. His friends didn't stir and Theo felt his attention wander to Clemmie's rhythmic breathing. Her neck already had a veil of perspiration, up past her defined jawline to the delicate hairs on her neck ...

Theo tore his gaze away and finished the beer in a single gulp. Avoiding looking at her, and with little else to do, time dragged its temporal corpse until the three of them suddenly gave shuddering breaths as they reached the mandatory limit and were ejected from SPACE.

Clemmie was the first to remove her rig, rubbing her eyes with the back of one hand as she yawned and stretched with feline grace.

'That was brilliant,' she grinned.

Baxter was next, immediately standing as he tossed his headset on the sofa.

'Out of the way, I need a slash!' was his only comment before darting from the room.

Milton hung his rig around his neck and scratched his hair. He beamed at Theo.

'That was cool. And Marv ... My God ...' He shook his head in disbelief.

Clemmie barked a single laugh of disbelief and nodded.

'I know. Marv. Christ, we were lucky to be there. That's the moment Eye of the Storm will be known for!'

Theo looked questioningly between them before realising that he hadn't been missed for the last three hours. His desire to share his worry was instantly replaced by an intense wave of loneliness.

'Yeah. Marv ...' he muttered.

'And then ...' Milton slapped his hands together to indicate the miracle they had all witnessed. 'Bam! Just like that. I bet System will come down hard on him.'

Theo was surprised. Invoking the name of the SPACE Admin System was only done in gross violations of SPACE's otherwise lax terms and conditions. He couldn't think of an actual violation, other than the murderous deletion of Slifs, which now carried with it the same prison terms as real-world murder.

Clemmie nodded. 'Lifetime ban.'

Baxter came back, zipping up his fly.

'Yeah. Makes you think, doesn't it?' The others nodded in solemn silence. Baxter picked up his rig and turned to Theo. 'Well, it's been real. I said I'd walk with Clem to the Tube.'

Theo didn't say a word as they gathered their gear and headed for the door, still chatting – odd comments about Marv and whatever the hell had happened. Then they were gone and an oppressive silence filled the flat.

Theo leaned against the door, various emotions pinging

his brain, chief of which was either disappointment or anger
– he couldn't tell. He was also painfully aware that his mum
would have usually been home an hour ago. He sat back on
the sofa and decided to wait up for her. He gripped his rig in
both hands, turning it this way and that to watch the light
reflect off the plastic. A tiny part of him was tempted to
jump into SPACE and find details about the Marv incident,
but his curiosity was extinguished by the icy threatening
words of the caller.

No. Ella would be back shortly and they'd work through
whatever situation she had got herself into. It'd be easy.

Theo woke with a start. His rig rolled from his lap and
bounced once on the floor.

'Mum?' he called out.

No answer.

He stood, about to call out again, but decided instead to
hold his tongue. As the fuzziness of sleep faded away he realised the sun was streaming in through the gap in the curtains.
Convinced he'd been roused by a noise, he padded into the
hallway. The front door was closed. He strained to listen.

Nothing.

The utter silence was made all the more powerful by
the building's excellent soundproofing. A blessing mostly,
unless you were screaming for help ...

Theo crossed the hallway to his mum's room. The door
was half open. Had she left it that way? He couldn't remember. He sucked in a deep breath and held it as he nudged
the door fully open. He was coiled, ready to lash out at the
slightest movement ...

The room looked as if a bomb had been detonated in the wardrobe, which had been its default state for as long as Theo could remember. But there was no sign of Ella. He quickly checked the bathroom and his own bedroom before returning to the living room.

'Where the hell are you?' he muttered, holding up his mum's rig in case there had been any further messages flashing on the visor. Nothing.

He sat back on the sofa, cycling through the limited options that presented themselves. Should he register her as a missing person? But she had only been gone less than a day, so he wasn't sure that was possible. Friends? Theo didn't know if she had any. That made him pause for thought. Was she as lonely as he was?

The clock in the corner of his AR visor read 8.30 a.m., the time Ella would ordinarily start work at the Conservation. She may have lost her job there, but didn't she say she was hoping to get reinstated? Or was that just wishful thinking? Whatever it was, it was his only lead.

Fetching a battered black canvas knapsack from his room, he shoved Ella's rig inside it and fastened the only buckle that wasn't broken. He donned his own and headed for the door, following an augmented map showing him the quickest route to the Conservation.

Chapter Six

Out of all the popular doomsday scenarios, from solar flares to unstoppable climate change, it was the near-extinction of the pollinators that almost eradicated mankind. Pesticides hit bee populations hardest and pushed the world to crisis as crops failed. The spectre of global famine sent governments into overdrive to reverse decisions based purely on commerce.

Just in time, the world was pulled from the brink.

However, despite all the good they do, Theo couldn't help but think of bees as stripy, noisy bastards filled with murderous intent, and all because he was stung by one when he was eight years old. It had hurt like hell at the time, but the pain had quickly been forgotten. However, he had no desire to repeat the experience especially as the Conservation around him was thick with swarms, circling like perfectly co-ordinated plumes of smoke, orbiting the hundreds of hives seventy storeys up, amid a man-made forest.

'Ella don't work here no more,' said a thickset person draped in a beekeeper suit and a hat that hid their face.

Even from their tone of voice, Theo couldn't be sure if it was a man or woman.

'I know, but she said she hoped to come back.'

He resisted the urge to swipe indiscriminately at the bees, which were buzzing all around him. Killing them carried a hefty fine.

'What, Ella?' The androgynous figure gave a snarky laugh. 'There's no chance that'll happen.'

What had she done? Theo looked across the rooftop. Two massive, heavily forested bridges arched from either side, the Conservation forming an island between them, built on the shared rooftops of four skyscrapers. Through the foliage he glimpsed more city skyrises and dozens of other rooftop Conservations, connected via the graphene-reinforced Parkways. For a moment he could see why the stillness had attracted his mother.

'Can I speak to your manager?' Theo said. 'Maybe they'll know more.'

'You're looking at the manager.'

Theo hesitated. He had been hoping for somebody carrying a little more authority.

'Do you have any idea where she might have gone?'

'Dead in a ditch is my best guess,' came the somewhat jovial response.

'She didn't come home last night.'

The tremor of emotion in his voice was unexpected, but it seemed to give the manager pause as s/he weighed Theo up.

'You her son?' the manager said, with sudden solemnity.

With last night's death threat ringing in his ears, he was

reluctant to admit the truth. But in the end he gave a shallow nod and took a step backwards.

'Theo.'

'That's right. She liked to chat about you. Sorry about the ditch thing – didn't mean it. But your ma didn't know a helping hand from a slap in the face. I took pity on her when she started here. She was looking to keep her head down and there's no better place in the city.' A gloved hand gestured around them. 'Places like this represent the new gold rush. You want to get rich – forget tech. Insects is where it's at. Ten floors beneath us, bugs is bred for food.'

Theo shrugged. His generation were au fait with insects as a food staple; it was the older generations who had a problem with it.

The manager gently plucked a bee from Theo's shoulder and released it into the sky.

'The hives on this roof alone are worth a quarter of a million quid, and that's just using them as pollinators. You know, to keep us all alive and that.' The manager's voice swelled with sudden pride. 'And I own ten sites across the city.'

'Then you can afford to give her her old job back.'

The manager gave a snort of derision. 'Therein lies the problem. Some roughnecks came in to talk to your ma, they did. I didn't hear what they were complaining about, but tempers flared. And then they did that.' A finger gestured over Theo's shoulder.

On the wall housing the access elevator, a hive stood abandoned. One side of the wooden casing had been splintered, creating a jagged hole.

'One bloke, a big blond fella with a dirty type of accent I ain't heard before, put his head right into it. Luckily they didn't kill me queen, but a hundred or so drones were completely crushed dead.' The veiled head shook sadly. 'That's why I had to sack her. The bastard who did it got several hundred stings all over his body and ball sack, though.' There was an unmistakable note of *schadenfreude*. 'Nothing he won't be recoverin' from any time soon. They scooted on out before security could collar them. Left Ella a right sobbing mess. It's difficult to fire somebody when they cry like that.'

'But you managed.' Theo felt a chill run down his spine. 'What did they want?'

'Moncy apparently. Isn't it always? From the way she told it, seems she owed a *lot* of it, too.' There was another lengthy sigh as the manager's tone softened some more. 'Look, Ella had a good heart, but I just can't be associating with crims. No offence. Whatever she was into, it wasn't loose change. Nor was it healthy.'

Theo's heart sank. This wasn't the direction he had expected his morning to take.

'Do you have any idea who they were, or where she went?'

The manager's hood shook from side to side, displacing several bees that had settled there.

'She never said. But I got the feeling it had been getting worse by the day. And another thing. She kept spending more time on her rig, despite the fact I don't allow that here.' The manager paused. 'But I made an exception for her.'

Theo sensed some deeper attraction in the voice and

couldn't help but read between the lines, whether he liked it or not. He made his excuses to leave and pondered his next move as he took the lift to the ground floor.

Shaded by the Parkways, the bustling streets were cold enough even in the summer to make Theo shiver and zip up his sweat top, stuffing his hands into its pockets. He was lost in thought as he weaved through crowds of tourists and business people, each and every one lost in their augmented worlds and all experts in avoiding collisions with fellow zombies. Further pavement hazards came from Wi-Fi repeater stations fashioned out of old red pillar boxes, that now ensured every square inch of the city was online. There was the occasional smashed-up repeater sprayed with a stylish CE logo, the entwined letters the symbol of the *Children of Ellul*, an anti-SPACE movement that preferred good old-fashioned vandalism to promote their cause.

What passed for a high street these days were mostly family traders since the larger superstores had moved into SPACE. Every shopfront was a café, pub, street food vendor or boarded up. The roads were crowded with electric vehicles, most of which swished silently by at speed. Theo had to be particularly wary of the homeless, who would leap out to surprise people by flashing QR codes printed on card, in the hope of accidentally inducing their targets to electronically transfer funds for a cup of tea. Even the destitute had to be online to function.

On a bench outside a charity shop, Theo took his mother's rig from his pack. A quick inspection revealed there were no messages or missed calls. Unlike his official Emotive Sony rig, Ella's was a battered plastic Nigerian knock-off. The casing was scratched and the battery level half of his own, but the functionality was pretty much the same. Rigs logged health data, location, calls, messages, ascensions – every part of a user's day-to-day life. If he could access it, he should have a full metadata trail leading up to the moment she removed it.

He traded his mum's rig for his own, and was greeted with a login screen as he attempted to access its home screen, but an 'UNAUTHORISED USER' message flashed across the screen. She'd locked everything to her biometrics, so there was nothing he could do, other than wait for another incoming call.

At home, Theo once again checked for any signs his mother had returned. But, satisfied nothing had changed, he lay on his bed and considered what to do. A picture was emerging from the little he had gleaned in the Conservation. It was a simple, yet desperate tale: his mother owed money to a loan shark and was unable to pay. Now she had fled and they were looking for her.

The call he received carried the positive message that indicated they still hadn't caught up with her. The downside was that she had abandoned him as collateral and a vivisection awaited him.

He tried to shove that thought from his mind. It was, he hoped, an empty threat. He had stumbled into a problem that his mother had created. He had just about enough faith in her to assume she was doing something to sort it out.

Stress and lack of sleep tugged at his body and mind. With a weary sigh, he slipped his rig on and decided to occupy himself with the last couple of hours of ascension before his limit was reset.

For the first time in memory, Theo looked around Nu London wearing a frown, a sense of displacement, and almost boredom.

He wandered the broad streets, with pavements that reflected chrome finishes and illuminated walkways to tempt visitors into shopping centres or game environs. Like the real streets, people were everywhere, except this time they walked with a sense of urgency. There were few time-wasters here.

The occasional Slif passed him. The gangly black-skinned creatures averaged a foot taller than a human. Their heads were more bulbous and plainly featured, with black horizontal eyes, a small slit-like mouth, and nostrils and ears that were nothing more than decorative bumps to help give a sense of humanity to them.

These synthetic life forms grew in the womb of SPACE, formed by the coding rules that surrounded them all and, as such, were able to sense avatars' emotional states as easily as a dog sniffing a scent. Whatever stress was flooding through Theo must have come across like an acrid taste because the Slifs even began crossing the street to avoid him.

A huge animated statue of Pac-Man chasing a Ghost floated outside a grand museum, advertising an exhibition of the largest and most complete history of gaming. Back in the day, he and Clemmie would have been charging inside to check it out, but right now he couldn't even drum up enthusiasm to watch the photorealistic *Pakkuman* tearing apart the wailing ghost with more graphic gore than Theo recalled in the original game.

After more listless ambling, Theo was ejected from SPACE and back on his bed. A quick check revealed his mother was still absent. Then he noticed a message flashing on her visor. He had missed an anonymous call.

He kicked himself for leaving the rig in the living room. His awareness was activated, but it was just out of earshot.

Anonymous.

That had to be the loan shark. He groped for some good news; it indicated they hadn't found her yet. Theo's stomach knotted. Waiting for her to show up was a road to nowhere. Who knew how close the unscrupulous creditors were to catching her up? He had to do *something* ...

Going straight to the police was, at this stage, perhaps overkill, but nosing around for advice would be the smart step. Which meant talking to Clemmie's father.

He knew Clemmie's parents reasonably well although the exact details of her father, Martin, were hazy. He was some sort of detective who specialised in cybercrimes, rather than the more glamorous street cops who kicked down doors and arrested criminals on the mean streets of the Midlands.

Over the years Clemmie had boasted how she had picked up little tricks and back doors from him, and Theo knew she had secretly watched him access the secure police server from his study. At the time it was all rather mundane stuff, until Milton had been slapped with a parking ticket the very day he passed his test. Fearing his strict parents would take away his car – and the others would lose a potential free ride – Clemmie had erased the ticket from existence.

Theo placed Ella's rig into his pack, put his own back on and hesitated as he called up Clemmie's contact card. This wasn't something he wanted to explain over a call.

Hurrying to Stepney Green Tube station he searched her social media stream. As expected, she had posted ambiguous comments and photos mapping out her lazy day so far. On the platform, her feed was a welcome distraction from the constant stream of commercials bombarding his visor as he passed the trigger points. New musicals in town pelted him with sound bites; fashion models suggested he consume an energy drink genetically modified to define your abs (Theo had already tried it, and all it gave him was acute diarrhoea).

There were few clues in Clemmie's images to her where-abouts, but the blurry background of the latest picture, posted thirty minutes earlier, looked distinctly like the coffee shop around the corner from her house. It was a start.

Chapter Seven

The toxic silence bored into Theo's skin.

'Look, I'm sorry. How was I supposed to know it was a date?' he said softly, sipping his double shot macchiato. 'He could've stayed.'

'It was *not* a date,' Clemmie intoned through gritted teeth, her focus on the visor of Ella's rig, which she was attempting to sync with her own.

'Okay, okay,' Theo whispered under his breath, desperate to avoid another one of her killer glances. A change of subject was in order, he realised. 'Thanks for doing this.'

For a moment Clemmie said nothing, her attention solely on a single line of code flashing across her own visor. With subtle eye movements and thought impulses via the wetware interface she began to edit the code. Theo assumed she hadn't heard him so opened his mouth to repeat himself, but Clemmie beat him to it, her tone gruff from concentration.

'When somebody threatens your life – and it isn't me – I feel obliged to help.'

A ghost of a smile tugged at Theo's cheeks.

'Making your life difficult is *my* job,' she added quietly.

Theo sifted through the sentence for any deeper meaning, before she added, 'Seeing as you're my pet stalker.'

'I'm not stalking you!'

'So how did you find me here?'

Again, she avoided eye contact.

'Your streams. I recognised this place.'

'I've never been here with you.'

'Well ...'

He didn't have a ready answer to counter.

'And you could've pinged my Echo.' She glanced up to see Theo shrug. 'But that would've warned me you were coming, right?'

Theo's jaw was working, but the words didn't form. He hated the way she read his mind; it was an old habit and her skills were improving at an alarming rate.

'And that would've ruined your date, right?' he said.

'I said it wasn't a date,' she snapped frostily. Theo was saved when Ella's rig gave a harmonic ping. 'And as if by magic ... we're in!' She flashed a smile, pleased with her success. 'This is only in safe mode, so we can't access her apps or recall histories. They're still secured. But we can trawl system files —' she navigated through the file system on screen — 'and we can see what was dumped in the sump.'

'Sump?' Theo said. 'Did your dad show you all this hacker stuff?'

'I'm no hacker, Theo. Not by a long shot.' Was that a hint of regret? 'This is just primary school stuff. You don't grow up around a policeman without picking up a few things. I was always convinced my parents used to exploit this same back door to monitor me when I was a teenager. I had to get wise quick.' She tapped the side of Ella's rig. 'The sump is residual temporary optical storage. The temp files from the last conversation you had on this should still be here.'

Without further narration, Clemmie delved into a soup of temp files. Theo could just see the faintest reflections of the three-dimensional interface in her visor. With quick eye movements, she navigated to a decahedral icon and unpeeled it. A few seconds later she was listening to Theo's threatening phone conversation.

'That's somebody who was unloved as a child,' she finally said with a shake of her head. Behind her visor, her brown eyes met his through a sea of projected code. 'If this was my mum, I'd go straight to the fuzz while I still had this sump file. But as I live with my stepmother ...'

'What if that lands her in more trouble?'

Clemmie studied him for a moment, before refocusing on the files. Theo would have preferred an answer, something he could bounce his own doubts off. Did she agree? Or did she have a clearer idea what to do? As the silence stretched, he clutched at anything to divert his mind.

'So ... you and Roger Huntington-Stanley, huh?'

The words tumbled out before his inner censor could warn him not to be a prick. He tried to look away but noticed her whole posture had become ridged with tension.

'You know why people go away to uni?' she said distractedly. Theo shrugged, sensing it was a rhetorical question. 'Because it helps them discover what a small world the people they leave behind live in. Even in big cities ...'

'I didn't mean ...'

He trailed off, wondering exactly what it was he didn't mean.

Clemmie spun Ella's rig around on the table and slid it forcibly into Theo's resting forearms.

'There's a nav-sump file I salvaged. The GPS data of an address your mum was heading to.'

Theo scooped up the helmet so he could better see the augmented map projected inside.

'This was the last place she visited?'

'It was two days ago. Other than your flat, it was the last place she visited wearing her rig.'

He noted the time stamp.

'Same day she got fired from the Conservation ...'

'A lead's a lead.'

Clemmie took off her rig and gently laid it on the table before tousling her hair.

'So this could be where our mysterious caller lives,' Theo said, trying to sound confident.

Clemmie folded her arms and sat back in the chair.

'Could be.'

'Yeah.' Theo lacked conviction. 'I guess I better check it out.'

'Sure.'

'Could be dangerous.'

'Goes without saying.'

After an awkward pause, Theo stood and rolled his mother's rig into his knapsack.

'Well ... Thanks for helping out, Clem. It ... means a lot.'

Searching – and failing – for something more poignant to

say, he stood and stepped towards the door. Clemmie suddenly called out.

'Hold on, Theo.' She stood, quickly following. 'Some fool should come with you, to watch your back.'

Theo couldn't help but swallow a lungful of smugness as Clemmie followed him out.

They hurried down Shoreditch High Street. A Mecca for foodies, Shoreditch attracted scores of them in the warm late afternoon. It was said you could eat around the world from one end of the street to the other. Shoreditch's ubiquitous street art now covered almost every façade, turning the area into one giant mosaic that attracted tourists from around the globe and had even earned the district UNESCO World Heritage status, despite the odd Children of Ellul graffiti tag denouncing technology. The award had kept the spindly skyscrapers away. Instead, they circled Shoreditch like fortifications, hemming old London inside.

It began to rain warm fat drops they usually got in the September monsoons. Their water-repellent visors meant the rain didn't interfere with their AR, but droplets still trickled in from the tops of the rigs. Theo and Clemmie turned down a side road away from the silent traffic jams and crush of pedestrians. Even just a few yards in, the streets felt abandoned, if beautifully decorated. Theo followed Ella's footsteps via the archived map, the way ahead lit by a floating green arrow. As they approached the boundary to Spitalfields, rippling vectors spun across his visor, highlighting a steel double door marked with a Rorschach blot of navy blue paint. He pulled his rig down to his neck.

'That's where she went,' he said, nodding towards the building.

Clemmie didn't reply. She was absorbing the historical data streamed on to her visor from the borough's planning office.

'According to the records, that place has regularly bounced between owners and has been leased to dozens of companies in the last five years, from a private members' club to a few short-lived tech start-ups. It's currently registered as being owned by a property development company and is supposed to be unoccupied.'

From across the road they could see the fresh padlocked chain hanging from the door jamb. The innocuous two-storey red brick building was covered in a painting of a verdant jungle scene, complete with a fierce leopard perched on a tree limb, that gave no indication what lay within.

Clemmie studied the artwork.

'Now what?'

'I suppose we go inside.'

Theo tentatively made to cross the street, secretly hoping that Clemmie might try to talk him out of it.

'You don't seriously think we just walk up, knock on the door, and then demand to know if whoever's in there has seen your mum, do you?' Clemmie shook her head. 'Because that would be pretty stupid.'

Theo felt a knot of tension unravel in his stomach; thank God she was talking him out of it.

'There's a side entrance in that alley.' She pointed. 'Let's see if we can sneak in that way.'

Tension once again punched Theo in the stomach with

renewed conviction as Clemmie darted across the empty street. He followed with growing reluctance. The narrow alley was stacked with colour-coded recycling dumpsters either side of another smaller door. Clemmie approached it, her head scanning the wall around it.

'Not detecting any alarms,' she said.

Theo slipped his rig back on and looked around. A quick recalibration of his settings drowned out all the usual distracting streams: facial recognition, adverts and so on. He switched to an app that had been designed for DIY enthusiasts to detect studs and wiring behind dry walls, but was a well-known hack used by thieves to detect burglar alarms and near-field communication sensors.

'Power's on,' he noted as the display highlighted a few weak lines criss-crossing the walls. 'No NFCs, but there's a wireless network base station. An RTE421.'

Theo had no idea what any of this meant, but hoped that Clemmie did. Since wireless connection was provided for free by the government, and indeed was now a mandatory human right in most countries, only big businesses tended to have their own base stations, predominantly so they could move massive quantities of data securely.

'What did you say used to be here?'

Clemmie ran her hand across the door.

'Nothing recently. And certainly nothing that would require shifting that much data.'

There was no external handle on the fire escape. With the tips of her fingers, Clemmie managed to grip the embossed metal bevel around the jamb and pulled. The door swung open heavily on silent hinges.

Theo looked at her. 'What did you do?'

'Nothing,' she replied quietly, peering inside. 'It wasn't locked.'

'Why lock one door but not the other?' Theo checked his visor. 'And the network signal went down the moment you opened it.'

Clemmie shrugged and put one foot inside the building. She turned her head and flashed an excited smile at him.

'So, you coming?'

All he noticed were the dimples in her cheeks as she stepped through the threshold and into the darkness.

Chapter Eight

Clemmie wrinkled her nose and spoke quietly, trying not to taste the scent in the air.

'What *is* that smell?'

'Lemon?' Theo hazarded in a whisper. 'Reminds me of really strong floor cleaner – sort of a sickly smell. Somebody must have wanted this place cleaned up.'

'The homeless people around here must have raised their standards ...'

Her voice rose, echoing around the dark empty space.

'Ssshh!'

Shafts of sunlight speared through gaps in the boarded-up windows, highlighting three coils of heavy-duty industrial cable and curved scrape marks spread across the floor like black claws. A narrow brick archway led into a similar sized area, which Clemmie was already stepping into. She pulled off her visor to take a better look, letting it dangle from her hand by the straps.

The windows had been boarded up with large slabs of rust-tinged steel plate bolted into the masonry. A dozen rank mattresses were stacked in the far corner, their fabric stained with suspicious dark blotches that were thankfully undefinable in the gloom. Several spotlights with UV bulbs stood to one side, their power cables coiled around them.

'Was your mum into drugs by any chance?' Clemmie said all of a sudden.

'What the hell, Clem?'

He tried to sound offended, although she suspected he'd jumped to the same conclusion.

'Well,' she continued, 'this place looks like some sort of weed farm. Look at those lights.'

She nodded to five large lamps that stood six feet high and would look more at home on a film set. The rectangular lights were tinged blue, putting her in mind of a tanning salon. Next to them were six tarnished aluminium poles, which had been grouped together as if ready to transport. The tips were bent into blunt hooks holding empty plastic drip packets.

'Why would they leave them here?' Theo turned a full three-sixty, taking in the space. 'And the door unlocked ... unless they're coming back?' The words rattled from his dry mouth. 'We should get out—'

The unmistakable sound of multiple soles shuffling on the tiled floor emanated from the room they'd just entered from. Two people, in low conversation.

Theo was frozen to the spot, until Clemmie hissed in his ear and tugged his sleeve.

'Theo! Come on!'

She darted for another open doorway partially concealed by the mattresses, pulling Theo just behind her. It was a short dark corridor that stretched all of four yards before stopping at a heavily bolted door that she figured was an emergency exit on the opposite side of the building. She was about to voice her thoughts when they both became aware that the newcomers had entered the room behind them.

'I don't wanna touch 'em,' growled a man, partially moving into view. Theo and Clemmie both kneeled, hoping the cover of the mattresses and the darkness of the alcove would be enough to conceal them. 'They stink like shit, mate. It's most grievous.'

Theo stifled a gasp; his horrified gaze met Clemmie's. She had recognised the phrase and the Cockney whine too. It was unmistakably the same threatening voice from the call.

'You know you sound like an absolute dick when you say that?'

They caught a flash of shoulder-length blond hair from the speaker.

'I'm not getting elocution lessons from a bloody Afrikaner.'

Blondie harrumphed. 'And these stink because it *is* shit,' he stated, with a pronounced South African lilt to his voice.

He limped into partial view between the futons and the edge of the archway. Theo could just make out a pair of tan trousers, black jacket, but the rest of him was lost in shadows.

'Burn them.'

'You mental?' came the other voice. 'In 'ere?'

Blondie slapped a wall. 'Solid brick won't catch. They'll burn themselves out. Who'll know?'

The first man hesitated. 'Maybe.' He sounded unconvinced. 'Least I won't have to touch 'em.'

'I'll do it,' the blond man snapped irritably. 'You take the lamps. And double-check the base station cables are in the van. Don't leave anything behind.'

The Cockney rumbled up some phlegm in his throat and spat it out before giving a grunt of acknowledgement. A few moments later they heard the clink of metal and the rattle of lamps rolling out. Clemmie dug her fingers into Theo's arm as Blondie shuffled around the stack of mattresses with a pronounced limp. She sized him up, reckoning they could easily outrun him – *if* they had an actual escape route.

The South African took a metal cigarette lighter from his jacket pocket. It was the first time in her life that Clemmie had seen one outside an old movie. Smoking had been banned years ago – vaping was the only legal way to get a nicotine hit. The man flicked the lighter's hinged top with a satisfyingly heavy click, and a flame sprang to life. He held it against the mattress fabric until the material caught.

Clemmie sucked in a sharp breath as the flame illuminated the man's face. His right side was stubbled, handsome and angular, but the other was a pockmarked landscape of boils and red raw lumps that distorted his cheek and had swollen his eyelid to such a degree that it partially hooded his eye.

Then Blondie looked into the dark passage – straight at her.

Had the man heard her?

His gaze lingered before returning to the slowly spreading flames. Thick black smoke coiled from the fabric, causing Blondie to cough, and the next moment he was limping away after his colleague.

The flames danced across the bedding and Theo realised

they were effectively penned in. Clemmie spotted the alarm on his face.

'Don't worry,' she said. 'They're fire retardant. They'll burn themselves out in a few seconds.'

With a forceful *whump* and an accompanying blast of heat that pinned them both flat against the bolted door, the cheap mattress stuffing ignited in fierce orange flames that rapidly spread across the fabric.

Acrid smoke drifted into the passage and stung Clemmie's nostrils. Theo covered his mouth with his left forearm, using his sleeve as a filter; his other hand fumbled for the bolts on the front door. The growing bonfire behind intensified, providing just enough light to show the bolts had rusted into the keeps. Clemmie hooked two fingers behind the nearest bolt and pulled, but the metal only grazed her skin painfully.

'They won't budge!'

Clemmie glanced back to see the entire end of the passage was a hellish wall of fire. Black smoke flowed across the ceiling, steadily thickening in the enclosed space.

Theo tried the bolt, drawing blood as he leaned his weight into the attempt. His fingers slipped.

'Son of a—'

He kicked the door with such fury his rig jolted around his neck and struck him across the chin — and with it came a flash of inspiration.

He pulled his rig off and looped its back around the edge of the bolt. The stylish black carbon fibre weave glinted in the flames as he heaved. Still the bolt didn't move. Sucking in a lungful of foul air, Theo planted one foot against the wall and tugged again. This time he could have sworn there was a hint of movement.

Now the inverted sea of smoke was just overhead. Clemmie slid down the wall, sitting on her backside and coughing hard. Just a few more seconds and the stark choice would be between asphyxiation or barbecue.

Theo pulled again, at first bracing one foot against the wall, and then the other. The carbon fibre strap could easily hold his weight, and finally, with a sharp snap, the bolt came free.

'You did it!' Clemmie exclaimed as they both pulled at the door.

It didn't open.

Frantically, Clemmie checked the door up and down: and spotted a second tarnished bolt at the base so she followed Theo's lead and wrapped the strap from her own rig around it. She heaved, both feet pushing out against the wall.

Burning embers tumbled into the passageway as the mattress tower collapsed, sending a cloud of smoke billowing towards them. The embers bit into her cheek and exposed hands, but she refused to stop.

The bolt snapped back so suddenly that the screw heads severed and the lock dropped to the floor. They both lunged for the handle, heaving the door towards them. Weathered hinges cracked as they offered resistance from years of neglect, but it opened just enough for Clemmie to crawl through, Theo stepping over her, tumbling into the rain as the sudden onrush of air fed the flames with an audible *whump*.

He helped Clemmie stand and they staggered several

yards away, eyes streaming, sucking in lungfuls of air and coughing out nauseous fumes. The rain helped soothe their stinging eyes. After a few moments, they glanced around the quiet street as acrid smoke began to pour from the doorway.

'Let's go,' Clemmie urged. 'Before somebody thinks we did this.'

Theo nodded, but couldn't summon the words. He followed her into the network of side streets, both rubbing sore eyes and trying not to inhale the burning stench soaked into their clothes.

Chapter Nine

High-velocity water droplets felt as if they were stripping Theo's epidermis away. Despite the repeated punishment of the power shower, he could still smell the lingering smoke. After shampooing his hair for the third time, the odour diminished, although it was still coming from his discarded pile of clothes in the corner.

Not wanting to raise too many suspicions by travelling on the Tube, he and Clemmie had started walking home in the rain. But with each step their nausea had increased. The discussion had been sparse, skirting around the obvious fact that his mum was into something much nastier than he'd initially feared. The inevitable conclusion was that he'd simply have to go to the police to register her as missing, regardless of what the consequences would be. The rain intensified to the point Clemmie called an Uber, a luxury Theo couldn't afford, so he told her he'd prefer to walk the rest of the way and watched as Clemmie disappeared into traffic. Already feeling dispirited, the thirty-minute trudge back to his flat did nothing to improve matters.

Theo angled his head and lolled out his tongue, hoping

the water would cleanse his palate of the acerbic taste that refused to go. He peeked with one eye at his rig, indelicately sitting on top of the toilet, as it flashed to life with yet another incoming call from Milton. Theo hadn't answered any of them. He suspected Milton had spoken to Clemmie and now wanted in on the gossip. Theo wasn't in much of a mood to share.

He cut the water off and stepped from the shower, blindly reaching for his towel. The soft material felt good against his skin as he vigorously rubbed himself dry. Slipping on some fresh jeans and an *Army of Gort* T-shirt – their last album cover printed on the front, and on the back a list of the venues of a world tour Theo had failed to attend – he retrieved his rig and headed into the kitchen. The smoke inhalation had left him with an unquenchable thirst, and constant beakers of tap water failed to slake it. He wished they could afford some fresh juice, but that was a luxury these days. He placed his rig on the table next to Ella's and regarded them both thoughtfully, noticing the fresh scratches along his carbon fibre strap and the new grime that had embedded in the Emotive logo, lending it a certain depth and definition.

'My mum the drug tsar . . .' he mumbled to himself, struggling to believe it.

Ella had always lectured him about avoiding drug use, even though hard-core addiction had melted away to the fringes of society as SPACE evolved. Why bother with narcotics when a panoply of ultimate emotional highs could be had without leaving the house?

His rig pinged again. Milton.

With a sigh, he slipped his rig on and took the call. Milton faded into view, standing in the middle of the living room in a loud Hawaiian shirt and black denims. It wasn't really a projection of him – he could be sitting on the toilet for all Theo knew – but the hologram was the same realistic render used in SPACE, this time augmented into the real world and programmed to seamlessly step around furniture and objects to add a sense of *being there*.

'Theo!' Milton's hologram spread his arms. 'Where the hell have you been?'

'I've—'

'Scratch that, Clem told me you were both in trouble.'

'Not any more.' Theo tried to sound calm.

'Mate, she said you almost burned to death.'

'Well, maybe *choked* . . .' Theo said.

That was typical Clemmie, augmenting the truth. But then he felt guilty all of a sudden – the two of them could have died, after all. It was barely an embellishment, and to her credit, Clemmie had not once blamed him for putting her in danger.

'Is it your mum?'

'What did Clem tell you?' Theo asked cautiously.

Milton meant well but could hardly be trusted to keep his mouth shut.

'That she's gone missing. I checked the hospital databases to see if she'd been admitted as a patient.'

Theo stepped towards his friend, reaching out to clasp his arm before remembering he wasn't really there.

'Milton, you genius!'

That hadn't occurred to him. What if she'd just been hit by a car? Or attacked, or . . .

'Yeah, but I didn't find anything.' Reality crashed Theo's brief moment of euphoria. 'What are you going to do?'

Theo sighed.

'I'm going down the police station to file a missing person report,' he said, wearily rubbing his chin.

'Wouldn't it be quicker to do that online?'

'And have a bot-detective run the case?' Theo shook his head dismissively.

AI avatars had eased the weight off the under-resourced police forces and, in many petty crimes, they had resulted in swift arrests. But there were problems with crimes of passion and the motivations of missing persons cases, two elements machine learning struggled with.

'No thanks. I'd rather have some underpaid detective with a badge actually doing something about it.'

Milton nodded. 'Want me to come with you?'

Theo was genuinely touched by the unexpected offer. His first impulse was always to refuse offered help. The fact they bought things second-hand and relied on food banks was something he had always been careful to keep from his friends.

'I'll be fine.'

The swish of an open door made Milton's hologram look around.

'What was that?'

Theo frowned. 'Why you asking me? That came from your end.'

He drifted off when he heard shuffling feet in the hallway.

Somebody had entered through *his* front door – someone using the key card.

'Mum!'

Theo ran into the living room for a better view down the hall, as Milton's avatar dutifully stepped aside and around the sofa to avoid a collision.

But it wasn't his mother.

A familiar shock of blond hair, a smart black suit jacket and tan trousers – oh, and that unmistakable half-face – stepped into the apartment, gun in hand.

'Don't move, mate.'

But Theo did move, instinctively stepping back into the living room and momentarily out of view. He berated himself for thinking it could be his mother. The door key was stored securely in both their rigs; this guy had obviously hacked the lock.

'Who is he?' Milton asked, unheard and unseen by Blondie.

'The bloke from the warehouse,' hissed Theo, scanning the room for any object he could use as a weapon.

'Let me see!'

Milton could only see a virtual representation of Theo in his own house, but a flip of perspective meant he could now see Theo's point of view just as the man limped inside, leading the way with a matte black handgun, the 3-D printed kind criminals used so they couldn't be traced.

'I said don't be a *poephol*,' Blondie growled, twitching with tension and pain from his gammy leg.

The Afrikaans word confused Theo, before the translation scrolled across his rig: *arsehole*.

Blondie continued, undaunted.

'And we'll get on just fine, *Theo*.' His eyes scanned Theo up and down and he gave a derisive snort. 'You're a lanky shit all right, just like your mama described.'

'Get the hell out of my home!'

Theo was surprised that he sounded one hundred per cent braver than he felt.

The man glanced around and sniggered.

'What, this dump? Makes you wonder what she actually spent all that cash on.' His aim didn't stray from Theo. 'And you cost me a couple of quid too. I wagered you wouldn't be stupid enough to hang around here, and yet ...' He waved the barrel of the handgun in a circle. 'Here you are.'

'Where is she?' Theo said, his confidence beginning to waver.

'I was about to ask you the same thing.'

Theo tried to hide his surprise. So, they still *hadn't* got to her. The news allowed him to channel a confidence he didn't know he possessed. Perhaps it was because he was on home turf, but the sight of the ugly bastard threatening him in his own living room enraged him.

'She must have just gone out.'

Blondie took a step forward.

'I see you got your smart mouth from her. Her jaw is the first thing I'm gonna tear off after what she did to me.' He indicated his scarred face. '*Anaphy-fucking-laxis* poisoning.' He patted his lame leg with the side of the gun. 'The docs say I could have permanent nerve damage, because that *bitch* threw a beehive at me.'

'She never was much of a conversationalist.'

Theo's quick comment was badly timed. The rage in Blondie's eyes flickered like static and the gun was raised again, this time at a sideways angle often favoured by old-fashioned TV gangsters.

'You think that's funny?'

'I think a scar suits you.'

'I'm in no mood, *dwankie*.' The word *retard* flashed up on Theo's visor. 'Bossman says if I don't find her I have to find you. Then you know what I'm going to do to you? I'm gonna peel away little pieces of you. Stick pins in your eyes so you can feel just the smallest hint of my pain.' He ran his fingers down his swollen face. 'Little pieces of you will be chucked around London like chum until that whore mother of yours resurfaces.'

Theo took another couple of steps back into the kitchen. The man angled around so he didn't lose sight of his victim, drawing slowly nearer.

'You must see this isn't gonna end nice for you.'

Each word was emphasised by a gesture with his gun. He'd clearly watched far too many mafia B-movies.

Drawing closer, Theo noticed the end of the gun barrel sported a horizontal slit rather than the normal round bore-hole. It was a taser, he realised, designed to knock a person out, not kill them. His gaze swept around the kitchen. A knife block stood behind Ella's helmet. The blades had long ago blunted, but still ...

'Want me to call the cops?' asked Milton, his phantom avatar angled to look at the intruder.

'Not yet.'

'Who you talking to?' Blondie frowned, before noticing

an icon in the curvature of Theo's rig. 'You on a fucking call?' He raised the weapon. 'Hang up now!'

'Too late, dickhead. Everything you just said, your whole confession, is being streamed live into SPACE.'

He was lying, and hoped his acting skills were up to par.

The thug raised his weapon again.

'You *domkop*.'

Idiot, dunce, fool scrolled across Theo's rig before he closed the annoying translator.

'Theo!' Milton suddenly cried out. 'Make this a party line!'

Party lining was an old trick that exploited a bug in the NFC protocol. A holographic call could be unexpectedly thrown over to a passing stranger without their needing to accept it. It was a glitch that made Halloween extra fun and still hadn't been patched by the telecom companies.

Theo tossed the call straight into Blondie's rig, achieved with an AR paper aeroplane animation that flew between them. The guy gave a startled scream as Milton appeared in front of him in a garish Hawaiian shirt and flailing his arms like a cartoon ghost.

Blondie lisped an expletive and twisted the gun around to take a shot. A pair of Tesla darts shot harmlessly through the augmented avatar and embedded themselves in the wall before a lightning spark tore between them with a fierce crackle.

Theo ignored the knife block, instead bolting for the rear kitchen door, which automatically unlocked as he approached.

Blondie quickly wised up as the ruse became apparent.

'You little *bliksem*!'

His injured leg slowed him just enough for Theo to make it outside on to the external balcony, which Ella had decorated with half a dozen colourful pots, only to let the plants wither and die.

It was a dead end – thirty-three floors above the street.

Theo fumbled for the balcony rail, his fingers locating a carabiner dangling from it, just as Blondie filled the kitchen door.

He smirked when he saw his quarry was cornered.

'That was the shittiest rush for freedom I've ever seen.' He loaded another Tesla clip into the stun gun and pulled a face as he peered over Theo's shoulder. 'Even up here it's a shite view. What were you hoping? That you'd grow wings and fly?'

'Something like that,' Theo spat back.

Then he threw himself over the rail, screaming at the top of his lungs as he plummeted towards the pavement.

Chapter Ten

Theo's heart thundered in his chest. His stomach experienced the butterflies of weightlessness. And he was *absolutely certain* he had shit his pants.

A sharp pain wrenched his arm and he was abruptly pitched a full one-eighty degrees from his head first plunge. The carabiner he had fingered on the balcony was connected to a graphene-woven cable, which he had wrapped around his wrist seconds before taking the plunge. The jump-cable was wound through a smart gear system housed within the balcony rail that controlled the rate of descent. Designed as a cheap life-saving device for high-rise towers, the whole system was supposed to clip into a body harness to provide safe descent for young and old alike. It was *not* designed to be wrapped around a limb. The cable bit tight, cutting the circulation to Theo's hand.

Now the right way up, Theo continued to plummet fast enough to flee danger from above, but just slow enough that it wouldn't break his legs on impact. Blondie leaned over the rail, hurling down abuse. He aimed the stun gun and shot straight down. In the rapid formulation of his plan, Theo hadn't factored in being a hanging target.

The first dart grazed the flesh of his shoulder, the same arm that was being torn by the cable. The fresh wave of pain at least took away from the throbbing agony of the graphene biting his wrist. The second dart narrowly missed, shattering into the pavement below. It was a rare moment of good fortune, as without the two nodes impacting in close proximity the Tesla darts couldn't unleash their crippling electric pulse.

Theo's bare feet hit the concrete with force and he crumpled to his back, cursing that he hadn't had the time to retrieve his trainers following his shower.

He used his teeth to slacken the cable from his wrist. His hand looked like a giant prune and his entire arm was numb. He glanced up and saw his attacker had retreated back inside. Theo staggered to his feet and broke into a run.

'That was wild!' screamed Milton in his rig. Theo had completely forgotten they were still connected.

'Jesus, Milt! That was terrifying! I'm heading to you now. But I need a favour. I need trainers. And maybe some clean jeans and underwear ...' He paused. 'Please don't ask.'

'No problem. Hey, if he doesn't know where your mum is, that's good news, right?'

Theo reached a junction and ran diagonally over the cross-roads, ignoring the horns from electric cars as they shot past him. He made it to the other side without stopping, eager to put as much distance as possible between himself and the thug.

'It's certainly something,' he agreed. 'But I still don't

know where she is. She's completely off-grid without her rig.'

Theo guessed that was part of the reason Ella had left it behind.

'Clem said she found some useable data on your mum's rig. We can try to piece together her movements.'

Theo stopped dead in his tracks.

'Bollocks!'

'What?'

'I left her rig in the kitchen!'

'Why would you do that?'

'Because I was busy psyching myself up to jump off the bloody balcony!' Theo snapped.

He turned back in the direction of his home, debating whether he should return. No, Blondie didn't look that incompetent; he would have taken it already.

Theo turned and continued running, his bare feet already sore on the coarse pavement – his punishment for losing the only clue he had to locate his mother.

'Christ, what were you thinking?'

'I was *thinking*,' Milton snapped back, 'that I was helping you.'

Theo yanked the belt on his new jeans in an extra notch in an attempt to hold them up. The fabric swelled around his legs like a bloated parachute two sizes too big.

'They're all I could find in Dad's wardrobe.' Milton was on the defensive, and Theo knew it was unfair to antagonise him. 'And anyway that look's sort of coming back into fashion now.'

'Yeah, thanks,' Theo muttered and sat back down on the edge of the bed.

He regarded the floating head in the centre of the room, crafted from an augmented face creator app normally used by game designers.

'It's not too bad,' he admitted.

The resemblance to Blondie was there, albeit in a vague kind of way.

Milton shrugged, attempting to hide his pride.

'I mess around with this stuff for my stream all the time. I customised Kaiju Killer myself, you know.'

'Yeah, I saw your *Avasta* review,' Theo said as he studied the sculpture. 'The left side of his face was screwed up worse than that. A bad reaction to being stung by a swarm of bees.'

'Not a common thing in London. If we can search the hospital admissions maybe we can get a match.' He paused. 'Good review, wasn't it?'

Theo pulled a face. 'I think your two-finger review method is a tad limited.'

'Count the subscribers, baby,' Milton said with obvious pride.

'Can you search the hospital admissions for him?'

Milton shook his head, his cheeks turning pink. 'I could if I had a name, like I did with your mum. But the police could do it.'

Theo glared at the giant head, repressing the overwhelming urge to punch it. Ella had left her rig to go off the grid and Blondie had yet to locate her, so all the police would be doing was tracking her down when she *wanted* to hide.

Which raises the question: why hadn't she gone to them in the first place?

He caught Milton staring at him and, as if by the power of their long-standing friendship, Theo was able to read his thoughts: *You're not planning on telling the police, are you?*

Theo sighed and lay back on the bed. His back was aching, his shoulder killing him from where he had pulled the dart out, and now the red-raw strap marks around his wrist were as itchy as hell, no matter how much antiseptic cream he smothered on.

'If she fell into drug dealing then going to the police right now seems wrong. Even if she had decided to get out.'

'Which is what it sounds like she was trying to do,' Milton chimed in.

Theo nodded. 'But she'll still be implicated. And that means prison time.'

Milton walked around the floating mugshot and slapped it to make it spin like a roulette wheel.

'I agree with everything you say,' he said thoughtfully, pausing long enough for Theo to lift his head and look at him expectantly. 'But *you* were the one receiving the death threat. *You* were the one having the Elephant Man here kicking your door down and forcing you to take a swan dive out of a block of flats, not your mum. She did the smart thing and legged it. And remember, she didn't even bother warning you.' He shook his head. 'That's harsh.'

Theo sat back up. Milton had tried to sound sympathetic, but couldn't completely hide his vitriol. And it was true.

Milton shot him a pitying look. 'I mean, where are you supposed to live now? She must have thought of that.'

Theo shrugged, then gave a vague gesture to the room around him.

'Oh, no.' Milton shook his head. 'My parents didn't even want *me* home for the summer. I'm already getting under their feet, and I hate it. Never move back in with your parents.'

Despite the fact they owned a six-bedroom house sprawled across four levels, Milton's parents were ultra-conservative. The last time Theo could remember being invited to stay over was back when they were both ten.

'Look,' Theo countered, 'I can't stay with Baxter. His folks are having loads of problems with his sister and Rex. Remember that stoner boyfriend of hers? They're still together. And Clemmie, well ...' He stood, gently rubbing his throbbing wrist. Only now was he understanding just how isolated he was. 'What about your uni room?'

Milton shook his head. 'We all get booted out every summer. I'm in a whole new building when I get back.' He took a step towards Theo in a vague hint of camaraderie. 'Look, I know this is all a bit shit, but maybe your mum *expected* you to go to the police? At least they'd be able to keep an eye on your flat in case he comes back.'

He waved a hand towards the floating head.

Theo knew it was the right thing to do.

And yet ...

'I said I'd come with you to the police station if you want,' said Milton. 'Baxter won't, not while he's still doing community service.'

'He's doing that because of Rex.' Theo gave a dry chuckle. They had both met the notorious boyfriend dozens of times. He seemed harmless enough and fashioned himself as a fixer, straddling the law, although they had yet to actually see any of his alleged handiwork. While in uni, Baxter had been caught in a nightclub selling thirty-minute extension packs to SPACE. Known on the streets as *staves*, they were illegal mods that allowed users to stay beyond the mandatory three-hour limit. Even with such a short extension, the risk of Lag or a complete mental breakdown was high, but people seemed willing enough to pay for it.

Luckily for Baxter the mods he'd scored from Rex were buggy, so didn't work. That formed the spine of his defence: that he was only running a *scam*. That landed him community service over a prison sentence. Although he never actually named Rex, Baxter's parents suspected the truth and it had caused fractions in their family, with Anna, his sister, eventually leaving home to live with Rex in some squalid bedsit in Bermondsey, just south of the Thames.

An idea struck Theo.

'If Rex had my mum's rig then he might have been able to hack deeper into it. I mean properly. Or at least find somebody who could.'

Milton shrugged. 'Maybe. But that's moot anyway because you don't have it.'

Theo stood and approached Blondie's giant floating head. He reached a hand out to stop it from spinning.

'Yeah. But *he* does . . .'

Theo saved the mugshot file and slipped his rig off, rubbing his tired eyes. The familiar, distant rumblings of a migraine were making themselves known, driven from the wells of stress building in his body.

'If I find him I can get it back.'

'Or he could lead you to your mum ...' Milton paused as Theo nodded in agreement. 'And then he can kill you *both*.'

Theo ran a hand through his hair. Milton removed his rig and tossed it on to the bed. He crossed to Theo and gripped his shoulder.

'Stop overthinking this. You jumped out of a fucking window. He almost burned you and Clem to death. This is a serious gangster we're talking about. You are not. You work in a burger hut, Theo. You're not even close to his level.' The comparison felt like a punch directly to his pride, but Milton ploughed on with his half-arsed motivation speech. 'You've done all you can, which is run. Report this mess before it gets any worse.'

Theo inhaled slowly, in part to ease the building pressure in his head, but mostly to refrain from saying anything snarky to Milton. After all, his mate was only trying to help, even it was with the full force of the brutal truth.

He clapped Milton on the shoulder. 'You're right.' He sat on the bed to slip on the trainers Milton had lent him. They were his father's too, and were a size too big, but he was in no place to complain. 'I've got a shift tonight. I better go.'

Theo slid his rig back on and gave a nod of thanks.

'Cheers for the crappy jeans and shoes.'

'Any time.'

Theo left as quickly as he could. He really did have a shift in forty-seven minutes, so his first call was to message in sick.

His next call was to Clemmie to warn her he was coming over. Just in case he was about to crash another date.

Chapter Eleven

Clemmie's house was an old Edwardian semi-detached nestled on a sloping road in Muswell Hill, and far less palatial than Milton's. However, it was spacious enough and was beyond anything Ella could afford. In fact, Clemmie's father could only afford it on a police salary because 3-D printing had plummeted house prices to something more affordable.

Clemmie hadn't tried to talk Theo out of coming around when he'd called from the Tube, already halfway to her home. But from the tone of her voice he wasn't convinced she was all that happy about it. Or was that just his imagination?

'Nice outfit,' Clemmie commented when she answered the door in a loose-fitting grey sweat top and black jeans. She looked him up and down critically. 'Let me guess – you've come dressed from the nineties?'

Her parents, on the other hand, were nothing less than charm personified, which had the effect of making Theo feel all the more self-conscious. Clemmie's stepmother, Augusta, insisted he join them for dinner and laid another place at the table for him. She had a hint of Polish in her accent, and was either approaching, or just into, her fifties – Theo couldn't tell. Clemmie had never got on with her – it was rather an open secret – yet Theo couldn't understand why, as she had always been very warm and welcoming to him. Maybe it was because she had replaced her real mother.

Theo had seen pictures of her, a raven-haired beauty with alluring almond-shaped brown eyes, full lips and flawless mocha coloured skin that promoted her high cheekbones. She had been raised in France and her DNA clearly flowed through Clemmie's veins. From what he'd pieced together over the years, her mother had had an affair and left when Clemmie was an impressionable nine-year-old – the perfect age to be screwed up by your parents.

Clemmie's father, Martin, entered the dining room from his office at the back of the property, muttering under his breath as he stroked his stubbled chin. He was mid-fifties, a handsome blend of his Welsh mother and Pakistani father. A smile washed over his face when he noticed Theo standing awkwardly at the dining table.

'Theodore!' he said, immediately reaching to shake his hand. 'I didn't know you were coming. Haven't seen you in a while.'

It was close to two years, but Theo didn't want to dwell too much on that.

'Sounds like you've had a bad day at work, Mr Laghari.'

Martin playfully shook Theo's shoulder.

'How many times do I have to tell you to call me Martin?' He gestured for him to sit at the table. 'Work never leaves me alone.' He took a casserole dish from Augusta and laid it in the centre of the table. 'But you know all about that, right? University isn't the easy ride it was when I was your age.'

Theo sat and Clemmie opted for the seat next to him.

'Theo didn't go to uni, remember.'

'Oh.' Martin sounded genuinely surprised as he relayed a stack of plates from his wife and laid them out. 'Really?'

'My mum needed me home ...' Theo said quietly, feeling embarrassment searing across his cheeks.

All his friends' parents knew one another from the numerous school evenings and events they had attended together for over a decade. Milton's parents remained indifferent and aloof towards the others, while they had all collectively attempted not to engage with Baxter's, who seemed a bit *down to earth* for their tastes. However, Ella and Augusta had always got on well when their paths had crossed.

'Well, it is *extremely* expensive,' Augusta said, returning with a water decanter and taking her seat next to Martin. 'I'm amazed anyone can afford to go these days.'

'Exactly,' Theo politely replied as Augusta ladled out some sort of chicken onto his plate. His stomach grumbled noisily in response to the smell, reminding him that he hadn't eaten since the previous night. He felt everybody's eyes fall on him. 'Smells really good.'

'Chicken chasseur.' She served Clemmie next. 'When did you last eat?'

Theo opened his mouth to reply, but was stopped by Clemmie's fingernails digging into his thigh.

'Theo works at *Synger* now,' volunteered Clemmie.

Her parents exchanged unimpressed looks.

'Clémence, try to be nice.' Clemmie pulled a face, an

automatic reaction to anybody who dared use her full name. 'Please forgive her manners. University seems to have instilled in her a streak of arrogance.'

Clemmie scowled. She flicked a look at her father for support but none was forthcoming. In fact, it looked as though he was avoiding the conversation entirely.

'Mixing with the wrong sort,' Augusta continued. 'And learning to ride a motorbike, of *all* the deathtraps ...'

Theo frowned at Clemmie.

'You ride a bike?' he said.

She nodded, her eyes fixed on her plate as she tried to keep a lid on her anger.

'That's so cool,' he whispered in genuine awe.

'It's motocross, *mother*. I'm not a Hell's Angel just yet, so that shouldn't give you a stigma with anybody in the Mayor's office. I know how those *types* get all uppity at the slightest thing.'

Augusta bristled.

'That's enough, Clem,' Martin snapped, avoiding looking at either woman. Clemmie lapsed back into her silent fume.

Augusta rested her sharp chin on steepled fingers as she studied Theo.

'And how's your mother these days?' she said.

'I ...'

Clemmie gave him a gentle thump on the leg, as if to say *stick to the script*.

During the brief call on the Tube, Theo had sketched his plan to use her father's police computer to ID Blondie. Clemmie had used it in the past, almost exclusively to dig up gossip about people she knew. The knowledge that somebody else's parents had committed driving offences, and in one case, tax fraud, was a good deterrent against bullies. Clemmie had used it without mercy, even if it meant relegating herself to the bottom of the popularity table.

'She's good, thanks.'

Theo projected the words with confidence and took a fork full of tender chicken, which drowned the dry smoky texture he had been putting up with all day.

'This is wonderful! I can't remember the last time Mum . . .' *made anything* hung in the air, reminding him he had been living on a diet of synthetic meals from food banks for far too long.

'The last time I bumped into Ella, she was working in one of the Conservations.'

Augusta started eating, her glance constantly appraising Theo as if probing for details.

'She enjoys it,' he said. 'Anything to take her out of the city, you know. She always said it was her favourite place.'

'And genuinely important work,' Martin added with a nod. He guzzled down the food as if it was his last ever meal. 'Bees are extraordinary insects. They can be trained, you know.'

Clemmie snorted a cute laugh that momentarily distracted Theo.

'Trained?' she said. 'What, like a dog?'

'Yes exactly. Like a dog.' Martin ignored her pout of disbelief. 'Scent is the new weapon in the streets, you see. Pheromones travel huge distances. They even have electronic pheromone detectors modelled on bees. Incredible. We've got a unit training them to sniff out drugs.' His eyebrows shot up and he couldn't help smiling when Theo laughed. 'I'm serious. Their noses are about a hundred times more powerful than ours. And forget sniffer dogs – bees come back and communicate the location to the rest of the hive. AI interprets their dance.' He swayed his shoulders, making Theo grin. Even Clemmie smiled, although her mother's face tightened with disapproval. Martin swooped his fork through the air. 'And we can follow the flight plan back to the stash. It's remarkable.'

Theo was surprised.

'Drugs? Who still uses them? We have SPACE for all of that. All the highs and none of the problems.'

'There's still some people who like to go ...' Martin paused. '*Old* school.' He shook his head and thoughtfully dissected the remaining chicken on his plate with his fork. 'And you know what, at times I miss that. At least you knew where you were with a good old-fashioned crim with a gun. A dealer pushing cocaine was something solid. Now everything's getting so damned twisted with SPACE. I know your generation never fault it, but it has its problems, trust me.'

'Martin has been promoted to lead the vCrimes unit.' Augusta flashed a proud smile across the table at him. 'A superintendent, leading a special task force within the vPolice,' she added with a wink.

'Since when does stopping second-skins needs a task force?' Clemmie asked.

'There's a sound reason skins are banned.' Martin waved his fork at her for emphasis. 'But there are bigger prob- lems.' A dark look crossed his face. 'Gangs who smuggled out second-skins are now porting weapons out of gaming bubbles and combining them with modified police code to make killers.'

One of the safeguards placed in SPACE was a curb on the emotional feedback. Sure, users could feel sensations, including pain to a degree, but not enough to *kill* them.

Too many times had a notorious criminal appeared in public SPACE arenas, looking exactly the same as they did in real life as they openly mocked the law and flaunted their illegal gains. Nothing could be done to stop them as their precise location in the flesh couldn't be traced and their access into SPACE couldn't be blocked.

The solution was to bring in police-controlled virtual weapons that overwrote that safety protocol. Shoot a criminal with an overwhelming emotion stimulant in SPACE, and you could effectively cause a seizure in The Real. A seizure strong enough to kill them. Simple and lethal.

Theo frowned. 'Surely System would reprogram that?'

'You'd have thought so –' Martin's brow furrowed – 'but apparently not. The whole SPACE ecosystem has grown out of control, beyond anything James Lewinsky envisioned. AI, Slifs, emotion smuggling ... It's simply far too complex at this stage to be unpicked. And even if they could be, alterations can't be made now Slifs have their own legal rights.' He sighed and noisily dropped his fork on his plate. 'Bloody Virts!'

Theo almost choked as he swallowed. He hadn't been expecting him to use such racist language. *Virts* was the most politically incorrect term to describe SPACE's now sentient virtual residents.

Clemmie slapped the table with her palm and snapped at her father.

'Dad! That's terrible!'

'Well ... you don't have to deal with them like we do. You don't understand,' he added with quiet contempt. 'They have their own cloned system architecture now that runs on separate orbital quantum servers. They live in SPACE, but they're not part of it.' Before Clemmie could react again, he continued, louder. 'And black market pax are just getting out of hand.'

Theo frowned. 'What's a pax?'

Augusta pointedly cleared her throat. 'Is that really a discussion for the dinner table?'

Martin forced a smile and waved his hand dismissively.

'Sorry. No. You see, work just has a habit of getting on top of me.'

As if on cue, Martin's rig, hanging on a peg in the hallway, suddenly rang. He puffed out his cheeks and sighed as he stood to answer it.

'See?' he said finally.

He disappeared into the hall to take the call, while Augusta filled his absence with small talk about holiday plans over Christmas. Theo could barely think beyond the next day, so he nodded and made the appropriate noises until Martin returned, pulling on an overcoat, his black police-issue rig across his eyes.

'I have to go to the station,' Martin announced. 'Some bobbies found another Den.'

Augusta pushed her plate back.

'That's such a shame. I was hoping to enlist Theodore into a game of Monopoly.'

She eyed the battered board game tucked under a sideboard. Theo remembered it was her favourite, and had spent many evenings with Baxter and Milton all trapped in the house playing it for hours at a time.

'Lucky escape,' Clemmie whispered under her breath.

'Need a lift to the Tube?' Augusta asked her husband. 'I was going to pop in and see Susan anyway.'

'Please.'

She rose to fetch her jacket and rig.

'Will you still be here when I return?'

Theo shook his head. 'I don't think so. I wasn't planning to stay long. I have to get back.'

'Going back home? Well, send my love to your mother. And don't be a stranger! You're welcome here any time. Tell her I would love to see her.'

Clemmie remained seated until she saw the headlights of their car reverse from the drive and merge with the main road. Then she jumped to her feet and hurried to her father's study.

'We have an hour,' she said. 'Maybe ninety minutes. Come on.'

The study was a cramped room with a bookcase lining the entire length of one of its walls, crammed with yellowing paperbacks and dog-eared magazines. Theo was momentarily taken aback; he'd never seen so many books in one place before. In all his years they had been friends, Clemmie had never allowed him in her father's study. She caught his reaction as she sat at the desk.

'My dad's *real* old school,' she said. 'He loves paper.'

'How does somebody so out of touch get to lead a vCrimes unit? Don't get me wrong, I like your dad, but—'

'You heard him. He'd rather unplug the whole world.'

She carefully took a rig from a stand on the desk. Unlike the fashion-conscious sets worn on the street, this one had a pair of chrome arms that curved over the wearer's skull like the antennae of some monstrous insect. An umbilical cord as thick as Theo's thumb ran from the back of the rig to a port in the floor. Even with wetware security measures, the police found old-fashioned hard cabling was best to avoid hackers. Instead of a curved glass visor it was a solid geometric shape; there was no need for augmentation when the user was about to be plumbed into the access corridors of SPACE.

Clemmie poised the helmet over her head.

'This is configured for Dad's emos, but he never locks it. Fingers crossed ...' She placed the rig down, and Theo watched as she repositioned herself to get comfortable with the additional weight. 'Hey presto ... I'm in. I'm going to tether you. Ready?'

Theo acknowledged a tether request that popped on to his visor, floating above Clemmie's head. As soon as he did so he experienced a sickening sensation, as if his whole body was being sucked through a drinking straw. Light blasted his retinas and he suddenly found himself floating in a world of geometric shapes, each with streams of code flashing across their surfaces.

'Welcome to Foundation.'

Clemmie's voice echoed around him. Theo looked around

but couldn't see her avatar. A quick check revealed he was completely bodiless too, just a lump of floating consciousness bobbing in a sea of data. If anything, this made him feel even more nauseous.

'This is what they used to call cyberspace,' Clemmie narrated inside his head.

Theo was aware of Foundation – it was the programming language James Lewinsky had literally built SPACE with. It was also the hard-core coding dimension used by System, games designers, mod creators and criminals. It was the place where things got done.

'We're in the City of London Police system now. They've had a major refurb since I was last here.'

'This is a refurb?'

Theo felt as if his voice wasn't his own, like he was having an out-of-body experience.

'Okay.' Clemmie ignored him. 'Criminal records should be over here.'

There was a sudden lurch as Theo was propelled between a dozen geometric shapes that loomed over him like skyscrapers. It was like being on a roller coaster with no way to control which way they twisted and turned, the spiralling sensation made all the worse due to no defined horizon.

Clemmie spoke again, without any indication she was feeling queasy at all.

'Don't forget Dad works for the City of London Police, not the Met. They protect the inner heart of the City of London, which is, like, one square mile. It's tiny.'

'That's weird,' Theo managed, fearful any further words would make him vomit.

'It's cool!' Clemmie shot back brightly. 'The City of London is an enclave. A separate county, and has been for hundreds of years. It's run by a corporation – I guess that's why they were chosen for vCrimes.' She glanced up at one of the shapes. 'Here we are. The Criminal database.'

They skimmed the side of a colossal diamond – the coding on the side informed Theo he was looking at the 'Personnel Admin Block' – then a massive icosahedron hove into view in front of them like a small moon. A myriad of coloured lights flowed over it, indicating heavy access from other users. As they watched, the shape slowly rotated and grew a little in bulk.

'Nice timing. They've just updated it. It's shared with every other police force in the country. Now upload your call with Milton.'

Following her instructions, Theo had used the time travelling to Clemmie's house to retrieve the sump file of his call which contained video footage of Blondie. The wetware interface read his mental intentions and retrieved the video file, which appeared in Foundation as a two-dimensional video clip. He tossed it at the icosahedron. The clip struck the surface of the Criminal database and vanished with a small flash.

There was a flurry of luminosity around the impact point, a visualisation of the database's AI interrogating the file. Within moments it threw back an answer.

One was a picture of Milton, complete with a full fact file to one side outlining what looked like every single byte of information about his life, including a link to his father's file indicating he was currently undergoing a tax audit. The other file simply had the message: 'Insufficient quality for positive ID'.

'What the hell?' snapped Theo. 'He was literally right in front of me.'

'Let me see the video.'

Theo threw the file so it floated in front of them, as big as a drive-in movie screen. The footage started from the moment Blondie entered the room, but his head was a swirling mass of pixels and his voice nothing more than crackling static. The virtual Milton, by contrast, was perfectly preserved.

'What the ...?' Theo repeated, puzzled.

'The bastard's wearing a scrambler!'

'I thought they were just an urban myth.'

'Clearly not. And they're expensive.' Clemmie clicked her tongue thoughtfully. Then her tone changed as she mimicked something she had heard on a streaming channel. 'Used by celebs, spies and killers ...'

'I have the mugshot Milton put together.'

He threw up the augmented photofit he had shown Milton.

'Mmm, not bad,' remarked Clemmie. 'But I doubt the system could get any useable biometric data from Milton's artwork. I'll cross-reference it with hospital admin, anaphylactic poisoning, see what matches.'

Again, Theo tossed it into the database. After another flurry of activity, a record popped up from the Queen Elizabeth Hospital: RECORD EXPUNGED.

A further message flashed up on the Criminal database: NO MATCH FOUND.

'Oh, for Christ's sake!'

Theo was struck by an intense wave of dizziness and felt as if he had been given a pair of black eyes as he suddenly found himself standing back in Martin's office. A little more used to being suddenly ejected from the system, Clemmie wasn't suffering and had already removed the rig and placed it heavily on the desk.

'Who would expunge a record?' she snarled.

Theo stood and staggered into the bookcase, only just stabilising himself in time to prevent a torrent of books from falling on his head. Clemmie noticed and flashed an apologetic smile.

'Sorry, Theo,' she said. 'I forgot. If you're going to throw up please use the toilet across the hall.'

Theo forced himself to swallow hard.

'I'm fine,' he lied. 'So, what does it mean for Blondie?'

'It means *Blondie* is what they call a bad actor. And my dad's told me enough over the years to know that expunging a record needs assistance from high places. Which indicates this is more serious than we thought. I hate to tell you this, but I think the time's come for you to report it.'

Theo slid his rig around his neck and wiped the sweat from his brow. Clemmie joined him and gently brushed the damp strands of hair from his brow, standing so close she smelled exquisite – whether it was shampoo, shower gel, some perfume or just *her*, he couldn't tell. Her brown eyes seemed to dispel the nausea he was feeling.

'Theo, I'm serious. Before something happens to her, let's go to the police station. Now.'

Theo wanted to hold her hand and lean closer. Instead he nodded – and quickly dashed to a plastic rubbish bin under the desk and filled it with an ungodly quantity of vomit.

Chapter Twelve

The three-storey orange brick Georgian aspect of Bow Road Police Station was a charming relic of historical London: site of the world's first professional police force, and a recent recipient of a Brown Plaque to ensure the UK's heritage wasn't lost to modernisation. Even the road in front had been dug up and the old cobbled surface recreated to hark back to Victoriana. It certainly stood out from the bland half-finished printed buildings across the street that could have been copied and pasted from any city in the world.

This late in the evening, the construction site was quiet. Four huge bright red JCB mobile printers stood idle. The bloated machines sat on caterpillar tracks, with long articulated printing arms connected to enormous tanks of composite material. Poised, they resembled prehistoric mammoths in the darkness, ready for dawn when the onboard AI systems would once again set out to build London.

However quaint the station looked from the outside, inside it was as busy and grim as Theo had anticipated. Preservation had succumbed to practical necessity and it had been rebuilt from scratch. Green plastic bucket seats were bolted to the grubby white walls, forming a waiting area from which a plump desk sergeant eyed Theo and Clemmie through an acrylic glass window that stretched to the ceiling. To the side, a single blue door led deeper into the station, accessible only by the biometrics of the officers on duty.

Theo occasionally shuffled his feet when his oversized trainers kept sticking to the dirty floor, all the while attempting to ignore the reek of alcohol from the dishevelled man in an expensive business suit next to him. To his left, Clemmie sat fending off the evening chill in a slightly too large khaki combat jacket, which was covered in Korean military patches an uncle had once bought her on a trip to the East. She was lost in social media feeds that danced across her visor, oblivious to the lecherous gaze of an older man sat opposite. Theo had pegged him as some form of sexual predator but when the freak was called, he broke into tears while registering his missing dog.

A migraine was banging Theo's forehead like an angry toddler, making him increasingly irritable by the second. It was a convenient excuse for habitually labelling people in such a negative light. He berated himself; being physically isolated from his friends for so long had clearly had a corrosive effect on him.

'Theodore Wilson?'

Theo only registered his name when a uniformed gangly sergeant read it louder to him the second time around. The officer was glaring directly at him; the facial recognition on his police issue rig had already picked Theo out from the crowd.

'Huh? That's me.' Theo stood and followed the sergeant's gesture to the blue door. After two steps he noticed Clemmie wasn't following. 'Clem?'

'I'll wait here if it's okay with you.' Her tone made it clear he didn't have a choice. 'I don't want my name put down on that report.'

On the way to the station she had told Theo to leave her out of the equation. He was to say he had been acting alone, that she hadn't been with him in the abandoned building, and neither of them had sneaked into police records. The moment her name was registered, even as a witness, Clemmie was convinced it would be flagged up on her father's system, and then all hell would be unleashed.

Theo followed the sergeant through the door and down a flickering fluorescent-lit corridor lined with interview rooms. He opened the door to room six and motioned Theo to enter.

Inside was poky, with barely enough room for a table and four chairs. A lone ceiling light cast a yellowish pall across everything, and the single window was covered by a grubby grey blind.

'Take a pew.'

The sergeant indicated the seat furthest from the door. He waited for Theo to sit, before settling opposite and resting both elbows on the table. From his rig the copper read Theo's initial statement, taken when he'd first entered the station.

'You wish to register a missing person? You know you could have done that with a bot?'

'It's my mum,' Theo said.

The sergeant tapped his rig. 'All I'm doing here is record-ing our conversation and the software is logging everything.'

Just like a bot, was the unspoken end of his sentence.

'I don't want to be messed around by a bot.'

The sergeant sighed. 'Yeah, it's much better to be bug-gered around by human error. Right. My name is Sergeant Jones. Can you confirm these details are correct?'

A file flashed up in the room between them. It showed all of Theo's personal data, address and wafer-thin job history. It linked to another file showing his mother's name and pic-ture, but her data were redacted.

'That's correct,' Theo confirmed.

'When did your mother go missing?'

'Last night.'

'And it's taken you all day to report it?'

Theo shifted in the hard plastic seat.

'I was in SPACE when she received a call.' He noticed Jones's questioning frown and quickly explained. 'It was on her rig, not mine. She'd left it at home for some reason. At first I thought it may have been something about a job. She'd ... recently lost hers. It was actually a voice call. No ID, nothing. A man ... threatening to cut me up if Mum didn't pay money she owed, and return something she'd taken. I don't know, it was all very confusing.' Theo's mouth was suddenly parched as the call replayed in his mind. 'May I have some water?'

'Carry on,' the sergeant said.

Theo took a moment to collect his thoughts.

'I had no idea she was involved with a loan shark. I waited up for her. When she didn't come back this morning I went to where she used to work.' A little disconcertingly, additional intel popped up between them, highlighting Ella's last known place of employment. 'Her boss hadn't seen her since she was sacked.'

'Sacked?'

Theo cleared his throat and nodded. 'The loan shark turned up demanding money and she ... Well, she threw a beehive at him.'

Sergeant Jones winced. 'That could land her a hefty fine.'

'Forget the fucking bees!' snapped Theo, instantly regretting his outburst. He softened his tone, but it was clear from the cop's reaction it wasn't enough. 'This bloke threatened to kill us. Then he turned up at my flat demanding to know where she was.'

Before Jones could interrupt, Theo dropped the recording of Blondie entering his flat and it hovered between them. The sergeant watched it with an increasing frown, then a final 'wow' of incredulity as Theo escaped and the clip cut off.

'You jumped off your balcony?' he asked with a measure of admiration.

'I was scared.'

'And using a scrambler.' His eyebrows raised. 'That's pretty high-end for a loan shark. Even an extremely well-connected dealer would struggle to get that.'

Theo discreetly wiped his damp palms on his jeans, conscious he had avoided mentioning his and Clemmie's encounter, as well as any possible drug-related connections. After all, that was speculation on his own part and he had no desire to overcomplicate things.

Jones drummed his fingers as he thought.

'It seems to me that your mother may have in fact *wanted* to go missing.'

'I thought that too,' Theo said. 'But he has her rig now. He might be able to use it to trace her movements, locate her. He may have already found her for all I know!' His mouth was dry again.

'Let me get you that drink.' Any previous animosity in Jones's tone had now vanished. He flashed a thin smile of admiration. 'This is clearly a serious situation. You did well not to bot it. I'll get somebody assigned to the case.'

Theo nodded his thanks. The moment the sergeant left the room, he felt his arms turn to jelly, and he slumped across the table with his head nestled in his arms as fatigue swamped him. Closing his eyes, he felt the welcoming tendrils of sleep reaching for him and he mentally kicked himself for not reporting the whole mess sooner.

He tried to call Clemmie to update her, but for security reasons there was no connectivity inside the room. He removed his rig and rolled the knuckle of his index finger between his eyes to null the pain that was still gnawing him. Without any painkillers, sleep would be the only way to rid himself of it.

The gentle click of the door's latch roused Theo from a microsleep. How long had he drifted off? Minutes or seconds?

He sat back and stretched, knots in his shoulders crunching. At least his migraine had receded to a more palatable throb. Sergeant Jones returned with a cup of water, which Theo eagerly accepted. Jones was joined by a smaller man wearing a mustard shirt open at the neck, his belly flopping over his belt buckle. He self-consciously masked his portly frame with a baggy black leather jacket, but it served only to highlight his short stature. His rig hung from a Velcro strap attached to his belt. He had a pleasant smiling face, a fringe of black hair orbiting the back of his head, highlighting a smooth bald scalp. As if to make up for it, he'd grown a moustache that dominated his top lip. He looked more *sidekick* than the *go get 'em* figure Theo had been hoping for.

'Theodore, this is DCI Frasier.'

Theo gave a quick nod as he gulped the tepid water.

'I read your statement, Theo,' Frasier said with a ruthless Cockney accent as he sat down. 'You don't mind if I call you Theo?'

'Sure,' Theo said.

Jones made no attempt to sit, but stood to one side as Frasier's smile widened.

'From your statement −' Frasier tapped Theo's rig on the table − 'it seems to me your mother may be involved in something a bit more −' he waved his fingers in a circle as he searched for the word − '*extreme* than upsetting a couple of loan sharks.'

'What do you mean?'

Frasier indicated to the sergeant. 'Don't record this. It's a very sensitive vCrimes operation.'

Jones hesitated for a moment, then removed his rig. Theo's migraine throbbed harder; what had Ella got herself into?

'What do you know about Dens?'

Theo shook his head and shrugged. Frasier chewed on his bottom lip.

'SPACE uses synthetic emotional stimulus to give us a kick up the arse, right?' Theo nodded. 'Which is great. And more importantly, regulated by the System. The thing is, some criminals found a way around this regulation. They worked out a means to mainline real human emotions straight into SPACE.'

Theo's eyes flicked between the sergeant, whose brow was furrowed with concern, and Frasier, who was staring straight at him, seeking a sign that he understood.

'I heard about that on the news. So what?'

Frasier's eyebrows raised. 'It's like injecting heroin.' He shook his head. 'You're too young. In my day heroin was the East End's illicit drug of choice, if you wanted to snuff it young, anyway. The System limits emo-feedback, meaning if I poke you in the eye in SPACE, you feel it, it hurts. But not as if I had done it for real. The pax's – the *emotional package's* – feedback is capped, and all you get is an uncomfortable sensation.' He paused long enough for Theo to indicate that he understood. 'Now if I feed you a raw, unfiltered, pax of some poor sod bleeding to death—'

'Unpleasant, but it wouldn't actually kill me.'

'But it would, Theo. This is an *unfiltered* pax, remember? Hacked. It bypasses the System. After all, police weapons in SPACE –' he pulled an automatic pistol from a concealed shoulder holster beneath his jacket and put it on the table with a heavy thud – 'are just as lethal as this is here.'

Theo eyed the brushed grey steel of the gun. He'd never seen one in real life. It looked far heavier than he'd imagined.

'It works by exploiting a feedback loophole in the emotion architecture.'

'So close the loophole.'

Frasier laughed. 'Now there's the issue. We can't, because of synthetic life. Who would have thought that would be a problem? The Slifs are up in arms, objecting to closing any loopholes or bugs because it would alter their ecosystem. One change could potentially have a devastating effect on them. Imagine fixing one tiny bug and it ends up committing genocide across all virtual life. The same emotional channel that gives them life is the same bleedin' one these crooks are usin' to inject raw emotional content into SPACE.'

Theo pressed two fingers against his temple and sucked in a breath as pain shot through his skull. He noticed the sergeant's concerned reaction.

'Immersion migraine,' Theo said quietly. 'If you've got some paracetamol or—'

'Sorry, we can't offer you any medication,' Sergeant Jones said, rolling his eyes. 'Health and safety. I used to get them. Found sleeping it off was best.'

Theo took another deep breath and felt weariness seep through his limbs. He didn't want to be listening to a lecture, he wanted to be home in his own bed.

'I'd really like that.' He looked at Frasier. 'So, that's fascinating stuff, but what's it got to do with my mother?'

Frasier raised his hand to slow Theo down.

'I'm getting to that. What we're seeing is organised gangs settin' up these so-called Dens. Usually large rooms, basements, old warehouses, that sort of thing. They snatch poor unfortunates off the street and they place them into drug-induced sedation, in a sort of limbo between here and SPACE. Then they make the poor beggars have *experiences*. Except they're unable to resist, unable to take control of the situation. But they feel every emotional and physical twist and turn and all that mental, physical and emotional data is squeezed into a raw pax –' he pointed to the ceiling – 'so those experiencing it in SPACE can do so with no limitations.'

He paused to let his words sink in, then leaned across the table as he continued, his voice lowered.

'Sometimes they kidnap to order just to satisfy some rich sod's morbid taboo. How about torturing some poor homeless sod in a warehouse in the East End and recording that into a pax. Then, you slip the pax into your victim's rig.' He tapped the side of his head. 'They don't even have to be in SPACE, just AR, but they experience *the very same torture*. Every moment of pain right up to the point they croak. Then we have a corpse in The Real with no physical signs of torture. Like it or not, there is a growing market for snuff vids. You ever wanted to experience what it is like to die?'

Theo glanced at the gun, then shook his head.

'There are some dickheads who do. They feed your avatar a pax and push you to the very moment of death – then yank the plug away.' Frasier mimed the action. 'So you live ... but have experienced the verge of death. Meanwhile, the poor bloke who died for your entertainment is thrown into the Thames.'

Goosebumps mottled Theo's arms. He leaned back in his chair, feeling worse than he had all day and wishing he could distance himself from Frasier.

'And my mum?'

Frasier quickly waved both hands.

'No, no, no. It doesn't always work like that.' Theo

glanced at Ella's AR file still hovering over the table. 'Your mum's a pretty bird. Unfortunately for them, the pretty ones look just as good up there. They're raped. Continually.' He ignored Theo's distressed look. 'You ever had sex up there?'

Theo shook his head, although he and everybody he knew had done so countless times. Simulated sex – *smex*, as the kids called it – was a rite of passage.

Frasier smirked again, easily seeing through the lie.

'Sure, it's fun, but now, with a pax you bypass the system. You can fuck your heart out for *real* and experience not just your pleasure, but theirs simultaneously. The ultimate kick, double the thrill.'

His lingering gaze made Theo uneasy. He glanced at the sergeant, whose expression was unreadable, but he clearly didn't approve of Frasier's raw interpersonal skills.

Theo could barely find his voice.

'And you think my mum is part of this?'

Frasier sighed and tapped Theo's rig.

'The suspects who visited your mother in the Conservation bore a resemblance to a gang who are harvesting Dens across the whole of London. Part of their money laundering routine is to lend cash to desperate people – easier than investing in some crooked business. And if they can't pay them back, they end up in a Den.'

Frasier paused to allow Theo to process everything. Theo put his head in his hands.

'You think she ran from one of these loan sharks?'

Frasier nodded. 'Considering your financial straits, and I bet she was more than aware of what they would do with her.'

Jones suddenly spoke up. 'This is a lot to take in, Theo. Dens are a big problem, but it's something the government doesn't want broadcasting right now, so details are confidential. Would you like a counsellor, or ...?'

'No. I think you may be right. What I didn't mention was ...'

The word *we* formed on his lips, but he corrected himself at the last second. A micro-twitch from Frasier made him wonder if the Detective Chief Inspector had noticed.

'I found a file on her rig, before it was stolen. GPS data. It led me to her last known location, just after she got fired. A building in Shoreditch. I sneaked inside.'

Frasier leaned back in his chair and folded his arms, nodding for Theo to continue.

'There were a few mattresses, metal stands, I guess like drip stands, big lamps—'

'UV lights,' Frasier confirmed. 'Even in a coma the brain needs light to regulate the body clock and produce emotions. The drips just keep them alive for as long as possible.'

'The place smelled odd,' Theo said. 'Like strong lemon-scented floor cleaner.'

Frasier nodded. 'The methohexital and amobarbital cocktails they use smell a little like that. Well, they do before you pass out.'

Theo closed his eyes in an attempt to force his headache aside.

'We picked up a network base station. An RTE421.'

'*We?*'

Frasier hunched on the desk, ready to press for an answer.

'An RTE421?' Jones repeated with a low whistle. 'That's

a *lot* of bandwidth. Farming emotions creates a lot of data.'

Frasier shot him a look, irritated that he was derailing the conversation.

Theo looked into the middle distance, recalling the events.

'There were two men there clearing the place out.'

Frasier turned back to Theo, his cockiness all but gone.

'Did you get a good look at them?'

'One of them. They burned the mattresses. Almost killed me. I put together a photofit of the bloke I saw.'

Theo called up Milton's sketch of Blondie. Frasier sighed and lifted his rig from his belt, holding it briefly to his eyes so he could see the augmented display. Jones put his back on and leaned forward for a closer look.

Frasier issued a single chuckle.

'This could be a breakthrough in the case, Theo, good lad.'

Theo wasn't listening. He was replaying the conversation back through; something Frasier said had only just registered with him.

'You said the suspects who visited my mum in the Conservation bore a resemblance to a gang linked to these Dens. How do you know what they looked like? That wasn't reported. I didn't tell you.' Frasier sighed as he fastened his rig back to his belt. Theo realised the DCI hadn't been wearing it when he described Ella. 'And how did you know what she looks like?'

Frasier picked up the gun and shot Sergeant Jones through the right eye, shattering the rig in half.

The report from the single bullet was so loud that Theo jumped from his chair and landed hard on his arse, knocking the wind from him. The blood from the exit hole in the back of Jones's skull spattered the Venetian blinds before the sergeant's body took a few crooked steps and crashed to the floor, arterial fluid spurting from his mashed-up face like a garden sprinkler.

Frasier swivelled the gun at Theo.

'Sorry, matey, but this is most grievous. You've just become a cop-killer.'

Chapter Thirteen

She knew it was futile, but like most people her age, Clemmie was addicted to her social media streams. Yet every time she viewed them she experienced despair. Everybody else appeared to lead a much better life, experience a more thrilling weekend and be cloaked with a tighter set of friends. They generally just had it better.

A couple of messages from Baxter came in, asking why she and Theo had disappeared. He seemed eager for another ascension, especially after the monotony of community service. He was desperate to discover the fallout from the Eye of the Storm incident – something that no longer interested Clemmie due to the day's crazy turn of events.

She rolled her eyes when another incoming call from her stepmother popped up. Since coming home for the summer, the cloying restrictions imposed by Augusta once again throttled her. University had given her a new lease of life, which had almost been stripped from her in the last couple of weeks. She parked the call with a quiet 'screw you' that gained her an evil eye from the woman taking up the two seats next to her.

The lack of quality sleep had left her feeling wasted and before Theo called that evening, she had planned to have an early night. A quick check showed that he'd been in the interview room for thirty minutes. The desk sergeant who had escorted him in reappeared and hurried down another corridor. She stifled a yawn. The protracted police system could easily keep Theo in there for another couple of hours. She knew the drill regarding interview rooms. Acoustically insulated against augmented listening devices and electronically sealed to prevent eavesdropping. She dropped an air-graffiti message in the middle of the seating area in three-foot-high flickering letters that only Theo would be able to see:

Tired. Heading home. Sorry. x

She hesitated, wondering if she should leave the kiss, but the return of the sergeant interrupted that chain of thought. He was carrying a cup of water and talking animatedly with another officer, this one in plain clothes. She caught the Cockney detective say 'It's most grievous ...' as he passed her by.

Clemmie stopped dead in her tracks. She felt as if the blood in her veins had turned to ice. She quickly rewound the AR's passive recording before it could self-delete after three seconds.

'It's most grievous ...'

A quick juggling between apps and she replayed Theo's threatening call, the waveforms of both clips overlapping and matching perfectly on the phrase '... *most grievous* ...'

She jumped to her feet before the blue access door could fully close and saw the men enter an interview room halfway down the corridor. Then the door between them closed with a solid clunk.

Fear had an unexpected effect on Theo. As the pistol barrel arced towards him, time seemed to slow and the panic he was experiencing receded, replaced with a clinical analysis of the situation. Every sound was fine-tuned and distinct: the shuffle of Frasier's shoes on the smooth floor; the raspy edge to the detective's breathing. The wet plop of blood dripping from the window blinds.

'That bitch mother of yours has been a real pain in the arse. All she had to do was play along, but no. She decided to push back.'

'Whatever she owes you—'

'What?' Frasier laughed. 'You'll get it for us? I don't think so, mate. I've seen you in *Synger*. I know how little you make.' His smile broadened when he noticed Theo's reaction. 'Oh, that's right. We've been watchin'.' He circled around Theo, the gun casually aimed, his voice modulating with fake sympathy. 'Oh, your poor ma. She ain't no saint. She took a loan with the wrong people. Happens all the time. Except, she chose to pay it off by recruitin'. Y'see, this isn't even about the money.'

Theo eyed the door, calculating the chances of reaching it before being shot as next to zero. The DCI lifted both hands, palms up.

'Go ahead,' Frasier said, spotting Theo's intentions. 'I'll give you a head start. It gives me a better excuse.'

'Recruiting who?'

Theo locked eyes with Frasier. He was playing for time, but also driven by morbid curiosity.

'She was good at sourcin' young skirts for the Dens. Like a pimp. But then she started having second thoughts.' Frasier sniffed deeply. 'However, I do have some good news for you. Somethin' to put your mind at rest. We found her.' Theo's involuntary gasp kick-started his breathing again. 'Thanks to you. That rig of hers—'

With a crunch so laden with bass it pummelled Theo's ribs, the window and a large section of the surrounding wall suddenly cascaded in. Old brickwork crumbled as it fell, partially crushing Sergeant Jones's corpse. A cloud of dust rolled into the room like a sandstorm, followed by what looked like a long-necked sauropod, spewing steaming vomit.

Although he couldn't define any details in the dust, the whine of servo-actuators told Theo the beast was, in fact, an enormous robotic arm. It twisted around like a snake, its vomit actually the distinctive acrid chemical odour of 3-D printing-concrete. The polymers sprayed across Frasier's chest as he turned to face the intruder. With a shriek, he back-pedalled across the desk. Theo snatched his rig and swung it as hard as he could on Frasier's gun hand – mashing fingers between the steel and the unbreakable desk.

The DCI howled as his fingers broke and his gun dropped to the floor. Frasier jerked wildly as he thrust his mangled hand into the hot liquid, attempting to tear away his scorched clothing.

Theo instinctively reached for the fallen gun, but stopped himself at the last moment. Having his prints on the murder weapon was going to reinforce his guilt and no matter what soundproofing the room had, the initial shudder from the building's structural integrity would have police hurrying their way in seconds.

This was his only chance to escape. He sprinted towards the hole in the wall, ducking under the printing arm as it continued to writhe and spray hot polymer across the walls. Without thinking, Theo leaped blindly through the hole.

His knees buckled as he landed on the pavement. He rolled twice before stopping hard against the caterpillar tracks of the enormous mobile printer. The flexible printing arm lashed this way and that, chipping away at the brickwork. Free of the room's air conditioning, the night-time humidity sucked the breath from him.

'Theo!'

He waved vaguely back into the room.

'He shot him . . .'

'No time,' Clemmie said, pulling him to his feet while checking around to see if anybody had yet spotted them. 'Let's go.'

Theo had no objections as, half-dragging his arm, she led them into the dark shadows offered by the streets.

Chapter Fourteen

It wasn't until they were far enough away that Theo and Clemmie stopped to catch their breath. Distant sirens from emergency responders shrieked into life as, gulping for air, Clemmie quickly explained how she had ID'd Frasier and, guessing Theo's life was in danger, improvised the escape plan.

She felt particularly proud when she worked out the construction printer's AI software could be spoofed at close range, enabling her to change its clock settings so it rumbled back to work thinking it was dawn. With a tweak of its GPS printing co-ordinates, the heavy machine trundled across the road and into the police station to begin its routine.

Theo crouched against the wall, his legs trembling. With the back of his jacket, he wiped beads of perspiration from his brow. The exertion and humidity were rapidly sapping his strength. Jones's graphic execution refused to leave his mind's eye. He could barely get the words out when he informed Clemmie that he was now branded a cop-killer.

'Was Frasier alive when you left him?'

Theo nodded. 'Burned up a little, but yeah, alive.'

'Pity. Then he's probably splashing your name across the National Crime Agency as we speak.'

And mine with it, she thought. All they have to do is see who Theo entered the building with.

She hoped that the situation was moving too rapidly for anybody to think of checking that.

'They have her.'

Theo gripped her arm, his fingers digging deep, but she didn't flinch. She slid down the wall to draw level to him.

'Then we have to find out where they're keeping her. Where the Den is.'

She lapsed into silence as a pair of police drones, blue lights flashing, raced down the end cross street. Only when the echoing buzz of rotors had receded, did she speak again.

'They were winding that Den down this afternoon. Can't be a coincidence they closed it days after your mum visited.'

Balanced on the balls of her feet, Clemmie put her head in her hands. Was it only this afternoon they had almost been burned to a crisp? It was not yet midnight and she was already on the run with a wanted fugitive.

'Maybe if we use my dad's rig again to search for them—'

'Turning up at your house is not the smartest option at this moment in time. Besides, if the police knew where the Dens were, they would have closed them down already.'

'You need to keep your head down.' She took his rig from him. The visor now sported a small spiderweb fracture from where it had struck the gun. 'If you use this, go anonymous. Even so, that's not infallible.'

Anonymous mode was commonly used, masking a wearer's digital ID from everybody, including the police.

It was one of the many benefits gleaned from the draconian overhaul of personal data laws.

'Baxter,' Theo said. 'I'll call him.'

She handed his rig back and thought about that. Baxter was the obvious choice for steering away from any contact with the authorities.

'He's been messaging me all night.'

'Does he know what's happening?'

Clemmie shook her head. Theo nervously drummed his fingers on his rig and looked pensive.

'What is it?' she asked.

Theo huffed a long sigh. 'Detective Frasier said Ella had had second thoughts. That she was going to blow the lid off everything.' When he lapsed back into silence, Clemmie nudged him to continue. 'So she *was* planning to go missing. What if her last visit to the Den was some sort of ultimatum to them?'

'Makes sense they'd abandon it. What's your point? They could have snatched her then, when she turned up, but obviously they didn't. Why let her walk away?' Clemmie was held by his gaze. Even in the street lights his eyes twinkled a beguiling soft grey, like his mother's. She had always wondered what his dad had looked like – devilishly hot no doubt. 'She must have had something on them. Or at least that's what they think.'

Theo snapped his fingers. 'So what if Blondie turned up at the flat not for me, not for her rig, but for something else? They didn't know she'd left her rig behind. They hadn't taken her at that point ...'

Clemmie nodded encouragingly. 'Precisely. What could she have left in your flat?'

Theo shrugged, then flinched as a police siren sounded alarmingly close in a parallel street, driving past at speed. It prompted them to keep walking. Clemmie hooked her arm through his, holding him closer than usual.

'My flat is a mess,' he admitted. 'I wouldn't be able to find anything in there even if I knew what to look for.'

They had been moving as randomly as possible and only realised where they were when they turned on to Burdett Road. The main road followed the length of the dark Mile End Park. The shadows may have offered cover but they kept to the busier side of the street, blending in with people in various states of drunkenness evacuating pubs and filling the parade of chip shops, kebab houses and burger bars that still favoured using real meat. The occasional whirl of delivery drones, coming and going from the drone-hives built on the restaurants' roofs, made them twitchy. They both slipped their rigs on to help mask their faces and maintained a fast pace, weaving between drunks and verging on breaking into a run, but fearful to do so in case it attracted unwanted attention.

'If they have your mum now, then they either have whatever it was she took, or she was faking.'

'I'm not sure. Why did Frasier kill that sergeant? If she knew nothing, it would be easy to shut me up. He wanted to find out what I knew.'

'Which is nothing.'

'Look, Ella has many, many, *many* bad attributes. But

she is anything but stupid. Where do you think I get my razor-sharp wit and intellect?'

Clemmie rolled her eyes witheringly. Across the street a Day-Glo flash of a pair of uniformed officers walking their beat on the edge of the park caught their attention. Luckily the officers were busy helping a girl, wearing a dress size too small, throw up over the pavement while her hen night harpies crowded around taking pictures. Thank God binge drinking was still a thing.

Only when they were much further down the road did Clemmie begin talking again.

'Wouldn't she leave a clue for you?'

Theo shook his head dismissively. 'She's not stupid, but she's also not exactly proactive either.' He noticed Clemmie's sceptical look. 'What?'

'I always thought she was smart. She loved crime shows.'

'Did she?'

'Are you serious? We used to talk about the *Midsomer Murders* reboot every time I was at yours waiting for you to get out of the shower.' His blank look surprised her. 'Come on. It's your *mum*! You should know this. That certificate she had ...'

Theo stopped dead, his linked arm pivoting Clemmie to face him.

'What about it?'

Clemmie unhooked her arm and stood arms akimbo.

'I thought you two were supposed to be close? It's an EMIV Diploma – Level 2.'

She wasn't sure why she felt so indignant when Theo shrugged. She had always suspected there was *something* between them, but Theo was always difficult to read. Maybe he was just one of those guys who was indifferent to everybody.

'Jesus, Theo. It's a vCrimes qualification: Emotive Investigation?' His blank look almost made her stamp her foot in frustration. 'There are only four levels. She was training to be a *detective*.'

'What, Ella? Mum? She worked in a bee farm. She did ... *adult* stuff, just to pay the bills.'

He looked away, embarrassed, but Clemmie had already heard the story from Milton and it had only made her respect Ella's steadfast courage and determination even more. She sucked in a breath to curb her irritation.

'My dad always said she shouldn't have quit the course when she had you. He reckons she could have gone on to great things.'

Theo took off his rig and wiped his eyes – or was it perspiration?

'How do you know all this?'

Clemmie waved a hand. 'She told me one time when I was sat waiting for you. I thought you knew, it wasn't a secret. Apparently she couldn't afford to study and raise a family. My mother – my *real* mother – tried to get her a grant to study but then she ran off ...'

They lapsed into an awkward silence.

'A clue,' Theo mumbled. 'She left a clue.'

'What?' Clemmie said, looking nervously around hoping that their altercation hadn't attracted any undue attention.

Theo tapped her visor. 'I was trying to think why she left her rig behind.' Clemmie shook her head, not following his train of thought. 'When I was a kid, at Christmas or birthdays, she used to leave messages around the flat. Riddles that made me run from room to room to find the next clue and the next – which led to the present she'd hidden.' He smiled as he recalled the distant memory. The laughter and innocence of the moment seemed all too unfamiliar these days. 'It always made her laugh, like she was getting more of a kick out of it than I was.'

'You think she left it on purpose?' Theo nodded. 'But we don't have it.'

Theo's eyes widened as something occurred to him.

'We don't need it. The rig itself was the clue!' Clemmie's frown made him smile. 'The riddle was *why* would she leave it behind. Don't you see? She left it as a pointer. Whatever she had, she left in SPACE.'

Clemmie broke into a smile. 'In a geo-locked position – the park in Nu London!' The park they always ascended to while in Theo's flat was in the same general location shared by his estate. 'Let's go. We can ascend now.'

Theo hesitated. 'We don't know how much ascension time we'll need up there. I don't want to waste it on virtual travel if we ascend from here. We should get as close to my gaff as possible.'

Because of the elastic nature of virtual distance Clemmie knew he was right; even a mile in The Real could see them crossing five times that in Nu London. Still, she was torn.

'Your flat is a definite no-go zone right now. I guarantee you the police will swarm it the moment they link that dead guy to you. But I'm pretty sure they haven't yet.'

'What makes you say that?'

'The lack of panicked calls from my parents, for one.' She raised her hand, lifting his visor over his face. 'Call Milton. I'll call Baxter. Get them to meet us close to yours. And tell him not to use their Echoes, or any social sites. We need total blackout on this.'

She felt an unexpected thrill. The situation was dire, but they had a plan. A mission.

Hope.

All of which had long been absent from her life.

They had to wait eighteen minutes for Milton and Baxter to eventually roll up, grumbling about the state of the night Tube's service (though Theo suspected this was more about steering the conversation away from his predicament than an actual complaint). It was half past midnight when they reunited in a small children's playground two streets from Theo's home. The block of flats still had a few lights blazing from behind curtains, but looked almost identical to the other cloned buildings around it.

Although Theo and Clemmie had sketched out the day's events to the two newcomers, it took a further fifteen minutes for them to answer an incredulous Milton's constant list of questions.

Clemmie had since been monitoring all major social media streams as well as the news. She expected a flood of calls from her parents at any moment, but everything was eerily silent on the Bow Road incident.

'Perhaps they didn't know you were even there, Theo?' offered Milton by way of explanation.

Since arriving he had been bristling with nervous energy

and commenting on how this all felt like a game.

'Don't be a dickhead,' Baxter cut in. 'He registered at the front desk with all his details. They'd know exactly which room he was in. And even if this bent copper is dead too, they'd have noticed only two stiffs in the room and worked out that he'd legged it.'

Theo interrupted. 'Thanks for that, Bax.'

He didn't want any more reminders about the loss of life. For once, Baxter didn't answer back; instead he fell silent and looked grim.

'You okay being here?' Clemmie asked Baxter.

Getting wrapped up with anything illegal, no matter how trivial, while being on community service would extend his punishment. Being implicated with a murderer would land him a heavier sentence than litter picking.

'I'm fine,' Baxter mumbled in a tone that clearly wasn't. 'But this smells like a sting to me.'

His head slowly turned as he scanned the playground with its nightmarish – at least in the darkness – cartoon hedgerow characters standing sentinel over the swings and slides. His nervousness was clearly infecting Theo too.

'What do you mean, a sting?' Theo followed his gaze.

'Look around. There's nobody here. Where's the Old Bill? They're running silent. If that DCI is crooked, makes me wonder who else is.'

Theo and Clemmie exchanged a meaningful look. That had been the unspoken elephant in the room ever since they'd fled the police station.

Baxter continued, oblivious to the discomfort he was causing.

'Think about it. What if they expect *him* –' he gave Theo a none-too-gentle punch on the shoulder – 'to ascend? Why chase him through London when they can just lie in wait?'

Milton gave a mocking snort. 'Why bother?'

'To see what I find.' They all looked at Theo, whose gaze was firmly fixed on the dark window of his flat. He cleared his throat and flashed a thin smile at Clemmie. 'That's why I'm going in from here. Just far enough out.'

'We're all going in,' Clemmie assured him.

'Not all of us.' Theo looked meaningfully at Milton. 'We need eyes out here. Someone to keep lookout.'

Milton wanted to object, but he was more than aware of the risks of ascending in public. There were stories about people being robbed, assaulted, or worse, while lying prone in public parks or sitting on benches. He agreed and watched as his friends sat on the grass, back to back in order to support one another. Their bodies slumped as they transferred into the virtual.

'Have fun,' Milton muttered to himself.

Despite the warmth of the night, he still pulled his sports jacket tighter as he sat back on a bench and loaded up a game on his AR visor, keeping one eye on his friends and the other on the augmented robot warlords suddenly erupting from the park around him.

Chapter Fifteen

Theo smiled as the feel-good upload signature massaged his brain. How ironic that this was the best he'd felt in the last two days. The Nu London skyline came into focus and he felt a tremor of dislocation in finding himself in an unfamiliar area. He was outside the park, the side he had *never* visited, which was a further quarter of a mile away from the city. Since every trip into SPACE had sent him in the direction of downtown, he had never had cause to simply turn around. He was undoubtedly a creature of habit, and it was disconcerting to think just a few hundred yards was making him feel completely lost. He felt a shove in his back.

'Theo!' Baxter barked at him. 'What are you loitering for?' His avatar appeared from behind, followed by Clemmie's. He gestured to the park. 'Are we going in?'

The curved hillocks rolled away from the path, the trees shimmering with their usual blue, casting a soft light to banish the darkness. There were few people around, most having already plugged in earlier, and most businesses were shut down for the night, consigning the Slifs to their own suburbs. Even the usual air-skaters had disappeared. If anything it added credence to Baxter's ominous warning.

'This way.'

Theo led them across the park towards where he guessed he usually appeared, but every step was unfamiliar. The grass underfoot rippled with simulated bioluminescence as he crested a small hillock.

A dull rumble came from a blimp-shaped billboard orbiting the park, playing looped commercials at full blast. Each was specifically targeted, so Clemmie and Baxter saw different adverts and Theo wondered why the hell he was being shown an ad for running shoes. Was the virtual world having a joke at his expense?

'Isn't this the spot?' asked Clemmie, glancing at a vaguely familiar field ahead.

Theo eyed the skyline. He took a few strides to the left and the trees appeared to snap in line to his memory.

'I think it's about right.'

He looked at his feet. The grass shimmered and a few experimental prods with his foot felt soft, like foam, sending out neon ripples that quickly faded.

He kneeled and began tearing the grass. Large luminous clumps came away in his fists and dissolved into pixels. Moments later they almost instantly reformed as the turf he'd just destroyed.

'This is impossible!' he yelled.

'I guess that's why there are no keep off the grass signs here,' mused Baxter.

Theo was gripped by a sinking feeling.

'She can't have buried anything! This is a waste of time!'

That didn't stop him continually hacking at the ground until it was nothing more than a rippling blue pool of light.

'Can I help you?'

They all looked up in surprise to see a willowy Slif on the path just yards away. It was walking a six-legged cross between a wolf and a sloth on the end of a leash. The custom pet, a sign of the Slif's wealth that would have made Milton giddy, growled a warning at the humans.

Theo had only been this close to a Slif on a handful of occasions; their paths never needed to cross in the brief time he had in SPACE. He couldn't take his eyes off its head, tapering to a cone-like cranium. Black horizontal eyes – a default evolutionary tactic that avoided any uncanny-valley feelings people might experience when dealing with a sim – stared unblinking. The slender neck was twice as long as a human's and while the torso was basically simian, its stick-thin arms ended in nothing more than three tentacle fingers. The creature's legs were similarly lean, ending in a pair of long splayed ungulate-esque toes with a third fat stubby heel to maintain balance. It wore no clothes and lacked genitalia – although it sounded male.

While their expressions were limited, a Slif's skin was an elaborate moving swirl of colours, like oil on water, representing emotions: emotions which – in an emo-driven world – were as tangible as cheap aftershave. It meant that Slifs were terrible liars, which made them welcome players in any poker game. In this instance Theo felt the sim's irritation.

'I said, can I help you?' the Slif asked again, this time with a touch of impatience. 'You cannot destroy the park.'

It wagged a chiding hand.

'Piss off, *virt*!' snarled Baxter, taking both Clemmie and the Slif by surprise.

'I beg your pardon?'

Baxter took a step to intercept the Slif.

'I'm sorry. Which word didn't you understand?'

The Slif became rigid, its basic features conveying immense distaste. A feeling that was accompanied by a slight emotional wave that left them all in little doubt about how perturbed it felt.

'I should report this!'

The Slif turned quickly away and rejoined the path, leaving nothing more than a wake in the grass.

'Report what? Not destroying the park?' Baxter shouted after it.

The Slif sensibly refused to argue and continued on its way, yanking the leash of the sloth-thing as it continued to growl at the avatars.

Clemmie glowered at him. 'That was harsh, Bax.'

Baxter's hard man image wavered under her scrutiny.

'We don't want anybody nosing around. Who knows who he'd tell?'

He scanned around with the same level of suspicion he'd had in the playground.

'Exactly! You've just drawn more attention to us.' Clemmie noticed Theo was still kneeling in the grass, stroking it in wide arcs with the flat of his hand. 'Theo, stop petting the grass.'

He looked up at her with a broad smile.

'You can't see?'

Clemmie and Baxter watched the grass flare up under

Theo's palm, he looked like a kid playing with a paint box.

'Oh God, he's having a breakdown,' whispered Baxter.

Theo laughed, then sent them a clone request. It allowed groups to see exactly the same things on their rigs from their own points of view, both in AR and VR.

Now they could all see that, when Theo moved the grass, the neon blue was accentuated with a dash of red. As he widened his reach they could see a red arrow form, pointing towards the city.

Theo felt a surge of unexpected pride for his mother. He had struggled to label her as anything other than a vaping boozer, but clearly she had hidden depths. He was trying to come to terms with Clemmie's revelation that Ella had been forced to abandon her dreams to bring him up. The irony of his own situation wasn't lost on him. It must have hurt Ella to watch her son abandon his own ambitions too.

He tracked the arrow towards the skyline in what would be the geographic south. He stood up and pointed.

'This way.'

He moved tangentially away from where the Slif had disappeared from view. His visor's head-up display (HUD) briefly appeared so he could check the countdown. They had already ascended for just over twenty minutes. One o'clock in the real world on a Sunday morning would place most people in clubs. Maybe he shouldn't let Baxter's paranoia affect him so much.

'Milton, you listening?'

Milton's reply sounded as if he was caught mid-yawn.

'Yeah. Still here. Bored.'

'Good. Nothing in The Real?'

'Nope. The real world is *really* dull. You?'

'We're chasing arrows.'

'Huh?'

Robot Warlords had failed to hold Milton's attention for any length of time and he was already formulating Killer Kaiju's review on the AR game. A single middle finger salute, perhaps? Although the game did have some charms – he was beginning to wonder if Theo had a point about his limited rating system.

Instead he switched to his social media stream and was delighted to see his *Avasta* critique had already ticked over two and a half million views and counting, with a stream of fanboy – *fangirl*, he corrected himself with a thrill – comments about how brilliant he was. He was intrigued by the occasional thread suggesting he should have a co-host or guest reviewer. He'd been considering the unique combination of doing it with a Slif. So far sims had yet to make an impact in the entertainment world, but maybe it would be better to recruit one of his – no doubt hot – fangirls. He'd never been successful with the opposite sex, not even hanging with Clemmie, who didn't have the common decency to have any attractive friends.

A noise behind Milton jolted him from the bench. He felt his heart in his throat as a graticule in his visor highlighted a figure just feet away. He gave a loud yelp before realising he'd just scared the shit out of a fox.

The canine made an abrupt and silent U-turn and sprinted into the darkness. Milton's hands were still shaking when he slumped back down on the seat. A quick check revealed his friends were fine; at least the fox hadn't urinated on them, he supposed. Nobody else was in the park and there was still no sign of the police. All was well.

He stifled a yawn and checked the time. They'd been in there for ninety minutes already ...

The route Ella had laid had been circuitous through the south of the city. While Nu London retained the name, there were no similar suburbs or districts, just an amalgam of structures and architecture removed from cultural aesthetics or physical rules. As a result, society had placed its own labels on areas, and as such they were entering the zone simply known as 'The Market'.

Its geographic twin followed the confines of the Thames, meaning that very few people ascended directly into it unless they were aboard a boat. Instead, visitors approached the towering fortifications constructed with a design ethic that put China's Great Wall to shame, the surface bedecked with swirling adverts, and the multiple entrances engineered to channel avatars into a network of narrow streets crammed with shops that were reminiscent of a North African souk if it had been designed by some trendy London hipster.

Being in SPACE, there was only a passing nod to physics. Some stores were only accessible by a series of zigzagging slopes that wound up or down to further levels. Junctions angled off in every direction – including vertically – as the whole of the Market was powered by its own localised Physics Engine. One level was even completely inverted, just to attract visitors rather than for any practical reason.

Nu London had become the world's shopping destination. It was said that you could buy *anything* here.

Ella's trail had transformed from hidden arrows through the park to more prominent air-graffiti as they entered the streets. It was still visible only via Theo's rig, but he suspected the closer they were to their goal, the less his mother had worried about security.

Even at this late hour, the Market was packed with avatars from all around the globe, using valuable ascension time to port across SPACE just for the chance to shop. The narrow streets restricted access, stopping any one destination from being overwhelmed by a DoS mob.

Theo led them into the upper tiers of the Market, where the tourists thinned out. They lost count of which level they were on, before the final arrow pointed towards a plain red door. Nobody else appeared to be paying any attention to it, and Theo wondered if perhaps only he and his friends were able to see it.

'Shall we knock?' Clemmie asked after remaining silent the entire trek.

Baxter looked around to check they were being ignored.

'No,' was his reply as he kicked the door, effortlessly breaking it off its hinges.

Clemmie shot him a look. 'Let's just hope we're not required to close that again.'

Ignoring them both, Theo peered into the inky blackness. Whatever was beyond the door wasn't merely in the dark, it was actively devoid of light.

'What is this place?' Theo asked as he pushed his hand inside, watching as it vanished into nothingness.

Alarmed, he quickly extracted it and was relieved to see it was still there. Not that a missing virtual hand couldn't easily be re-rendered.

'Let's find out,' said Baxter, pushing Theo firmly between the shoulder blades.

With a wail that was abruptly silenced, Theo vanished, the void swallowing him whole.

Chapter Sixteen

The mosquito whine of a drone swarm sweeping overhead roused Milton off his Killer Kaiju site. His visor highlighted eight drones flying low towards Theo's block of flats. They skimmed over the road, keeping pace with three menacing armoured electric police vans, running with blues and twos off and with only the sound of all-terrain tyres chewing up the tarmac.

Milton jumped to his feet as he watched the drones fan out around the tower block.

'Guys? Oh, guys, we have police.' He fed the video from his rig so they could see too. 'We have *a lot* of police.'

'That's a Trojan unit,' Clemmie commented ominously.

Milton was too caught up in the drama to ask her for clarification. Instead he quickly Wiki'd them to discover that Trojan, or more formally SCO19, were the Metropolitan Police's heavy-duty firearms team and only brought out in *severe* circumstances.

Milton glanced at his three prone friends, realising that while a passer-by probably wouldn't notice them concealed behind the bench and foliage, they were clearly visible from the air.

'You have to get back here.'

'Negative, mate.' Baxter sounded preoccupied. 'We've lost Theo.'

'What do you mean *lost him*?'

A feed from Baxter's point of view popped up in the corner of his visor. Baxter was experimentally pushing his hand in and out of the black doorway, watching it vanish.

'He walked in. Didn't walk out and now he's not responding to comms.'

Milton watched how the transition of Baxter's hand through the space was sharply defined, an instant transformation.

'I think that's non-rendered.'

'English please, Milt,' Baxter snapped back.

'A barrier to segregate areas so only limited data can pass through. It means you can't eavesdrop or spy. It's a completely private zone. Not easy to create.'

'Yeah, well, somebody thought it was worth the effort,' said Baxter, pulling his hand out for the last time.

Milton focused back on the police vans. Armed officers were filing out of the vehicles and running towards the flat.

'It's getting serious down here,' he said, relaying the stream back to the others.

'Oh my God!' wailed Clemmie. 'Have you seen the newsfeeds?'

Instantly a dozen separate windows filled Milton's vision. Whichever one he looked at played the audio of that particular anchor. Scanning across it was like listening to a news report stitched together from unconnected channels – but all saying roughly the same thing.

'... calling them the Bow Street Runners. One victim was identified as Sergeant Ian Jones, shot in the head at point-blank range. The injured man is a Detective Chief Inspector whose name has not been released.' The images variously switched to police gathered around the mobile printer wedged into the wall of the police station. 'An unidentified second suspect broke through the wall to release the killer, who is identified here as Theodore Joseph Wilson ...'

No one spoke for a few moments.

'Theo's middle name is *Joseph*?' Milton said in disbelief.

A picture of Theo appeared from his out-of-date sixth-form college ID card. Milton recalled that his vacant expression was an attempt to hide the hangover he had been experiencing. All Milton's feeds showed Theo's face – except one window that had cut to a dog food commercial.

'... are advised that he is armed and dangerous ... *Put the bounce back in your dog with* ... do *not* approach.'

Milton cleared the streams.

'We're fucked,' he said. Although intellectually he knew helping his friend would put him in trouble, actually seeing it on the news brought home the severity of it. 'Maybe we should think about turning ourselves in?'

Even as he said it, he didn't think it was a sensible move. He was pragmatic enough to know it wouldn't be so simple. Even as he weighed up his options, another wave of drones appeared from the west. Twenty of them, breaking formation like a murmuration of starlings as they spread over the surrounding streets with clear intention: a manhunt. Three of them were slowly heading towards the playground.

'Shit!'

'We see it,' said Baxter. 'This non-rendered zone.' He pointed to the doorway leading to the void. 'Is it safe to pass through?'

Milton ran to his three friends, shoving Baxter's prone figure to the ground.

'What do you mean?'

'I mean, are we going to go schizo if we go through?'

'How the hell do I know?'

Milton hooked his arms under Theo's armpits and grunted as he dragged him towards the metal tangle of a climbing dome, crowned by a grinning cartoon rabbit that looked demonic in the shadows. With her back support gone, Clemmie toppled on to the grass. As he shoved Theo between the rusting bars, Milton hoped the drones were not using thermal imaging or all of this effort would be pointless.

He returned to Baxter and Clemmie, then checked the drones' progress. Two had diverted over roads, while the third resolutely headed towards the playground. After a warm day, a thin mist seeped from the earth, highlighting a red laser thread that scanned the ground.

Milton had no time to move Baxter or Clemmie; they were about to be caught.

On impulse he dragged Clemmie parallel to Baxter and rolled her on top of him in his best attempt to make them look like they were having sex. He had enough presence of mind to cut his feed so they couldn't see his act of degradation.

'Sorry,' he whispered to Clemmie, before running in the opposite direction from the drone as fast as he could. He already had a stitch as he passed through the playground gate.

That was when he also realised he had lost contact with Baxter and Clemmie.

Chapter Seventeen

Baxter felt physically sick as he walked through the non-rendered space and was plunged into utter darkness. An alarmingly loud hiss of static crackled through his ears and every limb tingled unpleasantly, as if squeezed to cut off the blood.

Seconds later he was out of it and standing in a bare room. Behind him, the dense black doorway obscured the street beyond. Clemmie stepped through it and shivered.

'Well, that was horrid,' she commented dryly, taking in the new room.

It was an empty lobby space, the blank grey walls recognisable as one of hundreds of off-the-peg default textures across SPACE. Ideal for those with no wish to waste time with design. A door in the far wall was partially open, a letter T floating in front of it. Baxter was unsure if it was visible to everybody or if they were still connected to Theo. Either way, it was the only way forward.

Motioning for Clemmie to follow him, Baxter led the way through.

'You feel that?'

Each step felt strange, as if they were walking through treacle.

'This is not right.' Clemmie looked around, trying to locate the source of the problem. 'Milton, are you still there?' Nothing. 'We're completely isolated.'

Baxter tentatively pushed the door wider. Theo was inside, kneeling over something on the floor.

'Hey, Theo!'

Theo turned around, wearing a look of bewilderment. He opened his mouth to speak – then suddenly popped into a cloud of shimmering pixels and vanished, dropping the hexagonal box he was holding.

Clemmie pushed past Baxter.

'Theo? Huh ...?' She froze and blindly reached out for Baxter's shoulder, pulling him closer. 'Christ, look at the time!'

Baxter focused on the time readout discreetly tucked away in the periphery of his vision. The seconds were whipping by so fast they were a blur. Minutes ticked rapidly over as if they were in some bad time travel movie.

Then a disembodied voice spoke up.

'Ejection protocol initi—'

A pain struck Baxter between the eyes and he tumbled backwards.

He fell back into his flesh and bones so hard he spasmed, winding himself because of the weight of whatever was smothering him. The pain in his head was crippling. As his vision swam back he saw he was visor to visor with Clemmie, her lips an inch from his as she straddled him.

'Well, this is awkward,' he grinned. 'You should have said, Clem.'

'Sshh!' she hissed at him, grabbing both his wrists and pinning him to the ground as a drone shot over her head.

For a second it paused to sweep a laser across them, before continuing on its way. Only when it had cleared the park did Clemmie finally climb off Baxter and offer a hand to help him up. She took off her rig to massage her temples.

'Quick thinking,' Baxter mumbled shyly as he removed his own helmet, hoping the pain would recede.

'Lucky for me I'm not your type, hey?' Baxter was thankful the darkness hid his blushes. 'More importantly, my pride isn't damaged.'

She scanned the park to get her bearings.

'Theo?' she said. 'Milton?'

'You're back!' Milton's exhausted voice came over their rigs.

'Where are you?'

'Near the Tube station. I hid from the drones under a bridge. I'll loop back to you.'

They heard the clang of metal as Theo swayed drunkenly to his feet and clambered from in between the spars of the climbing dome. His foot caught on a low bar and he fell face first into the rubberised safety floor. Clemmie ran to help him stand.

'Theo, what happened in there?' She clenched her teeth and winced in pain.

'Migraine? Don't worry. I get them all the time. It should go soon,' Theo assured her. 'That room was in a time slur.

149

We were accelerating like crazy. Ejection is much tougher after that.'

He removed his rig and stretched.

'I thought slurs were only used as time forfeits in games,' Baxter said as he joined them.

Racing games in particular carried time penalties that were very real. A slow time slur could easily eat away precious minutes in SPACE. For those watching, it would appear you were moving in slow motion, but for the victim it was undetectable.

Baxter cracked his neck by twisting it to the right.

'What did you find? Something from Ella?'

Theo nodded and swayed as the playground wobbled around him. He started to reply but stopped when he noticed something beyond Clemmie and Baxter. Baxter followed his gaze.

Theo's block of flats was illuminated by powerful flood-lights. Police and news drones swarmed around it as armed cops evacuated residents, no doubt conducting a door-to-door search of the building.

Milton joined them at a run, once again fighting for breath.

'I guess they're not messing around. And I suggest we don't sit and wait to see what they will do next.'

Hurrying from the playground, they quickly got lost down Tower Hamlets' streets, hoping that the police would continue searching for two, not four, people. Even in this borough, the roads were quiet after three o'clock, and the sky was just hinting the pale blue of dawn. The last thing

Theo wanted was to be on the streets when the city's morning shift started. He had watched the news streams dubbing him, and the still unidentified Clemmie, as the Bow Street Runners, ignoring the historical fact that Bow Street and Bow Road were historically and geographically different. Even Theo knew that, but there was no substitute for sensationalist journalism. His face was plastered everywhere and with virtually everybody walking around with AR assistance, it would be a matter of minutes – not hours – before he was identified. They needed to get under cover.

His own flat was out of action, and Clemmie's house seemed a dreadful option. Milton refused to harbour a wanted fugitive and before Baxter had the chance to do the same, he had volunteered Rex's garage.

His sister's boyfriend owned a small lock-up under the arches in Bermondsey, where he pimped motorbikes. He was usually only there in the evening and Baxter felt confident the hike across town would be worth it. By the time they arrived, and Baxter had used a broken concrete post to batter the ageing padlock off, it was daylight.

They set about making themselves comfortable. A fridge was filled with bottled water and cheap imported beer. The only other luxury was a cramped toilet with suspicious stains baked in.

'Play that again,' Clemmie said thoughtfully as they finished watching Theo's recording from inside SPACE.

'In a minute,' Theo said, putting his rig on the floor then hanging his head between his knees.

They watched him gently bob, and Milton subtly edged aside, expecting him to throw up.

'Still got a migraine?' Clemmie moved behind Theo and massaged his shoulders. 'Mine has gone.'

Despite the nausea he was feeling, her touch was electric. She was no masseuse, yet the tension knots in his shoulder crunched away as she jabbed them. The new pain was a welcome break from the one splitting his skull apart.

'It's how I imagine Lag feels.'

Baxter stretched out on an oil-stained blanket and fought to stay awake. Fatigue made Milton monosyllabic in his responses.

Theo had no desire to put his rig back on, so he placed it on the workbench in front of him and played the recorded video on to his visor so they could both watch it. Clemmie continued circling her thumbs into his shoulders.

On screen, Theo's hands reached for the hexagon. Activated by his touch, a holographic image of Ella appeared on the screen, recorded in their flat. Theo couldn't identify the particular day, but suspected it was while he was working his arse off in *Synger*. She sat on the sofa wearing a shapeless dark green cardigan drawn tight over her low-cut top. She was pulling a pair of black boots over her ripped blue jeans, and her face was a picture of fear.

'Hun, I feel so bad about this. It's not something I wanted to drag you into. Jeez, it's not something I wanted to be a part of. This is me, screwing up as usual.' She tried to smile but her voice cracked with stress. She yanked one boot partially on and stamped her foot angrily on the floor to fit it snugly. 'But this has gone too far. I borrowed money to keep us afloat. Then I had to get more to pay for the interest payments ...' She rolled her index fingers around one another. 'Et cetera, et cetera. You're the smart one. You know where this is going. And these are bad people ...'

She slid the second boot on and leaned back with a regretful sigh, staring at the ceiling for a long moment, almost forgetting the camera was on.

'So they asked me to do some bad things to pay it off.'

Another long pause hung in the air.

'You see the problem,' Theo said, pointing to the screen. 'She likes her melodramatic pauses.'

Clemmie nodded. 'Not ideal in a time slur.'

Since the message had been left for Theo in SPACE, he assumed the time trap had been set by her too. Smart thinking to stall those on her tail, but not great when it came to imparting long rambling confessions.

Finally, Ella continued speaking.

'They made me recruit young girls. You know the type — straight off the train and lost in the big city. I didn't want to know what they wanted them for. But I'm not entirely thick.' She looked at the camera and forced a smile. 'Just naive. And it was starting to pay things off.' She waved her arms helplessly. 'What was I supposed to do?'

She leaned forward, arms balanced on her knees, almost mimicking Theo's pose.

'They used the girls in Dens. Forcibly extracting their emotions straight into SPACE.' She pointed to the roof. 'Up there they have these places, Joy Divisions they call them. You can judge me, hell, I judged myself, but I thought it was better they abuse some poor girl in SPACE than in the streets.' She lapsed into silence and peered beyond the camera as she recounted the horrors she had witnessed. 'I just didn't know how they really treated them. No ... I didn't *want* to know.'

Her voice became quiet. Distant. She pulled herself together.

'Girls were starved. Abused 24–7 while they're doped up so they can squeeze every last endorphin from them until the body can produce no more. By which time they're practically husks. Emotionally dried up, physically on the brink of death. Lagged to hell. But they did worse things too ...'

Again, a long silence. They could both hear Milton's rhythmic breathing and the occasional snort from Baxter as he sank straight into a deep slumber. Clemmie stopped the massage and sat next to Theo, her head propped on his shoulder. He in turn leaned against a shelf of engine parts which was uncomfortable at best.

Ella slapped her knees in an attempt to galvanise herself.

'When I saw what they were doing, I wanted out. They wouldn't let me, of course. They threatened to hurt you if I did. I was trapped.' She covered her mouth and let out an involuntary sob. 'Sorry.' She wiped a tear from her eye. 'I don't deserve sympathy, I know. I couldn't watch what was happening to those people. It wasn't just girls. They snatched people for all kinds of kicks.'

The wave of sorrow was suddenly replaced by fierce determination.

'So, I gathered information about their operation. The Dens, who was involved, how to bring the bastards down. It went further than I thought. The people involved were ... names we know. Trust. There are people in power you wouldn't believe would do such things, but they do, in plain sight. That's when I made the mistake of going to the Old Bill. That's when I found out how deep their tendrils go and I saw the full scope of their plan.' She shook her head. 'It was inevitable they'd come after me so I took what I had and spread—'

At that moment the video clip glitched and stopped as Theo was ejected.

'Great timing.' Clemmie stifled a yawn.

Theo leaned against the top of her head. She smelled of fruit and sweat.

'I need to go back in and see the rest of it.'

Which meant hiding for twenty-four hours until his ascension limit was reset, by which time the manhunt would no doubt have gained momentum, making their movements in the streets and in SPACE almost impossible.

Clemmie didn't say anything. Outside the patter of rain became a constant drum roll against the door. Theo weighed up their thin options. Leaving the garage was risky, and it was only a matter of time before Rex returned and found them. A low gasp from Clemmie told him she had finally succumbed to sleep.

He closed his eyes. Stuck. Trapped.

Asleep.

Chapter Eighteen

The falling sensation ended with an abrupt slam into the ground.

Theo spasmed awake; his kicking feet narrowly missed hoofing Baxter in the balls. It was Baxter who had been shaking him awake.

'He's coming!'

Awareness that he had fallen asleep across the workbench spooning Clemmie, whom he had accidentally woken, was followed by the previous day's events, which slammed into his cortex like a freight train. Theo was already spinning off the bench before he registered who the *he* was.

The garage's side door was yanked open with great force, admitting a fierce shower of rain, and the fully formed bulk of Rex powered inside, swinging the broken chain and padlock as he bellowed, issuing a fountain of spittle.

'You twats!'

Waving his arms for attention, Baxter threw himself between Rex and Theo.

'Rex! No! It's me! It's me!'

The transformation from rage to amiability was instant as Rex regarded Baxter with a smile.

'Hey, bruv!' Then the rage returned with a snarl. 'You smashed my bloody lock off!'

'We needed a place to lay low.' Baxter indicated Theo.

Rex frowned as he vaguely recalled Theo and Clemmie.

'Oh, yeah. You lot ...'

'Hi, Rex,' Clemmie said, still half asleep. She gave Milton a sharp kick to wake him. 'Thanks for letting us hang out here.'

'I didn't exactly let you ...'

Rex pulled the door shut to prevent more rain from spattering across the floor.

'We'll buy you a new lock,' Theo said nervously, aware they needed to keep Rex on side.

'Yeah, one that's burglar-proof,' Baxter assured him.

Rex prowled around to make sure nothing else had been disturbed. He crossed to the machine hidden by a dust cover that nobody had bothered to remove and snapped it away, revealing an antique cool blue Indian Scout Bobber. The beach-brown saddles were covered in protective plastic and the wheels had been removed; the bike itself was held upright by four metal clamps. The petrol engine had been replaced with an electric one.

Satisfied nothing had been touched, he looked suspiciously at the others.

'Why did you need a place to crash? You're not getting drunk, are ya?' he added with a cheeky wink.

Baxter was offended. 'I'm twenty already. You and my sis came out with me to celebrate.'

Rex groaned when he saw the carefully arranged tools on the bench had been shoved aside.

'Come on! Everything in its place, bruv.' He began sliding the tools back to their abstruse positions when a thought struck him. He stopped and stared wide-eyed at Baxter. 'It's not drugs, is it? Tell me it isn't the hard stuff.'

'It's not drugs!'

'I can't have the Old Bill finding any crap like that here. I'm clean!'

'Rex. It's not drugs.'

Milton finally stood and stretched, every joint in his back cracking.

'Don't you watch the news?'

Rex gave a shrug of indifference and returned to aligning his tool set. Milton was about to explain when Clemmie held up her hand to cut him off.

'Good. It's boring anyway.'

'Sure is,' Rex confirmed under his breath. He crossed back to the Indian and folded his arms. 'What do you think? I'm gonna whack a pair of Commander twelves on there and take it for a spin before my client takes it back.'

Clemmie ran a hand admiringly over the handlebars.

'It's a beauty. 2015 model?' Rex nodded, impressed. 'You kept the original detailing.'

'Natch.'

'Why twelves? They're double width.'

'Client's got it in his head to take it off-roading.'

Clemmie shook her head as she admired the engine.

'That's nuts. But it would be sweet. I do motocross but not on anything like this.'

She kneeled to inspect the engine.

'I installed two-wheel drive and jazzed the torque to ten thousand Newton metres.'

Clemmie gave a low chuckle of appreciation.

'That's some monster torque.'

Theo quietly watched, trying hard not to show how Clemmie's engineering knowledge was making her increasingly attractive.

Milton ruined the moment by leaning in and whispering, 'I was wondering how your mum got her hands on a time slur? I mean, she's not exactly tech-savvy, right?'

Theo was loath to admit he was right. Baxter joined them, picking up on the conversation, ignoring Rex and Clemmie porning over the Indian.

'You know Rex deals in second-skins.' Milton nodded at him. 'He knows about these things.'

'He's got a point,' Baxter said. Then louder, 'Rex. Where could we get our hands on a time slur?'

Rex stiffened. His eyes darted to the door. Satisfied the police were not about to burst in, he relaxed and stroked the wiry growth on his chin. He regarded Baxter curiously.

'Why're you in the market for a slur? It's a serious piece of kit.'

'We're just curious.'

'They're expensive to port out of games. Illegal too.'

'So *you* can't get one?' Baxter played to his ego.

'I can get anything, bruv. Skins, trackers, geo-blockers. But slurs are up there with lethals.' Even mentioning weapons that could kill in SPACE was taboo. 'But we're talking serious cash. Like, two grand.'

'Where would your mum get money like that?' Clemmie asked, although her expression told Theo she was thinking the same: stolen.

Milton wanted clarification.

'So to get that gear any other way than the black market you'd have to be connected to the police?'

'Totally. Police, military, mafia ... You get caught with that stuff up there ...' He shook his head. 'Instant ban. At least in jail you eventually get out. Who wants to be banned for *life*? Not worth it, mate.'

He returned to arranging his workbench, conversation terminated.

Baxter rubbed his stomach as it rumbled.

'Man, I'm starving. Rex, can Theo stay here while we get some food?'

Clemmie retrieved her rig from the bench before Rex had chance to move it.

'Why aren't you all going?' said Rex without looking up.

'We can't.'

Clemmie's voice was ice. She had put her rig back on and something had hooked her attention. She indicated the others should rig up.

Milton, then Baxter, quickly followed suit.

'I missed thirty-six calls from my parents,' Milton said with a monotone that betrayed his fear.

'Two,' said Baxter, taking his rig off.

Theo looked expectantly at Clemmie. She shook her head.

'You don't want to know.'

Theo hesitated, then checked his own.

'Two calls,' he announced. 'Both from the police.'

He double-checked that he was still in anonymous mode. Untraceable – unless he had decided to answer, in which case an assault team would probably descend upon him in a matter of minutes.

'Same newsfeeds though,' said Clemmie, scanning through for any mention of her name. 'Just you and one other anonymous scumbag.'

Milton was trembling so much he had to sit on a stool to steady himself.

'I bet when my father heard your name on the news this morning he shit the bed.' He rocked slightly on the stool as he thought. 'But nobody actually knows I'm with you. I wasn't at Bow Road for onc.' He tapped Baxter on the elbow. 'If we say we were out together all night. Just the two of us.'

'Aiding and abetting,' Baxter said with a snort. He nodded at Theo. 'He goes missing, then we do too? It's not rocket science.'

'They haven't mentioned our names.' Milton was scrambling for excuses.

Baxter regarded him with pity. 'I see. A little trouble and suddenly you wanna turn your back on your mates?'

Milton couldn't meet any of their gazes.

'It's not like that,' he mumbled quietly.

Baxter gave a snort of derision. 'Sounds exactly like that.'

Milton removed his rig and stared at the bike, refusing to take it any further. He had paled.

'If you want to go, go.' Theo gestured to the door. 'Nobody's forcing you to stay.' He realised his tone was too harsh and instantly regretted it. 'Sorry, Milt. What you've done so far – that's above and beyond a real friend. But I can't let you dig yourself into any more trouble for me.'

Milton nodded, but didn't meet his gaze. Baxter and Clemmie stared defiantly at Theo. Baxter took a step forward, gunning for a fight.

'Are you telling us to piss off too?'

Theo stood to block him.

'If it gets you out of trouble, yes. This isn't a game, Bax. It's not another dash through *Avasta*. This all has real-world consequences.'

Baxter gave a hollow laugh. 'That's always been your problem, Theo. Think you can do everything on your own. Maybe that's why you ended up printing burgers.'

Theo wasn't sure where that dig came from, but it hurt more than expected.

Clemmie leaned against Baxter. 'He's right. You can't do this without us.'

'If they catch us—'

'Then we tell them the *truth*!' Clemmie interjected. 'Exactly what we'd tell them if we turned ourselves in now.' She shot Milton a meaningful look. He gave a slight nod. 'Nothing changes, except you have your back covered by us. That means we stand a chance at finding Ella before it's too late.' She flinched, regretting her choice of words. She took a step nearer to Theo and gently took his hand. 'If it was my mother ... Okay, bad choice. My *dad*, then I'd want you all busting a gut to help me. Right?'

She looked at the others for support.

Baxter nodded. 'Sure.'

Milton pulled a face. 'If it was my dad ... maybe not.' He

reached a decision then nodded firmly. 'But yeah. We're up to our arses in it right now.'

Theo wanted to return a warm smile of camaraderie, maybe even a team fist bump to stoke up morale, just like in the movies. But his stomach was fluttering and his bowels stirred uncomfortably.

They all suddenly became aware Rex had been watching the exchange with increasing puzzlement.

'Wait a sec. What have I missed?'

Chapter Nineteen

Waiting out the mandatory time restriction was interminable, especially as they would have to wait until past midnight for the clock to reset. With Rex's growing insistence, they had little choice but to explain the situation to him. He listened, twiddling his beard with increasing excitement, ending up in high-fiving Clemmie when they described breaking from the interview room.

Agreeing to let them hide out and not tell Baxter's sister their location was one thing, but paying for some takeout turned out to be an impasse that almost brought the coalition down. In the end, Rex begrudgingly agreed to splash out for five meals.

The rest of the day was spent with Baxter and Milton resting and surfing social media while Clemmie helped Rex put the Indian together and run engine diagnostics. Theo tried to help, but couldn't focus on the most basic tasks. Instead, he resigned himself to checking news updates. The Bow Street Runners had slipped news ranking as a British political scandal, threats of a civil war in evangelical-torn America and a real war in Central America ate up the headlines.

As night fell, Rex was preparing to leave when he dropped a bombshell on them.

'Why didn't you guys ascend earlier to get the rest of that message?'

Baxter sighed. He was lying on the oil-stained sheet, curled in the corner of the garage, trying to snatch a moment's sleep.

'Told you already. We used up our allocations and we're still unsure if we have enough to replay the entire message.'

'Yeah. So? You could've staved it, bruv.'

Clemmie, who had been slowly spinning in a circle on a battered swivel chair, lashed out her foot and spun around to face him.

'Shut the front door! You can do that? I thought the ones you got him to push were nothing but mal-code?'

Rex had the decency to avoid Baxter's scowl.

'They were naff, sure. But since then I managed to get my hands on some pure staves. You didn't ask.'

Theo stood up and held out his arms helplessly.

'But that's illegal.'

Clemmie arched an eyebrow teasingly.

'Says the cop-killer.' She punched Theo playfully in the arm. 'We only have to hold back ejection time for one of us to see the rest of that message.'

Baxter held his hands up, not wanting to be part of this plan.

'Not again. I was lucky the shit you had me scalping didn't work. If it did we'd *both* be behind bars. I can't risk getting caught with a real stave.'

Theo was intrigued. 'How do we know these will work?'

Rex feigned being offended. 'This is no dodgy code that's traceable. These staves trick the System by lacing somebody else's ascension time with your own.' He interlocked the fingers of both hands as a demonstration. 'So it thinks you're two separate people and therefore expands your time.'

'Brilliant!' Milton exclaimed. 'And we don't go crazy from staying in too long?'

Rex grinned. 'Nah. That still happens.'

'Then not so brilliant.'

Rex caught Baxter's disapproving look. 'Mate, these can't be traced to us like that last lot.' He turned to Milton. 'And you only go wacko if you keep doing it. Like all good things, moderation.'

'Have you ever done it?' Clemmie asked.

Rex extended his arms like a showman and flashed a yellow-toothed smile.

'All the time, babe. And there ain't much wrong with this.' He pointed to his own head.

Theo and Clemmie exchanged a look, unconvinced.

'Can you buy me an extra hour?' Theo looked at his friends. 'If I go through the slur on my own I can use the time to hear the whole damn message.'

'And only one of us goes mad,' noted Milton without a smile.

'I can get you an hour. Clarion trades the best black market tech, but one of you'd have to go there to trade it straight into his rig – it's got to pair with Theo's biometrics.' He held up his hands. 'And before you ask, I'm just the middleman, so I'm not doing that. And it'll cost you.'

'If I use my cred, I'll be tracked. We all would be.' Theo

sighed. 'Besides, I don't think I'd have enough.' He knew for a fact his personal account was already overdrawn. 'And if I step out of here ... I risk getting arrested.'

'Then no can do, mate. I put myself on the line letting you stay and buying you lunch. Shelling out for a stave is a favour too far.'

Clemmie finally spoke up. 'I can do it.' Theo's questioning look made her laugh. 'What? I have a crypto-account on the side.' She noted everybody's surprise. 'If your dad was in the police, then you'd learn how to avoid your every move being traced.'

She looked at Rex and raised an eyebrow.

'So, *bruv*. What do we do?'

Industrial dubstep vibrated Clemmie's chest as she followed Rex through the crammed dance floor. She felt out of place in her combat jacket, jeans, and an oily satchel from Rex's garage thrown over one shoulder. Everybody else was either in vanta black – cloth that literally sucked the light from the room, making the wearers resemble silhouettes under the harsh strobes – or clad in pixi-cloth, a fabric that played random video images over every curve like a piece of walking street art. It was notable that nobody in the club wore their rigs. That was Pulsar's policy; using rigs would get you thrown out. It was one of a number of growing niche venues around the world trying to wean visitors from their tech and back into the tangible real world.

Baxter stuck close to her, uncomfortable with the music. His tastes veered more towards K-pop.

Rex followed the curving bar towards a set of booths. He stopped and shouted to Clemmie over the music.

'Wait here!'

Within a couple of paces he melted into the crowd.

Baxter looked around with a scowl, then eyed the bar.

'We should get a drink.'

Clemmie had to strain to hear him even though he was inches away.

She shook her head. 'They won't take crypto.' Bars seldom did. 'Do you trust Rex?'

She had to repeat the question at the top of her lungs.

'I think so! He's a complete tit, but Anna likes him.'

Clemmie scanned the crowd. Since leaving the garage, they had walked to Bermondsey Tube and travelled three stops without incident. Yet she was convinced they would be stopped at every turn.

'Nobody's looking for us,' Baxter reminded her.

'Not officially.'

At the Tube she had pointed out that Rex would have to pay their fare so they wouldn't be ID'd. Once they were on their way, Rex was less argumentative, almost keen on getting to the club on time.

They waited close to the bar, but the servers were all attending the crush of customers at the far end and paid them no attention. Clemmie noticed one gorilla of a bouncer checking her out, but he looked away the moment she scowled at him.

Baxter must have sensed her nervousness.

'Relax. Rex's got too much to lose by turning us in.'

Clemmie thought she saw a flicker of doubt cross his face – or was it the strobes?

'Us, maybe. But Theo?'

She hadn't been happy about leaving him behind with Milton, but the risk of being identified was too great. Although, looking around the rig-less crowd, maybe this was the one place he could be truly anonymous.

After several minutes, Rex reappeared and motioned they should follow him.

'We're on.'

Skirting around the dance floor, he escorted them between a series of booths. One was larger than the others, positioned against the wall to give it the best view across the club. Sat in the middle, on a throne of black chrome, was a woman a little older than Rex. The wheelchair she was sat in blended seamlessly with the booth. She had a shock of white hair and alabaster skin from which her fulsome blood-red lips pouted alluringly. An ethereal otherworldly beauty poured from her. Her hands were folded on the table next to a bottle of Fuller's London Porter. Only her eyes, piercing blue, moved to study the newcomers.

She was flanked by three androgynous goths sporting perfectly tattooed make-up that had been accentuated with threads of copper and silver metal woven between their pores. One of them had inked the whites of his eyes, while another wore contacts that constantly shifted through the spectrum.

'Clarion, these are the ones who want to trade—'

Rex was shouting the last two words against a sudden backdrop of silence. For a second, Clemmie thought the music had stopped, but a quick check over her shoulder revealed the dancers were still pounding across the dance floor.

Clemmie indicated the ceiling with her finger.

'An anti-noise cone? A little overkill, but it's nice not to have to listen to more dubstep.' Clarion watched her without comment and Clemmie was damned if she was going to be intimidated. 'So are you willing to sell me a stave? I need an hour.' Clemmie cocked her head in a well-polished look of indifference. 'Or are you wasting my time?'

Clarion reached for her beer with one hand. She took a slow swig, the bottle held close to her face as if she was trying to peer through the brown glass.

'Why would a girl like you want to spend any more time in that hellhole?'

She placed the beer back down, then steepled the fingers of one hand against her fine chin.

'I don't share my reasons.' Clemmie shot Clarion her best defiant look. 'And some of us see the future in SPACE.' She gestured around. 'Not in a basement class club.'

One of Clarion's eyes narrowed. 'I used to think the same as you. I spent all my time up there, wasting my life away.'

As she spoke, Clemmie and Baxter sucked in a sharp breath but tried not to react further. Half of Clarion's mouth didn't move; they could see she had been masking the right side of her face with the bottle when she first spoke. Everything, save her eye, was completely paralysed. Any muscular movement on the healthy side of her face pulled the skin over atrophied muscles on the other. It shattered any illusion of beauty and, in the pulsing black light, made the stagnant side of her face look almost skeletal.

Clarion gestured to the side of her face with one hand, and Clemmie assumed her other hand was just as immobile as her face.

'This is what Lag does to a healthy mind. I stayed in far too long and suffered a massive stroke when I wasn't much older than you. It fried the nerve endings in half my body. It stole my future and put me in this.' She tapped the touchpad on her wheelchair with a single black nail-polished finger. 'But worse than the physical was this.' She rolled several fingers through her snow-white hair. 'It prevented some of my mirror neurons from firing. I see from your expression that means nothing to you. It should.'

Clemmie flicked a glance at Baxter, who watched on, intrigued.

'They help us interpret other people's behaviour. I was always good at reading people.' She gave a short laugh devoid of humour. 'They also control emotional states, such as empathy.' Her eyes flicked to the rig hanging from Clemmie's belt. 'Those crowns of lies use those very neurons to ferry emotional feedback. So now I feel nothing up there or down here.' She tapped the table. 'Every time you ascend, those vital neural pathways are slowly being desensitised over time. Imagine a future, a society of cripples like me, drained of empathy and emotion. The inverse of the caring society that James Lewinsky promised us.' She patted the chair for emphasis.

Clemmie licked her lips. The little speech had rattled her, but she didn't want to admit it.

'I assume you don't go any more?'

Clarion shook her head. 'And if I had my way I would delete the whole system.'

'I think the Slifs would have something to say about that.'

171

Clarion waved her hand dismissively and half her face twisted into a disbelieving grimace.

'Programs with attitudes. Not with souls. Just because some politician on a crusade thought Slifs should have rights, while conveniently overlooking what ascension was doing to people like me.' She looked away in disgust. Then her face softened. 'But I have no quarrel with the Slifs. They are welcome to inherit the kingdom without us. That's what some of them want anyway. Others simply wish to keep the status quo.'

Clemmie's fingers drummed the table as recollections of past conversations with her father and occasional newsfeeds came back to her.

'You're one of those killjoy neo-Luddites who have been trying to screw up SPACE for everybody, aren't you?' The name came to her and she snapped her fingers. 'The Children of Ellul! I knew it was something stupid.' Without her eyes leaving Clarion's, she inclined her head to Baxter. 'Remember there was a glitch last New Year's Eve. Two hundred thousand people booted out because somebody had laced an optical server farm with a hundred pounds of Semtex?' She pointed an accusing finger at Clarion. 'Exhibit A.'

Clarion tilted her head in acknowledgement. 'I prefer to think of us as freedom fighters following in the footsteps of the great French philosopher Jacques Ellul.'

Baxter was incredulous. 'You are freedom fighters, fighting against a new world of freedom and possibilities?'

'Ellul battles for all of our emotional liberties.'

'If you're so opposed to it all, then why sell your time?'

172

It took a moment for Clarion to focus back on Clemmie and she shrugged one perfect shoulder.

'If you can't beat them ... Besides, what use do you think the world has for a cripple like me?' Her eyes flicked to the rig around Clemmie's neck. 'I would rather talk you out of not extending your time. If I can't do that, then I will happily take your money to further our cause.'

Clemmie pulled her pack from her shoulder and took out Theo's rig.

'It's not for me. It's for a friend.'

She placed the rig in the centre of the table.

Clarion ran a painted fingernail over it, circling around the crack in the visor.

'You must really hate him.'

'I'm not the hater here.' Clemmie snapped back.

There were always groups, usually concerned parents, trying to ban SPACE use and she despised all their ham-fisted attempts to take freedom from her, as had happened so many times in the country's recent past. Now she was face to face with somebody who had become militant in such narrow thinking, she was angry with herself for feeling so bad about her plight. All Clemmie wanted to do was make the trade and go.

'An hour, you say?' Clemmie nodded, provoking a sigh from Clarion. 'That will be two hundred pounds.'

Clemmie's hand shot out and pulled the rig towards her so Clarion couldn't reach.

'Are you fucking with me? Two hundred? Did he tell you I was paying in crypto?'

'He did. And that told me you were somebody with

something to hide. Two hundred and you receive an hour of my life.'

'Of your *virtual* life. The one you have no use for.'

Half of Clarion's lip curled. Her paralysis made it difficult to tell if it was in admiration or contempt.

'The price can climb—'

'One-twenty.'

'You are in no position to haggle.'

'Why not? Rex here knows a ton of other people willing to sell.'

Rex opened his mouth to refute the claim, but Baxter silenced him with a sharp elbow. Clemmie pressed her advantage before Rex could screw it up.

'One-twenty and let's face it, you know I'll be back for more.'

Clarion seemed to consider as she threw an angry look at Rex.

'One-fifty.'

'One-thirty,' Clemmie said without thinking, surprising herself by how much she was pushing her luck. 'Because I'm not the only one with something to hide.'

Threatening the figurehead of a militia group wasn't the best idea she'd had.

Clarion stared at her for a long hard moment. Then she gave a terse nod and indicated to Blackeyes sat next to her. The henchman slid on a pair of thin AR glasses and stood, leaning across the table. Clemmie put her own rig on and leaned forward, calling up the crypto interface. She did her best to lock Blackeyes' gaze as her own retina was scanned and the money shunted along the blockchain. Now she understood how useful Blackeyes was – great at receiving payments but difficult to retina-hack.

Clemmie removed her visor and slid Theo's rig to Clarion. When Blackeyes nodded to confirm the transaction, Clarion held the rig over a sensor on her chair, then rolled it back. Clemmie caught it before it fell from the table.

'That's it?'

She checked the visor for any message, any sign time had been transferred.

'That's it,' Clarion confirmed with a half-smile. 'I hope he enjoys.'

Clemmie placed the rig into her pack.

'And how do I know you've traded your time?'

'Your dear man will know.'

'How do *I* know now?'

Clarion took a swig of beer and smiled. 'Trust, my dear. Trust.'

Clemmie wanted to punch the woman. Rex gave a nod of confirmation, his eyes pleading that it was time they left. Clemmie swung the bag over her shoulder and turned to go.

'A pleasure doing business with you,' Clarion called after her just as they exited the anti-noise cone and pounding bass struck Clemmie's eardrums with vengeance.

'Thanks for backing me up!' she shouted to Baxter, who doggedly followed her.

'You were doing great. That woman may be a terrorist, but you *utterly* terrified me.'

His comment cheered Clemmie up a little as she circled

around a bouncer patrolling the fringes of the dance floor. With any luck they'd be back in the garage in forty minutes and just in time to ascend.

Chapter Twenty

After a brief reunion in Rex's lock-up, it was agreed they should get as close to the Market as possible so as not to waste any ascension time. Even with the stave, Theo wasn't confident he'd enough time in the bank. They'd have to take a risk and go on foot.

The walk from Rex's garage to Lambeth was punctuated by a heavy downpour of warm summer rain. At times the fat raindrops stung as they fell, forcing them to take shortcuts through alleyways that had been covered by plastic shelters to prevent the bins from flooding, as they often did when the monsoons struck. The heavy rain thundered on the covering, turning any conversation into a shouting match. On the plus side, the cloaking darkness gave them further anonymity that helped fox AR cameras and the city's dense network of surveillance cameras. For anybody running ID scans, they would simply flash up as anonymous, like half the people in London.

With just two of the so-called Bow Street Runners still reported, the foursome didn't particularly stand out from the Sunday night revellers and they made it to Lambeth Bridge with ease. The rains abated just as sharply as they arrived.

Across the dark – and recently cleansed – Thames, the Houses of Parliament were lit up, unchanged over the decades, while the skyline opposite had grown into an arterial nest of linked skyscrapers edged with neon strips of primary colours in a vain attempt to try to outshine its virtual counterpart. To the south, towards Vauxhall, a network of overhead Parkways soared across the city, connecting Hyde Park to Greenwich in the east, and curving away to join Battersea and Richmond parks to the south-west.

Milton overlaid the augmented map of the Market over the Thames and vaguely indicated an area just to their left.

'As far as we could tell, the building you found in the Market is over there, on the fourteenth level.'

While waiting for the others to return, Theo and Milton had made the most of their time matching the SPACE footage Theo had recorded in Nu London to a map of London. It wasn't straightforward as the virtual space between was somewhat elastic, like an Einsteinian wet dream. The fact the Market was bound by the Thames at least helped them narrow down their search.

Theo indicated a rubbish-strewn alleyway behind them; the plastic awnings had made it the only dry space around.

'I suggest we crash there. Keep awareness on and ascend together.'

Closer examination of the alley revealed a smell that had Milton gagging, but to his credit he didn't complain, knowing the stench would disappear the moment they ascended. After moaning about living his life in the trash, Baxter found several cardboard boxes that would provide some notion of comfort on the floor, while concealing them from view. With less fuss than usual, they settled down, logged in, and ascended.

Theo sprinted through the ovoid archway in the wall as fast as he could. Although technically in the virtual he had no muscles to punish, the wetware convinced his brain he *was* running, so pretty soon his legs ached.

He stopped in a square, packed with tourists, shoppers and an assortment of Slifs, some walking weird insectoid pets. Clemmie had kept pace with him, but grabbed his shoulder to stop him moving off once he had found his bearings.

'Wait up! Let the others catch up.'

She jerked a thumb towards Milton and Baxter, who were on the far side of the square. Milton had stopped to catch his breath and admire the custom pets.

'We need to keep moving.'

They may have ascended anonymously but somewhere their presence in SPACE had been logged. Theo had expected vPolice to appear the moment they set foot in the Market, but nothing bad had happened yet.

'You're literally running off paranoia,' said Clemmie as the others caught up. 'Has the stave registered yet?'

Theo shook his head. 'No. My clock's ticking as usual. Same countdown.'

The doubt in his voice confirmed Clemmie's fears that she had been ripped off. Seeing the disappointment on her face, Theo smiled.

'But that doesn't mean a thing. Time will tell.'

That got a smile from her and an impatient cough from Milton as he caught up.

'Does any of this look familiar to you?'

All the streets looked identical, differentiated only by the variety of signage and garish flashing banners that were a visual assault on the eyeballs. Nothing looked familiar. Theo decided they should continue up to level fourteen, following the rough directions on Milton's hastily configured map.

After thirty-eight minutes of navigating sloping passage-ways, doubling back, throngs of avatars to nudge through, and multiple crossroads leading deeper into the labyrinth, Theo stopped and indicated a store showcasing designer pets.

'That looks familiar.'

'Wow!'

Milton dashed to the open frontage where a printer was busy laying down 3-D life-codes which writhed like maggots as they interlocked together, slowly building the creature from inside out, like watching an autopsy in reverse. Each strip was bespoke and carried with it as much data as a strand of DNA, indelibly marked with the creator's stamp and time of creation. Beyond the printer, two parents held back a bouncing eight-year-old girl, who was watching the process with impatient excitement.

'I've never seen a code printer before,' Milton said with a trace of awe.

Creating virtual life was governed by strict codes of conduct, so stores like this one were rare. The animated signage, Odin's, unleashed a torrent of subconscious metadata informing them that it was one of the most highly regarded artisans in London.

Theo didn't pay attention to Odin's as he circled the junction before identifying a street sloping up. It was less crowded and with far fewer open shops.

'This way.'

He broke into a run.

Milton was glued to the spectacle of the printer finally producing a super-cute kitten-puppy combo with a rolling tongue and wide Manga-esque eyes. The *kuppy* sprung to bouncing life and leaped from the printer into the arms of the delighted girl, who squealed as it licked her face.

'Milton!' Baxter yelled.

With a sigh, Milton forced himself away from the shop and followed. They were all oblivious to the Slif standing across the street, its skin rippling in a chameleon effect as it blended into the neon graffiti on the wall around it.

'This is it.'

The blackness beyond the still-broken door was unmistakable. Theo braced himself, noticing that the few avatars who passed by didn't stop to gawp at the darkness. They were seeing a normal, undamaged, doorway.

Clemmie patted him on the shoulder. 'Go for it. Remember, there are no comms in there.'

Theo took a deep breath and vanished into the non-rendered void. Milton looked critically at the portal.

'I would have added sound, or some kind of cool animation.'

He wiggled his fingers to indicate a sparkly effect and made a tinkling noise. The pitying look from the other two shut him up.

Typically blind to aesthetics, he thought morosely. What a dull world it would be if they were in charge. His mind drifted back to the kuppy. If he wasn't going to spend his life behind bars when this was over, Odin's would be the sort of place he wanted to start. After the first week in university, and to great consternation from his father, he had switched from an English Lit degree to double in virtual biology and Foundation architecture, which he found much more engaging. The irritating thing was that none of his friends were aware of the switch; not a single one of them had asked about his studies or any new friendships he had forged. It was as if they didn't care. Yet here he was, putting his liberty on the line for them ...

Clemmie leaned against the wall with Baxter standing close, supporting himself with one arm planted close to her head. He wondered what had happened with those two since they had left for university together, and tried to ignore the irony that he hadn't bothered asking.

He turned away, and took in the street that sloped away at a good forty-five degree angle before it joined the bustling square three hundred yards away. When they were in SPACE they were either gaming or partying hard. Never had they taken time to stop and take the amazing place in.

Milton ran his fingers across the uneven wall next to him, designed to resemble an old mud brick surface. He closed his eyes, feeling every dimple and pit. The smell of the Market crept up on him. After the stench of the alleyway it was a treat to sample alluring odours such as fresh bread from stalls that would have it drone-delivered to your home before you had time to remove your rig. His parents still marvelled that they lived in a world where delivery was faster than the shopping experience itself. A sweet concoction wafted by, designed to lure people into a nearby vintage clothing shop by stimulating nostalgia. It struck him hard, bringing back wonderful memories of a holiday in the Lake District when he was ten – a time when he regarded his father as a role model. He knew it was just a clever marketing technique – nostalgia was a powerful weapon that generated huge sales.

Woven among all that was the subtle background new car smell that permeated SPACE and was the signature scent of all Slifkind. That odour was particularly prevalent in the street.

Milton opened his eyes and peered down the incline. Something felt amiss.

People criss-crossed in the square beyond without so much as a glance in his direction. A couple of avatars walked past, deep in conversation while another made her way briskly down the hill. No Slifs around, and yet ...

His vision shifted. Although SPACE was a fully rendered world, the System still relied on localised *foveation* to stop the geostationary servers from going into meltdown. That meant the areas the users looked directly at were rendered in full 32k resolution, *more real than real*, as Emotive's slogan went. But peripheral vision, as in real life, suffered from lower quality.

As a result, the moment Milton's gaze ran across a scrawled street tag on the wall, the image suddenly shifted and a three-dimensional figure hove into view like a moving autostereogram.

It was a gangly Slif who was standing motionless and staring right at them, recording everything on a small spherical drone that hovered at his shoulder. As soon as the creature realised Milton was staring with an open mouth, the Slif spoke quietly in a language that resembled the whistles and clicks of an ancient modem.

At that same moment, a loud crackling sound came from the opposite end of the street. A drone, about the size of Milton himself, banked into view at the apex of the street. Its nose-mounted weapon pod crackled as a gravity wave charged up – then spat right at them.

Baxter used his supporting arm to shove Clemmie to the ground as he dropped to his knees. Milton was rooted to the spot. This was the sort of thing that only happened in games, not the virtual streets. The wave shimmered the air over Baxter and struck the wall next to the doorway Theo had vanished through.

Chapter Twenty-One

Theo swore aloud as Ella's hexagonal vid unit began to play her message from the beginning. He turned it this way and that, trying to find a way to fast forward it, but the hologram stubbornly continued.

He glanced at his clock. It was rapidly counting down as the slur chewed up his immersion time. With still no indication he had been allocated any extra minutes, he scooped up the vid and ran into the entry room, intending to leave the slur altogether. The moment he passed through the door into the lobby, the vid disappeared from his hand, instantly reappearing where he had picked it up and forcing him to start the message from scratch.

'Oh, come on!' he yelled to the air, not willing to try that move again.

Instead he sat cross-legged, rested his head in his hand, his elbow balanced on one knee, and watched his mother's crisis unfold. Again. When she finally reached the new section, Theo craned forward and listened intently.

'That's when I made the mistake of going to the Old Bill. That's when I found out how deep their tendrils go and I saw the full scope of their plan.' Ella addressed the camera with iron determination. 'It was inevitable they'd come after me so I took what I had and spread it out. No one vault would be safe enough from these people. They have too much blood on their hands.'

She leaned back on the sofa and tousled her hair.

'But I'm not there yet. Who's pulling the strings? Who is at the very top? I have my suspicions and when I leave here, I plan to come back with the evidence.'

Again she stopped, gazing wistfully off screen. Theo impatiently drummed his fingers, glancing at the blurring figures on his timer.

'If I don't come back ... Well, that's why you are watching this. I may be a screw-up, Theo, but I did all right with you. Know I love you.'

Theo felt a tear trickle down his cheek as he was overwhelmed with a tsunami of emotion. He was unsure if she had embedded her own emo-stream into the recording or if it was something genuinely welling up inside him; either way love was a taboo word they'd never used in any world.

Ella pulled herself together. 'So, right now I'm going to deposit some of my evidence in the place I found a new me.' She flashed a twinkling smile. 'And however brief that was, I wish I was still there. I'm sorry for what I did. Bring them down, Theo.'

The image went blank.

Theo sat in silence. He had half-expected her to punch the air and demand he claim vengeance, but that wasn't her way. But what was her way? It was evident that he had never really got to know her, and the little he thought he knew was wrong. Studying to be a detective? A bright young woman with a dynamic future ahead of her, before he had come along and scuppered her dreams. However, she was wrong about one thing – she was still alive. The fact the unseen enemy had instigated a manhunt just to find out what he knew was enough to convince him that they would keep Ella breathing to use as a bargaining chip, and he would tear the cities apart to find her.

His timer was still a blur.

'Shit!'

He leaped to his feet, berating himself for eating through valuable time by moping. Reaching for the vid unit, he pondered how he could destroy it – just as the entry room suddenly exploded.

The shock wave from the detonation tore the dividing room door from its hinges, forcing him to duck as it whipped overhead and splintered against the far wall. Theo swayed as a wave of dizziness swept over him and the room seemed to flex as if it was projected on a plastic board.

A circular hole had been blown in the lobby wall, revealing the street beyond. The curtain of non-rendered space had vanished and the slur had been destroyed. Theo hopped through the hole – and slipped on the rubble, falling hard on to his back.

'Theo!'

It was Clemmie, screaming from somewhere to his right. Dazed, he rolled to his feet as she and Baxter ran towards him. The air was thick with smoke, which billowed aside as a drone pushed through it. The menacing aircraft angled to face them.

'Run!' Clemmie screamed as the weapons pod lit up from within and another gravity pulse crackled towards them.

It slammed high into the wall opposite them. A circular five-foot section of wall was destroyed with a loud pop as the gravity wave focused the impact to a single point with the force of a localised black hole, while the section around it exploded outwards, tossing masonry shrapnel in every direction. They sprinted down the hill, skidding to a halt when they found Milton half-covered by detritus.

Theo grabbed his friend's hand.

'Milt, are you alive?'

'I don't know,' came the groggy reply.

Theo dragged him to his feet, bricks and dust flowing off him.

Clemmie eyed the drone as another gravity wave charged up.

'Now's not the time to debate!'

She picked up a brick and hurled it at the weapons pod.

It glanced from the drone's nose and the entire aircraft swayed, firing the pulse wide across the plaza beyond. It struck a shop; the entire building crunched into a single pixel, while the buildings either side blew apart in opposite directions.

'There!' Milton yelled, pointing at the Slif fleeing towards the square. 'He was spying on us.'

Theo looked between the drone and the Slif. They had the information they needed, so ejection was the smartest move right now, yet Milton's accusation had him intrigued. He shoved Milton forward.

'What are you waiting for? Let's get the bastard!'

The Slif was remarkably fast as it entered the square and ploughed through the crowd of avatars, roughly shoving them aside.

'Stop him!' Theo bellowed as he shouldered a larger avatar from his path.

The big man was left spluttering obscenities in Russian as he floundered head first into an energy-screen window and bounced off it in a mass of ejection pixels.

The Slif darted sideways down a branching street. Clemmie overtook Theo and leaped halfway up the wall, aided by her Nike Airs, briefly using the vertical surface to run along before dropping back to the ground.

This narrower road was crammed with traditional market stalls filled with bric-a-brac that people were selling from the comfort of their own homes. The Slif smashed through one table at speed, hurling the items behind it to slow Clemmie down. But she was now in her stride, resolutely gaining on the snitch. Irate shoppers and stallholders tried to reach out for her, but she nimbly jumped onto a table and bounded from stall to stall, scattering simulated goods.

Baxter glanced behind to see the drone swoop low into the street. Another grav-pulse discharged from the aircraft, straight at Theo.

Theo shouldered into a shopper, whose hulking form refused to budge and instead sent Theo reeling sideways into a stall of vintage porcelain figures which shattered on impact.

'You stupid—' was as far as the hulk got before the pulse struck him in the chest. The startled man was sucked into his own chest, then oblivion.

Baxter stopped in shock, his eyes wide as a man imploded in front of him. Too late did he realise the section of wall next to him had also been caught in the blast. It exploded apart, a huge chunk of masonry clobbering Baxter across the head.

'Bax!'

Theo watched as his friend erupted in a mass of ejection detritus. He scrambled to his feet and followed Clemmie as the drone gained ground.

With a curt *phut*, a dart shot from the drone's wing tip. Theo heard it whine past his ear and it struck Clemmie in the neck. She continued with nothing more than a blind swipe at whatever was annoying her.

Theo glanced back to see the drone bearing down on Milton. Fuelled by virtual bravery, Milton jumped onto a stall — and quickly changed his direction as he leaped straight for the drone, uttering a primal scream.

The aircraft pierced him like a missile, completely undeterred as Milton's pixel dust bounced from its fuselage.

Clemmie was focused on the Slif as it made a break towards a branching side street. She tackled the creature around the waist. Her momentum pitched them both hard against the wall. A writhing three-tentacled hand pushed into her face in an attempt to lever her off.

'No you don't!' she growled, pulling the hand away and shifting her weight to drag the Slif to the floor. Pinning the creature down felt like wrestling a slug. Her hands slid from its torso, forcing her to renew her grip. The Slif uttered a series of unintelligible squawks, before she noticed it had freed one arm to thrust a shock baton into her ribcage. The voltage blurred her vision with blistering pain.

Chapter Twenty-Two

'Jesus Christ!'

Clemmie writhed across the filthy alley floor and tossed her rig aside. It took a few seconds of frantic eye-rubbing to confirm her eyeballs hadn't melted like cheese under the grill. Then she probed her side, searching for a physical wound from where the Slif had shocked her. Finding nothing, she concentrated on shallow breathing to slow her racing heart. Her neck gave a psychosomatic itch from where she had been stung.

Milton stood over her wearing a look of concern. He absently rubbed his chest.

'Are you okay?'

'What happened?' Clemmie refused his offer of help to stand; instead she hauled herself up using a recycle dumpster. 'That felt worse than any game—'

They both jumped with fright as Theo screamed himself back to reality. He plucked his helmet off, lying on his back like a startled tortoise, his face drenched with sweat.

'That was intense.'

They only realised Baxter had been standing on the main

road when he sprinted back into the mouth of the alley.

'Hey! We have to go!'

The urgency in his voice was such that nobody challenged him. Milton helped Theo up and they ran to join Baxter. He had crossed the main riverside road and was leaning against a steel rail, peering up the Thames.

'See him?'

A speedboat was skipping across the shallow waves in an aimless arc. The pilot was at the wheel, a second figure standing, hands braced on the windscreen for support.

'When I ejected I heard the boat. Saw them circling, looking for something. That's when I noticed the bloke standing had a radio control unit.'

As he drew near they could see the controller hanging from his neck. His face was masked by his rig, but there was no mistaking the shock of blond hair and the half-swollen face. Theo had shown them all the footage of his escape from his flat so nobody needed to be told.

Baxter voiced his suspicions. 'Blondie was flying that drone.'

'In SPACE? From *here*?' Milton wasn't convinced – he hadn't ever heard of such a crossover.

'I bet one of you broke his toy?' Milton nodded. 'He was swearing about that.'

'That was me,' said Theo with a hint of pride.

Blondie twisted his head along the riverbank, searching this way and that – then looked directly at them. He pointed to the pilot and shouted orders. The speedboat veered in their direction.

'Shit!'

Theo turned and ran, the others following moments later.

'Theo, it's going to be a piece of piss outrunning a speed-boat on the streets!'

Baxter put on his rig, calling up a street map.

The screech of tyres made them all stop and face Lambeth Bridge as a pair of Audi SUVs skidded on to the embankment road. Rubber crunching the road surface was the only sound they made as they converged at a set of concrete steps leading to the water.

'This way!'

Baxter led them down a street perpendicular to the river.

Behind, one vehicle skidded to a halt as Blondie rushed up the quay steps and jumped in. The second vehicle roared ahead to pursue their targets. It jumped the kerb, almost broadsiding a trio of rusting archways poised on the corner as some sort of art exhibit, before the driver regained control and jounced back on the road.

'Down here!' yelled Theo, overtaking Baxter and darting down a narrower road to the left. It ran between two buildings, the space only wide enough for a single vehicle. The building to the right was covered in scaffolding, slender fingers reaching skywards to an aerial Parkway that grazed the rooftop. 'Up!'

Theo began clambering up an access ladder. Baxter hesitated, fighting a genuine fear of heights.

'Bax!'

It was Clemmie who looked back down and saw he had frozen. Above her, Theo and Milton had already reached the first floor and were now sprinting along a slatted walkway erected against the frontage, towards another ladder, like a giant game of Donkey Kong – except this ladder led directly to the roof.

The lead Audi performed the turn into the narrow road at speed. The driver handled it well this time and didn't overshoot the junction – although he probably wished he had.

The savage acceleration of the electric vehicle jolted the bulky SUV forward, on to the narrow pavement. The driver's side of the car smashed through the supporting scaffolding, knocking metal spars aside like skittles, fracturing the windscreen and pummelling the bodywork.

Everybody screamed as the entire wall of scaffolding shuddered with an ungodly metallic creak. Theo's feet slipped as he ascended the long ladder and he dropped – only saving himself with a looped arm around a rung. His flailing ill-fitting trainer narrowly missed punting Milton in the face.

The Audi continued demolishing the spars, passing just beneath Baxter's feet as he cleared the first ladder, which was unceremoniously snatched away an inch from his foot. Baxter fled along the trembling structure.

A falling pole speared straight through the vehicle's windscreen, impaling the driver in a blast of crimson that spattered the inside of the spiderwebbed window. A quirk of physics snagged the leading end of the pole down into a small broken drainage grid – and the still accelerating car flipped like a pole-vaulter, clear off the pavement.

Baxter reached the second ladder and began climbing just as the SUV was flipped through the first-floor platform like a massive steel metronome. The vehicle arced past inches from him. Wood splintered as the Audi swept through more scaffolding before twisting away from the building and slamming into the wall of the office block opposite, where it remained lodged, crumpled into the brickwork.

The second Audi skidded to a halt at the end of the street. Blondie exited and hesitated as the scaffolding swayed precariously from side to side with a shriek of metal grinding against metal.

Theo reached the sixth floor and powered on up. Baxter was two floors behind them all, aching limbs forgotten. He pulled himself flat against the swaying ladder as sections of scaffolding sheared loose from above and speared past him. The hollow tubes made almost melodic sounds as they bounced from the street like cabers. He pushed on up.

Blondie retreated behind his SUV's door as the first six storeys of scaffolding on the far side began to collapse like a house of cards, blocking the street below.

Baxter couldn't even summon a scream of terror as he watched section after section crash into the floor in a slow inexorable wave towards him.

At the last moment, he closed his eyes and clung on for life.

Seconds passed and the noise receded.

When he opened his eyes again, he gave a dry laugh of incredulity. The wave of collapsing scaffolding had stopped just feet away from the ladder which, for safety, had been bolted independently to the building. Now the remaining top three floors of scaffolding were only supported by the skeletal fingers of the remaining poles.

Baxter's relief was short-lived as those remaining levels inexorably peeled away, toppling like a felled tree and striking the top of the building opposite, where they wedged in place. Baxter felt the ladder holding him, Milton, Clemmie and Theo shudder as the weakened bolts holding it to the wall sheared and, like a peeling sticker, it too rolled away from the wall.

They all gripped the rungs hopelessly as the ladder crashed into the building opposite. The whole structure shuddered to a halt at an awkward thirty degrees across the street.

Baxter was now halfway up, inverted on the wrong side of the ladder.

His arms and left leg were caught between the rungs, hanging him in place. He experimentally moved his right leg around to the other side of the ladder ... which flexed alarmingly. A quick check showed that his friends were in the same predicament and all slowly crawling around to the safer side. Their combined movements pulsed slow stress waves through the ladder.

With his right leg now hooked around the rungs, Baxter freed his right arm and slowly moved it around. His other arm took the brunt of his weight and with a quick shuffle he heaved himself on to the safer side of the ladder. The entire structure creaked alarmingly, but Baxter was now able to spread his weight on the incline and catch his breath. Bad move.

A gunshot echoed through the street.

Darkness and dust from the collapsed scaffolding masked the street below, but Baxter caught the muzzle flash from the direction of the remaining Audi. A bullet pinged from a nearby spar, galvanising Theo, Milton and Clemmie into action. They continued their ascent, ignoring the wild swaying of the ladder.

Any apprehension regarding heights evaporated as Baxter double-timed it to follow them. Four more gunshots sounded, three striking metal close by. The dust below was clearing, enough to see Blondie clambering over wreckage to gain a better angle on his targets.

Theo reached the rooftop first and reached down to drag Milton the rest of the way. Two more shots rang out, both smashing an office window between Baxter and Clemmie. She didn't look back as hands reached down to haul her on to the rooftop.

A flood of adrenaline powered Baxter to the lip of the building. Clemmie and Theo tried reaching for him as a quartet of shots rang out, forcing them into cover. Baxter felt something whip his leg, but concentrated on scrambling on to the turf-covered roof.

His fingers frantically searched his leg. Finding no blood, he risked taking a look. The bullet had slit a hole in his jeans' inside thigh, just missing his flesh. He swore under his breath. Crouching on the grass, Clemmie spluttered in a giggling fit, more from a relief of stress.

'What's so funny?'

'You almost had your bollocks shot off!' she gasped between breaths, tears streaming down her face.

Baxter sat upright, searching for anything amusing about that.

'That's not funny.'

She patted her chest with her palm. 'Sorry.' Between gulps of breath she added, 'I think I'm just hysterical.'

Theo and Milton returned to the edge of the building, trying to unjam the ladder. They recoiled as bullets kicked up spurts of masonry near their feet. Theo dropped flat so he couldn't be seen from below and began booting the top of the ladder. It gave a warning groan.

Milton joined the frenzied attack and they were rewarded as the ladder gave way, crumpling into the street below. Nobody wanted to risk peering over the edge to see if it had crushed their assailant.

They sat in silence and caught their breath. Theo was the first to stand and nodded to a fire exit in the far corner of the roof.

'It's not going to take him long to figure a way up here.'

Nobody required further explanation. From their rooftop the Parkway bridge, as wide as a motorway, extended east over the building they had originally climbed, and west, arcing high over the river where it joined another distant rooftop.

Theo indicated north-eastwards.

'We need to go that way. And hope he doesn't follow us.'

Clemmie frowned. 'What's that way?'

'Something I hope my mum left behind.'

The darkness ahead was intense, the street lights far below unable to offer any assistance. They activated their rigs' low-light mode as they made their way along the elevated Parkway. The edge was lined with mighty oak and willow trees, their roots and branches elegantly draped over the side. The ground was carpeted with knee-high grass and wild flowers, which were damp from the rain shower.

Despite a path mowed through the centre, their shins and feet were soaked and uncomfortable. Occasional movements in the gloom betrayed hedgehogs rooting in the soil and, on one occasion, a lone badger hurrying away.

Milton indicated nervously behind them. 'He was using *real* bullets.'

Theo led the way. 'And I bet he has more.'

'He was trying to kill us!' Milton insisted. 'For *real*. And in SPACE, that drone? I swear the gravity wave was a killer. And he was controlling it from *here*!'

Clemmie gave him a curious look. 'What's your point?'

'My point is, this is getting out of control. We should hand ourselves in.'

Baxter sniffed and nodded. 'I think he may finally have a point.'

Theo stopped and turned to face them. 'I'm pretty sure Ella hid something in the Conservation.' He pointed over the river. 'And whatever it is almost got us all killed.'

Milton looked away, never comfortable with direct confrontation. 'All the more reason to tell somebody.'

'Who?' Clemmie held out her hands in a gesture of hopelessness. 'We have one crooked policeman searching for us and that guy is *not* a cop.'

Milton was dismissive. 'You don't know that.'

'That was a private boat he was in. Those SUVs are not police issue. The tech he is using smacks of military.' Clemmie counted off each point on her fingers.

That sparked Milton's interest. He reluctantly nodded.

Theo sighed, his tone betraying the weariness he felt. 'Ella said whoever is behind the Dens is well positioned.'

'This is major organised crime,' Clemmie insisted. 'And the sheer fact they tracked us in SPACE and have kept our faces —' she indicated Milton and Baxter too — 'out of the news shows they have some serious official power. They're trying to lure us out.'

Baxter wasn't following her logic. 'Why?'

'To see what we know.'

Everybody turned. It was Milton who had spoken quietly. He raised his visor and rubbed his forehead as he addressed Baxter.

'Like you said before, they know we're running with them. They're not dumb, they're just hoping we're naïve enough to think they are.'

'You've changed your tune. So you now think we need to see this through?' said Baxter slowly.

Milton gave him a thin smile. 'I suppose I do.' A thought struck him as he looked at Theo and Clemmie. 'And don't forget that Slif. Whoever he works for —' he jerked a thumb behind them — 'they also have Slifs working for them up there.'

While they openly mingled in SPACE, it was rare, beyond big business, for Slifs and people to work together. They were two deeply segregated societies and their interactions were often founded on mistrust.

Milton peered thoughtfully across the city as something occurred to him.

'More importantly, how did Blondie know where to find us once we ejected? That is supposed to be impossible.'

Clemmie rubbed her neck. 'Just before I tackled that Slif to the floor I felt something hit my neck.'

'That was in the virtual,' Baxter pointed out. 'There's no way it could magically become real.'

Clemmie looked away; she didn't know what to think.

'We're wasting time speculating.' Theo continued walking. 'Whether Blondie gets up here or not, he knows where we are. Let's just hope he doesn't know where we're going.'

Without another word, he walked on to the Parkway that arched over the river. The others exchanged looks, then reluctantly followed him into the darkness.

It was possible to convince yourself that you were very far from the city when walking through the aerial Parkways. Up here there was no hum of the city, no light pollution. The rain clouds had cast aside, unveiling a waxing moon that bathed the wild scrub with ethereal silver beauty. The air was alive with the hoots of owls and the occasional swish of bats swooping through trees; the rustling of branches as the wind riffled through them was almost hypnotic.

After ten minutes they reached another flat rooftop thirty storeys up, from which a further four walkways blossomed out across the city. The buzz of distant police quadcopters had forced them to hide in a copse of ash trees until they assured themselves there was no danger.

Theo shared Ella's message across their headsets, which ate up time as they neared the Conservation.

'Has it occurred to you that we could be walking straight into a trap?' Milton pointed out after he finished watching. 'For all we know they may have found ... whatever it is, already. That Slif, out of the whole of SPACE, managed to track us there.' He let that hang for a moment, especially as it was supposed to be impossible. 'They could have beaten the information out of her.' He caught Theo's pained expression. 'Sorry. But ... we don't know.'

Clemmie cupped a hand around her neck where it was still itching and rubbed it thoughtfully.

'Milt's right. We could be.'

Theo walked to the start of the Parkway bridge that led directly to the distant Conservation. Even with his visor's digital magnification he couldn't see any sign of movement or light.

'The only thing that appears to be stopping the police from crashing down on us is that they – whoever *they* are – have no idea how much we know.' Theo turned to the others and couldn't shake an unfamiliar sense of hope that stirred in his chest. 'And that's why I'm convinced she's still alive.'

'This is starting to feel like one of those conspiracy theories.' Milton waved his hands to indicate how spooky it was. 'Bi-world tech, mysterious killers, sex farms.'

Theo was beginning to feel pissed off with his constant downbeat attitude, but held his temper in check, reminding himself that none of them had to be there.

'What's your point?'

'I don't know. I don't have one.' Milton's frustration was building. 'I'm tired, grumpy and about to walk into some bees in the dead of night to look for God knows what!' He clenched his fists. 'I'm scared, Theo. I'm bloody terrified.'

Baxter lightly punched Milton's shoulder.

'So am I. But look.' He gestured around. 'We're still alive. They're not good enough to touch us.' He held up his hand, waiting for Milton to high-five. 'You do realise this is the only time in our history that I'm not going to be a dick to you.'

His hand hadn't wavered. Milton reluctantly slapped it.

'Aw, I love a good bromance.' Clemmie snorted, relieved the tension had dissolved.

Theo nodded his thanks to Baxter and caught a fleeting look – one that said Baxter was barely holding it together himself.

Chapter Twenty-Three

Halfway across the bridge a message flagged in the corner of Theo's visor warning him that there was an infrared sensor ahead. He stopped in his tracks as the app made the light visible.

'Okay, there's motion sensors.'

As it was part of the park system, the Conservation had no fences, no real delineation from the rest of the wild areas to prevent access, but they had anticipated security around the apiary due to the bees' sheer value. Clemmie had spotted several prominent cameras positioned at the end of the bridge, and was sure there would be more discreet ones among the hives themselves.

They stopped to consider their next move. Blundering in there would set off untold silent alarms, bringing security down on them.

'This doesn't make sense,' Clemmie said. 'Are you certain she hid whatever *here*?'

'You saw the vid. Where she "found a new me". This is it. She told me this place had changed her life.' Clemmie didn't look convinced. 'What?'

'This was the first place those crooks came looking for her. It's the first place *you* came looking for her. Surrounded by cameras and security. Does that feel right to you? Does it sound like she was able to hide something here, in the most obvious place?'

Theo wanted to point out that Ella was under pressure, racing against time, but he had to admit his mother was also operating with a savviness that he would have previously thought beyond her. Hidden messages, time slurs, even a crisis of conscience wasn't anything he'd normally attribute to her. He was reluctant to admit that Clemmie had a point. She would have been smarter than that.

'Somebody's coming!' Milton suddenly hissed, shoving Theo towards the deeper shadows of a knot of trees.

The others bent low as they ran to join them, peering from behind the thick, twisted, moss-covered trunks to try to spot their pursuer. In the amplified light of their visors, several tall slender figures approached with leisurely confidence.

'The *bastards*. They followed us,' whispered Baxter, looking around for a rock or anything to form a weapon.

Theo's heart was in his mouth as they drew nearer. Then he stood for a better view.

Clemmie pawed at his arms to pull him back.

'Theo!'

Theo smiled as eleven slender fallow deer, no more than five feet high, sauntered through the grass. Three of the large bucks sported impressive antlers, their ears twitching as they stared directly at him. The does weren't perturbed by the humans and stopped to nibble acorns from the floor.

'False alarm,' Theo said quietly.

Clemmie stood to join him, fixated on the animals.

'I've never seen a real deer. My whole life and they're right here. They're beautiful.'

As she watched, one of the bucks swished its tail to disturb a swarm of midges bothering it.

Theo turned back towards the Conservation.

'Animals must trip those sensors all the time, so they must be calibrated specifically for people. That's not cheap tech.'

'Are you suggesting we go in wearing a deer costume?' Baxter quipped, joining them.

'No. But it reinforces Clem's point, doesn't it? Walking in there takes us straight into jail. Do not pass go, do not collect two hundred quid.' He looked around thoughtfully. 'So, what if she didn't hide anything there. But there instead?' He pointed straight up as his mind worked overtime. 'What if this point is geo-locked? Not just the location, but the height too.'

The default arrival anywhere in SPACE was at ground level, but they'd all heard stories about private clubs and secret floors in virtual places only accessible by exploiting the full three dimensions.

Baxter peered over the bridge sixty storeys above the street.

'We're at one of the highest points around here. There's nothing this tall in Nu London.'

As land was not a premium in the virtual, and with no need for physical office space, there was little call for skyscrapers. All the impressive towers that had been built in the financial districts, where they soared two hundred or more storeys high, were built for bragging rights and usu-ally housed cloud data. They were expensive – paid for by the bit – serving as visual power plays in a world where size was irrelevant and ingenuity was all.

'I'm not talking about *tall*,' said Theo, sliding back to the floor and making himself comfortable against the tree. 'You guys keep watch. I'm going in without the safety net.'

The safety net was a basic safety protocol that meant wherever somebody ascended from, they would appear on what passed in SPACE as the ground level. It prevented users from suddenly appearing half a mile above and plum-meting to the earth, something that had happened in the early versions of the software.

Raining people was both painful and distracting.

'I'm coming with you.'

Clemmie sat next to him, so close their legs pressed to-gether and he could feel the tingle of her body heat.

'You realise that if I'm wrong, this is going to be a very short trip that's going to end with us meeting the ground, face first?'

Clemmie pulled a face. 'Would you believe, I've had worse recently.' She slipped his hand into hers and squeezed. 'Let's do this.'

Theo kept his eyes closed as he ascended. The little emo-tional spike on the way in was welcome – although he was expecting to suddenly free-fall back to the ground and briefly mused if he'd have time to eject before impact. Sure, it wouldn't kill him, but it would still hurt like a bastard.

They ascended.

Then they fell.

Theo's stomach lurched – but he landed on his feet a second later. He opened his eyes and found they were standing in a black corridor. The surface resembled shiny plastic, the corners blunted to form a shallow hexagon. Theo guessed the location was geo-locked several feet lower than the bridge and, judging from their orientation, ran in a direct line towards the Conservation. Wherever they were, somebody had matched it perfectly. A massive door, some three times larger than necessary, blocked their way. And in front of it, a red 'X' rotated.

'X marks the spot,' said Clemmie, who was cloned to Theo's rig. 'Your mum really does have a flair for the dramatic.' Behind them the corridor stretched several yards to a dead end. 'Curious. This is a dedicated arrival zone.' That meant ascending into the room was prohibited. They slowly approached the door. 'What do you think this place is?'

Without warning the door rose open in front of them like a portcullis, blending seamlessly with the ceiling, complete with a hiss acoustically designed to project quality.

They entered a huge circular chamber with seating booths around the perimeter that were a cross between mid-twentieth century retro and modern goth, upholstered in black and white leather. Everything was bathed in a light that strategically splashed purple overtones around the joint, adding to the sense of expense.

Central to it all was a raised circular stage, some two feet off the ground and eight feet in diameter. The area around the dais was slightly bevelled like an amphitheatre in order to give visitors a clear view of the performers.

Clemmie walked clockwise around the empty chamber.

'Did Ella often frequent jazz clubs?'

'Not that I'm aware of,' said Theo as he circled in the opposite direction. 'But what do I know?'

There were no windows and the door they had passed through was the only exit, and it had silently closed behind them.

Geometric shapes revolved on the ceiling above the stage, forming impossible optical illusions. As Theo watched, a pair of Penrose pentagons that appeared to have an infinite surface no matter what angle he observed them from, twisted together, then unlinked moments later as they morphed into Penrose triangles. It was a hypnotic display of mathematics.

'I think it's safe to assume she wanted you to come here,' said Clemmie as she ran a hand along the seats, searching for anything amiss. 'But God knows why.'

Theo kneeled on the stage and searched the smooth surface, looking for anything hidden, any defect.

Clemmie hopped on to the stage.

'The question is, what do you expect to find in a private karaoke bar?'

Theo shook his head and looked up at her, perfectly lit without a single shadow despite the absence of any spotlights – another SPACE rendering trick. Bespoke lighting like that didn't come cheap. Clemmie performed a little jig that had them both snickering. Even in the virtual, her eyes sparkled when she laughed and for a moment, Theo was happy they were alone together here ...

Clemmie noticed his dreamy expression and kneeled down, bringing her face closer to his.

'You look star-struck,' she teased.

But Theo wasn't looking at her any more. Something above her, among the shifting impossible shapes, had caught his eye. He clambered onto the stage.

'What now?' There was a note of resignation in Clemmie's voice.

'Give me a boost.'

Clemmie cupped her hands, supporting them with a crooked knee. Theo placed one foot in her hands and gripped her shoulders.

'On three. Ready? One ... two ... three!'

He sprung himself upwards, and Clemmie followed through with a powerful shove. Thanks to the lite-physics of SPACE, Theo shot several feet into the air. A rotating hexagon clipped the top of his scalp as he snatched a small square stuck to the ceiling.

A pair of revolving Penrose hexagons suddenly interlinked around his outstretched hand. The impossible shapes merged through his forearm and held him like a clamp. He cycled his legs uselessly, hanging from the mathematical gantry. Pain shot through his arm as the optical illusion continued rotating, threatening to break his bones – then his hand was suddenly freed as the shapes continued to morph. He crashed onto the stage, landing on his backside with a crunch.

Clemmie dropped to her knees to check him.

'Theo?'

'I'm okay. Just chewed up by geometry.'

'It's been one of those days,' Clemmie confirmed, helping him stand.

'But maybe worth it.'

He held up the small cube he had retrieved. It was gunmetal grey and had basic shapes recessed on each side – unmistakable control buttons.

Clemmie took it, and examined it more closely.

'It's a remote data dump.' She caught his expression. 'If it's not a game, technology just passes you by, doesn't it? They hold separate packets of information not stored here.' She gestured around. 'It's not in *this* System, just like the Slifs are now on separate protected servers. This data is held outside SPACE architecture, but only accessible with it.'

'What's the point?'

Clemmie was warming to her subject. 'It's a portable security vault that can't directly be hacked here, or in The Real. We access it here, then the data is quantum entangled wherever it is stored. That could be anywhere and is untraceable.'

'I see you found it,' came a thick South African accent behind them.

They spun around to see Blondie had entered the room, his avatar's face boil-free, revealing classically handsome features. A pair of Slifs, armed with wicked-looking rifles, flanked him. Theo suspected one of them was the same creature they'd pursued in the street, but couldn't really tell.

Blondie extended his hand. 'I'll have that, if you don't mind.'

When Clemmie made no move to hand the data dump over, Blondie indicated to one of the Slifs, who raised his gun fractionally.

'Or she'll vaporise you on the spot. Oh –' he tapped the

barrel of the rifle – 'these are killers.' He noticed Theo's re-action. 'You're wondering where you've seen them before? We port the designs out of games before we mod them.'

Now Theo recalled the design. 'It's a BFG1138 from *Avasta*.'

Blondie held out his hand again, impatiently beckoning with his fingers.

'Whatever. That's just a game. This is *real*. You'll die wherever you are.'

Chapter Twenty-Four

Baxter lay flat in the grass as he watched Blondie. His rig sat several feet away from where it had landed after Milton had accidentally knocked it off his head while hauling him into the grass. The deer had fled the second the thug appeared, galloping through the Conservation and no doubt triggering a dozen motion alarms.

'What should we do?' Milton's voice was barely a whisper next to him.

Baxter wasn't sure. He tried to calculate if both of them could bring the trained hit man down. Blondie jogged past them to the edge of the bridge, stopping short of entering the apiary, as he searched for his targets. He turned around, intently scanning the bridge and looked straight at Baxter . . .

Through pure luck Blondie failed to see them hunkered under a tree. Irritated, the man shifted his weight from one foot to another with obvious uncertainty; he stared at the ground in a familiar zoning out most people did when taking a call. They couldn't hear what he said, but the short conversation ended with him dashing to the bridge rail and slumping against it, ascending before he even had time to sit.

'That's one bloke in a hurry,' Baxter commented as he stood. Milton motioned to stop him, but Baxter batted his hand away. 'It's okay, he's out for the count. Come on.'

Milton reluctantly followed. Searching around, Baxter found a fallen branch, torn off by the wind. He picked it up and weighed it against his palm, satisfied that it would serve as a blunt-force cricket bat. They trod lightly as they drew nearer.

Milton frowned. 'Your plan is to whack him across the head?'

'Then we can throw him off the bridge,' Baxter said quietly. 'That would make our life a lot easier.'

Milton shot him a look, not quite sure if he was joking or not. Then he spotted something poking from the guy's jacket and put his arm across Baxter's path to stop him.

'Gun!'

Baxter nervously eyed the pistol grip protruding from beneath the linen. Blondie had slumped to his side, wedging the weapon between his body and the ground. Licking his suddenly dry lips, Baxter motioned forward but Milton stopped him again and spoke with barely a whisper.

'If he has his awareness on ... he'll know.'

Baxter swore silently and handed his club to Milton. He edged closer, each step weighed with trepidation. The grass rustled against his shins; rain-sodden earth gave a squelch that seemed overly loud in the stillness. He was now so close he could hear the man's shallow breathing.

With aching slowness, Baxter kneeled at his side,

balancing on the balls of his feet and supporting himself with one hand. He slowly reached for the pistol, as the pollen stirred by the man's fall began to irritate his nose ...

Theo met the man's blank stare.

'Who are you?'

There was a brief flicker of surprise across the man's face.

'If you haven't worked that out already, then you deserve to die just outta sheer incompetence.'

Theo feigned a knowing smile, mustering every acting muscle that had lain dormant since the school nativity play.

'But that's the point, isn't it? You have no idea what we know and who we have told. Your whole operation —' he circled a finger indicating the room — 'is about to implode.'

The man tensed, rolling his fingers on the weapon's grip as if expecting Theo's comment to be a cue for an assault ...

Nothing happened.

'It's about what *you* know. Yes. Not what the *stukkie* knows.'

With a jerk of his wrist, he shot Clemmie.

The energy blast from the gun seared Theo's eyes. He just caught movement as Clemmie vanished from his field of vision. A sickening primal rage gripped him, wresting conscious decisions from his mind. With a roar of fury, Theo pounced for the thug.

Adrenaline brought every movement, every motion, into razor-sharp slow-motion relief. Blondie started tracking his gun back to Theo, but then sharply turned his head to the right, switching targets towards an unseen assailant.

Theo's knee crumpled into the man's solar plexus and

he felt simulated ribs crack from the brute force. The pistol dropped from his grip. Theo's arm locked around the man's neck and he bounced from a Slif and rode him down to the floor in some half-arsed back-breaker. They slammed into the polished floor – and Blondie exploded into a cloud of pixels. Now awkwardly placed, all of Theo's weight crashed painfully on his knee and he unceremoniously rolled several times before sliding to a halt against a seating booth.

Dazed, he looked up in time to see the two Slifs had opened fire to his left, presumably at Clemmie, who must have survived. Their first shots tore part of a shutter open, revealing a floor-to-ceiling panoramic window. The glass behind shattered under the deafening volley. Theo kept his head low, not wishing to be their next target.

Baxter's fingers were inches from the hilt of the pistol when he sneezed.

He froze, praying the man was fully immersed. He wasn't.

With practised discipline, Blondie's head twisted towards the sound and his elbow snapped out, clipping Baxter's jaw just as his fingers closed around the gun. Off balance, Baxter was flung backwards – plucking the weapon from Blondie's shoulder holster. As he landed on his back, the weapon slipped from Baxter's grasp and was lost among the long grass.

With an acrobatic grace that belied his muscular figure, the hit man arched his back and flipped to his feet, adopting a crouched fighting stance.

'Real dumb move, you *drol*!' he growled at Baxter, then

spun around, bringing the heel of his boot down in a perfectly executed kick intended to crush Baxter's larynx.

If he was there.

Baxter felt the ground impact as he rolled aside. He lurched again as Blondie followed through without pause – this time a punch that would have shattered his face. The man's fist expertly stopped short of punching the ground itself.

With a grunt, the assassin twisted his body back upright and spun around, arms raised at an angle in some form of martial arts pose. Baxter rapidly crawled backwards on all fours to gain distance, then felt himself back against the bridge's barrier. With a tree to one side and a six-hundred-foot drop behind, he had painted himself into a corner.

Blondie threw two practice punches and the air actually swished to emphasise the power behind them. Then he advanced on Baxter.

'You're sushi, mate.'

He didn't hear Milton approaching from behind, swinging Baxter's rig with such force that it shattered in half across Blondie's skull.

Theo jumped to his feet and blindly reached where he thought the pistol had landed. There was nothing there – belatedly he remembered it would have vanished the moment Blondie ejected.

The Slifs were focused on the stage, which was now a smashed mess of pockmarks and bubbling simulated plastic. They seemed puzzled that there was no sign of Clemmie.

Theo wasn't. He saw movement above them – a flicker of light from Clemmie's Nike Airs, which propelled her to the twisting geometrics above. One Slif spotted her and fired. A forming Dalí cross suddenly morphed into a box-within-a-box – a tesseract that absorbed the impact and saved Clemmie's life. Stray fire bounced off the moving Penrose shapes, ricocheting in all directions. One wayward pulse forced Theo to duck and the booth behind him was shredded apart.

With a crunch, one side of the damaged geometry display gave way and swung down like a hatch, batting Clemmie aside. The Slif who had taken the shot shrieked a warbling multi-frequency lament of agony as a Penrose triangle impaled its chest. The revolving shape acted like a drill bit, tearing through the Slif's innards, spraying blue liquid and glitching strands of code that lit up like a Christmas tree.

The dead Slif wore a mask of surprise as the revolving shape vanished, and it slumped to the ground amid a growing pool of blue ichor. Unlike people in SPACE, when a Slif died, its body remained. Its mere presence was an affront to the surviving Slif, whose feelings of pure hatred oozed through the air and rippled jagged red tattoos across its skin. He stalked towards Clemmie, who rolled to a halt close to the broken window. Screaming a string of Slif obscenities, it opened fire.

Blood spattered Milton when Baxter's rig split in two across the hit man's head. For a moment, he was more surprised the headset had broken than he was about having just bludgeoned a man half to death with it.

Blondie stumbled into the barrier, his hand probing the bloody scar on the side of his head. The plastic stem of his own rig, looping behind his ear, was cracked open, the wet-ware interface sparking.

'Sons of ... bitches ...'

His words were slurred. He lashed out at Baxter, his once precise movements now jerky and wild. Despite that, one punch clipped the side of Baxter's temple, drawing a trickle of blood.

Baxter followed through, grabbing the man's fist and forcibly locking it against the side of his own body with a violent snap he prayed would break bone. Apparently, that only happened in movies. Instead, Blondie's momentum knocked Baxter straight for the Parkway balustrade. Baxter lost his balance on a rock and was pitched over the railing, dragging the dazed man with him.

Grappling the Slif from the side was like running face first into a punchbag. Theo knocked its weapon aside. With its finger jammed on the trigger, the creature blasted more of the window apart, then raised itself to its full height, loom-ing a good two feet taller than Theo. With his arms still looped around its gangly neck, he was hoisted from the floor, feet kicking.

Clemmie was back on her feet in an instant, delivering a high kick recalled from some long-forgotten self-defence class. It struck the Slif mid-body, but she was uncertain what, if any, damage it would inflict.

The creature snarled as it attempted to swing its weapon in her direction. Hanging from its back, Theo entangled his arm in the rifle strap and shifted all of his weight. His body arced back as his knees pressed into the Slif. The strap tightened, choking off the Slif's vocal barrage and crushing the length of the barrel against its face.

Continuing to strain, Theo clamped his legs around the Slif and lent all his weight into strangling it. The data dump fell from his hand and skittered across the floor.

'They don't breathe!' Clemmie looked around for another weapon they could use. 'You're just pissing it off!'

Theo twisted his head in surprise as the ghost of Blondie ascended back into the room, his movements twitchy and erratic, at times showing his arms and limbs in radically different positions at the same time. Struggling to gain definition, he was ascending and ejecting several times a second, something Theo had only heard about in urban horror stories about how SPACE turned people insane.

Theo unclamped his legs and swung them around the Slif, his pendulum action forcing the creature to twist to counter the movement—

Blondie's gun fritzed in and out of existence, unleashing a staccato volley of energy bolts. While some phased through, others pocked the creature's chest with fist-deep cavities of burning blue flesh-code; the smell put Theo in mind of *Synger*.

The Slif crashed to the floor, tossing Theo from its back and straight out of the window.

Clemmie started towards him. 'Theeeeooo!'

His plummet was short-lived. The rifle strap pulled taut around the dead Slif's neck. Still hooked under Theo's arm, it yanked him to an abrupt halt. With his legs cycling air over the six-hundred-foot drop, Theo had an unprecedented view of how the club floated high over the city, blending into the sky to be invisible from the ground. It offered a magnificent view of Nu London, a network of multicoloured lines and contours that belonged to a psychedelic hallucination.

Clemmie's head appeared at the window, precariously crouching at the edge. She reached for him.

'Give me your hand!'

Theo braced himself, then experimentally freed one hand and reached out. With all his weight on one shoulder strap, the pain was becoming unbearable. He strained ... his fingers inches away from Clemmie's.

'I can't—'

The strap suddenly jerked and he slipped a foot lower. He gripped the strap with both hands, unable to do anything.

The Slif slid towards the window, lubricated on a trail of its own internal fluids. Clemmie positioned herself between the window frame and the creature to stop it. Then she saw something in the room that Theo couldn't see.

'He's going for the data!'

Clemmie looked back down at Theo and treated him to a sweet smile as he desperately stretched his hand out to her once again.

'Sorry, hun.'

She gave a little wave and retreated from the window edge, hopping over the Slif as it slid out of the window – leaving Theo to plummet towards his doom.

Baxter's fingernails raked across the wet curved graphene surface without leaving a mark. The side of the bridge was a six-foot long shallow curving slope that ended in a gutter to prevent small animals from accidentally falling off. Lying face first, with the weight of the man crushing him, Baxter slid slowly, yet inexorably, towards the edge.

Faintly conscious, Blondie shuddered as every muscle spasmed wildly. He issued a faint moan, trapped between two worlds.

'Milt!' Baxter yelled through gritted teeth as he tried to roll the hit man off him. The edge hove into view; a one-way trip to the brightly lit street below filled his vision as he was slowly drawn over the edge. 'Get this fat twat off me!'

Desperate, Milton gripped the balustrade with his left hand and lunged over the rail, snagging the man's twitching ankle on the third attempt, preventing him from sliding any further. Milton heaved, but lacked the strength to pull them both away from the edge.

'I can't ...'

Theo suddenly raced to his side and assessed the situation.

'Jesus ...'

'What happened to you?'

'Oh, you know, Clem chucked me out of a window.'

He leaned over and gripped the man's leg as it began jerking with greater fury. With a co-ordinated effort, they both managed to tilt Blondie to the side. Baxter wriggled from under the increasingly spasming man, aware that a single slip could spill him over the edge. On his hands and knees he crawled away from the edge, then scrambled gingerly up the incline, the damp soles of his trainers squeaking on smooth graphene. He slid backwards—

'Oh, shit!' Baxter snapped, his splayed palms finding no purchase.

Theo released Blondie's leg and snatched at Baxter's T-shirt. He dug his fingers deep and heaved Baxter towards him. They both ignored the laboured sound of cheaply made seams popping. Baxter gripped Theo's arm with both hands, then finally latched on to the balustrade and clambered back on to the Parkway.

'Holy shit!' was all he could repeat.

'Uh, guys? A little help?' Milton was still clutching Blondie's thrashing leg.

'You'll have to let go,' Theo said.

Milton instantly released his leg.

'No!'

Theo darted forward, wildly flailing to grab Blondie as he slid at an angle towards the edge, now propelled by his own thrashing. He was already beyond Theo's reach.

'I didn't mean drop him off the edge!'

'You said to let him go,' Milton protested.

They watched with horror as the man crept towards the edge, but they lacked the motivation to risk their own lives to stop him. Blondie's head lolled over the gutter ... then his body slumped motionless and he stopped sliding.

'Shall we help him?' Milton asked.

They were suddenly aware Clemmie had joined them.

'What did I miss?' She peered over the edge and glared at the man. 'Is he dead?'

Theo eyed her with a mix of admiration and disbelief for letting him fall.

'That depends on what you did to him.'

She bit her bottom lip before answering. 'I kicked him out of the window and left him hanging there.'

'You're making a habit out of that.'

He could just see her dark eyes searching his.

'Sorry,' she said without a hint of an apology.

'What did you lot find?' asked Baxter, his eyes never leaving Blondie.

'I'm not sure,' Theo admitted. 'He turned up with two armed Slifs ready to kill us. It was a data dump but ... I lost it.' He hung his head regretfully.

Clemmie playfully slapped his arm. 'Cheer up. You might have lost it −' a smile crept across her face − 'but *I* didn't. I've stowed it some place safe.'

With a flush of gratitude, Theo threw his arms around Clemmie and delivered a crushing hug.

'You are brilliant!'

She laughed in delight.

'We better go,' said Milton urgently.

His head was cocked towards the far side of the Parkway as he watched the distant blue strobes of an approaching police quadcopter. His gaze returned to Blondie.

'He must have triggered the sensors when he stumbled into the Conservation. What do we do with him?'

Baxter spat at the man. They could now see his chest fall and rise with shallow breaths.

'Kick him off the edge.'

Theo regarded his friend sternly. 'That would make us murderers. Do you think you have it in you?'

'To do it?' Baxter nodded. 'Hell, yes.'

'I mean to live with it afterwards.' Theo had watched a man die the night before, he remembered suddenly − could that be right? It seemed like a lifetime ago. 'That's not something you're going to forget.' He saw the hesitation in Baxter's eyes. 'That's not us, Bax.'

Baxter gave a defiant snort and turned away. He was playing tough, but there was no mistaking the relief in his eyes. Without another word, they hurried back the way they had come, disappearing into the darkness.

Chapter Twenty-Five

Being on the run was not fun. It wasn't just the constant paranoia that the police were about to collar them. News streams had moved on to other stories: a gang knifing in Dagenham; an automated car plant in Bromley crippled by a virus that sent the bots into a repetitive synchronised dance routine; and a surge in the Virtual Index, the stock market tracking businesses in SPACE, had boosted the UK's economy ahead of Europe's, although it still had quite a way to beat China.

Nobody was interested in a cop-killer unless he resurfaced. However, that still meant Theo couldn't be seen in public. Although Clemmie had yet to be publicly identified, they suspected all their faces were loaded on police ID scanners, just waiting for them to reappear so justice could pounce.

Isolation proved to be the biggest killjoy; the fact they had nowhere to go made the whole experience dispiriting. Baxter suggested returning to Rex's garage, but Theo still wasn't entirely sure he trusted him.

They descended from the Parkway as fast as they could. The cops must have been distracted by Blondie, buying them enough time to hit the streets and get lost across town while it was still quiet. They reached the relative tranquillity of Regent's Canal behind St Pancras Station just as dawn was breaking. They broke into an uninhabited narrowboat that was listing in the water and surrounded by so much duckweed it looked as if it had sunk in grass, not water.

Inside, the owners had cleared personal possessions as water reached a depth of two feet, canting the boat a good twenty degrees before the leak had been patched up. There were enough raised bunks and tables for Theo and the others to keep dry. While, like the rivers, the canals had been cleaned and fish stocks introduced, the boat's prevailing dampness still kicked off Baxter's armada of allergies.

Baxter and Milton fell into deep sleep almost instantly, but the pulse-quickening excitement of the evening and night kept Clemmie and Theo wired and awake. They sat on bunks across the hull from one another. Clemmie wrapped her combat jacket around her knees to fend off the slight chill, and wriggled into a comfortable position on the bunk. Theo had no such luck. His legs were curled at an awkward angle as his bunk, obviously designed for a child, had been shortened to make room for the stove in the adjacent galley.

'Rex can really help us,' she told Theo for the third time.

'I know, I know ... but one argument with Baxter's sister – and you've met her.'

'Fickle,' Clemmie agreed with a smile.

'You're being kind. That's all it takes for him to switch loyalties like that.' He snapped his fingers, then glanced at the other two. They were deeply asleep. 'Are you sure you stored the data dump safely?'

Clemmie gave a lazy half-smile and stretched, cat-like.

'Safe and sound in SPACE. Relax, I can get it instantly. Besides, we've all got a little time left to check it out when we're awake enough.' They looked at the other two. 'Did that stave work?'

'Let's put it this way – when you let me fall to my death—'

Clemmie held up her hands. 'How many times can a girl say sorry?'

Theo ignored her. 'I was minutes away from ejection. So, I decided to take fate into my own hands before I had a face-to-face with the ground.'

'So I could've been ripped off?' She rubbed her neck and yawned.

Theo nodded. 'Another reason I don't entirely trust Rex. Guess we'll find out later.'

He had desperately wanted to see what was on the data dump, but the others had been exhausted so they'd all agreed they'd check it out after a long rest. It would be a literal waste of time watching it while fighting sleep.

His thoughts drifted to Ella. The hit man's comments had convinced him she was still alive. The only question was *where*. Back in Rex's garage he'd had time to surf for information about Dens, but it was too harrowing to read. Clearly, they were still a little-reported world which was wrapped in mythology. Stories abounded of gangs hawking children for sport or to make rich businessmen feel younger through piped emotions. Deaths performed to order so some rich fuckhead could experience the joy of killing – or some screwed-up weirdo could know what it was like to experience the brink of oblivion. One thing was clear though: the poor conditions in the Dens meant Ella's lifespan could only be measured in mere days.

It seemed while the world was repairing itself, humanity was becoming an increasing warped collection of misfits.

He became aware Clemmie had been talking.

'Mmm?'

'I was thinking about those Slifs.'

'Yeah. Never seen one die before.'

He was conscious that killing a Slif now bore the same ramifications as killing a human, but in the circumstances he thought it best not to mention it.

'I meant, working alongside people. I thought they had some kind of baked-in morality about harming people.'

Another urban legend, Theo thought. Asimov's Three Laws of Robotics apparently didn't apply to artificial life. Scientists, programmers and philosophers argued that they would have to obey the rules of SPACE, unable to inflict real pain on avatars, duty-bound to follow orders, basically becoming slaves. It had sounded a terrific deal to the rest of mankind.

Of course, with people being people, groups began to form demanding Slifs were granted the same rights as captive animals, which soon developed to the same rights as humans. When the Slifs themselves began to argue for complete independence, things became heated and stories started to appear about them attacking avatars, stealing Bitcoin transactions and generally acting as screwed up as humans. Which, of course, was a natural evolution when your creator is a caffeine-fuelled twenty-something from a code farm in Bulgaria.

It wasn't what James Lewinsky had envisioned when he bequeathed SPACE to the world as a brave new universe for people to live without fear of war, boundaries, prejudice or labels. He also didn't expect his son, Dominic Lewinsky, to stab him in the back. Unhappy with the billions they made from Emotive manufacturing the wetware to interact with SPACE, Dominic started legal action to wrest SPACE back into private hands. Corporations, games companies and undeserving individuals were making fortunes out of his birthright.

His father died at the height of the legal battle and Dominic was cut off from any inheritance. Emotive was passed to the board of directors under the strict policy that SPACE always remained free to the world. The last Theo heard about Dominic Lewinsky was when he launched a hard-right anti-Slif movement that ultimately fizzled into obscurity. Before the servers went orbital, it was rumoured he was behind the explosive-laden truck that had crashed into a server farm, killing the driver and thousands of Slifs with it.

SPACE had broken the Lewinsky family, created simulated life, and given the world new pleasures and, as Theo was discovering, new nightmares.

'Slifs are like people. They can be bastards too,' he said with a shrug.

Clemmie studied him carefully. 'It turns out they can be killers. The question is why? What's in it for them?'

'They're being paid.'

'They're richer than we are.'

With almost ninety per cent of global financial transactions now happening virtually, that was inevitable.

'Somebody with deep pockets?'

'Maybe,' she said thoughtfully.

She recalled what Clarion had said about them: some wanted complete independence from humanity ...

Theo frowned. 'You keep rubbing your neck. Are you okay?'

Clemmie looked at him questioningly. She hadn't realised she was doing it.

Theo pushed upright in his bunk, feet dangling inches over the water. He was on the raised side, so the lip of the bunk was the only thing preventing him from rolling off. He reached across to Clemmie and gently stroked her neck as she angled her head so he could see. There was a faint red rash where she had scratched.

'That's where the drone shot something at me.' She laughed off his look of concern. 'It's psychosomatic. Don't worry about it.'

'What if it's not?'

She frowned, not understanding. Theo reluctantly removed his hand.

'I was on some clickbait site a while ago—'

'Ah, the source of serious journalism.'

She leaned back in her bunk, propping her head up in her hand as she languidly studied him.

'Some paranoids were claiming the government was spiking people in SPACE. You know that feel-good feeling?'

'That's just your dopamine popping when you engage with the wetware interface. Fact.'

'Sure. But what they were saying was that virtual

injection triggered the brain into releasing pheromones in the real world.'

He couldn't read her expression, but her brow creased at the implication.

'They were *sniffing* me out?'

'The articles I saw said the effect didn't last very long.' That didn't seem to placate her. His thoughts jumped track. 'Bees!' Now she looked even more perplexed. 'Your dad was saying how they were using bees to sniff out drugs. He mentioned they can do it with sensors now. What if the Slif had injected you with a virtual stimulant?'

'That made me stink in the real world?' she said coolly.

'Undetectable without a scanner. And on cue, Blondie turns up. We could have been anywhere in London. In the country. The world. But he zeroes in on that one alleyway.'

Clemmie gave an involuntary shiver. 'Christ, Theo. That's serious Big Brother stuff. Emotional tracking? That's not even tech I've heard of.'

'You don't read the kind of high-quality clickbait I do.'

But she had a point. That was exactly what had been bothering him. Milton's and Baxter's excited recount of the fight with Blondie – no doubt slightly embellished – nevertheless painted the combat moves of a trained professional. A soldier, not a cop. He ventured his theory.

'So it's military tech.'

'Christ, this has escalated from organised gangs to the police to the military very quickly.'

'You said yourself he wasn't a cop, probably military. I'm not saying they're behind it, but Blondie didn't appear on the police database, right? His medical file was expunged.

Maybe they recruited him from somewhere else?'

'We should've cross-indexed the government database,' she muttered, dropping her head flat on the mattress.

'You can do that?'

She closed her eyes and nodded. 'Theo, you're beginning to really scare the shit out of me. Is this punishment for dropping you out of the window?'

'This is only the start of it.' He lay back on his bunk, propping himself against the lip so he didn't roll out. He yawned. 'When this is over I'm going to challenge you to a rap battle ...'

Clemmie reached her hand across the boat, her voice now sleepy.

'I can't stay awake. Watch over me ...'

Theo's heart skipped a beat as he reached out and tangled his fingers with hers. Clemmie didn't respond because she was already asleep.

Chapter Twenty-Six

Theo woke first, feeling refreshed and hungry. Noticing it was almost eleven o'clock, he roused the others. Not daring to leave the narrowboat in broad daylight, Theo, Clemmie and Milton used what little time they had left to ascend into SPACE while Baxter sat back, miserably toying with the two broken halves of his own rig.

Once they had found a nearby plaza in which they could sit without being bothered, Clemmie retrieved the data dump from the sole of her Nike Airs. By bonding the cube with her avatar's costume, it had effectively become part of her inventory – and undetectable when she ejected the previous night. The device would have simply melted into her avatar's code, reappearing the moment she set foot back into SPACE. In a world where there was no need for pockets, stowing it on her avatar was a complicated solution for something that would have been easy in The Real.

Once activated, the data dump had drawn them into a virtual recording that Ella had stolen from a security feed. Like a game, it existed as a separate bubble in the SPACE environment, except this time their avatars had been left behind and a second identical set rendered inside the recording, wherever that was stored, like a series of matryoshka doll avatars.

Theo, Clemmie and Milton stood to the side of a packed circular room – the very one Theo had taken a nosedive out of the night before. This time it was rammed with people watching the central stage. The group all looked well-heeled. Handsome men wore tuxedos that shimmered and flared just enough to hint at their wealth. The women were all impossibly beautiful, sporting dresses over curves that couldn't possibly be natural. The window shutters were wide open, displaying a gorgeous sunset over Nu London. But the three friends, like the holographic avatars around them, didn't care about the view. Only what was on stage.

An exceptionally pretty blonde teenage girl was standing miserable and naked. An unseen host conducted an auction; the bids were up to £5,000 and climbing. Theo couldn't see any counterbids being made in the room – no subtle nods of the head or half-raised hands. He assumed the vultures were making such discreet bids via their rigs.

He turned his attention back to the girl as the bid reached £7,000. There was something odd about her. Only when the auction concluded at £8,000 did the girl suddenly vanish in a flicker of glitching blocks, only to be replaced by a young Chinese girl, who looked equally forlorn as the auction started again.

'They're not avatars. They're live holofeeds from The Real,' said Clemmie with disgust.

'Makes sense,' said Milton, who was surprised by their confusion. 'You can make an avatar look like anything.' He lashed out at the hologram of a buxom woman next to him, his hand passing harmlessly through. 'That's a second-skin she's wearing. If they're selling slaves then you need to know what the real deal looks like.'

'How can you tell they're second-skins?' Clemmie asked.

'Because they look like cartoon characters! Trust me, I know skins.'

With Milton's alter ego harvesting serious revenue with his game review channel, they accepted his word when it came to crafting second-skins.

'This is a slave market,' Milton said with an edge to his voice.

As the Chinese girl sold for £6,000 and was replaced with a muscular twenty-something black man, his mood darkened.

'They're selling so cheaply.'

Clemmie gasped in shock. 'For fuck's sake, Milton. Are you offering to promote their business for them?'

'That's not what I meant. Watch.' The guy was sold for £4,000 and promptly vanished. 'I mean, to these people, life is cheap.'

Clemmie nodded in agreement. 'This is how they get their kicks.'

'Precisely. It's not even about the money. It's like drugs, the Dens hooking in kids off the street for cheap smex – profits build and build.' He indicated another boy who had appeared on the stage. 'But these guys are not in the Dens, are they?'

The penny dropped for Theo.

'They want them for something specific.'

Milton pointed to a middle-aged man with movie star

looks, courting two Barbie-sculpted blondes and a Mexican man whose muscular physique was certainly unobtainable in reality.

'When the last guy was sold, that bloke over there got a hard-on about it.'

Milton walked through the holograms, straight for the Movie Star. The others followed. He held up his hand. A floating set of controls materialised under his fingertips and he scrubbed back along the recording's timeline. The entire holographic surrounding rewound until he released the control.

'Got him!' whooped the American-accented Mr Movie Star, punching the air as the black guy vanished from the screen.

'What are you going to do with him?' asked Barbie Clone #1, with a thick Australian accent. She had been hungrily eyeing the exhibit as rich women once did with gladiator specimens.

'You've never stabbed a man to death before?' Mr Movie Star asked disbelievingly. 'It's such a rush! And you need a stallion like that to last long enough so you can really feel the kick.' He thrust his hand in a stabbing motion. 'Forget hunting elephants! Any pussy can do that. You walk away from a stabbing experience like that and you're on a high for the whole day. It's fantastic!'

'I feel sick,' Milton said, feeling the taste of bile in his mouth and wondering if his paralysed real-world body had somehow puked.

Clemmie moved away, her face scrunched in disgust. Still the auction continued on the stage.

'They're from all around the world,' she said with a hollow voice.

Theo nodded, wondering why his mother had chosen this security clip to steal. What was so special about it?

'Is there any way to find out who's behind a second-skin?'

Milton gave a hollow laugh. 'Not really. And definitely not from a recording.'

Theo moved away, scanning every face he passed, looking for someone familiar. Some hint ...

'Ah, shit, Theo. My time's—'

Milton suddenly vanished in a cloud of pixels.

Clemmie looked equally annoyed as she too vanished, leaving Theo on his own. He glanced at his own clock. After using far more time in the slur, he should have popped out first. He hadn't been paying attention to the numbers, but he now noticed they were running backwards. Then he noticed a completely alien symbol on the display – a minus sign. His readout told him he had twenty-seven minutes before he hit zero.

'My word, Rex, your stave worked.'

He felt a tinge of guilt for doubting him. He didn't have that much extra time left; his last thirty minutes had been running on reserve. He continued circling around, studying each face.

Had he missed someone at the beginning? He called up the floating controls and noted the clip was only forty-five minutes long. It had started midway through the auction, so Ella had even gone so far as isolating a specific period. Why?

He turned his attention to the victims on stage. They were

all perfect specimens, mostly young, naked and despond-
ent. Reasoning that he didn't know anybody he'd consider
perfect, Clemmie aside, he turned his attention back to the
crowd.

The door opened and a willowy woman sashayed in, looking every inch a supermodel, with sharp cheeks and a cascade of red hair. While he agreed with Milton's assessment
that everybody here was clad in a second-skin, the woman
following the supermodel was definitely *not* wearing one.

It was his mother.

'Mum!'

He raced across to greet her, only remembering after
several steps that she was just a ghostly recorded image.
He stopped as they walked towards him, the supermodel
eyeing the people in the room as she quietly spoke.

'The lists are encrypted in your rig.'

Ella's frown deepened. 'Mirri, you promised me I had
almost paid off my debt.'

Theo remembered the name from the original threatening
phone call. So, this was Mirri. He studied the supermodel,
searching for any hint of who she really was under that skin.

Mirri regarded Ella with amusement. 'Almost. My dear,
you're far too good at what you do. We would very much
like to retain your services.'

'I just want the debt paid, then I'm out of all this.' Ella
looked around with disgust.

Theo looked around to see Blondie had entered with them,
his perfect face creased in a permanent glare as he took in
the room. The way he was standing close to Mirri screamed
bodyguard. He obviously didn't feel the need for a skin, so

Theo guessed either he was somehow well-placed not to fear public exposure, or that everybody in the room knew who he was and operated under the thumb of fear.

Theo circled him, almost nose to nose like a championship fighter. Blondie's face was perfect without anaphylactic deformation.

'Who the hell are you?

Mirri continued. 'We need some Japanese girls for a client with *specific* tastes. Here are some samples.'

Theo stepped away from Blondie and tried to see what she was talking about, but the interaction was in a sub-virtual level, so there was nothing for him to see – but Ella could. She tried to hide her reaction.

'Pretty. Young too.'

'Sixteen to nineteen, he's flexible.' Mirri tilted her head, unconcerned. 'The client pays, that's all that counts. A means to an end.'

'And what does he ... *specifically* want them for?'

Mirri flashed a perfect smile. 'My dear, what does anybody want meat for? To devour!'

Ella looked around the room. 'Is he here?'

'Good Lord, no. Even with a second-skin it would be taking a chance. You know his feelings about SPACE. Besides, he would never frequent a place like this. When you obtain a sample, you have his address. He prefers to check out the merchandise in the flesh. He's rather old-fashioned that way.'

'12 Bishops Grove, Hampstead,' Ella recited.

The woman shot her a look so fierce it marred her impossibly exquisite face.

'Never repeat that!'

Ella looked away, sufficiently humbled. 'Sorry. I was just checking. You wouldn't want me delivering to the wrong address now, would you?'

'You wouldn't be that incompetent.'

Mirri's gaze bored into the back of Ella's head and Theo swore that was the moment his mother's days were numbered. Why had she said that aloud? The only reason he could think of was that she wanted *him* to hear it. Which meant that she had planned to steal this clip to hand him a solid lead. A real address. It displayed a maturity and cunning he'd never believed Ella possessed.

With a sharp flick of the wrist, Theo exited the hologram and was left sitting on a bench in the corner of the public square in SPACE where they had first started watching it, except now both Clemmie and Milton had been ejected.

He looked around the plaza, satisfied that nobody was paying him any attention. A large statue of James Lewinsky, some forty feet tall, dominated the area. It was said this point was geo-locked to the exact spot Emotive's creator first dreamed up his breakthrough idea. A fountain spat colourful plasma around his feet, and the sculptor had even added some artificial pigeons to fly around, occasionally perching on the great man's head – but never, *ever*, pooping on it. The ubiquitous billboards lined the buildings, rolling targeted commercials that were ignored by many of the people passing through.

A few Slifs walked among the humans, usually in pairs and talking intently to one another in their own language. They had never bothered Theo before, but now the sight of them put him on edge. A crowd of people had gathered on the far side of the square, around a stage playing a holographic band. Unlike the bespoke billboards, everybody could see and hear the boy band playing an impromptu free promo gig. *Blasted!* were the kind of crap K-pop Baxter loved listening to. Theo even vaguely recognised the tune.

He was loath to sink while he still had some time in the bank, but for once it was more important for him to be in the real world with his friends. He savoured that thought for a moment; never would he have considered it a possiblity.

He prepared to sink and glanced at his countdown.

It had stopped.

The clock *never* stopped. It was integral to the System, yet the numbers were frozen at −54:57. With his palm he tapped the side of his head in the desperate belief it would alter the display. Had living on borrowed time somehow corrupted his avatar?

It must be a glitch, he assured himself. He sank from SPACE.

The peppy boy band continued unabated.

He looked around the square. He was *still* here.

Theo stood up and tried to sink again. A passing group of kids gave him a funny look as he strained, even half-crouching as if that could possibly help. He heard the words '... shit his pants ...' and the boys laughed mockingly.

Theo felt a rising panic. He'd heard stories about people getting locked in the virtual and driven mad. Again, clickbait stories with no presented facts. He'd always assumed they'd been dreamed up by parents with overactive imaginations and a desire to ruin their children's lives. Yet here he was.

Then a godlike voice boomed from *everywhere*.

'Theodore Wilson, this is the vPolice. You are under arrest.'

Chapter Twenty-Seven

Theo was on his feet and looking around the plaza in panic. His face suddenly appeared on every billboard, framed by the vCrime unit's 'most wanted' logo. The boy band on stage vaporised, replaced by a spinning hologram of him.

Heads twitched as people searched for the criminal among them. Theo saw the gaggle of kids were pointing his way. More and more gawping avatars were turning towards him.

With a loud *whump* that shook the air, a circular police cruiser swooped down from the sky, slowly rotating like a bad sci-fi B-movie UFO, blue police strobes flickering around its circumference.

He'd never seen a cruiser so close. The ships, easily the size of a private jet, were the workhorses for the vPolice and could generally be seen overhead. Rather than have a dedicated pilot, any copper on board could fly them. It also explained why his timer had frozen.

To prevent suspects from simply sinking out of SPACE, the cruisers emanated a retention field that prevented anybody from baling out. Everybody around would be experiencing the same problem. Only when the cruiser was out of range would the field cease to work.

'You are unable to sink!' boomed a voice from the police cruiser. 'Raise your hands!'

Theo did so, slowly turning, seeking any opportunity to escape. He heard the heavy steps of the police troopers echoing from the buildings before he saw them emerge from a side road opposite.

Each identical vPolice avatar was an intimidating eight feet tall and impossibly muscular. Two carried distinctive rifles: real world police-issue Killers. These guys were not messing around. The others wielded shock batons, the tips of which crackled with menacing sparks.

Time was running out – or at least Theo wished it was. They'd soon be upon him. He had to act *now*.

His first response was to stream a video link out to the others. They'd be able to see exactly what was happening, even though they would be unable to help.

'You are under arrest for the murder of a police officer. Do you understand?'

'It wasn't me! I've been set up!'

It was pointless arguing and he knew it wouldn't get him out of this mess. The billboards switched to images of Clemmie, Baxter and Milton revolving in 3-D and labelled as 'accomplices'.

He completed one last revolution of the crowd, noticing several Slifs among them. Most regarded him with suspicion, but one stared intently at him, a tiny drone hovering at his shoulder. The Slif's skin subtly shifted patterns when it felt Theo's gaze locked on him.

'Bastard,' Theo muttered.

He was certain that it was the same slimeball they had chased through the Market. It must have tracked him here and alerted the cops. Desperation suddenly kicked in.

'Sod it.'

Theo dropped his hands and ran straight for the Slif spy.

'FREEZE!' boomed the voice of authority.

A cry from the crowd behind informed him that the cops had given chase. People ahead tensed as he approached. Some edged away while others – displaying bravery they lacked in The Real – stood coiled ready to intercept him.

Theo shoved his hand in his jacket as he sprinted towards them.

'I have a bomb!'

As ludicrous as the idea was, the crowd in front of him suddenly dispersed into wails of terror as they attempted to flee. Even the hint of being mildly hurt turned them into a pack of wild animals.

Theo turned a corner, slipped through a set of ornate supporting columns and ducked into a narrow pedestrianised parade. From somewhere behind he heard the rumble of the police cruiser, but took a morsel of comfort that it was too large to follow him. However, he was still caught in the retention field. He needed to get further away.

A main avenue cut his path ahead, heavy with streams of vehicles thundering past at speeds both illegal and impossible in The Real. Hover cars were used on specific arteries to cut down travel time and stop the menace of flying public traffic that had plagued earlier versions of SPACE. While teleporting between cities was common practice, it was prohibited in the cities themselves. Having people pop up wherever they liked was discourteous and played havoc with the System's bandwidth. If only he could get into one of the cars ...

Three monstrous vPolice turned the corner in front of him, blocking his escape route. Without missing a step, Theo made a hard right straight through the arched doors of a shopping mall.

The precinct was huge, much bigger on the inside than the outside as the retailers were forced to expand. It stretched twelve storeys high, each level housing a specific range of consumer goods and accessible by circular blue grav-pads that flung people to the floor above with great precision, a much faster and fun alternative to an escalator. It was crowded with shoppers from around the globe, drawn by massive digital banners declaring it was 'slashing summer half-price sale throughout the mall!'.

Theo elbowed shoppers from his path.

'Excuse me! Move! Out the way!'

He hopped onto a grav-pad and, with a soft *boing*, was gracefully pitched on to the first floor. He immediately hop-scotched onto another pad, propelling him up again – just as a platoon of pursuing cops burst into the mall. Theo clocked fifteen of them before he lost count.

'Stop! We are authorised to use deadly force!' bellowed a vCop with a rifle and attitude.

He fired as Theo took a running jump onto another pad and bounced clear over the open atrium on a preordained arc. He was already running the moment he touched down on level three.

A chunk from the column behind him exploded as pulsing energy bolts struck it. The authorities were obviously not messing around, even in an environment filled with innocent avatars.

Shoppers stopped and stared as the posters around them were replaced with Theo's wanted profile. The words 'armed and dangerous' flashed ominously.

Theo sprinted along an avenue decorated with colourful plants that danced and writhed in time to the store's ambient music. One, with a Venus fly-trap-like mouth, coiled towards him and spoke.

'Are you looking for a special gift for the girl in your life?'

Then it gave a strangled scream as an energy bolt ripped it apart. Another narrowly missed Theo's ear as it impacted against the wall, leaving him wondering what mysterious advice the plant was going to impart.

He reached the end of the avenue and skidded to a halt as he noticed the walkway was shaped like a tear, with him at the narrow apex. It turned sharply back on itself, following the opposite curve of the mall. Any further and he would be running in circles.

The cops knew this as they spread out, already hopping up the grav-pads to pincer him from either side in an almost comical chorus of sound effects.

Theo had trapped himself. He dashed to the balcony and considered jumping down the three floors, but with no prospect of ejecting, what damage would the fall do?

'Theodore!'

The sibilant hiss made Theo spin around, expecting to

see an officer with a gun to his head. Instead, it was the Slif sneak, and he held a pistol in his hand. Theo raised his hands in surrender.

'Don't shoot.'

'But I must,' lisped the creature.

Then he raised the pistol higher and fired.

Theo twitched, thankful he had met the worst shot in SPACE, but realised the target had been a copper springing up from the floor below. Theo watched in astonishment as the cop spun to the ground, disappearing in a cloud of pixels as he struck the tiled floor.

The Slif shot another officer running towards them, winging him in the leg. The man went down, howling in pain and clutching his limb.

'If you wish to live, you must trust me,' the creature said earnestly.

With little choice, Theo nodded. The Slif rushed to his side and peered over the edge.

'Jump.'

'Are you mad?'

It pointed to a green pad on the edge of the balcony that Theo hadn't noticed on his way up.

'Jump!'

The Slif led the way, its lanky legs allowing it to jump with ease. The pad immediately transformed into a long green chute that continued to form just feet ahead of the Slif as it twisted to the ground level, like a white-knuckle helter-skelter. The creature slid down while still standing, its gun blazing.

'What kind of shopping centre is this?' Theo muttered as

he pitched himself head first in pursuit of the creature.

The Slif dispatched several more cops as they twisted down to the ground, the slide automatically writhing one way, then the other, to avoid shoppers and cops bouncing up a floor.

The chute vanished the moment they reached the ground. The Slif continued running, while Theo rolled across the floor several times before he was able to pick himself up.

'Stop right there!'

Theo's field of vision was filled by a rifle barrel. There was a flash of light – but it wasn't the rifle. The Slif had shot the cop point-blank, obliterating him and pushing through the dispersing particle cloud to reach the exit. Theo paused to retrieve the cop's gun, but it too vanished along with the officer.

'Will you stop killing people!' screamed Theo.

The Slif shot him a puzzled look. 'Police avatars can still eject, the flesh isn't harmed.'

Without missing a beat, he fired over Theo's shoulder as a policeman emerged from the department store. The copper's head exploded a split second before his body.

They ran back out on to the avenue that was still packed with speeding vehicles. The crowds ahead quickly parted when they saw the gun.

Theo followed the Slif towards a wide crossroads ahead, jammed with traffic that had been forced to stop due to the police activity. So focused was he on the vehicles, he almost ran into the Slif, who had abruptly stopped. Dead ahead, the police cruiser banked into view, sirens wailing and re-sponder lights blazing like azure supernovas.

'The craft is blocking your ejection,' said the Slif, looking around for any other escape route.

Shots rang out behind them, one glancing the Slif's arm. It responded by peeking around the corner and blowing the assailant away. The others scrambled for cover.

Theo couldn't take his eyes off the creature's wound as blue liquid seeped from writhing strands of coding. It was what passed for a real injury in the Slif's world; he could even *feel* the wave of pain emanating from the creature.

'I will stop it,' the Slif said, eyeing the cruiser and ignoring his wound, although the pain was evident in his voice. 'Prepare yourself to sink the moment I do.'

'How?'

The Slif held up his pistol and Theo watched, impressed, as the small weapon rapidly extended in length and bulk, transforming into a rocket launcher. The creature took careful aim at the approaching craft, waiting for the launcher to give him a locking tone. Then he fired.

The energy pulse struck the cruiser amidships. With a colossal crunching noise, the disc was cleaved in two. It belly-flopped into the traffic below, crushing designer vehicles and tossing more aside as it ground towards them.

'Now!' yelled the Slif.

'What about you?'

What passed for a smile tugged the creature's lip. He nudged Theo.

'Go. Now.'

Without further pause, Theo ejected from SPACE as the stricken cruiser slid towards them, tossing cars and bikes from its path like a wrecking ball.

Chapter Twenty-Eight

'You saw it all!'

Theo wanted to tear his hair out – nothing made sense.

'I don't know what I saw,' Milton replied. 'Partly because I had my rig on the table so he could watch what was going on too.'

He gave a sharp nod towards Baxter.

'Only because you broke mine.'

Baxter slammed both halves on the table for emphasis.

'Yeah, saving your sorry arse,' snapped Milton.

'Will you both stop freaking out?' Clemmie demanded.

That brought some calm to the proceedings.

Milton sucked in a breath and tried to keep his voice level.

'My face – our faces – are plastered all over the news.'

The moment they appeared on the billboards in SPACE, streamed news channels had resurrected the Bow Street Runners story with additional details about Clemmie, Milton and Baxter, who were *wanted in connection*.

Clemmie laid a consoling hand on his shoulder.

'That was inevitable. You knew that.' Milton might not

have liked it, but he couldn't refute it. 'Don't forget, my dad's in the force. I've just probably killed his career too.'

'We should give ourselves in.'

Milton leaned back on the bench, which creaked under his weight.

Theo leaned across the table.

'Milt, why is that your first reaction to everything? We've just got our first solid clue. A real address.'

'Maybe he's got a point? We can't move here.' Baxter gestured around. 'We can't move there. What do you expect us to do?'

His comment triggered another round of silence. Outside a sleek international train trundled into the nearby St Pancras station, startling a few noisy ducks.

Finally, Clemmie spoke up.

'We need disguises.' They looked blankly at her. 'Here we can mooch about in the dark. Up there, we'll need second-skins.'

'Outside games and vlogs they're illegal,' Milton reminded her. 'And way too expensive, unless you're super-rich. In which case, they're still illegal. And we're not super-rich.'

Clemmie smiled. 'But at least we're wanted criminals, so we're halfway there.'

Milton pulled a face. 'Well, I don't know where you can port them into SPACE.'

'Luckily we know a man who can.'

'I don't think so,' said Theo, trying to cut her off.

'Theo, Rex is our man. He's complicit. Turning us in will buy him time in jail too. That stave he arranged for us, it was legit. He can help us.'

Theo tried to rationalise his arguments, but found he had none. He looked to Baxter for support, but he was nodding in agreement. With a sigh, Theo waved his hand in defeat.

'Whatever.'

'How do we get in touch with him?' Milton asked. 'We can't just walk out and knock on his door.' He waved his hands jazz-style. 'Wanted fugitives, remember?'

'Bax, you have his ID. Why don't you give him a call?'

Baxter indicated to his broken rig. 'Using telepathy?'

Clemmie delicately plucked Milton's rig out of his hands.

He snatched out for it. 'Hey! I don't want his sweaty brainpan in my rig.'

Clemmie offered it to Baxter, who took it with a reluctant sigh.

To everybody's surprise, Rex's improvised plan unfolded without a glitch. Baxter had spent a long time persuading him to help; with each iteration of the plea he painted Rex as a larger-than-life hero with balls of steel. Eventually, it was too much for Rex's ego to ignore.

As dawn broke, Rex arrived at Regent's Canal in a battered white delivery van that was masked under a layer of grime so thick it had tinted the windows. He thought it was inconspicuous, but Milton reckoned it had 'my owner is a serial killer' written all over it. They transferred inside and Rex drove them to his garage without incident.

Only when they were safely locked in did he announce that Baxter's sister, Anna, had dumped him. She and her parents went hysterical when Baxter was smeared over the media. He'd struggled not to tell her they'd crossed paths.

She had misread his dithering as 'not understanding' and promptly dumped him.

'Told you she was fickle,' Clemmie whispered to Theo.

Rex winked at Baxter. 'I reckon helping her fugitive bruv will have her on her knees, begging me back.'

His upbeat attitude was reinforced when he ordered Chinese takeout for them, without demanding a single penny. A drone delivered the food, and they all watched Theo's recording on their rigs as they ate. Rex even supplied Baxter with an old headset that lay dented on the shelf. It was bulky, almost a decade out of date, but at least it was functional.

'That's definitely the same Slif I chased,' Clemmie confirmed, picking every last rice grain from her carton.

'I don't get why a Virt would help now?' Rex jiggled his chopsticks in the air. 'They're notorious dicks. Has to be something in it for them.' He did a double take when everybody shot him a look. 'What? I'm being racist about a computer program? I don't get your point.'

Clemmie tossed her empty carton aside and leaned her chair back on two legs, feet on the table.

'We're misremembering.' She used a chopstick as a pointer, jabbing it towards Milton. 'You said he was watching us before the drone attacked.'

'Yep.'

'We chased *him*. The drone chased *us*. As I recall, those grav-pulses were not exactly surgically targeted.' She soared the chopstick to mimic their trajectory. 'Whatever they did to us, they could've killed him.'

Despite his hunger, Theo could only pick at his food,

choosing smaller chunks of beef and avoiding the tangled noodles. He put the carton on the table, stabbing the chopsticks inside as he leaned forward.

'You think he was trying to help even then?'

Clemmie swayed her head indecisively. 'If not help, then observe. Or, at least, not hinder.' Her frown furrowed. 'He jabbed me with a baton to force me to eject. He could have killed me. He might have even saved me from a grav-pulse.' She looked at the others, slowly coming round to the idea of a Slif saviour. 'And Blondie was flying the drone, and drawing closer to the alley. We needed to be back here.'

'Looks like it risked its life saving your neck,' Baxter pointed out as he scrubbed the video back to the crashing police cruiser. 'I mean, in the ultimate way. We don't even know if he survived.' He nodded approvingly at Theo. 'It seems we've got ourselves a guardian angel.'

'The question is – why?'

The others swapped looks, hoping for inspiration.

Rex popped the cap off a Heineken bottle.

'Maybe your mum asked it to help?'

'I can't see that. She doesn't . . .'

Theo was going to say *associate with them* but stopped short. It was abundantly clear he had no idea what type of person his mother really was.

Rex guzzled down a third of the bottle and burped, ignoring Clemmie's disgust.

'So you're all fugitives *everywhere*.' He cocked a finger at Theo. 'And you're a cop-killer. Well, we have one bent copper, who by the way was very much alive and well on the news talking about you lot.'

Clemmie groaned. 'So, the slime lives.'

Rex nodded. 'Some bee-stung ninja hit man with real sweet tech has been chasing you down to find out what your ma hid. He's involved in Dens, where you think they're holding your ma. We just don't know where, and you think she's got days to live.'

'She *had* days, days ago,' said Theo darkly.

'All you've got to go on is some address in Hampstead? And you can't even go to the police with all of this.'

'Beautifully summed up,' Clemmie announced. 'Which is why we came to you.'

Rex took another swig and flashed a yellow-toothed smile at her.

'I'm touched.'

'Because we're desperate.'

She rocked her chair back on to all four legs.

Despite the weight of events, Theo suppressed a chuckle. His admiration for her was climbing to unhealthy proportions.

Clemmie stood and started to pace.

'Obviously we need to get into that address.'

Rex took another swig of lager. 'You're planning on rocking up, ringing the bell and getting yourself invited into some mad murder club?'

'If that's what it takes.'

'No offence, but you're fucking crazy.'

'Do you actually know what "no offence" means?' Before Rex could reply, Clemmie continued. 'We're fucking *smart*. Ella laid out a string of clues for Theo to follow. She risked her life to expose their whole operation so she could save lives, knowing very well she'd go down with it. She's not going to let us walk into a trap.'

'We'll go to the address on the ground and at the same time we go in virtually to check out the geo-lock.'

Rex's bottom lip stuck out as he thought about it.

'Two-pronged attack. Okay. Except you don't know where that house is geo-locked *to* ... and you can't enter SPACE without every twat trying to arrest you.'

'That's why we need second-skins.'

Milton watched the uncertainty ripple across Rex's face.

'And a few more staves.' Clemmie smiled. 'Once we ascend, we can't risk coming back down until we find her.'

'That could take days,' said Rex.

'Ella doesn't have days,' Theo said softly. 'From what I've read about Dens, I'd be surprised if she had even one day left. And now the bad guys in all this know we found the data dump, they don't have much incentive keeping her alive.'

Another gulp drained Rex's bottle. He tossed it at a corner bin. It ricocheted from the lip and bounced off the wall. He didn't register the miss.

'Okay, I can get you the skins and the time.' He met Clemmie's eye. 'Clarion liked you. Said you reminded her of her.'

'I'm deeply offended.'

He looked pointedly at Theo. 'I feel I better warn you, an extra hour – maybe fine. But *hours* ... I said moderation, bruv. You're already way over, plus however long did the police retain you? You'll be popping brain cells before anyone else.'

Theo's Pavlovian response was to rub his temple the moment Rex mentioned it. His migraine had been constant since he'd left SPACE and, when the others were not look-ing, he noticed his hands trembled. Was this the onset of Lag, or just fatigue?

'What choice do I have?'

'We're going to need weapons too.'

Baxter remained seated and didn't meet Rex's disbeliev-ing look as he jumped to his feet.

'Oh, come on, bruv. That's hard-core. That's a line even I don't cross. Uh-huh.'

'Rex,' Clemmie said softly. 'We're not asking you to use them, or even buy them. Just ... facilitate.'

'Facilitate? I can go to prison for facilitating.'

'If we get caught, you're going to prison anyway,' Baxter pointed out. 'Least if we can defend ourselves, we stand a chance.' He finally locked eyes with Rex. 'Over the last few nights I've lost track of the amount of times I could've died. All we're asking for are some non-lethals. Something that gives us an edge.'

Rex calmed a little. His hands kept nervously, repeatedly forming fists.

'Non-lethals?'

'Absolutely.'

Rex reached a decision, then nodded.

'That could take more time.'

'We don't have it!' snapped Theo, his temper fraying along with his voice.

Rex held up his hands defensively.

'Bruv, I get it! I really do, but skins, staves, weapons ...

Clarion moves at her own pace.' He glanced at Clemmie. 'You met her. The whole Children of Ellul cult scares the shit out of me.' He pointed outside. 'And none of you can go sneaking around in broad daylight. If you're gonna move, it will have to be tonight.'

Theo and Clemmie swapped a look of despair. Baxter spoke up as the voice of reason.

'Sure. But you can get the gear tonight?'

Rex wasn't sure. 'I'll message Clarion. Tell her we're desperate.' He looked between the foursome and scratched his lank hair. 'I'd be well pissed off if my rescue party looked like you lot.'

Milton frowned. 'What's that supposed to mean?'

'You look knackered. If you're gonna do this, you're gonna have to be awake.'

They knew he was right and the mere thought of sleep was welcoming. Even as he thought about it, Theo felt his body sinking and his thoughts jumble in a soft fugue. He met Clemmie's eye and she gave a slight nod of approval.

Rex retrieved his jacket and walked to the door.

'Rex's Palace is at your disposal. Just don't touch nothing. I'll be back about nine, just going dark. We'll take the van down to Pulsar.'

Theo gave him a tired, but appreciative smile.

'You're all right, Rex.'

Rex opened the door and half-stepped through before stopping and shooting a cocky smile back at Theo.

'Who said I wasn't?'

*

Flashes of blue and green fire scorched Theo's eyeballs as he plummeted earthbound. Kicking wildly, he corkscrewed around in time to see the impassive face of the Slif who had saved him – before impact jolted him awake, startling Clemmie, who had been gently shaking him.

She clutched her pounding chest.

'Christ, Theo! Take it easy!'

Theo panted as hard as if he'd just been running. A lance of pain shot through his eyeballs from the lock-up's yellowing strip lights that had been left on all day. He looked around with alarm.

'What's happened?'

'Nothing,' said Clemmie softly, indicating with her hand that he should keep his voice down. A tilt of the head guided him to where Milton and Baxter had made their cots on the floor. Theo rubbed his throbbing forehead and felt Clemmie shove something into his free hand. 'Take these.'

He rolled a pair of paracetamol tablets in his palm and accepted a cup of water. He tried to ignore the stained coffee tidemarks in it as he knocked back the pills in one swig.

'I have no idea if they help fend off Lag.' She raised an eyebrow when he glanced at her. 'I've seen your hands shake. I had an idea. If we can find out who Blondie is, it might give us an edge.'

'Didn't we try that?'

Theo closed his eyes as the incandescent flashes at the back of his eyes slowly faded with the pain.

'Remember I said we could access the government database from a police one. Like my father's.'

'My photofit isn't good enough and our video footage is scrambled.'

'Not all of it ...'

She smiled when he suddenly latched on to her thinking. 'Ella's security footage.'

She tapped her visor. 'I already edited a loop.'

A 3-D composite of Blondie hung in AR between them.

'But how do we access the database from here?'

'We can't. But my parents will both be in work right about now.' Theo wasn't so sure, and his expression gave that away. 'Think about it. Dad probably hasn't left the station from the moment my name dropped, and Mum will be on damage control at the Mayor's office. She'd be more concerned about her own reputation, trust me.'

It was a hell of a risk, but the idea of identifying the bastard was too tempting. Tonight would be their final roll of the dice and Theo wanted all the odds to be on their side. Chance was left for fools.

'How do we get to your house without being identified?'

Clemmie gave a genuine laugh, the kind that made her eyes sparkle and her dimples show.

'The problem with your generation, mister,' she said, parroting a stereotypical elderly voice, 'is that everything is digital this, and virtual that. You don't get that sometimes the old ways are best. They may be simple ...' She retrieved a biker's helmet from the side of a tool cabinet. The tinted black visor reflected Theo's surprise. 'But they work.'

Speeding along the elevated North London Expressway was both exhilarating and one of the most terrifying experiences of Theo's life. That included plummeting from his balcony.

Sitting pillion, his grip around Clemmie's stomach had increased so much that their bodies were pressed flat together. He'd never been on a motorbike before, and when he had first put his arms around her and accidentally cupped a breast he felt mortified.

Rex had an assortment of helmets designed to slide over rigs, although the fact most were scuffed from previous prangs didn't help ease Theo's nerves. Neither did driving at seventy miles per hour, weaving through silent traffic on a silent bike with nothing but the Indian's newly fitted double-wide off-road tyres crunching tarmac and the whip of each passing vehicle sounding louder than the last.

'Slow down!' Theo barked, easily heard over the background noise.

'If we go slower, we'll draw attention,' said Clemmie, shifting her position so Theo wasn't constricting her too much.

True enough; the police often targeted slower drivers who often turned out to be drunks trying not to stand out.

Overtaking the eighteen-wheeler lorries was the worse. By law, they emitted a deep throaty growl from their powerful hydrogen engines to warn other drivers of their presence. Unfortunately, most truckers had a morbid sense of humour and fine-tuned their engines to sound like something just short of the gates of Hell rumbling open.

Clemmie proved to be competent in the saddle and soon had them taking the Haringey exit. Minutes later they were pulling up Muswell Hill without ever coming to a halt. She pulled up a hundred yards across the street from her home.

'No car,' she stated, so at least one parent was out.

They spent a few minutes sat on the bike, trying to spot any loiterers who may be staking her house out. Satisfied there was nobody paying obvious attention, Clemmie moved on and parked in a perpendicular street several yards from her house. She killed the engine and dismounted, keeping her helmet on.

'The moment you use your key, surely they'll know?'

Clemmie's house key was chipped into her rig. All she had to do was approach the door and it opened automatically.

'I only have a key for the front door and I've deactivated it. We're going in the back door.'

Without rushing, they strolled to a black wrought-iron gate that accessed an alley between the gardens of back-to-back semi-detached houses. Checking nobody was passing by, Clemmie scrambled over the locked gate with practised ease.

Jumping down the other side she called to Theo. 'Hurry up!'

He followed, managing to clamber over on his third attempt. Clemmie was already a quarter of the way down, standing impatiently at an unmarked wooden gate. Again she scaled it, and again Theo struggled.

He dropped down into her parents' back garden. Working so much, they had no time to tend it so it was overrun with damp grass and wild flowers. Clemmie rummaged under an old plant pot and finally produced a mud-splattered off-white card, which she held up triumphantly.

'This is how I used to sneak in and out when I was in college.' She sounded relieved it was still there. 'I never registered it, so my folks never knew ...' She touched it against a cobweb-covered scanner on the back door. There was a click as the mortise lock disengaged and she pulled the door open. 'Come on.'

Inside the kitchen she took her helmet off and placed it on the wooden table, wiping sweat from her brow with her forearm. Theo was relieved to remove his and reached for a plump green apple in the fruit bowl as his stomach growled. Clemmie slapped his hand away.

'They can't know anybody's been here.'

She led him to her father's office. As far as Theo could make out, nothing had changed since their last incursion. He felt a twinge of guilt thinking that her father might have spent the last few days in work, fretting over his daughter because of him. Apparently unencumbered by such worries, Clemmie sat and placed the hard-wired police rig on her head.

'He's still logged in. Ready?'

Theo sat cross-legged on the floor in anticipation of being tethered into Foundation.

'Go for it.'

The sense of displacement wasn't as bad as last time, probably because he had been expecting it, or maybe the last few nights in SPACE had desensitised him.

Swirling geometrics towered around them as Clemmie silently navigated them through Foundation, towards the Criminal database. The icosahedron appeared; each of the twenty sides was peppered with rapidly moving pulses of light, looking like rush hour.

'Busy day,' Theo commented dryly.

'Yep.' Clemmie was distracted. 'And we're the reason why. There's the Government access node.'

As she drew them closer to the spinning shape, Theo could appreciate the sheer scale of the database. Each side was not flat, as he had assumed, but covered in towers, spires and cubes – all sub-filing systems and AI subroutines – between which the pulses of user light zipped. Some of the edges between the icosahedron's sides resembled cities, with yet more users mining information.

Clemmie followed one such track which stopped at a small circular aperture where five of the sides came together. A shimmering red meniscus layer flickered over the opening. Theo knew a firewall when he saw one.

'Can we get through that?'

'Sure.' She couldn't hide the uncertainty in her voice. 'My dad's got clearance.'

'You've done this before?' Silence as they drifted closer to the portal. 'Clem? You've done this before, right?'

'*Precisely* this? No.'

'What happens if we don't have clearance?'

'Nothing. We just bounce off.' The tunnel filled their vision, as did the pulsing firewall. 'And maybe a load of alarms will go off too.'

Before Theo could stop her, they struck the firewall.

Chapter Twenty-Nine

'I'm hurt you doubted me,' Clemmie quipped as they passed through the firewall without incident. 'And I thought you loved me.'

She was teasing, but Theo didn't trust himself enough to reply.

After the briefest rush of a spiralling tunnel, they were suddenly inside a huge spherical cavern filled with users that zigzagged like fireflies around a spinning orange dodecahedron, its surface etched with lines and towers like its larger cousin.

'This is a record of all government personnel. We can only access basic details, but Dad said it was enough to liaise with the military during state events. Remember the King's wedding? They practically mobilised the army that day. He was in this thing for hours finessing arrangements. That looks like the interrogation point there.'

They drifted closer to a broad pentagonal side, with a cluster of towers poking from it that gently undulated like a sea anemone's tentacles sampling a current. Clemmie called up Blondie's holo-recorded image.

'Fingers crossed.'

She tossed the image towards the towers. The tentacles wrapped around it, the data packet flaring brightly. A swarm of red lights moved towards the base of the tower, circling in a predatory fashion as they digested each bit.

'Take your time,' Theo said sarcastically. Their previous search had been completed in seconds; now the swarm increased around the impact point until the centre of it appeared to burn. 'What's happening?'

A file suddenly appeared in front of them. Blondie's head slowly spinning, the picture taken from a personnel file some years earlier. The name Rutger Haugen appeared alongside. Theo quickly read the text.

'UKSF?'

'UK special forces,' said Clemmie in a monotone. 'Previously with the Recces?'

A sub-window informed them that was the South African special forces.

'Pathfinder Platoon ... service record redacted. Active status, Gold Command?' Theo read aloud. 'That is really not helpful.'

'Yes it is. It tells us he's still with the military. It also means he's working on some clandestine shit somebody in authority doesn't want people to know about.'

Theo thought back to the auction.

'Somebody not just rich but well-placed, with the power to subvert the police ...'

'Or *in* the police. Gold Command is a command structure to co-ordinate the emergency services during incidents, such as terrorism.'

'Or a manhunt.'

'They usually liaise with Parliament, updating COBRA meetings, that sort of thing. I've got to get this to my dad,' Clemmie suddenly said with urgency. 'Frasier is just a day-player. This guy is key.'

She saved the file then folded it up – a Foundation short-cut to email the file. Before she could send it, what looked like a spiky grey massage ball swooped from the outer wall and hovered between them and the floating file. The spikes stretched and shrank, reminding Theo of a cartoon virus. Then they all pumped out like a three-dimensional graphic equaliser in time to a voice bursting with gravitas.

'User TK421, you have unauthorised file access. Identify yourself.'

'Shit!' Clemmie exclaimed.

'Shit is not valid authorisation. Your access portal has been traced. Do not make any attempt to vacate your physical—'

They ejected from cyberspace so rapidly that Clemmie toppled from the swivel chair as she yanked the rig off.

'Bollocks. They're coming!'

Theo stood unsteadily up. 'What? How?'

'I think that was my dad's user ID. They'll trace it here. We've got to leave now!'

She half-dragged him into the kitchen.

'Did you send the file?'

Clemmie nodded as she retrieved her helmet from the kitchen table. She was pale, her fingers trembling. Theo laid a hand on hers.

'Clem. Relax. Even if they said they'd traced—'

His comforting words died with the whoop of a police

siren from the front of the house. Blue lights strobed through the glass panels in the front door.

'That was stupidly quick!'

'Come on!'

Clemmie shoved his hand away and bolted for the back door. Theo scooped up his own helmet and gave the front door one last look, making out the frosted shadows of people running up the pathway. By the time he was through the kitchen and out into the garden, he heard the first thump of police officers attempting to batter open the front door.

Clemmie had already reached the garden gate and had enough presence of mind to unbolt it so they could enter the alley unhindered. She charged to the black gate, slamming her weight into it as she snapped the single bolt back.

In an instant they were at the motorbike. Clemmie grasped the handlebars and fluidly tossed her leg over it like a gymnast. She already had the engine engaged by the time Theo took his position behind her. They both looked up as a drone flew overhead. Bedecked with green and blue Met Police decals, it was almost as large as their bike, and a pair of powerful propellers made it half as wide. It homed in on the back of Clemmie's house . . .

Then suddenly it stopped as the AI registered something. It drifted sideways then suddenly turned, tracking the open gates and locking on to the two targets sat on the bike. Its siren blared to life, blue strobes pulsing.

The ubiquitous synthetic police voice of authority cried out, 'You are under arrest—'

Clemmie didn't wait to hear the rest. She gunned the engine with nothing more than a rising electrical whine, and the bike took off with such savage acceleration that the front wheel kicked up into a wheelie, almost pitching Theo off. His arm went around her neck and squeezed so hard she started to choke. She managed to push the bike back on to two wheels and croaked at him.

'You're strangling me ...'

When Theo didn't respond she butted her head back hard, cracking his helmet visor. He got the message and repositioned his arm around her waist.

Theo risked a look behind. Two more police drones had joined the pursuit, sirens blazing.

'Clem!'

'I saw! I saw!'

'What's the plan?'

Clemmie skidded the bike into a side street to the left and continued to accelerate past lines of parked cars. A driver-less Toyota saloon chose the inopportune moment to pull out of its parking space as its driver summoned it, forcing Clemmie to jink the bike to the right, just about sweeping around the bonnet before the car slammed on its brakes.

A T-junction loomed ahead, but she didn't slow – instead she made a hard left at speed, then a sudden right that had the tyres screeching. Before he knew it, Theo realised she had circled back on to the main road.

They accelerated up Muswell Hill, weaving between speed bumps designed for cars. The drone relentlessly pursued, fruitlessly demanding they stop. Another pair banked in to formation, following the leader. Behind those, two police cars joined the growing pursuit.

Clemmie overtook a red double-decker bus – a move that

drew them into the path of another oncoming double-decker.

'Whoa!' Theo and Clemmie shouted in unison.

Theo felt the pressure wave as Clemmie threaded the bike through the diminishing gap between the buses, clearing them by inches. The leading drone hadn't time to recalculate its route. Flying ten feet above the traffic, the aircraft was suddenly sandwiched between the top decks. There was a tremendous bang and a cacophony of shattering glass as one propeller chewed through the windows, while the other mashed against the aluminium side of the second bus and shattered its blades. The drone cartwheeled through one top deck, bringing the front half of the roof down on the passengers inside.

The vehicles swerved, grinding into one another in a cascade of sparks before jerking to a halt, blocking the road. The remaining two drones pulled up in time, continuing the chase. The police cars, however, had no way past.

Clemmie didn't have time to enjoy the victory. She was pushing eighty as they hit the slip road up on to the North London Expressway.

Straight into rush hour traffic.

Chapter Thirty

The stagnant ribbon of traffic had just begun creeping forward under the soundtrack of car radio dissonance and the artificial grumble of lorries.

Clemmie's speed flashed ninety-six on her visor as they snatched air cresting the access ramp. The Indian's newly fitted fluid suspension, a testimony to Rex's engineering prowess, sucked in what should have been a jarring impact. The wide off-road tyres secured their balance, preventing them from broadsiding a dozen cars as they rumbled over the cat's-eyes on the nearside lane.

The police drones effortlessly followed, blazing sirens causing every driver to try to locate where the action was.

A break formed in the traffic ahead, barely wide enough for Clemmie to swerve into the central lane and weave through the traffic. The slope of the expressway as it climbed over central London wasn't problematic for the powerful engine, but Theo was more than conscious that they were gradually rising to three hundred feet over the congested streets with few options for a quick exit.

'When you came on here, did you have an actual plan for getting off?'

Clemmie didn't entertain him with a reply. She was too focused on not killing them. Her rig's HUD highlighted the gaps ahead with a green trailing arrow actively threading between lanes, picking out routes just large enough for the bike. It was a useful app, but it was limited to what her rig's cameras could see combined with GPS data streamed from other cars. The constantly flowing traffic resulted in the arrow suddenly swapping one turn for another as a gap became too narrow, or the guide would suddenly vanish, forcing her to brake hard to match the sluggish pace of the traffic.

Theo craned around to locate the drones. He couldn't see them. He twisted around to check his blind spot, just as one aircraft sharply descended, pulling alongside them. Clemmie was too focused on the road to notice, as the breaks in the traffic began to increase as everybody accelerated forward once again.

'Clem!'

His warning came too late.

The drone broadsided the bike. Its propeller housing, the diameter of a dustbin, crushed their legs, forcing Clemmie to bank the Indian left in a frantic battle to stay upright.

The drone relentlessly bobbed around a massive Range Rover, the near miss causing children inside to press their gawping faces against the windows. Then it veered straight at them again. The propeller was large enough to chew both of them up, which was clearly the drone's intention, and not exactly 'by the book' police protocol.

Clemmie spotted the drone at the last second and squeezed the brakes. The bike responded immediately. The back wheel bucked off the road, almost flipping Theo over her. One arm squeezed Clemmie hard, the other reached behind and gripped the sissy bar to anchor himself.

The drone overshot in front of them, crashing into the trailer of a lorry that was changing lanes. The thin metal trailer ripped asunder, electrical goods inside toppling out to form a wake as the truck wildly snaked.

With the Indian's new ceramic brakes still screeching, Clemmie somehow managed to balance the bike on the front wheel before the rear end bounced back on to the road. She swerved around the lorry and its liberated cargo of refrigerators and microwaves spewing across the carriageway. With a flick of the wrist, she throttled forward.

Behind, the lorry jackknifed, blocking the southbound road to a chorus of car horns and rising black smoke as one car ploughed into it at speed. Theo's relief was short-lived as the remaining drone punctured through the cloud, smoke mushrooming through its propellers as it sped towards them.

'It's right behind us, Clem!'

Theo renewed his grip around her as they reached the expressway's apex over the Thames. Ahead, the road sloped down to the South Bank and the traffic had started to knit together again as drivers slowed for the steep descent. Movement across the river caught his eye. He squinted against the sun glaring from the blue water – another pair of drones were zeroing in.

Behind, the pursuing drone's warbling siren rose in volume as it skimmed over car roofs, on a direct collision course for them. Theo swore in all the police chases he had seen on *Police, Gotcha!* streams that it wasn't policy to ram people off their rides.

An unfamiliar icon suddenly flashed in his rig. A message read:

INCOMING DOWNLOAD: #UNKNOWN ID.

'Are you seeing this?'

'Seeing what?' snapped Clemmie.

She leaned over the handlebars and decided to accelerate down the incline, rather than slow like any other sane person.

A small spinning AR shape, like a pineapple, formed a foot away from Theo's head. Mystified, he reached for it. The wetware interface made him feel cool smooth metal as his fingers wrapped around it. That was odd. Such sensations were limited to SPACE alone, yet here he was experiencing some sort of augmented hybrid. A countdown hovering over the object began: 5 ... 4 ...

It dawned on him he was holding a grenade.

Virtual or not, his first instinct was to hurl it at the pursuing drone. As it ticked down to 1, the grenade splattered on to the aircraft's fuselage like a mud pie. Black tendrils erupted from it, expanding across the drone like a fast-moving cancer.

Naturally the aircraft didn't respond to a virtual grenade only Theo could see – until, with an abrupt ascending pitch, the propellers spooled up far too quickly. The drone shimmied in turbulence of its own creation before the engines exploded, orange flames draughting through the propellers, spitting out behind like dragon flame. The burning drone carcass belly-flopped into the road on the opposite carriageway, causing traffic to swerve violently aside.

Through her mirror, Clemmie caught the drone ripping apart in a second fiery detonation.

'What did you do?'

Theo was wondering exactly that as the two new drones rose over the side of the expressway ahead and swerved towards them. The message flashed up again, indicating another download. This time when the grenade formed, he noticed the completion message briefly pop up:

AUGMENTED VIRAL GRENADE #DOWNLOADED

Somebody was fusing AR tracking technology to lock on to the drone's rapidly changing position, then hacking them in real time from SPACE. He'd never heard of such a thing, but his mind went straight to Milton. In case Baxter and Milton awoke before they returned, he'd left air-graffiti outlining their plan. He assumed Milton must be tracking them and had somehow reached out to Rex and Clarion in their hour of need.

Theo tossed the grenade at the lead drone as it levelled out in front of them, destined for a perfect collision course.

'Theo!'

'Don't wimp out!'

Again, the drone didn't respond to the augmented impact of the grenade, and it clearly had no intention of moving aside first. Now Theo understood the tendrils smothering the drone were merely a visual representation of the hack. As it reached the engine cowls, whatever virus had been implanted dicked around with the rotor management system so they spontaneously combusted.

With a forceful boom, the engines dutifully exploded, twisting the drone in different directions, causing it to tear apart in mid-air.

Clemmie screamed and ducked her head behind the bike's visor as they shot through the cloud of debris. Burning metal and plastic struck the windscreen hard, spiderwebbing the reinforced acrylic. Theo felt something bash his helmet as he pressed himself against Clemmie.

In an instant, they were through it.

The remaining drone overshot them, rising in a steep climb to avoid its fallen comrade. They had now caught up with traffic ahead, and weaved through it as the gaps once again diminished as the mass slowed down. At the bottom of the expressway the branching spaghetti snarl of junctions was blocked by five police cars lined end to end, strobes blazing.

'I hope you have some more tricks up your sleeve!'

Clemmie slowed, sliding the bike between a pair of delivery vans. A quick check up over her shoulder revealed the police drone corkscrewing through the air towards them.

Another grenade appeared in Theo's rig. He chucked it at the drone. Distracted by the roadblock, his aim was off. The grenade fell short and struck the bonnet of a slow-moving black cab. Seconds later the taxi skidded to a halt as flames sprouted from the electric engine. The driver jumped out moments later, staring incredulously as the flames took hold.

The drone jinked aside, abandoning its attack run to avoid the pillar of smoke rising in front of it. The manoeuvre was so violent, the cabbie threw himself to the floor to avoid decapitation.

Theo waited for another grenade to replenish, but nothing happened.

'We're thin on options,' he warned Clemmie.

'How thin?'

Theo spoke after the briefest of pauses.

'Like "having to ram the roadblock" thin.'

Clemmie decelerated with such abruptness that Theo figured she had reached the same conclusion he had: their time was up. Capture was now inevitable.

He kicked himself for agreeing to the reckless plan and only hoped the name they had uncovered would be enough to persuade Clemmie's father they were innocent.

Traffic ahead was now gridlocked bumper to bumper. Officers on foot were approaching through the narrow aisles between traffic.

No sooner had Theo become resigned to his fate than Clemmie suddenly yanked the handlebars, throwing her body weight back so violently that he was pinned against the sissy rail. At the same time, Clemmie stood in the saddle and applied the throttle, kicking the bike on to its back wheel. The chunky front tyre slammed on to the boot of the BMW in front. Rex's two-wheel drive system and enhanced torque allowed the Indian to crawl up and over the vehicle – buckling the roof as it did so – before dropping on to the bonnet and mounting the next car in front without a hitch in speed.

Theo clung tightly on as the bike swayed. A message flashed on his visor, taking his attention from the carnage they were causing. Another grenade was downloading.

Gaining confidence, Clemmie applied more speed. Her front wheel shattered a Ford's rear windscreen as they rolled on to the roof. Ignoring the yells of the driver inside, Clemmie powered on – up and over a dozen vehicles and past the first wave of startled police officers, who flinched as side windows popped from the pressure on their buckling roofs.

As the police drone drew alongside, Theo reached for the AR grenade, his hand passing through the ghostly shape. It had yet to be fully downloaded. A message warned: BANDWIDTH ERROR!

The buzz of rotors increased as the drone angled towards them. Desperate, Theo kicked out, slamming the propeller casing hard enough to make the aircraft shudder. The far rotor glanced off a stationary van, shattering its protective casing. The exposed rotors gouged through the Transit's thin bodywork like a circular saw before it recovered, made a swift adjustment and swung towards the bike again.

Theo raised his foot for another kick – just as their bike bounced up on to the roof of a taller 4 × 4. He missed the propeller casing and lashed out over the vicious rotors. The fierce pull of the air tugged at his jeans, sucking his leg downwards. The heel of his oversized trainers grazed the top of the blades, slicing a salami of rubber sole. Theo lost his balance – but luck navigated his foot on to the relative safety of the spinning central propeller spindle.

At the same time, Clemmie spotted a new peril ahead.

A pair of cops at the roadblock were armed with bulky cylindrical bazookas raised to their shoulders. Rather than a hollow barrel, the weapon tips were copper-coloured geodesic balls – EMP-rifles, used by traffic police to stop vehicles.

Before she could react, they fired a precisely focused electromagnetic pulse at the bike. She and Theo felt nothing, but the Indian's electronic systems failed immediately. Deceleration was instant as they pitched from the roof of another taxi. Clemmie was hurled from the unresponsive bike, head first into an estate car's rear window.

Theo was thrown sideways as the bike toppled. The sole of his trainer squeaked across the rapidly spinning engine spindle. Pure momentum carried him clear of the lethal blades and on to the drone's fuselage.

The aircraft wasn't designed to carry a payload and Theo's weight forced it to belly-flop. With a jarring crunch, the drone skipped like a stone from the roofs of gridlocked vehicles. Theo caught sight of the sheer drop to the fresh blue-green Thames to his right as the machine edged nearer with each hop. The port side blades sheared as they struck a lorry, pitching the drone sideways – and over the edge of the bridge. Theo let out a scream as he hugged the broken drone and plummeted towards the river.

Chapter Thirty-One

The Thames was surprisingly warm, reflecting the long hot summer. But the impact hurt like hell.

Theo sucked in a lungful of air a second before striking the clear water. His next moments were a turmoil of bubbles, unable to tell which way round he was. The flaming police drone narrowly scythed past him like a torpedo as it sank, scattering a shoal of fish. However, it gave him the orientation he required and he kicked to the surface, gasping for air.

Half a minute later, he was dragging himself through the mud and weed on his hands and knees. Every desperate breath stabbed his side. He suspected he'd broken a rib or two, but was too relieved at still being alive to care. Even his rig was still functional as he poured water from it and plucked a strand of weed from the battered winking Emotive logo.

'What're you grinning at?' he muttered, catching his breath. 'This is all your bloody fault.'

Theo squinted up at the expressway sixty feet overhead. People were craning over the edge, pointing and shouting. He wondered if Clemmie was okay. The last he'd seen, she had been thrown from the motorbike and through a car window.

He put his rig back on. The HUD impatiently flashed an arrow upwards and to the right. He followed it. The arrow reoriented until it was pointing to stone steps leading from the riverbank to the raised embankment road. A second later, Rex's van skidded to a halt, Milton slid the side door open and stared open-mouthed at Theo. Baxter peered from the driver's seat.

'Jesus Christ!' Baxter finally exclaimed. 'We thought we'd be scooping your corpses out of the water.'

'Not today,' said Clemmie from behind.

Theo turned to see her striding from the river like a rising Venus. Her clothes clung to every curve under her sodden combat jacket. She yanked her rig off, and shook it to dislodge any water while looking up at the fall she'd taken. She gave a low whistle and absently ruffled her hair before noticing Theo was staring at her.

'What?'

Theo followed her gaze up to the expressway. A crowd of faces were peering over, pointing and shouting.

'You're okay,' he managed, before hissing as pain played a concerto across his ribs.

She shot a half-smile. 'It's not as if I haven't fallen off a bike before.' She glanced up at the bridge. 'Although jumping after you was a first.'

'It would be an idea not to hang around!'

Milton pointed across the river. Three more drones were skimming towards them, so low they kicked up curtains of water in their wakes.

Theo and Clemmie made it up the steps as fast as they could, Theo clutching his ribs and Clemmie limping, blood oozing from a network of cuts on her cheek from face-planting the windshield.

Milton helped them into the van before following. Baxter stomped the pedal even before the side door closed. He twisted the steering wheel so savagely the van almost lurched on two wheels as it entered a narrow one-way street the wrong way.

'How did you find us?'

Theo found it hurt to speak while sitting with his arms splayed against the bulkhead to stop sliding around.

'We picked up your Echo,' Milton said, climbing into the front passenger seat.

Clemmie was confused. 'We didn't send an Echo.'

'One of you must have. That's how we zeroed in on your co-ordinates.'

Theo and Clemmie exchanged a puzzled look.

'What exactly has happened since we left?' Theo asked. 'And Milt, where did you get those grenades from? That was an awesome move.'

Now it was Milton and Baxter who exchanged a look.

'Grenades?' Milton tutted. 'You must be brain-damaged, mate.'

'And if you're not, I'm certainly going to make sure you are!' growled Baxter. 'What were you thinking, slipping out like that?'

He took another corner at speed, rubber squealing. More police sirens blared.

'Where's Rex?' Clemmie asked. Baxter and Milton

exchanged another look, but neither spoke. 'Where is he?' she asked more firmly.

Milton chewed his lip. 'He went thermonuclear when you nicked his bike.'

'How did he know? He wasn't supposed to be coming back until tonight.'

Milton hooked one arm around the back of his seat so he could turn and address them directly.

'It's all over the streams. News drones tracked your joy-ride. He woke us up screaming.'

'That's the first we knew about it.' Baxter spoke through teeth gritted in both anger and concentration. 'But it didn't take the Bill long to trace the registered owner, who thought his bike was still in the garage.'

Milton nodded. 'We only just got out when the police raided it. There was a blocked doorway connecting it to the lock-up next door. They arrested Rex. We took the van, then caught your Echo to pick you up.'

Theo zoned out as Clemmie filled them in on discovering Blondie's identity and their subsequent escape. If the AR grenades were not from Clarion, then who?

'Somebody else is trying to help us,' Theo finally said out loud.

The others stopped their heated exchange, which was mostly Baxter bitching about how inconsiderate they'd been. He kept his eyes on the road while Milton and Clemmie regarded Theo, waiting for him to reveal more.

'I reckon the Slif who sprung me out of the shopping centre is watching over us. My money is on him sending the Echo and bringing those drones down.'

They listened in silence as Theo outlined his theory on how the AR grenades worked.

Milton finally gave a low appreciative whistle and shook his head.

'Nice. But it doesn't stack up.' He held out one fist. 'Real world.' He held up the other a few inches away. 'SPACE. We can look at one from the other, but the virtual can't really affect The Real. We have priority. We win every time.'

'Not true.' Clemmie was thoughtful as she scratched the rash on her neck. 'We can trade emotions from one to the other. They have weapons that kill in The Real.' She tapped her neck. 'And we think our friendly neighbourhood hit man, Mr Rutger Haugen, may have tracked me by injecting a pheromone stimulant in the virtual.'

Silence filled the van as they contemplated the implications. Baxter began to shuffle in his seat, craning to see the passenger mirror.

'What's wrong?' Milton followed his gaze.

Baxter sounded worried. 'There's nobody following us. *Nobody.*'

Theo was confused. 'The first good news of the day and you're questioning it?'

He positioned himself between the front seats, so he could better see through the windscreen and the mirrors.

'The coppers were swarming,' said Baxter. 'Dozens of them. Now it looks like they've been sent packing in the wrong direction.'

'Our guardian angel strikes again,' said Clemmie quietly.

Baxter briefly released the wheel so he could crack his knuckles, releasing the tension.

'What now?'

'It's only going to be so long before somebody recognises this van.' Theo drummed his fingers on the seat as he considered their meagre options. 'We need to pay Clarion a visit and hope Rex put his order through.' He turned to Clemmie. 'Remember the way?'

Clemmie gave a reluctant nod.

Rex had been arrested dozens of times, something he regarded as a badge of honour although he never elaborated to others the specific range of petty misdemeanours. The plain-clothes detective opposite him read them on his rig, slowly shaking his head and sighing.

'You're a real tough arse, aren't you?' He chuckled, but that seemed to hurt his throat.

Rex tried to scratch his beard, but his cuffed hand wouldn't extend that far and snapped to a halt. He indicated them.

'Are these really necessary, bruv?'

'Sadly, we ain't blood related,' the detective said with another snigger.

Then he relented and pushed his thumb against the fingerprint scanner on the cuffs. They snapped open, and Rex rubbed his freed wrists. He glanced around the drab interior of the police truck that had been jury-rigged into an interview room.

'I'm parched. I need a drink.'

The detective sat opposite. 'Let's not get too friendly just yet. I see some reckless driving on your file. Well, fuck me sideways – thirty-two in a thirty zone.' He whistled sarcastically. 'Several formal cautions for faulty headlights. Ooh, look at this – arrested for carrying a knife.' The detective regarded him with a frown. 'You are a regular hard man. Oh wait, says here the charges were dropped when it was confirmed you were on your way to your mum's Women's Institute bake sale.'

Rex looked away – why should he feel ashamed for failing to stab anybody?

'But we know you, Reginald Cline. Suspected time-trader. That's a little more serious. Suspected trafficker in second-skins. Sounds to me like you're trying to join the big boys' club. I mean, harbouring wanted fugitives – that's gotta be a personal best for a career crim like you.'

Rex held the detective's gaze for a long moment, then forced a dry laugh, proclaiming his innocence with a shrug.

'I don't know what you're talking about.'

He'd seen Baxter and Theo escape in his van while he was outside and, as far as he knew, he hadn't been spotted with them.

'Theodore Wilson, Clémence Laghari, Edwin Baxter and Milton McCarthy were hiding out in your garage. They stole a bike from your garage. Then they stole *your* van from *your* garage.'

'I don't know anything about that. Baxter, sure, I used to go out with Baxter's sister. She's bipolar I think. She dumped me.'

The detective leaned back in his chair and pulled a sympathetic face.

'Aw, didn't it go well for you?'

'Anna is a complicated but great lady. I never liked her

brother, though. Little wanker. He's been to the garage before, so he could've easily broke in. You know *he* was arrested for selling staves?' Rex bit his lower lip and sadly shook his head. 'I mean, I don't want to get mixed up in that shit. Shouldn't I have a solicitor or something in here?'

Rex knew all he had to do was play dumb, but his heart seemed to keep pace with the detective's drumming fingers on the table.

'There's one on the way. So, fine, they broke in without your knowledge. Stole the bike, then your van. And you had no idea. You look stupid enough for me to believe that.'

Rex placed a hand on his heart.

'I'm the victim here, detective.'

'Detective Chief Inspector, mate.' He nodded in agreement. 'And indeed you are, Reg – sorry, Rex, isn't it? So, explain, if you didn't know they were hiding out in your garage, why did you buy them food?'

Rex only realised his jaw was hanging slack after a few seconds of silence. He closed it, then gave a quick shrug, feigning confusion.

'It was delivered straight to your door. That happened *twice*. Both times bought using your chip.'

'They must have stolen my chip.'

'The one in *your* rig.' He indicated the rig on the table between them. 'This one you were wearing when we arrested you.'

'They cloned it then. Happens.'

'That makes sense. They cloned your chip and were so hungry they made five separate orders.' He held up his hand, fingers splayed, two of them held in rigid moulded plastic splints. He waggled them for emphasis. 'Five. As in, one of these kids is doing his own thing.' He lowered four fingers until only his pinkie was raised. 'And he's the one currently going down on behalf of a cop-killer.'

Rex felt beads of sweat roll down his back, making him shiver. The air had suddenly become thick, almost chewy.

'I need that drink.'

'I need answers. The clock is ticking. This isn't a game, this isn't a jolly in the virtual. Somebody died. You are complicit and tying yourself into deeper knots with each lie.'

Rex avoided his gaze as that sank in. The detective put his elbows on the table and steepled his fingers across his mouth.

'I see people like you take the fall all the time. I know you're good people, Rex. You're a bloody good mechanic, I saw what that bike of yours did. You can turn that skill into something truly on the straight and narrow instead of spending a decade in the nick.'

Rex took in a double-breath as he repressed the burgeoning anxiety inside.

'I didn't do nothing.'

'I know that, Rex. They came asking for help, didn't they?' He cocked his head to the side to better see Rex's sheepish expression. 'That's because Edwin knew you'd do a friend a solid. You're that type of bloke. But they abused that – *they're* the ones who broke the law. All you did was warp it a tiny bit as they used you. What is it they asked you to do?'

Rex flopped back in the chair, manspreading defiantly. He slapped his palms on the table, leaving a trail of sweat.

'I don't have to tell you nothing until my brief arrives.'

He sounded cockier than he felt.

The rear doors opened and another man entered, again wearing plain clothes. He carefully closed the door behind him and spoke in a thick South African accent.

'DCI Frasier. Is the prisoner chirpy?'

Frasier slowly rose from the chair, unconsciously running a light hand across his scalded and bandaged chest.

'Not very, Mr Haugen.'

Rex stared at the intimidating blond, especially at the half of his face riddled with red-raw boils.

'My God, the Elephant Man lives . . .'

Haugen tutted and held up Rex's rig.

'You're hurting my feelings, mate. Shame, I was going to give you this back as a gesture of goodwill.'

He circled around Rex as Frasier leaned on the table.

'Is your solicitor your final word?'

Rex crossed his arms. 'Absolutely.'

His rig was suddenly thrust on his head with such force he sprained his neck to compensate. Before he could move, Haugen's vice grip crushed both his hands and painfully crossed them tightly over his chest into a straitjacket repose.

'What the fuck? This is police brutality!'

Frasier issued a sharp laugh. 'Isn't it, though.'

Despite the pain, Rex tried to focus on sending a distress message to Baxter, but his interface refused to obey any of his impulse commands.

'We disabled your rig,' Haugen whispered close to his ear. 'You're now just an audience. Have you ever been to the theatre?'

The image of an Asian man, a few years younger than Rex, appeared in front of the door. It was a perfect AR projection. He wore jeans, a designer polo top, and his wrists and legs were bound to a chair with plastic ties. Instead of a rig the small wetware interface components had been attached directly to the skin around his ears, temples and between his eyes. He appeared to stare straight at Rex, hyperventilating in terror.

Frasier gestured to the phantom, clearly visible on his own rig.

'We had to drag this poor reprobate out of a club in Uzbekistan, just for your entertainment. See how many people you're inconveniencing?'

The holograph suddenly gave a shrill scream as a knife appeared at the edge of the image. The six-inch blade sliced into flesh just above his kneecap.

Rex screamed, his leg kicking out as he simultaneously felt the white-hot stab sever nerve endings as it passed through flesh, muscle and cartilage. But his own scream remained locked in his skull. While his parched throat worked, no sound came out.

The blade was slowly extracted so that every ridge on the blade scored through more meat, issuing pulses of constant pain, until just a fraction of an inch remained in the man's leg. Blood dripped steadily to the floor from behind his kneecap. Rex could feel every moment of intense agony as the blade was slowly drawn up the thigh, slicing the man's beige trousers and epidermis, leaving a wake of blood as it inched slowly and inexorably towards his groin. Rex could feel every nerve and fibre snap under the ridge of cold steel.

The man's screams rose in pitch – as did Rex's internal ones.

'The pain receptors of you and our pal here are one,' Haugen calmly narrated close to his ear. 'You're feeling everything – with the added bonus of turning down your volume. After all, we don't want to wake the neighbours, do we?'

The knife stopped two inches from the top of the Asian's inner thigh. The wake of flesh behind it slowly widened as skin pulled taut, milky blobs of fat oozing between the blood. The blade disappeared.

'Ooh, nasty!' Frasier wagged a finger, but couldn't wipe the smile off his face. Through his pain, Rex realised that the sick moron was getting off on this. 'As you said, you're the victim here. Has it loosened your tongue?' With his hands on his knees, he bent down to Rex's eye level. 'Oh, you can talk. You just can't scream.'

'You baldy bastard!' Rex blurted.

Frasier rolled his eyes. 'Oh dear, that was unpleasant.' His voice lowered. 'You're in a most grievous state, matey. Silence is not your friend.'

The knife reappeared next to the whimpering man's eye. The tip slowly pressed in the soft lower eyelid. Rex flinched as it pricked 'his' eyelid.

'This is interesting.' Frasier walked around the AR ghost to get a better look. 'Because he won't be able to see once his eye is sliced up, but you will be able to watch the whole thing. And the odd thing about the old noggin is, it makes you feel pain more acutely when you can see the wound.'

A pinprick of pain made Rex gasp as blood began to trickle from the victim's ocular orbit.

'All you have to do is speak to us, mate,' came Haugen's disembodied voice from behind.

'Okay! Okay!' Rex whimpered. The sensation around his eye immediately relaxed. 'They wanted to buy some staves.' Frasier's eyes widened, but before he could ask, Rex cut him off. 'And I don't deal that. I was just connecting them with a dealer. I'm a middleman.' He held his hands up in mock surrender. 'I wasn't even getting paid for it!'

Frasier clapped his hands together and rubbed them in delight.

'See how liberating honesty can be?'

'Where were you going to source them from?' Haugen asked.

'D'you know the Pulsar club?'

Frasier exchanged a look with Haugen.

'Yes we do.'

'There's a trader there. Goes by the name Clarion.'

'That was all you had to do,' Frasier said. 'But you had to make it complicated. Shame. I was planning to let you walk out of here. Hell, I even had a car I needed pimping up.' He shook his head sadly. 'What a waste.'

Too weak to do anything, Rex could only helplessly look between Frasier and Haugen, then to the pale Asian man, who seemed to glare through his one good eye at him. The knife appeared from the side again, stabbing the man through the heart in a frenzy of jabs. The screams became wet chokes as arterial blood sprayed in all directions.

Rex silently howled. His physically unharmed body jerked like a jackhammer as he mainlined the victim's pain, effectively watching himself be stabbed to death. Then a wash of unfamiliar sensations flooded through him as he consciously experienced what it was like to die ... moments before his own body followed suit.

Chapter Thirty-Two

Milton could barely take his eyes away from Clarion's piercing gaze as she studied him curiously.

'I expected you to be different in The Real,' Clarion said flatly.

Theo and Baxter shifted nervously, uncomfortable with the odd situation that had developed. They had abandoned the van when it became apparent that even their mysterious benefactor couldn't deflect the entire police force from them, and hurried the rest of the way to the club in broad daylight. Risking side streets and alleyways they had managed to avoid scrutiny from CCTV, which conveniently failed as they neared it.

In little over forty minutes they reached Pulsar and had been surprised to find it was already open with a dozen revellers already drinking. Clarion sat in her mobile throne, irritated that they had arrived without Rex. What's more, she had been following the progress of the convicts on the streams and wondered aloud why she shouldn't turn them in.

Clemmie had frostily retaliated that she would not only

make sure the Children of Ellul were brought down with them, but she'd also find a way to cram the wheelchair up Clarion's backside.

That had provoked her two henchmen to reach for their matte black 3-D printed sidearms secreted under the table. Clarion raised her good hand to stop them, her gaze locking on Milton. It turned out she used to be one of his loyal subscribers for his SPACE game review stream.

'Killer Kaiju used to be very funny,' she said without irony.

Baxter was unsuccessful in suppressing a snort of derision.

'I'm a barrel of laughs when people are not trying to murder me,' Milton shot back quietly.

Theo wasn't sure, but swore there was a flicker of a half-smile on Clarion's face and the henchmen sat back down, keeping their weapons visible on the table.

'Of course, I haven't watched it since SPACE tried to claim me as another victim.' She switched her gaze to Theo. 'For spending too much time there.'

With nothing to lose, Theo quickly filled her in on his search for his mother. She was intrigued with the identification of Haugen, and paid close attention when he gave the details of the Hampstead address. She soaked it all in without interruption. Only when he mentioned they had a Slif helping them from the other side did she break her silence.

'Are you certain?' She looked between Clemmie and Theo.

'As best as we can tell.' Clemmie rubbed her rash, which was becoming increasingly itchy. 'But don't forget, the others seem very much against us.'

Clarion indicated Clemmie's neck. 'Do you still feel it?'

Clemmie nodded. 'Don't worry, it's merely a side effect, it will fade. Pheromone tracking is real. We publish on message boards trying to alert people to the true dangers of SPACE, which people then label as conspiracy theories.' She fixed Theo with a look before continuing. 'The virtual stimulant triggers your body to produce specific pheromones which can be tracked with an app on that.' She tapped Theo's rig, which was sitting on the table with the others. 'Pheromones can carry for a few miles, but fade away within the hour. The rash is a side effect from the body being forced to create a chemical reaction.'

'Then I suppose the whole Children of Ellul is not just you being batshit bonkers? You actually know this stuff.'

It was the first time Baxter had spoken since they'd arrived and he was beginning to feel left out.

A smile grew on Clarion's face, her warm beauty shining out despite her disfigurement.

'I don't just sit here like some petty criminal trading black market wares. Ellul's philosophy is the principle of a movement that warns about the dangers of singularity.'

'Ah, that old chestnut.' Milton leaned back in his chair, shaking his head.

The runaway train of artificial intelligence was a favourite scaremongering argument bandied about by conspiracy nutters and eminent scientists eager for more funding. Despite decades of stirring the pot, doomsday had failed to manifest in the envisaged Skynet-computer-takes-it-all type scenario.

'It already happened. Right under our noses.' Their united confusion made Clarion half-smile. 'Precisely my point. Everybody was looking at robots and artificial intelligence to be the point of singularity, while over here –' she extended her hand, unfurling her fingers like a blossom – 'artificial life prospered and became sentient. *That* was the singularity, all made possible by Emotive.'

Theo held up his hand to stop her.

'I appreciate you have a higher cause, but I'm simply looking for my mother and for all I know, she might be dead by now. That –' he indicated to her still-blossomed hand – 'is not my concern. Sorry.'

'But it's your mother's.'

Theo leaned back in his chair, unable to hide his frustration.

'She was just trying to pay the bills. Got indebted to a loan shark, became a pimp for emo-thieves ...'

He stopped himself, realising just how bad a picture he was painting of Ella.

'And then she discovered the truth,' Clarion said simply.

Milton was curious. 'Which is?'

Clarion took time to look around the club. The dance floor was beginning to populate with dancers gyrating beyond the cone of silence.

'Humanity has a right to be free.' She fixed her gaze back to Milton. 'I have no issue with simulated life. But I don't believe the two should merge.'

'Merge ...?' Milton frowned.

'Technology finds ways to blur the boundaries in ways we never anticipate. We are infusing the virtual world not just with our avatars, but the chemical keys to our brains, our *consciousness*.' She lightly touched her forehead. 'Maybe our souls. The very thing that makes us human. Your mother witnessed the suffering in this world, and that guided her to the truth.'

Theo waved his hand in disagreement. 'No. That led her to being *kidnapped*.'

Clarion's ordinarily cool expression seemed softer. 'Theo, the very fact Slifs are helping those chasing you, while another is assisting you, shows there are divisions within SPACE. You have to ask yourself, what do both sides want?'

'Money,' Baxter said with a simple shrug. 'It always comes down to money.'

Clarion shook her head dismissively. 'Every emo-trader in the streets is looking to make quick cash. It's happened throughout history – bootleggers with liquor, drug dealers – but those at the top did it for power.'

Milton was beginning to lose track of the conversation. 'The power of what, exactly?'

'Control over the singularity. The merging of both worlds.'

Clemmie dabbed a napkin over the glass grazes on her cheek and was relieved to see there was no more blood.

'A bunch of influential people are using an ex-soldier and corruption in the police force to ... what? Seize control of that fusion?'

Clarion nodded. 'AR weapons in The Real, drones controlled between worlds –' she pointed at Clemmie – 'tracking you from SPACE to a back alley in London ... it is all coming together.' She looped her forefinger and thumb. 'SPACE is considered a basic human right. So if people here can control it, they can control the very fabric of global society.'

'And the Slifs?'

'I'm sure those aiding the singularity are no doubt think-ing they will have the upper hand when it's time. After all, money means nothing to them, so they pander to mankind's hubris, then at the last moment they will turn and bite the hand that feeds them.' She snapped her fingers. 'However, there is a small group of them that sees the dangerous game being played could lead to the destruction of SPACE, their very ecosystem. The end of their world.'

'And you know this how?' Clemmie asked. 'I thought you don't go there any more.'

Clarion cast a look at Blackeyes. 'We do our best to liaise with our allies. As I say, I have no problem with sims.'

Theo rubbed the pain mustering between his eyes.

'Somehow I don't think that kept my mother awake at night.'

'Then you misjudge her.' Clarion stared at Theo with her usual frosty attitude. 'She could have easily imparted news of her debts to you instead of leading you on a merry dance. Did you ever ask yourself why she did that? Why did the good DI Frasier frame you for murder rather than shoot you in the head? Why has Rutger Haugen, a trained killer, had such apparent trouble stopping you four.' She pulled a face. 'You are hardly SAS material.'

'Yet here we are,' Theo said, with as much sarcasm as he could muster.

The truth was that he had found Ella's little treasure hunt a waste of time – nothing more than an irritant to prevent in-formation from falling into the wrong hands. She could have easily written it all down and hidden it in the apartment.

A thought struck Clemmie and she sat up in surprise.

'Ella knows who's behind it all.' She looked at the others. 'I mean, not just who is running the Dens, but who is pushing for this singularity to happen. Remember, that was her last message. She was going to find that evidence. She thinks the answers are in that house.'

Theo felt a sinking feeling. He had pinned everything on finding his mum there, not another piece of the riddle. Clemmie reached across to squeeze his hand. He was too crushed to reciprocate. By the end of the evening his mother would probably be dead in some dingy Den, and he didn't want to waste time on a wild goose chase.

Blackeyes slid a paper-thin flexi-screen across the table. Clarion read it with a sweeping glance.

'You call it a house. I would call it a mansion. It's huge.' Theo saw an imposing ranch-like building on the screen. Clarion continued reading. 'Built on an old golf course, the deeds to the estate are held in a nest of corporate companies masking the owner's identity. We have always suspected a politician was behind it all.' She looked between them all. 'Somebody with influence, who has the police in their pocket.'

She stared into the middle distance, pondering all that had been said.

Theo could take the intolerable silence no more. He stood up and rapped his knuckles on the table to snatch her attention.

'I haven't got time to help Ellul's cause, but I need your help. Are we going to deal?'

Clarion's gaze never wavered from over his shoulder,

303

but her mouth parted in surprise. Theo spun around to see a dozen fully armoured police push the bouncers aside as they entered. It was the Trojan team that had raided his flat. Assault rifles raised, their green laser sights scythed across the dance floor. Haugen and Frasier pushed through from the back. Frasier held his badge high in the air as he shouted above the music, unheard by those in the cone.

'It's them!' hissed Theo, reaching out for Milton's shoulder to force him to stand.

Clarion's chair was already reversing through a gap in the back of the booth. Her henchmen stood, fluidly retrieving their weapons.

'Follow me,' Clarion commanded.

Theo edged around the table, glancing back in time to see Frasier wildly pointing in their direction and shouting. The lasers converged on them. He saw the muzzle flashes, but only realised they were shooting when bullet holes strafed across the table. The henchman with iridescent pupils violently convulsed as bullets ripped through his body.

Clemmie and Baxter dropped to their hands and knees to avoid the firestorm. Theo half-crouched as he followed Clarion, Milton keeping close behind.

Blackeyes brought up the rear, hunkering low and taking measured shots, forcing Haugen and Frasier to seek cover. One of the armed cops fell as his kneecap was blown off. Return fire caught the anti-noise speakers and a wave of dubstep, staccato gunfire and screams suddenly rolled over them.

A narrow passage sloped through the wall behind the booth and Theo sensed they were descending into a sub-basement. Behind, Clemmie and Baxter clambered to their feet as Blackeyes hit a panel on the wall. A reinforced door slid across with a clang, sealing them from the chaos beyond.

The passage opened into a windowless circular concrete room. Metal racks lined most of the walls, crammed with optical servers. Four techies clad in black jeans, high-tops and T-shirts sporting various anarchic logos ran in from a room opposite.

'The police have blockaded the front!' cried one young red-headed woman in a 'Lay waste to SPACE' T-shirt.

'Take what you can,' Clarion ordered, heading towards a roller shutter door that was already clattering open. 'We're evacuating.'

Milton stopped dead to watch two techies pull a large piece of hardware off the shelf, yanking the connections free as dry ice vapour seeped from its vents.

'Polariton superfluid quantum processors!'

He was impressed, never having seen the tech that formed the beating heart of SPACE in real life.

'We fight fire with fire,' Clarion commented as the techies irreverently tossed the server into the boot of a black Land Rover, one of three parked in the garage beyond the shutter. 'We're out in thirty seconds!'

Everybody turned as a loud repetitive thump came from the end of the passageway. The cops were attempting to batter the door down.

Clarion pivoted her chair next to the passenger door of the lead vehicle. The door opened and a hydraulic fork smoothly scooped the chair up, locking it seamlessly into the specially adapted passenger space. She peered at Theo.

'Your aims and Ellul's are one and the same. You have my help if you wish it. But by my rules.'

Theo glanced behind as a stressed crack sounded from the passageway. The door probably wouldn't hold much longer. Blackeyes took the wheel next to Clarion while the techies loaded up the other two 4 × 4s with more server racks and long black flight cases.

'All I want to do is find her,' Theo said resolutely.

'You will.'

Theo was still torn whether to take her word, but was in no place to negotiate. With a dull bang, the reinforced door into the club was blown apart. The distinctive clatter of heavy booted feet headed their way. Theo nodded and opened the Land Rover's rear door. Clemmie clambered in while Milton and Baxter made for the car behind. Theo joined Clemmie and hadn't the chance to close the door as Blackeyes stomped the accelerator. Momentum slammed the door shut for him.

The banshee wails of the electric engines echoed in the narrow spiralling ramp ascending from the sub-level garage. Theo craned behind to see DCI Frasier sprinting into view and opening fire. Shots sparked from the bulletproof coating of the vehicles, then he lost sight of him as they cleared the ramp's first turn and raced out into the streets of London.

Chapter Thirty-Three

Escape is easy. Staying free – that's harder.

Within an hour of evacuating Pulsar, media streams burned with footage of the police raiding a Children of Ellul terrorist cell in south-east London. Carefully framed angles showed alleged terrorists wheeled out in body bags, with no reference that they were innocent revellers executed on the dance floor.

Now Theo's picture, along with those of his friends, joined Clarion's as the manhunt widened. He was no longer a wanted murderer, he was a terrorist driven by radical idealism to destroy SPACE and bring down society. This was reinforced by footage of Frasier supervising the dismantling of the high-end tech that had been abandoned in Pulsar's basement.

In the back of the car, Theo spent the journey out of the city with Clemmie curled up next to him. She hadn't seen anybody killed before, and it rattled her. Theo was in worse shape, unable to hold back his tears, fuelled by thoughts of his mother. What the hell had she expected him to do with this information? He was just a failure who printed burgers in a fast food dive. An insignificant other.

Focusing back on the news, he watched Wayne and Kerry interviewed in their *Synger* uniforms, painting him as a quiet bloke who didn't socialise and kept himself to himself.

Jesus, he'd become the perfect terrorist stereotype overnight.

He hadn't been paying attention to where they were travelling, but noticed the Land Rover's bonnet had changed colour from black to red, then later to beige. The adaptive paint job told him everything he needed to know about Clarion; she had been preparing for this moment for a long time.

They eventually pulled over in a lay-by in some leafy Surrey suburb. Clarion's seat rotated one-eighty to face them.

'This is the moment you must decide whether you trust me or not.'

Theo and Clemmie held one another's gaze. Her eyes were wide with fear, but even so they reassured Theo; pools of chocolate that made his pulse quicken. He ran a delicate finger over the tiny scars on the side of her mocha cheek; even those looked good on her. He slowly inched forward, eyes locked, lips ready to dock ...

Clarion gave an irritated cough. They looked at her sour face.

'For fuck's sake, tame the hormones.'

Clemmie pushed herself upright, angry and embarrassed.

'I don't trust you at all, but it seems our options are *very* limited at the minute.'

That got a lopsided smile from Clarion.

'I was right about you. Smart.' She gestured around.

'These rather nice suburbs have the unfortunate distinction to be geo-locked to an area of Nu London that has been developed by sims. The locals are not entirely pleased about that, but it benefits us. The moment you ascend somebody may recognise you. Out here, the local denizens don't care so much. So this is where you will ascend and establish contact with the resistance. It is vital we co-ordinate an attack on the house from both sides simultaneously.'

Theo opened his mouth to interrupt, but Clarion held up a slender finger and continued.

'In all probability, your mother will not be there. What we hope to find are the people behind it and records of where the Dens are located. Then we can trace her.' She waited until Theo gave a curt nod of agreement. 'The four of you will ascend here. I will provide staves and skins so you can travel incognito. We have to move swiftly before the opposition can strengthen their position. While you are gone, we'll relocate for the ground assault.'

Theo hung his head, wondering if he had the strength to do this. Clemmie gently squeezed his knee twice in solidarity.

'Let's do it,' she said, pushing back into her seat to get comfortable. She wiped dried river mud particles from her rig.

Theo leaned back and studied his own headset. He had taken it off when the weight of news streams had started to crush his spirits. The rig was dented and scuffed, the white star-like crack on the visor had grown during recent punishment. He ran a grubby fingernail over the Emotive logo. The embossed winking smiley face was lined with dirt that made it more defined. He wondered if James Lewinsky had ever foreseen SPACE becoming the singularity not just of the mind, but life; had he ever dreamed it would be used for torture, twisted into an implement to overturn society?

'I'm staving you both an extra three hours,' Clarion said. Theo put his rig on and made himself comfortable, an almost impossible act with two broken ribs. 'Do everything you can not to use too much of it. You especially, Theo.'

Theo gave Clemmie one last lingering look. Even dishevelled, she still managed to look as perfect as he'd always remembered. He didn't take his gaze off her when she gave a thumbs-up to Clarion, settled back, and ascended.

Ascension was different this time. When arriving straight into SPACE it always took a few seconds to fully materialise. Uploading into a game was a swift experience as players arrived in a specially enclosed bubble, a waiting room housed on some gaming corporation's server. While it used the mechanics of SPACE to function, the world inside the bubble could be completely reprogrammed.

And now Theo found himself in a shimmering gaming cocoon, the walls just beyond arm's reach. Through them were the vaguest hints of the soaring Nu London skyline, as if viewed through constantly distorting translucent oil.

He couldn't move and had ascended in the same slumped horizontal position he'd adopted in the car, so he had a clear view across his chest, his arms resting in his lap and his legs sprawling away. His skin puckered and swelled as it deformed. He wasn't alarmed. This usually happened when wearing a different avatar skin, although unlike most games this one was not configurable.

His clothing changed to expensively tailored black trousers and tan boots. A fine cotton shirt formed across his chest, white with blue stripes – the uniform of a generic businessman. Even his hands appeared smaller, his pale fingers slender.

Then the bubble popped and he dropped a few inches to the ground – as did four complete strangers next to him. From their curious expressions as they held up their arms to examine them, he knew who they were.

'Stop looking so obvious, Milt,' he hissed to the shorter figure dressed in a plain grey tracksuit, who looked about forty and was already going bald.

'Theo? It's me. Bax.'

The new Baxter noticed a couple of passing people regarding them curiously. He poked a taller muscular man in the arm, who was standing next to him.

'Milton?'

Milton – or the prime figure of a man with chiselled movie star looks and wearing an expensive dark blue suit, his black silk shirt opened enough to show off his chest – stopped what he was doing and stared at Baxter. Then he burst into deep laughter.

'The state of you! You look like shit!'

Baxter scowled. 'No points for guessing who's her favourite.' He badly mimicked Clarion. 'Oh, I love your stream. Big fan—'

'Will you two shut up?'

They turned to look at Clemmie, or rather the image of Clarion a decade younger and without her debilitating paralysis. Her features had been refined beyond perfection,

311

and shaggy shoulder-length platinum blond hair writhed in a private stylish jet stream. Only the annoyed furrow on her brow gave any hint that Clemmie was inside. She wore a long flowing black trench coat, biker boots, jeans with an emoji of a growling cigar-chomping face on the buckle, and a black shirt with barely enough buttons to keep it fastened.

'What?' she barked.

Milton instantly sobered up and shook his head like a berated schoolboy. Theo self-consciously tore his gaze away and looked around.

'So, this is Synth-Town.'

In the distance, the towers of Nu London were rendered across the skyline. The simulated sun was less than an hour from setting, and the light possessed a volumetric quality only found in Hollywood movies.

The leafy real-world suburbs around them had been replaced by sprawling suburbs that were unmistakably Slif. The single-storey buildings all sported geometric quirks that would make M. C. Escher do a double take. There wasn't a right angle to be seen.

Brightly illuminated signs advertised products in a language of chirps and whistles. Even the alphabet was alien, formed from three-dimensional symbols that gave a different meaning depending on their axis and the way they shifted shape. It was a text only readable in the digital realm.

Avatars walked the streets, mostly gawping out of town tourists taking in the sights, but there were many Slifs, more than Theo had ever recalled seeing at any one time.

And one of them was standing to the side, studying them, his adaptive skin flashing through a series of patterns. Theo suddenly felt certain it was the Slif who had saved him from the police. He truly *felt* it – as if the patterns had triggered a surprising emotional response within him. This was confirmed when he noticed a chewing-gum-like blob covering the wound where the Slif had been shot.

'I'm Theo,' he said, stepping forward and offering his hand.

The Slif stared curiously at the extended hand for several seconds, but made no effort to shake it.

'Of course you are. Do you not remember me saving your life?'

Theo sheepishly retracted his hand. 'I looked sort of different then.'

'You all look the same to us. I'm Clive,' it said, giving a slight bow.

Baxter sniggered, gaining an inquisitive look from Clive. It was more than a look; Baxter could feel the irritation as physical waves.

'I just thought a Slif would have a more ... a different name, is all.' He lapsed into silence.

Clive abruptly turned and indicated they should follow.

'Clarion informed us of what is needed. We have much to do.'

Theo fell in step with Clive. 'She was a little fast and loose with the details.'

'We must weaponise. There are a number of tools that have been developed here to impact your world.'

'So it was you who dropped the AR grenades, sent the Echo, diverted the police?'

'I have been tracking you closely.'

'Why?'

'It was like playing a game,' Clive answered without a trace of irony.

Theo shot a look at his friends, each wondering if the Slif was joking. After a couple of yards, walking across a hexagonal plaza, they reached one of ten billowing gas doughnuts some ten feet in diameter, that pulsed a soft yellow. It was an official booster portal that allowed commuters to zip around the city without wasting too much valuable immersion time. Clive pressed what passed for his palm against a floating scanner and with a *whump*, the portal turned purple, indicating his preprogrammed destination had been confirmed. He gestured to it.

'Please follow.'

'Where are we going?' Clemmie asked suspiciously.

'Where we need to be.'

Theo positioned himself between the Slif and the portal.

'Why have you been tracking me?' he demanded, hoping his new skin was intimidating the creature.

'Because your mother asked me to,' Clive said simply, then pushed Theo out of his path and stepped into the portal. The Slif appeared to stretch as he was pulled into the void with a faint plop.

'Talkative fella, isn't he?' said Milton, grinning with the novelty of a new SPACE experience. He followed Clive without hesitation.

They portalled into the Market, just to the side of a busy thoroughfare. Theo instantly recognised the narrow warren of sloping streets, with other buildings twisting high above them. Clemmie picked up on his wariness as soon as she appeared.

'Relax, nobody's going to recognise us.'

She flashed him a smile which failed to hide her own reservations.

A frisbee-sized police drone silently cruised overhead without giving them a second scan. As they joined the busy street, they spotted several more drones snooping over the crowd, all displaying vPolice insignia.

'They're not taking any chances,' Milton said. 'They're everywhere.'

Taking a branching side street, Theo caught up with Clive.

'How do you know my mother?'

'She came to us for help. Which is unusual as Meats usually assume only they have the answers.'

'Meats?' echoed Theo, although the meaning was clear.

'When she told me what she had uncovered, I knew the time for action was upon us.'

They took another road which curved downwards and entered a tunnel crossing under the main avenue. Theo's internal map indicated the tunnel system was entwined, like walking through a hollow knotted lace. It opened into a new narrow avenue packed with both Slifs and people. More busy walkways criss-crossed above, giving occasional glimpses of the stacked levels. A majority of storefronts displayed old books with fading covers or antique collectable toys. Clive took another turn and Theo lost all sense of direction as they pushed further into the labyrinth.

'What did she tell you? Why you? What did—?'

Clive suddenly stopped, his head cocked to the side.

'You are a fountain of questions.'

'And you're not answering any of them,' spat Theo, instantly regretting his sharp tone. A kaleidoscope of tie-dyed ripples passed across Clive's chest. Theo looked at them and held out his hands helplessly. 'I don't know what that means!'

'Emoji has transcended,' Clive said, with a hint of pride that trickled across his body in a smattering of light green pixels, and Theo swore he felt it too. 'This indicates that I want to be short-tempered, but I should be patient instead.' He gestured to a door. 'We are here.'

Without further explanation, he entered.

'Wow,' cooed Milton as he looked around the geodesic room with wide eyes.

The shiny grey and black surfaces had a hint of iridesence occasionally flowing through them, giving the impression they were alive. Six large code printers stood in a circle at the hub of the room, five times larger than the one they'd seen at the pet store. Another Slif was waiting for them.

'Freaky up close, aren't they?' said Baxter quietly, nodding towards the Slifs.

At first Theo thought the mottled skin tones were the only difference, but as the two creatures conversed in their own language he could see many subtle nuances in the shape of their faces and body language. They were certainly two different entities.

Clive finally turned to the humans and introduced his companion.

'This is . . .'

He uttered a string of sharp high-toned whistles and clicks and looked expectantly at Baxter.

'Um ...'

'If you have a problem with the accent, you can call her Xif.'

'*Her?*' Baxter blurted before embarrassment kicked in. He pointed between them. 'Sorry, I just don't see ...' *the difference* faded on his lips.

'Keep digging that hole,' Milton muttered with an overbearing sense of smugness.

'The difference is optional,' said Xif in a definite female voice, then both the Slifs burst into interference, or it could have been laughter. It was difficult to tell.

Theo gave two quick claps for attention.

'Wonderful! Xif, it's a pleasure, but right now I need answers. Clive, why did Ella come to you?'

'I am the face of the resistance here,' he said simply. Then he indicated himself from head to toe. 'But I'm in disguise.'

Again Theo had no idea if it was another joke, so he let it go.

'How did she find you?'

'She's a very resourceful woman. You should be proud to be biologically connected.' Theo felt a pang of guilt as Clive scrutinised him. 'She said you took after her. That's why she chose to guide you into this through a series of steps. Although she made me promise to watch out for you as you would undoubtedly require assistance.'

Theo blinked, offended. '*Undoubtedly?* If you were watching me then you should've seen I needed help from the very first day!'

Clive circled the printers, checking each one as he spoke.

'Working in the Dens Ella came across the Joy Divisions.' He noticed Theo's frown deepen. 'They are the sites your people come to get their endorphin spikes. You would call them red-light districts.'

'Why haven't vCrimes shut them down?' Clemmie asked.

'It's not so simple. Partly because they are hidden in plain view as real locations in SPACE. You travel there, then you enter a bubble.'

'Like a game bubble?' said Milton.

'Except this is a bubble within a bubble, if you like. Free of interference from the System, and of course, the Meat.'

Baxter felt a little offended. 'Meat?'

'In a Joy Division, anything goes. Sex, murder and everything in between. They have been throwing innocents off buildings in The Real just so rich people can experience death, before being snatched out at the very last second, of course. Extreme hedonism. I don't see the attraction myself, but how you entertain or eradicate yourselves is no direct concern of mine.' Clive sounded as if he could have been talking about cattle. 'You think you are our gods here – the truth is we think of you merely as operating systems.' Their shock amused him. 'Emotive built a world that works on the synaptic impulses of your brains and the chemical sensations of your emotions, so things feel real. Including us.' He patted his chest for emphasis. 'We are the logical evolution of emotional artificial intelligence. We are the point when it is no longer artificial. The point at which symbiosis occurs.'

Clemmie was racing ahead.

'So without people's emotional stimulus ... you would all die.'

She carefully studied Clive's face.

He inspected a printhead with a little more thoroughness. His voice lowered.

'Extinct, I believe is a more accurate term. We need you alive to effectively feed us, in turn we keep running a world that sustains your society.'

The cattle comparison bounced back into Theo's head. Suddenly the Slif were farming people. Clive cocked his head and his eyes narrowed as he looked straight at him. Theo wondered if, somehow, his thoughts were being broadcast.

'You do know the Children of Ellul, the very group you're supporting, want to bring this all down?' Theo asked.

'No. They want to stop the singularity from expanding. As do I. There is a flipside to every ecosystem, which your mother spotted. SPACE was designed to channel the user's emotions. What they are doing with the Dens is flooding in raw, powerful emotional stimuli without the usual safe-guards and without any user actually experiencing it.'

Clemmie was the first to get it.

'They're overdosing the System!'

'Yes.'

Clemmie caught Theo's look. 'It's like an oil spill.' She pointed at Xif. 'These guys evolved with SPACE giving a balance – one person in with all their emotional baggage. Now they're piping in emo, without the people.'

'It is environmental damage at the highest levels. Too much is toxic, and it overloads us. Kills us, for want of a better phrase.'

Milton paced around the printers, examining them closely.

'That's why you need the Dens taken down.'

Now Xif spoke up. 'Without them, the Joy Divisions would cease to be, and the balance returns.'

Clemmie was thoughtful.

'But not all of you believe that, right? A couple of Slifs took potshots at Theo and me.'

Xif's head bobbed back and forth, a motion Theo belatedly realised was a negative shake of the head.

'No. They are working with the Meat—' Xif began.

'Excuse me,' Baxter interjected. 'I'm finding the term *Meat* a little offensive.' He looked at his friends for support. 'No?'

Milton shook his head. 'Not at all. Don't you call them Virts?' He smiled at Baxter's scowl, then gestured to Xif. 'Please continue.'

'People are using Slif labour to protect the Joy Divisions. Those Slifs are the ones developing the technology that reaches into your world.'

'The pheromone tracker, the AR grenades ...' Clemmie ticked them off on her fingers.

Clive gave an odd up-and-down head bob of agreement.

'All items we managed to steal to help our cause. They see their work as enhancing the singularity, which in time will see Slif triumph over human. Which brings us to this.'

He gestured towards the code printers.

A thought struck Clemmie. 'Partly because of what else?'

Milton gave her an impatient look – he was more interested in the printer set-up. Clemmie pressed Clive.

'I asked you why the police here hadn't closed down the

Joy Divisions. You said *partly because they were hidden in plain sight*. So what is the other part?'

'Because the vPolice are not governed from here. They have a single dedicated vCrimes unit that controls all of the UK's virtual hubs.'

'And where's that?'

'The new headquarters for the City of London Police.' Clive waved a finger at Theo. 'Your mother obtained vital information from the Dens about who led the corruption within the force. Information so sensitive we haven't even dared share it with the Children of Ellul in case they become compromised.'

Xif took over. 'There is a traitor within vCrimes who deliberately obfuscates every Den investigation. Somebody high up in the conspiracy to expand the singularity. They've always been one step ahead. Only you four have managed to blindside them. Beforehand, everybody who has attempted to expose them has vanished, like your mother, and died.'

Theo winced. Tact obviously wasn't a Slif strong point.

Xif continued without noticing. 'They have deleted files, concealed truth, wormed into the high levels of government to get their way.'

'Such as blackmailing people attending slave auctions, like the recording we helped your mother steal,' Clive said. 'Many who attend such auctions have been on the inside for a long time, but others, a few top politicians in that instance, were just in it for the taboo. That makes them easy targets to blackmail. The key influencers are in government, the military, the police and the media. Nothing is out of their reach. They can even conceal the details of an entire estate in Hampstead, which has been revealed as the hub of all our problems.'

Clemmie felt butterflies in her stomach and a rising sense of nausea.

'We still don't know who actually owns the property,' Theo said to Xif, although his gaze never left Clemmie.

'Oh, we do,' Clive cut in. 'Dominic Lewinsky.'

Only Milton and Theo reacted to the name. Milton regarded the others' blank looks with surprise.

'Seriously? Dominic Lewinsky?' He slapped his own forehead to emphasise his point, then extended his hands to indicate the entire universe around them. 'The son of James Lewinsky, the founder of all of this!'

Chapter Thirty-Four

'I have literally no idea who he is.'

Baxter responded to Milton's geek-fest with an expression verging on pity.

Milton sucked in a breath and calmly, but swiftly, explained.

'Lewinsky's son became bitter when his father announced he was giving away his creation for free. He saw that emotional interfacing was the next big thing, a new iteration of the web, so like Tim Berners-Lee ...' He stumbled to a halt when Baxter gave a little shake of the head. 'Do you know nothing of history? The bloke who practically invented the internet?' Baxter shrugged and Milton bit off the sarcasm ready to spew forth. 'Berners-Lee gave it away as a gift to the world. Lewinsky followed in his footsteps.'

'What knobs,' Baxter said in disbelief. 'But Lewinsky was a billionaire.'

'Later. Through Emotive, the wetware and optical servers, but the SPACE architecture he created, he ensured that remained in the public domain. His only son, Dominic, resented the fact his father had given away the rights to SPACE.'

Theo nodded. 'There was a big lawsuit about it when we were kids. He claimed his family owned SPACE and therefore everything in it. Including personal property, financial institutions, companies ...'

Baxter nodded, only now understanding the scope of the ousted son's rage. He glanced at Clemmie, who stood in the corner, arms folded. She had heard this all before but, despite herself, was finding Milton's recap useful. The Slifs' news about the City of London Police had upset her more than she cared to admit and now something about it was nagging on the edge of her conscience, a vague memory demanding attention. She avoided Theo's eye.

Milton paced the room. 'Only after James died about sixteen years ago, was it revealed that he hadn't left Emotive to Dominic, he had given it to the board of directors. Dominic had to deal with a trust fund.'

Baxter's lip curled. 'Poor rich bastard.'

'Dominic tried to win back the rights, but it was too late by then. That case bankrupted him.'

Clemmie finally spoke up above the gentle whirr of machinery as Clive and Xif started the code printers.

'My stepmother met Dominic Lewinsky once. I remember her telling me when we were in college. He was running for Mayor of London ...'

'Somebody with political aspirations,' Theo said, paraphrasing Clive.

Clemmie was lost in a maelstrom of conflicting thoughts and concepts as the code printer's articulated arms began forming lines of bio-code.

'He wants SPACE back.'

Milton joined her, watching the squirming strands of code issuing from the printheads as they were precisely arranged on a smooth cradle that constantly adapted to mould the creature's shape. It was as if the printer was piping lines of icing to form a cake, except this confectionery was already squirming with life. Milton was clearly fascinated with the process, but his attention was torn as the Lewinsky story was something he had studied with great interest.

'More than that. Lewinsky senior had seen the impact the internet had on the world. He foresaw SPACE would be even more encompassing. He didn't want governments or corporations getting in here.' He tapped the side of his head. 'He saw this as the seat of control.'

A family feud, Clemmie thought. All of this because of a clash of ideology. She stared at the printers weaving three-dimensional layers of moving code. It put her in mind of knitting, something her grandmother used to do. Her real mother's mother had been a rebel in her youth: a political activist, an animal rights evangelist, and an anti-war campaigner. Clemmie was certain she had inherited her firebrand mentality.

It certainly didn't come from her father, who was the poster child for the Keep Calm and Carry On meme that refused to die with each successive generation. She knew he had a steely determination, but had never understood how such a placid demeanour had allowed him to build such a high-profile career in the police, yet he was now a superintendent and, according to her stepmother, on the verge of becoming chief superintendent. That made her proud; her father had always been supportive. The one she looked up to. The very notion that there could be a traitor in his department worried her. Her involvement with Theo would undoubtedly ruin his career. For all she knew, he could have already been arrested on some trumped-up charge of aiding and abetting her, especially as she had used his secure rig to access a restricted military database.

Guilt weighed heavy on her. She had helped a friend at the risk of her family – how could she justify that? She looked sidelong at Theo. He looked preoccupied as Milton excitedly recorded its creation for use on his stream once the madness was over. In college she had been mortified to develop a crush on Theo. She had hinted at her university preference in a distant hope they could go there together and start afresh, but had finally consigned Theo to the scrapyard of friendship when it became apparent he had no ambition other than to work in a burger restaurant. Only in the last few days had she seen the old spark in him, the gluon to her quark.

Her focus was brought crashing back to the half-formed creature forming under the six revolving printers as it suddenly thrashed. It was a massive snake, about fifteen feet in length and, at the points where it was almost complete, two feet in diameter.

'What exactly is this?'

'A synthetic life weapon,' Xif said as if the answer was obvious.

'Do we need it?'

'Are you joking?' gasped Milton. 'This is next-generation stuff!'

Clemmie watched Clive and Xif supervise floating

control screens as they adjusted the printers' parameters. She thought it was an odd step backwards that she and the others could access their rigs' HUDs while in SPACE, but the life forms living here had to revert to traditional screens, albeit ones that could be conjured from thin air. She crossed to Theo, who had been taciturn for the last few minutes. Since jumping from the expressway they hadn't had chance to speak properly.

'How're you holding up?' she asked tentatively.

Theo forced a smile. 'Home-grown terrorist weapons weren't *quite* what I had in mind.' He lapsed into silence. 'Clem ... What they said about the City police ... Your dad.'

'They traced us to the house. Even if he wasn't there, they'd arrest him ...'

Her thoughts drifted to Frasier. A different force but very much part of the problem. If somebody as ruthless as he gained leverage over her father ... She shuddered at the prospect. She had considered asking the Slifs to find out if he'd been taken in, but the uncertainty was the only thing keeping her going.

'I've thought about this, trust me. I can't think of any way we can help him or your mum, other than by bringing Dominic Lewinsky down.'

'Sounds easy when you put it like that.'

Theo gave a thin smile, but she could see the fight was wearing him out. She tapped his arm to get a reaction.

'Chin up, soldier. We made it this far, didn't we?'

'By pure luck.'

'I like to think of it as accidental teamwork.' She smiled. 'Wasn't four people heading to the same destination our team strategy in *Avasta*? Who'd have thought when it really counted we could come together like this? Even those two.'

They watched Milton, bending to get a closer look at the printed creature's serpentine head. It was almost fully formed: wrinkled, with stubs of coarse hair which acted like sensors. He reached out a hand to touch – and was kicked up the arse by Baxter, pitching him forward. The beast's blunt head snapped at him, peeling open banana-fashion, revealing a mouth of jagged teeth that spun like circular saws. Baxter burst into laughter as Milton rounded on him with a battery of verbal abuse. Theo and Clemmie laughed hard while the Slifs watched on, completely perplexed.

They might be emotional beings, she thought, but they had yet to evolve a sense of humour.

The moment Clive received a message from Clarion informing them they were ready on the ground, the easy-going Slifs were suddenly possessed by a sense of urgency.

Theo, Clemmie, Milton and Baxter crowded around Xif as a hologram of an oversized woman's head slowly revolved over a workbench. A rig slid into place over the woman's face, then became a cutaway diagram to reveal the circuits and wetware interface.

'Why are we watching an instruction manual?' Milton asked impatiently.

'The ascension limit might be three hours, but Emotive's wetware interface was designed for a maximum of twelve.' Xif zoomed in on a set of sensors in the rig's stems that arched around the ears. Other sets were positioned between the eyes and temples. 'These interfaces directly stimulate your brains. Beyond twelve hours, simply removing the rig and disengaging the sensors *may* create biofeedback, causing a small amount of brain damage.'

The humans exchanged alarmed looks.

'Define *small*,' said Clemmie.

Xif dismissively waved off the question. 'That's irrelevant. But the damage is specific enough to put Meat ... a person,' she quickly corrected, 'into a coma they may never wake from.'

'They'd become a vegetable,' said Baxter. Then he caught Clive's question before he could ask it. 'Not *literally*. I mean ... It doesn't matter.'

Xif continued. 'It's known as Lock-in. The longer a user wears the rig, the worse it becomes. Your mother, and anybody else held in the Dens, will have been wearing them for *days*. Sudden ejection at that point could be fatal.'

'So how do we get them out?'

Xif and Clive exchanged a look. He gave her a head bob of encouragement.

'I have developed an app that helps filter the brain from receiving biofeedback.' They could feel the tangible pride emanating from her. 'The only downside is that it must be administered from here in SPACE.'

'You guys can do that?'

Clive moved his head negatively. 'It has to be *Me*— ... human to human. You essentially act as a sponge for the feedback.' Off their deepening concern he added, 'The feedback is manageable enough for two brains to absorb it via NFC without *real* harm. But it's imperative that you transfer the app here in SPACE, eject Ella and the others, before sinking back to The Real.'

Theo rubbed his chin thoughtfully. 'So even if we locate Ella in The Real, we can't eject her without also finding her avatar – which could be *anywhere*, not necessarily where we ascend to.'

Clive's head bobbed vertically up and down. 'You understand the difficulties.'

Xif replaced the headset schematic with a blueprint of the mansion.

'This is Dominic Lewinsky's residence. Clarion's people have identified private security and some powerful optical routers. We suspect they may have a temporary Den in the basement, a staging post as they move the more permanent venues around.'

'So it could be the one Clem and I found?'

Theo felt a surge of excitement. His head snapped up, but before he could ask another question, Xif held up a hand, her three fingers splayed, and rapidly continued.

'We don't know if your mother is among them.'

'Like a fence ...' said Clemmie, before realising everybody was looking expectantly at her. 'Criminals use them to temporarily hide stolen goods before moving them on.'

Xif's head bobbed. 'Yes. Setting up a Den is not something that can be done overnight. Having a temporary facility allows them to be more mobile. The house seems to have a few anti-drone measures installed, and this.' She highlighted a small server in a ground floor room. Wires feeding off connected to panels set within the roof. 'A military grade isolation shield. Similar to a firewall, it prevents any virtual or augmented attack from the outside.'

Baxter punched one fist into the palm of his hand as he studied the map.

'So we have to strike them hard on the ground.'

Xif zoomed in on the server. 'The Children of Ellul do not possess the strength of numbers. We must bring the shield down first.'

Theo, Baxter and Clemmie exchanged glances. Only Milton nodded in understanding.

'It's a geo-locked quantum server?' Xif's head twitched in acknowledgement. Milton was in his element as he explained to the others. 'The operating architecture is stored in a data house in SPACE. The data is entangled, which means if we can't get to the physical, we can with the virtual. Problem is the data house needs to be positioned in the same geo-locked location as the mansion, so we can't ascend directly from inside.'

'We find and hack it *here*, then launch a physical assault on the building,' Clive finished. He pointed at Baxter and Milton. 'You will both be on the ground. They —' a finger wagged at Clemmie and Theo — 'will stay.'

After that, Milton and Baxter were left with Xif to strategise their AR requirements for the upcoming assault, while Theo and Clemmie were ushered to an armoury bristling with weapons floating in mid-air in neat rows. Clive led them to a rifle that Theo had last seen from the business end. When the Slif hefted it into his arms, another immediately replenished the floating display.

'They're Killers,' Theo said with disdain. 'Posted from *Avasta*.'

Clive shoved the weapon into his reluctant hands. The metal felt cold and solid, possessing just enough weight to give a menacing impression. He tried to hand it back to Clive, who stopped him with a little nudge.

'There will be avatars and Slifs with these, all with the express purpose of stopping you.'

Theo didn't even have to wonder if he had what it took to kill; the very thought sickened him. He was surprised when Clemmie took another from the display, click-clacked the slider on the side to charge it up and raised it to eye level, peering down the barrel with the stock pressed against her shoulder. Exactly as she had done in countless games. She cocked a questioning eyebrow at Theo. He wisely said nothing.

Clive indicated a slider at the side.

'This controls the emo-charge. It is set to kill here.' He pushed the slider to the left. 'Now it's merely crippling pain.'

Something caught Clemmie's eye and she wandered to the far wall with a faint 'Wow!' of excitement. Clive took a rifle for himself then led Theo to another rack filled with small thin black squares, not dissimilar to antique mobile phones his grandparents used.

'Time slurs,' Clive explained.

'Like the ones you gave to my mother?'

'Exactly.'

Clemmie joined them, taking one to examine it. Her face lit up with delight.

'Wow, these are from *World Grand Prix IV*, the *Mad Max* mod!'

Now Theo recognised it. They had spent many a session in that game before uni. It was the last time they all had enjoyed one another's company – actually winning the gruelling post-apocalyptic race over several days, and getting drunk between ascensions. The chronicling of that game had spurred Killer Kaiju's virtual success. It had also been the moment Theo almost kissed Clemmie while both drunk in the kitchen. A moment nuked out of existence when Milton excitedly ran in to inform them that his stream was going viral.

Clive slid a finger to the right across the slur. A blue bar appeared and instantly began to recede.

'This creates a sustained field that speeds time, or ...' He slid the button in the opposite direction. The bar turned red. 'Red slows time. The field lasts for up to six weeks.' Before the bar completed its countdown, he cancelled it with a downward swipe of a finger. 'It covers a range of twenty feet.'

Theo scooped up six of the slurs; this time they were not replaced on the shelves. Each box snapped together forming a bandolier, which he tossed over his shoulder. The whole experience was reminiscent of arming up for a game, and he was warming to the experience. He picked up a familiar-looking sword straight out of *Avasta* and gave it an experimental swish through the air.

Clive gingerly snatched the blade from his hand and carefully placed it back on the rack, where it merged with its replacement. He attached a small carton to Theo's belt; it stuck as if magnetic. Theo flipped the lid to see two red eggs inside, their polished surfaces catching the light.

'Be extra careful with those,' Clive cautioned. 'Code interrupts. Whatever they attach to—'

'They freeze the code.' Theo finished the obvious. 'Question is why.'

'Handy if you want to walk through walls.' Clive took a spherical drone from the display and tossed it into the air, where it hovered and obediently followed him when he moved. 'Just be careful. You don't want to go falling through SPACE.'

The very notion had never occurred to Theo. What lies beyond the virtual world?

'What's this?'

Clemmie picked up a small cylinder the size of an asthma inhaler. Multiple segments could be rotated around, but gave no indication of their purpose. Clive snatched it from her hands and carefully held it in his palm.

'That is a Physics Engine. It's not wise to tamper with the laws of physics, even if they can be anything you wish them to be.'

Theo plucked it from Clive's hand before he could stop him.

'Sounds too useful to leave behind.'

He tried to attach it to his belt, but it wouldn't lock into place. With no pockets he resorted to keeping a firm hold on it.

The Slif's gaze lingered on the device before he decided not to argue. He looked between Theo and Clemmie, his skin rippling with a trace of jaundice. There was no mistaking the fear Clive was experiencing.

'Now, we fight.'

Chapter Thirty-Five

Not only had the adaptive paintwork rendered Clarion's Land Rover a sporty red; the vehicle's skin had lifted and tucked, altering its profile enough so as not to be identified by traffic cameras and passing police drones. Police automatically ignored loud paintwork; fugitives were supposed to be stealthy.

Milton ejected from SPACE with a start, his leg spasmodically kicking out. He was already suffering a headache like a knife in the eye. It was completely disorienting to find he was now in Clarion's car, with Blackeyes driving. Baxter was folded next to him, removing his rig and rubbing his eyes.

'Where're the others?'

Milton's mouth was fuzzy and dry and he welcomed the bottle of water offered by Clarion.

'We swapped you out.' Clarion studied them with concern. 'You have both been in for eighty-two minutes extra. How do you feel?'

'Like somebody kicked me in the ear,' said Baxter, wincing. 'Clem and Theo?'

'Still there. Theo at least has had some time to acclimatise himself.'

Milton closed his eyes and tilted his head back, hoping the unpleasant sensations washing through his skull would vanish.

'But if they spend too long—'

'They understand the consequences. And it gives us more motivation to act swiftly.'

Baxter peered out of the window. It was now night. Occasional grand houses, set back from fortified gates and long driveways, occasionally passed.

'I'm guessing this is Hampstead.'

Clarion nodded and revolved her seat to face the windscreen. Baxter checked behind to see only one other Land Rover was following them, a grey minibus behind that.

'When you said army, I imagined the assault party being a tad bigger.' He caught the briefest half-smile on Clarion's face.

'Surprise is our best weapon.'

Xif had kitted them out in SPACE and explained the plan which, at best, Milton had described as 'desperate' and Baxter had countered with 'suicidal'.

The trailing minibus contained thirteen Children of Ellul, picked up from other cells across the city, and armed to the teeth. The Land Rover with Theo and Clemmie had been repositioned at the far side of the estate, with the techies from Pulsar. There, they would co-ordinate drones and other technical aspects of the strike which all hinged on Theo, Clemmie, and the Slifs to deactivate the isolation shield.

'Confirmed – Dominic Lewinsky and Rutger Haugen are

in residence,' came a steady voice over their rigs. The techies were surveilling the house from afar. 'They arrived by a private aircraft. We count twelve armed security guards in addition to fifteen catering staff who just arrived via the front entrance. Looks like they're preparing for a dinner party. Sensors detect another thirty bodies in the basement. Their vitals are low.' Clarion and Blackeyes exchanged a look of concern. 'Highly likely the people they're transitioning from the Den.'

Milton leaned forward, his head between the seats in front.

'Is Theo's mum in there?'

'It's impossible to make any positive identifications,' came the curt reply.

Clarion consulted a display panel on the dash.

'We'll be there in thirty seconds.' She touched a discreet earpiece. 'All teams deploy. Launch the strike.'

A flashing warning light pinged in the corner of Rutger Haugen's rig. The perimeter alarm had been triggered to the south. He held up a hand to stop Dominic Lewinsky talking.

'What?' snapped Lewinsky, scratching his uneven black beard.

Since the acrimonious split with his father he had refused to wear a rig. He was fully aware of the emotional addiction people developed with the virtual and swore he would never get sucked in himself.

'Possible intrusion ...'

Haugen ignored Lewinsky's further questions. He despised the overweight tub of lard and everything he stood for. But he spent money like it was oxygen, so the mercenary couldn't ask for a better paymaster.

Haugen ran down the corridor and out into the elaborate circular entrance hall. He took the broad sweeping staircase two steps at a time to the first floor and turned left into a grand room that was having the final touches applied for the dinner party. His first instinct was that some of the catering staff had once again sneaked off for a shag in the extensive manicured grounds.

He sidled between a chatting pair of waiters, who were adjusting one another's bow ties, and opened the sweeping patio doors. The wide veranda offered southern views across the rolling lawns, swimming pool and helipad, which was currently occupied by Lewinsky's quadcopter. All framed against the distant illuminated pinnacles of London.

He scanned the grounds, waiting for his AR rig to pick out the strays. He was surprised when the graticules flagged movement at the top edge of his visor. He tilted his head skywards to centre the targets.

Drones. Three of them.

As his head moved, he gave an impulsive snort of surprise when his display suddenly began to fill up with more drones. Ten ... then thirty ... fifty ... just on the periphery of the ground's airspace, held back by the isolation shield.

An entire squadron continued to fill his AR until it was rendered useless as he could see nothing but a mass of graticules. With a bright flare, three pen-sized rockets arced from different points in the sky, straight for the house.

Under his guidance, the paranoid Dominic Lewinsky had installed aerial countermeasures to combat any inquisitive drones. The small automated EMP guns swivelled on their gimbals and silently blew the missiles out of the air as they crossed over the grounds.

With his display rendered useless, Haugen tugged it off and peered into the darkness. He could only see two drones leading the pack, keeping beyond the isolation shield's perimeter.

Rocket pods flared again. This time the missiles arced towards the building unhindered as the EMP guns recharged. Haugen felt the floor tremble as they fell short and impacted in the grounds. The explosions packed little punch, but as the trees erupted into flames he realised that wasn't the point – they were volatile incendiaries.

He was already running back into the house when the intruder alarms finally sounded. His hand knuckled around the grip of his shoulder-holstered Beretta. Despite the tech available, he knew cold steel and bullets were always reliable. He'd save the last one for Frasier if he was the cause of this new setback.

Blackeyes skidded the Land Rover to a halt halfway down the cul-de-sac as rolling clouds of orange fire silhouetted the grand mansion from behind. It was a huge building; no more than twenty years old, it was a fluid composition of Georgian styling accented with modern curves. A pair of impressive gates blocked the driveway, surrounded by a thick stone wall.

Baxter tumbled out of the car, his eyes wide at the spectacle.

'Wow!'

Milton followed, already adjusting his rig with the mods Clarion had supplied. On his display, a transparent dome appeared around the house.

'Shield is up,' he informed the others.

The second Land Rover and minibus caught up with them and fifteen mean-looking Children of Ellul exited with military precision and took cover behind vehicles parked in the road. Wearing rigs and bulletproof vests over their street clothes, and armed with automatic rifles, they were restless for action. Blackeyes joined them, assuming command from the front.

'Remember,' Clarion called out to them all, 'if you pass through the shield while it's up it will render all your tech dead and they outgun us.'

Baxter watched wide-eyed as another explosion lit up the landscaped front garden, before remembering his role in the attack. He launched a beacon app on his rig, sending an encrypted broadcast into SPACE revealing his position.

Milton leaned against the car and waited. He could do nothing with the shield up. He only hoped the drones would keep Haugen and his team busy before they discovered the truth.

Chapter Thirty-Six

Theo and Clemmie held on tight to the skiff's handrails as Clive raced along the fast-moving virtual express. The skiff was nothing more than a hovering platform with raised rails mounted behind a control console. The uninspired design was something they were coming to associate with the Slif community.

'Not much further,' he informed them as they zeroed in on Baxter's real-world beacon.

They sped along a curved banked road that looked more at home on a Nascar track. Theo and Clemmie knocked into one another as they adjusted their balance so as not to be thrown off. The Physics Engine rattled in a small glovebox, the only place on the skiff Theo could put it as the device continued to refuse to adhere to anything on his body.

Clive pointed to the warehouses off the expressway.

'They house virtual streaming centres. The beacon is coming from inside that one there.'

He indicated one with a roof twisted into a gigantic Möbius strip.

They took an exit ramp and brought the skiff to a stop

beneath the underpass. There was nobody around; there simply wasn't any reason for people to waste valuable ascension time coming to the city fringes.

They debarked and watched for any sign of activity. It was eerily calm. There was no simulated weather here, no rustle of leaves or wild animals searching for food, as they had become accustomed to in the Parkways. For the first time, Theo was aware of the chasm between worlds.

A ripple of pain passed through his skull and his vision momentarily blurred. He squeezed his fists tightly around the rail until he felt pain. That focused him back to the moment. A glance at his timer showed that he was fast approaching almost three hours of extra time. Countdown to schizo, he thought morbidly.

'Remember where we parked,' Clive said to Theo as they jumped from the skiff. 'This is your respawning point.'

'Funny,' muttered Theo.

He started walking towards the building.

'What's the plan?' Clemmie asked, keeping pace with her gun pushed firmly against her shoulder as she looked down the barrel.

Theo cockily balanced his rifle over his shoulder.

'We blast our way in. Blow shit up.'

Clive launched his drone ahead of them as he followed. The spherical aircraft's high vantage point projected into their rigs, giving them full coverage of the area. Still nothing stirred.

'Theo, Clem?' Milton's voice sounded strained. 'How close are you to bringing the shield down?'

Theo reached the massive hangar doors and gave them an

experimental shove. They were solid. He extracted a small red egg from the carton on his belt and weighed it in his hand.

'We're on our way in.'

'Good,' came the reply, followed by a grunt and a series of loud cracks. 'We have some seriously unhappy company down here!'

Theo chucked the egg at the wall. On impact it spattered like a burst water balloon, staining the door a slightly darker colour as it froze the operating code.

Clive raised his rifle.

'Let's go!'

Theo girded himself and ran for the wall, expecting to slam into it. Instead, the frozen code invalidated any collision detection, and he stepped through like a wraith.

'Down!' Baxter bellowed, yanking Milton around the waist and pulling him behind the cover of a car as bullets chewed the windows apart above them. Shattered glass, nothing more than chunks of white fragments, rained down on them.

Speaking to Theo, Milton folded himself into a foetal position and yelled into his rig.

'We have some seriously unhappy company down here!'

Baxter pressed his back against the vehicle. Next to him, Blackeyes raised his gun one-handed, blindly returning fire towards a pair of Jaguars that had skidded to a halt as they entered the cul-de-sac, sandwiching the Ellul team between them and the house.

Frasier exited the lead vehicle, using the door as a shield as he shot at them. The bullets hammered the vehicle around

Baxter. One grazed his rig with a whip-crack sound. His display glitched as he hunkered lower for cover. He'd been in many combat games before, and had considered them frighteningly realistic. But now, with his cover being systematically shredded around him, Baxter realised Emotive's *more real than real* tag line didn't really stack up. Reality was terrifying.

The resistance fighters increased their barrage as more passengers baled out of the second Jaguar behind Frasier's – rich dinner guests by the look of them, although guests who had come armed to the teeth, as they joined the shoot-out.

A pair of armed security guards crouch-ran from the house, taking positions behind the brick gateposts, and deployed suppressing automatic gunfire, pinning the Children of Ellul down.

The crystal chandelier above Haugen shuddered as something exploded in the garden outside. He crossed Lewinsky on the grand staircase as he headed for the front door. Counter to the grandeur around them, Lewinsky favoured jeans, white tennis shoes and a grubby checked shirt with a grey T-shirt underneath. Despite his scruffy appearance, there was no mistaking his arrogant confidence.

'Who is attacking us?'

Lewinsky snatched the lapels of Haugen's jacket to stop him from hurrying away.

'Frasier has the Children of Ellul pinned at the gates. His *fokking* amateur tactics led them here! I told you the man was an imbecile! And they have a hundred drone units orbiting the place.'

Lewinsky let go of Haugen and gave a pitying snigger.

'Drones won't get past the shield. They'll die if they try.'

'No, but their *incendiaries* might flush us out. They're going after the Den.'

The chatter of automatic gunfire outside intensified.

'I told Frasier not to bring them here!' Lewinsky snapped. Then his eyes narrowed. 'That Wilson kid? We should've just killed the bitch when she turned against us.'

Haugen slipped his rig back on, pulled out his Beretta and chambered a round.

'You told us not to – too afraid of what she might've said to people. Like a coward. Now outta my way!'

He shoved past Lewinsky and out of the front door.

He was halfway to the gate when a flock of drones circled overhead and unleashed a barrage of missiles into the driveway. One struck the wrought-iron gate, which exploded in a tangle of metal that slammed into the security guard shooting through it. His rig showed the sky was filled with drones, clogging up his display with icons attempting to track every single one. He fired at two targets, but it was impossible to get a range on the cluttered headset. He tore his rig off in frustration.

Three drones flew overhead, deploying another missile towards Frasier's car at the end of the road. The detective raced away as the vehicle exploded, barrel rolling end over end towards him. But that failed to hold Haugen's attention. He was staring at the sky.

He slid his rig back on. Dozens of drones zipped back and forth, the remaining security guard firing wildly at them, but when he removed the visor there were still only three, their undercarriages catching the street lights as they zig-zagged overhead.

'*Jou bliksem!*' snarled Haugen.

The penny dropped with an alarming thud – there were just a handful of drones, each ejecting chaff in their wake. The metal strips were designed to confuse AR rigs into thinking there were *swarms* of drones out there. A simple illusion, no hacking necessary. And it had succeeded in wasting Haugen's time.

Inside the data centre hundreds of towers, each four storeys high and constructed from dozens of doughnut-shaped data dumps, flowed with torrents of data like fireflies caught in a jar. Corkscrewing ramps spiralled to each level, allowing access to any crash points, and were populated by dozens of Slifs.

Theo took it all in with despair.

'Which one is the house?'

Clive shook a device in his hand and a blazing red trail highlighted, visible to only them as it snaked to the central batch of towers. Theo broke into a run as an intruder alarm began to wail.

A Slif high on a gantry drew a sidearm and shot at Theo, blasting the ground in front of him. Theo stumbled sideways – which saved him from a head shot. Clive twisted around and, with supreme marksmanship, blew the head off the gun-toting Slif. Blue ichor splashed, and the corpse tumbled to the floor. Every Slif around them began to squeal in panic, a high-pitched sound that inflamed Theo's headache.

At his side, Clemmie dragged Theo to his feet.

'Will you stop arsing around?'

Without another word, she broke into a run, following the trail. She was so focused on it that she didn't see a Slif step in front of her, firearm raised. Clemmie was brought up short. Heart pounding, she raised her hands in surrender.

'Don't shoot,' she pleaded.

The Slif's mouth did a passable impression of a sneer and its skin pulsed with vitriolic purple hatred.

BAM!

Clemmie flinched before registering she hadn't been shot.

The Slif looked down at the gaping hole in its chest that was the size of its head. It gurgled, then keeled over. She turned around, arms still raised, to see Theo holding the rifle. His hands were shaking after the kill.

Clemmie lowered her arms and gave him a curt nod of approval.

'Hurry!' Clive shouted as he rushed past without giving the dead Slif a second glance.

Yards away they could see their target. The tower's only identifying feature was the number forty-two etched into the floor. As they reached the foot of the ramp, the warehouse door blew apart and six armed vPolice officers ran through the gap.

'Keep moving!' Clemmie shouted, pushing him up the ramp as shots pinged around them, sounding like a popcorn machine going haywire as more cops flooded into the room.

Clive pushed past, shooting at anything that moved, and continued to the second level. A floor below, Theo glanced down and wondered if the entire vCrimes unit was descending upon them. There must be a hundred of them and counting. Some had already reached the base of the ramp; others took potshots from the back.

Theo and Clemmie joined Clive on the second floor. He had stopped at a section of the tower and was inspecting the surface.

'This is running the Isolation Shield,' he confirmed.

More shots clipped the edge of the gantry, forcing the three of them to crouch low. Holding their rifles overhead, Clemmie and Theo fired wildly into the crowd. They had reduced their weapons' power, preferring to stun rather than kill. Not that it seemed to make a difference.

Clive threw his rifle over his shoulder and connected the small control pad from his belt to the tower via a thin thread of coiling light that stretched between the two.

'Optical quantum security key,' he said thoughtfully. 'It may take a little more time. Xif, can you bypass this?'

'That is a distinct possibility,' came the clipped reply.

A section of walkway close to them finally collapsed under the onslaught, taking with it an escape route.

'No rush!' Clemmie screamed sarcastically.

'Time . . .' breathed Theo.

He snatched a rectangular slur from his bandolier. He thumbed the slider so it turned red and tossed it into the crowd below.

They felt a pressure blast as the slur expanded in an orange-hued dome, trapping two dozen cops in its grip. Caught mid-run, they were suddenly moving at a twentieth of their speed. The line of police behind couldn't stop themselves from passing into the slur, becoming stuck like flies in amber.

Meanwhile, the police compressed at the front of the bubble already had hands poking through, grasping for freedom at normal speed, while their bodies, still stuck behind, moved hyper-slow. For those at the edge who had feet and legs trapped on the slur's curving edge, it was as if they'd dipped them in concrete – their bodies carried on at regular speed while their slow-moving legs painfully shattered.

Still the police poured from every direction. Theo tossed another slur in the opposite direction, snagging both them and their hail of laser blasts that now shimmered in the air as they slowed to a crawl.

'You're in,' said Xif without any trace of urgency.

Clive concentrated on the pad in his hand.

'Turning the shield off now.'

'Go for it!'

Clemmie screamed as an energy blast scorched her arm. She dropped, clutching her red-raw shoulder. The pain was so intense she feared she might black out. Her second skin warped and stretched as it disintegrated in long streamers until only her avatar was left.

Theo twisted around to see the cop who had fired. With a snarl of fury, Theo shot the avatar in the chest. The surprised cop lost his balance and tumbled backwards into the frozen mob below, painfully entering the time slur which shattered his back.

More officers sprinted up the helter-skelter. Theo set a red time slur and let it slide down the ramp. The dull *thwomp* from below told him that route up was now temporarily blocked. He kneeled next to Clemmie.

'Are you hurt?'

She gritted her teeth and nodded.

'Theo!'

Clive's warning came too late. A volley of shots came from the walkway opposite as the police used other towers' ramps to avoid the slurs. Now on the same level, there was little cover.

Theo wrapped a protective arm around Clemmie and with the other he raked his rifle from side to side. Stunned cops dropped, while others fell from the balcony – yet more replaced them, closing steadily in.

They were trapped.

Clive crouched with him, still hacking the system.

'Done! The shield is down.' He put one hand around Theo, who felt a wave of sincerity oozing from the Slif. 'I promised Ella I would protect you. You must save her.'

Something suddenly bleeped close to Theo's ear. He twisted to see Clive had planted something on his shoulder. Before he could speak, the code forming his avatar erupted and he felt a cold pulse stab through his body as his brain reacted to the sudden stimulus. Then everything went dark.

Chapter Thirty-Seven

Washed in golden firelight, Baxter watched Frasier crawl across the road away from his blazing Jaguar like a cockroach, dragging a limp leg. He sought cover behind a row of parked vehicles which bore the scars of the battle. Baxter turned as Milton cried out.

'Yeah!'

Milton punched the air as the shimmering AR shield around the house fizzled and died.

'You did it, Theo! Clem!' Baxter reported, but when they didn't respond he felt the prickles of concern.

On Blackeyes' command of 'Let's go!' the Children of Ellul charged towards the broken gate. The remaining guard took potshots at them from the driveway.

Baxter and Theo remained at the Land Rover, now pocked with so many bullet holes it looked like a sponge. Baxter's glitching visor was beginning to irritate him. He snatched it off and noticed that a long section of the left stem had been gouged open by Frasier's bullet. A fraction of an inch closer and it would have been in his skull.

He flinched as the Land Rover behind him suddenly moved. Clarion had taken the wheel and accelerated straight at the security guard.

Baxter put his rig back on and watched in alarm as the display suddenly lit up with threat warnings from the grounds, drawing his attention to four football-sized sentry guns popping from recesses on the perimeter wall posts. They spat heavy calibre bullets. Clarion's already weakened car dented with every hammer blow. It was only a matter of time before it gave out.

She struck the remaining guard. He flipped on to the bonnet and ricocheted from the windscreen in a splash of blood.

Without warning, a set of steel bollards erupted from the ground several yards behind where the gate used to be, just as the Land Rover passed over. They violently struck the underside of the car, flipping it into the air. The 4×4 smashed on to its roof and continued skidding in a shower of sparks as it ground to a halt.

The automated guns swivelled to track the vehicle.

'No!'

The bellow came from Milton, who rushed from concealment.

Baxter reached out for him. 'Milt! Get back here!'

He watched as a small AR sphere bobbed over Milton's hand. He hurled it at the nearest gun as hard as he could. The orb unpacked and the creature Xif had printed unfurled from within, extending into a huge twelve-foot worm that swam through the air.

Baxter spotted Haugen approaching Clarion's car from

the shadows. The hit man froze as the huge worm slithered across his path and burrowed head first into the nearest sentry gun.

The sentry gun vibrated, then exploded. The augmented worm flew sinuously from the fireball and seamlessly into the second gun, dealing a similar fate seconds later. The augmented creature seeped into the remaining defences' electronic system and delivered a targeted payload that fried processors and pushed the sentry's systems into over-drive. It was over in seconds. Then the worm squirmed as it sensed the wireless systems within the house, and with jaws snapping, it shrank as it spiralled into the security camera over the front door.

Seconds later the house was plunged into darkness.

Haugen hesitated, then he reacted as the drones, now unhindered by the isolation shield, flew over the house, deploying more incendiaries into the upper floors. Flames sprang from the windows as expensive furnishings ignited. Haugen shot one drone down, before hurrying back into the building.

Baxter broke from cover to join Milton at the totalled Land Rover. Blackeyes was already there, kneeling as he reached inside. Baxter and Milton skidded in the gravel drive as they dropped to help.

The vehicle's cab was a mess. Acrid electrical smoke seeped from the dashboard, forming a haze. Clarion lay at an awkward angle on the roof; she hadn't been wearing her seat belt when the Land Rover flipped. Although the roof had retained its integrity, it was her wheelchair that had broken free and crushed her back.

Blood trickled from her throat, forming a perfectly straight linear track down her alabaster skin. Her eyes had lost their piercing intensity; instead they stared into the infinite. Milton couldn't stop a choke of grief. He heard Blackeyes suck in a staccato breath as he stood, his hands shaking.

Then without a word, Blackeyes signalled to the Children of Ellul, cocked his gun, and walked purposefully towards the front door, from which catering staff were now fleeing. The civilians howled in terror when they saw the guns, but were ignored by the rebels as they entered.

A tear rolled down Milton's cheek as he looked at Clarion. 'Thank you . . .' he croaked.

Baxter spotted a dead security guard and retrieved his rifle. It felt heavier than anything he'd used in a game. The barrel and grip were still warm and it carried with it a sense of death. Or maybe Baxter was projecting that? Maybe he had spent too long in the emotional vortex of SPACE. But the one emotion he was definitely feeling was a thirst for revenge.

Milton and Baxter jogged into the grand entrance hall – and straight into a gunfight.

Their rigs enhanced the low light enough to spot security splayed flat on the circling balcony overhead, pinning the rebels down with chattering automatic gunfire. Another pair hunkered behind doorways on the ground floor, and another was tucked behind an elegant marble column that supported the vaulted ceiling. Two of their colleagues were sprawled on the floor in growing pools of blood.

From the darkness, a hand pulled Milton roughly to the

ground as more shots whipped past him. Above, thick black smoke pooled in the domed ceiling as the flames spread across the first floor. The ornate chandelier shuddered on its chain then fell, shattering on the tiled floor like a detonating star, sending crystal shrapnel in every direction.

Blackeyes, who had saved Milton, indicated for him to take cover behind a column. Milton couldn't see the man's pupils, but from the tears seeping from his inked eyes, he was suffering from the smoky haze that made breathing difficult.

'Go!'

Blackeyes wiped his eyes with the back of his hand then emptied his clip, buying Milton cover to scuttle behind a column. Once exhausted, Blackeyes ejected the clip and rammed a new one home while the guards took turns in replying. It was a stand-off, a race to see who would run out of ammo first.

Milton tried not to look at the corpses. His parents, like many, bemoaned that games were desensitising children. Across the generations it was the very same argument parents launched at children. The rise of SPACE had intensified the discussion, and Milton had even suspected that it may be true.

Until now.

The sight of real blood, the scent of burning, the dull throb of each bullet, all mounted to something that the simulated world somehow couldn't quite reach.

This was, unquestionably, reality. An unforgiving place. No extra lives, no respawning, no reboot, just a one-shot deal. Perhaps that's why people turned to SPACE to experience death. It gave them the ultimate opportunity to cheat reality.

He glanced across at Baxter, who had taken cover in a recess. The three-hundred-year-old antique cabinet that had been there was now a mass of splintered wood. Baxter pointed to his rig, then to the guards. He spoke, but his damaged rig only sent hissing static and nonsensical syllables.

Milton shook his head blankly. Baxter repeated with growing frustration, then mimed a wave motion with his hand, pointing to his own rig. Milton gradually understood. It wasn't a wave – he was mimicking the worm.

With a gesture, Milton summoned the AR ball in his hand. Up close it was a tiny cute version of the worm, coiled tightly together with its tail clamped in its mouth. He tossed it at the nearest gunman. It unfurled in mid-air, half as large as last time. The guard twisted to shoot the incoming nightmare that filled his visor. He screamed as the jaws of the creature folded around his head.

Dropping to his knees, his rig's visor displayed nothing but darkness, while the wetware interface *convinced* him he could smell the beast's vile breath and feel the heat from its maw as it painfully chomped his neck. The powerful emo addition of raw terror pumped straight into his cortex. Sobbing, he tossed his weapon aside and yanked the helmet off – suddenly realising there was no threat. Now an open target, he raised his hands in surrender.

Blackeyes slowly lowered his weapon in awe as he watched the augmented worm coil for its next victim. One by one, opponents fell to the phantom. Screaming, each man tore their rig off, relieved the creature was mere illusion. Blackeyes shot a guard who stumbled from behind a column, firing wildly as his arms flailed. The others threw up their hands in surrender.

Baxter was the first to the partially open basement door. He stopped short and peered into the Stygian darkness. Milton joined him, retrieving a torch from a stricken guard. Coughing from the acrid smoke, they entered the basement, taking each step with trepidation.

Even down here smoke was already seeping in, turning the flashlight beam into a lance of light as it swept over the unconscious women arrayed on grubby mattresses, each wearing a rig wirelessly connected to a suitcase-sized router in the corner. A handful of drips had multiple tubes running from them into five women at a time.

'Oh my God ... Are they alive?'

Milton jumped the remaining steps and dropped to his knees next to the closest woman. He could feel the bones beneath her grubby shirt, which barely moved with her shallow breaths. He didn't dare remove her visor in case it caused irreparable brain damage.

Baxter checked another woman.

'She's out cold.'

Milton looked around. 'Is Ella here?'

They quickly and methodically checked each woman, a range of ages and ethnicities, but all so deeply comatose they didn't respond to the hardest shaking. Many were so malnourished their collarbones pressed through parched skin. None of them was Theo's mother.

Blackeyes entered, stopping a few steps down as he took in the room.

'Christ ...' He called up over his shoulder. 'They're in here! We need to evacuate now!'

'There's twenty-nine of them.'

Baxter snatched the torch from Milton and swept it around the room, angling behind pillars in case they had somehow overlooked Ella.

'They detected thirty bodies down here!'

The growing density of smoke in the room curled as it was caught in his beam, almost as if it was flowing ...

He aimed the light further back, highlighting a distinctive channel of smoke caught in a faint breeze. It led to another door in the far wall, which hung slightly ajar.

He flicked a meaningful look at Milton, then raced over. A few short steps led up and out into the garden. Baxter, Milton and Blackeyes sprinted across the lawn. What was once an expensively tended oasis was now an inferno, lit by blazing trees.

Ahead, a luxury six-seater quadcopter sat on the helipad. They could just see Haugen riding shotgun, gesticulating wildly to the pilot. The aircraft sprung vertically up with a chainsaw buzz from the rotors. The downdraught blew a fury of glowing embers at them. Blackeyes shielded his face with one arm and raised his gun to shoot, but Baxter knocked the barrel aside.

'Look!' He stabbed a finger towards the aircraft.

As the quad rotated, the interior lights revealed Frasier and Lewinsky in the middle row. Ella was slumped in the back, unconscious and still wearing her rig. The lights snuffed out and the machine soared away from the house. Within seconds they had lost track of it against the dark city.

Ella was gone.

Chapter Thirty-Eight

Theo lay face down, gripping the ground as it rotated under him, convinced he was going to be thrown off. Was he back in The Real? Had the car containing his body been involved in some sort of accident?

He sat up unsteadily. Everything flickered like a faulty fluorescent and it didn't stop until he thumped the palm of his hand against the side of his skull.

Everything fell into sharp relief.

He was outside the warehouse, back where Clive had parked the skiff. His timer was deep into minus territory as it ticked over an additional four hours and counting.

'Respawned . . .' he muttered to himself.

A classic trope that had been ported from games when a character died, he now understood what Clive had meant. The Slif had linked the respawn point to the skiff just before they entered, anticipating they may require a rapid exit.

As he watched, a square formation of vPolice marched from the broken warehouse door, weapons poised. In the centre of the pack, Clemmie and Clive were pushed along on glowing red octagonal containment pads that held them in invisible confinement. Theo reached for his rifle, but felt nothing. It had vanished, along with the slurs, code freezers and the rest of his armoury.

With an ominous rumble, a police cruiser soared overhead so low that Theo ducked, expecting it to clip the overpass. All thoughts of riding to Clemmie's rescue were immediately terminated. He'd be torn into binary before he made it halfway across, and he doubted so many cops would miss a kill shot.

The cruiser landed close to the group. The disc's front section peeled back, like watching Pac-Man open his mouth, and a gangplank extended. Clemmie and Clive were unceremoniously shoved aboard to a pair of waiting figures: Frasier and Haugen.

He activated his comms.

'Anybody read me?'

To his surprise, a sudden clamour of voices acknowledged him, all talking over one another.

'Milton? Bax?'

'We're here,' Baxter confirmed, his voice grim.

'Xif here.'

'Xif, the cops have Clemmie and Clive. They're loading them aboard a cruiser. Can you track it?'

'He's still alive?'

There was a trace of relief to her words and it occurred to Theo that she and Clive must be an item – however that translated in Slif relationship terms.

'Yes, but possibly injured. Can you track them?'

'No. Police vehicles are heavily encrypted. You will have to get on board or we'll lose it.'

'We found the Den,' said Baxter.

'Ella ...?'

The pause was enough of a portent to know bad news was coming.

'She wasn't with them.' Baxter hesitated, having trouble finding his words. 'Haugen took her. They flew out. They could be heading anywhere in the country. Sorry, mate.'

'Haugen is on board that cruiser. I just saw him. There's a chance my mother is too.'

He suddenly gasped as a stabbing pain sheared through his forehead and his body twitched.

'You all right?' Baxter suddenly said. 'Mate, get out of there, there's nothing more you can do.'

Theo fought the pain aside as the ship began to close up.

'If I leave now, they will be trapped here until they ...' He couldn't bring himself to say 'die'. Desperate, he looked around for anything that would give him an edge. 'Xif, how do I get on board?'

'It's impossible.' Her reply was typically blunt.

Theo watched in despair as the cruiser began to rise. He'd lost his mother, and now he was about to lose Clemmie.

Chapter Thirty-Nine

Clemmie stood in the middle of the police cruiser's circular chamber, the walls nothing more than bland white curves that offered a harsh illumination from within. There was no sense of movement and no other sound.

She tried to move, but the red octagonal pads she stood on effectively bolted her to the ground in a vertical confinement field. Only when she pounded the invisible wall did it fleetingly appear as fading ripples around her fists.

The effort caused a wave of dizziness. Closing her eyes just made the pain in her head increase. Her jaw felt strange – tingling, almost – and when she moved her hand, she noticed there was a slight delay between her intentions and the avatar. It was less than a second, but noticeable: textbook Lag.

A pain in her shoulder fought for attention. She gently moved the burned circular patch of sleeve to peer beneath. The digital flesh was puckered and ragged, but it had stopped painfully haemorrhaging code.

'Well, aren't you a handful?' DI Frasier said, stepping into her field of vision.

He regarded her with a lecherous grin, nudging her containment octagon with his foot. It slid like a puck on ice, revealing Clive alongside, trapped in another confinement field.

Clive spoke up. 'Dominic Lewinsky's crimes are exposed. All you can do now is run, and how long do you think you can do that for?'

Frasier's smile vaporised. Without warning he punched the Slif hard in the stomach. Or at least the approximation of it. The blow hurt Clive, but he couldn't resist a defiant snarl. Clemmie noted the detective had no problem reaching into the confinement field, indicating that it only operated one way.

'Your knowledge of Slif physiology is pathetic,' Clive calmly stated.

Frasier snarled and punched Clive in his throat. The Slif gurgled in pain and hung his head, but with no need to breathe it was little more than a token injury.

'You're only alive so we can track down the rest of the Children of Ellul. When we're done, I will personally delete you and everyone you care for.' He lifted Clive's head so he could look the Slif in the eyes. 'And when Lewinsky finally gets the keys to his rightful kingdom back, your kind will be the first to go.'

'That's genocide!' Clemmie spat.

Frasier's mouth twisted in disbelief.

'Do you ever listen to yourself, darling? Genocide?' He gestured around. 'We're in a computer simulation.' He poked a finger in Clive's chest. 'None of this is real. All we'll be doing is eradicating some stray programs.' He shot the

Slif a hateful look. 'Stamping out a virus in the system.'

Clemmie stared defiantly at him. 'You're pathetic.'

Frasier backhanded her across the face. She felt the pain as sharply as if it had been real.

'And you're just another soft liberal snowflake. The product of a faulty generation who never knew hardship, but still feel they have the right to moan about it. You think you and your pals have actually done anythin' to stop us?'

The despair on Clemmie's face served to fuel his delight. He turned her around so she could now see the area behind her. She gave a sharp intake of breath when she saw Haugen, Dominic Lewinsky and Mirri quietly talking as they cast dark looks in her direction. But it was Ella, her containment field just feet away, who surprised her most.

'Ella, it's Clemmie. Can you hear me?'

Inwardly she was monitoring every word, and there was a definite slur. Her mouth and tongue were not quite co-operating.

'Ella?' She noticed a slight roll of the head. Ella's painted lips parted, but no words came out. Clemmie couldn't shake the unsettling feeling she was watching her dying throes. 'Stay focused. We're coming for you.'

Frasier gave a little laugh. 'Nobody's coming for either of you, darlin'. You don't win this game. All we need to know now is where you are.'

'I'm right here.'

'You know damn well what I mean, sweetheart. Where is this fine body located in The Real?' He slowly ran his gaze up and down her. 'It would be most grievous if anythin' happened to it. All you have to do is open your mind, ping me an Echo so we can trace you. Then I personally guarantee you can sink back down and save that beautiful mind of yours.'

Clemmie pretended to consider.

'Do you know what you remind me of? One of those desperate shopping channel hosts trying to sell useless shit after midnight.' She arched an eyebrow. 'Maybe that could be a new career for you? If you ever survive being gang-raped in prison, that is.'

His lip trembled with repressed fury. Then he laughed and addressed Mirri.

'You said she'd be trouble.'

He held out his hand and a golf-ball-sized orb floated over his palm. A series of interlocking golden rings slowly revolved around a small red flare of light.

'You know what this is?'

Clemmie shook her head.

Frasier casually tossed it in the air and caught it.

'It's what all the kids on the street want. It's a pax. A whole packet of emotions delivered straight to the noggin.' He tapped her head again, two slow solid thumps. 'Your pal, Rex, tried one. Experienced the full emotional gauntlet of being slowly carved up a piece at a time until he ...' He placed his free hand over his heart and patted several times, each slower than the last. 'Died. Quite painfully too.'

Clemmie sucked in two halting breaths, fighting every urge to cry out. Frasier raised the pax so she could get a closer look.

'I am told by those who specialise in such things, this is a real eye-opener. A cardiac arrest. The good news is that it's not going to kill you – the old dear who supplied this survived. The bad news is, you're going to wish it did kill you.'

He slid the pax towards her. She tried to pull back, but butted the confinement field. It felt like a white-hot blade was piercing her forehead as Frasier pressed it into her skull.

Chapter Forty

Milton and Baxter carried the last of the women from the basement and laid her with the others on the front lawn, a safe distance from the burning house. They were all still locked in ascension, unable to be safely freed until their avatars could be tracked down.

With a squawk of sirens, flickering blue lights of police and fire engines appeared from the end of the cul-de-sac.

Blackeyes shouted and gesticulated. 'We need to go! Now!'

He hurried to join the Children of Ellul retreating around the side of the house.

Milton motioned to join them, but noticed Baxter hadn't moved. He was looking between the rescued women and the approaching cars.

'Bax, come on!'

He flinched as a burning section of the roof collapsed inside the house, sending up a swarm of embers.

Baxter indicated the women. 'We need to tell the Bill about what really happened here.'

'There's no time!' Milton's hand fluttered, encouraging

Baxter to join him. 'Lewinsky's already infiltrated the police force! They're not going to listen.'

'So we need somebody we can trust. Clem's dad needs to know what's happening to his daughter.'

Theo's voice suddenly cut in. 'That's a bad idea, Baxter. We don't know if he's been framed too, or if they're waiting for one of us to approach him.'

Firefighters were first out, tackling the blazing cars blocking the road. The police were amassing just beyond as the water hoses struck the wreckage. Milton silently pleaded with Baxter, but it was clear his mind was set.

'I've already called him, Milt. In case things go tits up with them.' He nodded to the approaching police, 'Then it's up to you.' He gave a shallow chuckle. 'Who the hell would've thought I'd sacrifice meself?' He shook his head in disbelief.

Milton gave him one final look ... then disappeared into the shadows.

Theo listened in despair as the cruiser rumbled overhead, following the motorway. In seconds it would be beyond his reach. He kicked the skiff in frustration. Something clattered in the vehicle's glovebox. Curious, he reached inside and extracted the small cylinder he had placed there earlier.

'Hey, Xif. How do I program a Physics Engine?'

There was an acute feeling of disembodiment as Clemmie doubled over. She clawed her chest, the muscles contracting like a vice. An involuntary gasp stuck in her throat as her heart jackhammered. The constricting sensation increased, becoming a black hole of pain sucking every breath and muscle around it towards a single point of excruciating pain.

Rivulets of sweat dripped down her nose and flashes of lightning burnt brief after-images across her retina. Her lips involuntarily peeled back, teeth gnashing painfully together just short of biting off her tongue.

Clemmie's peripheral vision warped, swirling Frasier's expression of fascinated delight. Everything else was a soft-focus blur as the System's foveation became useless. She pounded one fist against the shield, but her movements were so severely Lagged, she looked like a jerky stop-motion animation.

Frasier activated an exterior panel on her confinement unit that only he could see from the outside, and Clemmie was sent sprawling to the floor as her field collapsed. She doubled over, her entire body quaking.

The detective kneeled by her side, running a hand through her damp hair.

'Does it hurt?' Every muscle in Clemmie's body contracted, intensifying the pain. 'I can make it go away. See?'

He held his hand out, palm up, and the swirling pax drifted from her head. The pain instantly ceased and she lay sprawled on the floor, too weak to move.

'Now, try harder. Call up your location. Send me that Echo.'

'Fuck. You.'

Her defiance came in barely audible sound bites.

'People are more likely to survive a heart attack if they receive critical aid within minutes. I can have emergency responders on your location very quickly. Just Echo ...'

Clemmie wanted to fire off a volley of abuse, but she didn't have the energy. All her willpower was focused on the tiny part of her mind separated from the pain – a form of fight or flight that was stuck firmly into *fight* gear.

Weakly, she pressed just below her collarbone to alleviate the pain. The movement distracted Frasier from her other hand, the arm of which was crushed under her body, as she slipped it into her inner jacket pocket – a rare fashion addition in SPACE. With Lag it was as if she was operating in a thick liquid, compounded by trying to locate the pocket's narrow opening by delayed touch alone. But persistence paid off, and the sudden feel of cold metal confirmed the device she had taken from Clive's armoury was still there. Thank God Frasier was lazy enough to believe a containment field meant he didn't have to search her.

Her silence infuriated Frasier. He edged the pax closer to her face.

'Next time, I'll ram this so far into your cerebral cortex and play it on loop that you'll be eating through a straw for the rest of your miserable life. So, last chance. Where the fuck are you? I need that Echo.'

Without warning, the entire cruiser violently shook, pitching Frasier to the floor. Clemmie just saw the startled expressions on Lewinsky and Mirri, before hearing Haugen yell out:

'The *fok* is that?'

A blur of white phased through the walls like a phantom. It stopped in the centre of the room, forming into Theo. His second-skin had gone, replaced by his avatar – or how his avatar would have looked after a decade in the gym and some serious plastic surgery. He was muscular and taut, every inch a hackneyed superhero.

Haugen raised his arm, a pistol materialising in his hand.

'Theo? You think you're *fokking* Superman now?'

Rapid energy pulses spat from his gun. Frasier rolled on to his knees and joined in the fray. Theo was once again a blur, their shots passing harmlessly through him and striking the hull. In his ghostly form, he swung a right hook – and his arm kept extending like rubber. He punched Frasier so hard the man was lifted off the ground and cartwheeled through the air, smashing into the wall.

At the same time, Theo's other impossibly long arm lassoed around Haugen's wrist, forcing him to direct his fire towards Mirri and Lewinsky.

They vanished in a cloud of pixels. Clemmie wasn't sure if they had been shot or not, and didn't care. She had other plans. Free of the containment field, she could now see a red vertical panel suspended over Clive's octagon. It had a single round button on it. She summoned all of her energy and lunged for it. His shield immediately collapsed and the freed Slif sprung for Frasier.

Theo swung Haugen hard into the ceiling, then back down into the floor with such force the deck cracked. Before he could dole out more punishment, Haugen let off a shot point-blank. In Theo's new physics he moved faster than the energy bolt. He raised his arms to deflect the shot into the ceiling—

But not before the bolt struck the Physics Engine secreted in his palm. Pain singed Theo's hand and he dropped the cylinder, throwing himself forward as it rolled across the floor. Haugen tackled his legs, pulling him down as both men scrambled after it.

Clemmie staggered towards Ella. Punching the containment release she caught her in mid-fall, but she was too weak to support her, and they both collapsed in a heap.

'NO!'

This was from Haugen, his eyes blazing with contempt when he saw Ella was free. He vanished in a plume of particles as he ejected.

Seconds later Ella disappeared, presumably force-ejected by Haugen from The Real.

'MUM!'

Theo groped for the dispersing pixels. Such a forcible eject could have killed her.

Frasier, caught in Clive's tight bear hug, sneered as he prepared to eject.

Clive repositioned his grip.

'I think not.'

He unfurled his palm, revealing the pax. He slammed it hard into Frasier's ear. The detective's eyes widened in shock and he spasmed. The Slif dropped him, watching with contempt as Frasier clawed at his chest as the cardiac arrest seeped through him.

Theo tore his gaze away and dashed to Clemmie's side.

'Are you okay?'

She rubbed her chest, feeling weaker than she ever had in her life, but managed to nod. She traced a hand down his immaculately defined muscular chest.

'You're a superhero now?' she said weakly, managing a faint smile.

Theo squeezed her hand, but couldn't summon any cute comeback. He looked back to where Ella had been, only yards from him.

'I've lost her ...'

'No.'

With great effort, Clemmie shook her head. She held up a palm-sized pebble-shaped device with three barbs poking from the end. It was the item that had caught her eye in Clive's armoury.

Clive angled for a better look and nodded approvingly.

'A pheromone tracker. Impressive thinking for a human.'

Without warning, the entire craft around them began to shudder with such violence they were all briefly tossed in the air. Alarms warbled as the cruiser banked sharply, sliding them into a heap against the wall.

'There's nobody flying it!' said Clive with an urgency they hadn't heard before.

There was another ear-splitting bang, followed by the world around them suddenly going apeshit crazy. The craft began to spin like a centrifuge, crushing them against the wall. Then a series of bone-jarring impacts had them repeatedly flipped like pancakes to the roof, walls and floor. Stress cracks raced across the hull – then on the fourth bounce the front tore open.

The cruiser had come to rest against the entrance of an online banking consortium. A large crowd of spectators formed as Theo, Clemmie and Clive walked unsteadily out, holding one another for support.

'Anybody hurt?' Theo asked.

The Slif had a blue scar down his head where a piece of shattering debris had glanced off him.

'I'll survive.'

Theo examined Clemmie with concern. She was acting drunk. Each step was an effort as her legs crossed clumsily, almost tripping her.

'Clem, you have to eject.'

'You nee ... me he ...' She was barely coherent.

Theo turned her so they were nose to nose.

'Clem. Time to go. We'll eject together. On the count of three ... two ...'

She surprised him by suddenly ducking in and kissing him full on the lips. It was more of an unco-ordinated pressing of flesh, but the intention was clear. A smile flickered on her face, then she combusted into particles.

'Milt, Bax, you hear me?'

He frowned when neither replied. With the cruiser down and Clemmie ejected, communications should have been re-established.

'Theo?'

Theo looked at Clive – who was looking at the crowd as they were jostled apart by vPolice running from every direction.

Hundreds of them.

Then they saw why the comms had been severed. Some thirty police cruisers approached fast, filling the sky.

Theo and Clive slowly raised their hands in surrender.

In the back of the Land Rover, sandwiched between an inert Theo and Clemmie, Milton felt numb as the Children of Ellul fled the mansion. Blackeyes drove like a demon while they picked up the police chatter concerning Baxter's arrest.

Milton checked his Killer Kaiju stream was looping the footage of the Den he'd recorded. Pre-recorded moments before, his avatar solemnly narrated the terrors and trauma of emotional harvesting – a difficult thing to do when you look like a 1980s pop icon – but he reckoned he'd pulled it off with enough dignity and gravitas, although in retrospect he regretted giving the clips a 'triple thumbs-up' rating. However, the views were ticking towards three million and it was going viral. Any joy he felt about that was over-shadowed by the fresh memory of Clarion lying dead in her car. The cost of it was simply too high.

He suddenly leaped in his seat as Clemmie sharply jerked awake next to him with a faint scream. The car swerved as Blackeyes turned to see what was going on.

'Keep those blackies on the road, pal,' said Milton as he helped Clemmie remove her rig. 'How're you feeling?'

Her head twitched as she tried to open her eyes.

'She's ejected but in bad shape,' he relayed to Blackeyes. 'Clemmie?' He gently slapped her face, and couldn't help but smile when she weakly returned the gesture and lightly slapped his. 'I think you have severe Lag.'

'And a heart attack ...' she whispered.

'What?'

'A pax. He gave me a heart attack ...' She clawed feebly at her chest.

'We need to get her to a hospital!'

Clemmie shook her head, which shuddered erratically

due to Lag. She managed to grip the top of his T-shirt to pull him closer.

'No! Ella ... I injected her with a pheromone tracker.'

Milton's face lit up with the first bit of good news he'd heard.

'Brilliant! We can tell your father!'

Clemmie's face screwed up. 'No! Somebody in the police must have been covering the Dens. Somebody highly placed ...'

'Wait.' Milton was desperately trying to process the accusation. '*Your father?* But the other person on the loop was a *woman.*' Then it hit him. 'A second-skin! Jesus!'

Tears rolled down Clemmie's cheeks; she was utterly devastated.

'We can't tell him anything.'

'Um ... We may have a problem about that,' Milton said darkly.

Baxter scratched the rash forming on his wrists. He evidently had an allergy to being handcuffed.

He sat in the small interview room – no, not room, he thought, more a cube with grab grey walls. The table, and the chair he sat on, were moulded hard plastic and bolted down. He placed his hands in his lap and shifted his butt cheeks to stop them falling asleep.

Superintendent Martin Laghari sat opposite him, arms folded and brow knitted.

'I don't know where to begin.' He didn't take his eyes off Baxter. 'Murder. Harbouring a fugitive. Aiding and abetting criminal activities with Virts. Aiding and abetting an armed raid on private property with a known radical terrorist group. Arson—'

'It sounds bad when you put it like that.'

Martin looked to the ceiling for a moment, then back to Baxter.

'And mixing my daughter up in all of this ... By the time you serve your sentence, I swear the sun will have collapsed into a red dwarf.'

'Are you forgetting about that police corruption we uncovered?' Baxter was too exhausted to remain polite. 'And exposing Dominic Lewinsky for being the pile of shit he is. Oh, and the Dens *you're* supposed to be doing something about are the ones *we* just collared for you. You're welcome, *Martin.*'

'That's Superintendent Laghari to you,' Martin snapped back.

Since surrendering at the house, Baxter had transmitted the footage of the liberated women straight to Martin, complete with a message about corruption in the Met and, quite possibly, the City of London Police too. Martin had responded immediately, arriving in a police quad so Baxter could surrender directly to him. That annoyed the Met officers on the ground, who pointed out that the Superintendent's jurisdiction didn't extend beyond the Square Mile. That hadn't stopped Martin from bending the rules and exercising his vCrimes privileges.

'Why pick me up if you didn't believe me?'

'To find my daughter.'

Martin placed his hands on the table and shifted in his chair. He replayed Baxter's footage on his rig. Baxter's helmet had been confiscated the moment he'd been arrested and he was starting to feel naked without it.

'Ella Wilson is not with these women.'

Baxter sighed. 'For the hundredth time. They took her. She opened up the whole can of worms on these creeps, and they took her because she knows stuff that scares them. Knows how to bring them down. She can identify the conspirators like that Frasier bloke. She nailed Lewinsky.'

'She can identify *everybody* involved?'

Baxter rubbed his eyes and nodded. 'Pretty much. Some politicians too.'

Martin drummed his fingers thoughtfully.

'This is a lot to accept, Edwin. Without further evidence it doesn't vindicate my daughter, Theo, Milton, or you. Where's Lewinsky now? Where's my daughter?'

Baxter leaned back, unsettled by Martin's sudden intensity, and further irked by an uncomfortable thought nagging at the fringes.

'I'm wondering why Ella didn't just come to you for help.' He placed his cuffed hands on the table and stared levelly at Martin. 'She knew there was corruption *everywhere*. Not just the Met.' Martin's gaze cooled. 'I mean, if I was going to run Dens and sell hardcore paxes to the ruling elite, then I'd have the fuzz in my pocket. Especially the ones who are supposed to be *closing* them down. And if you're thinking of doing anything to shut me up, remember people know I'm with you.'

'Nobody knows where you are, Edwin. I kept your announcement off the grid because you never know who is listening.'

Baxter chuckled. 'You're right. Just you, me, Milton ... and Killer Kaiju's millions of subscribers.'

Martin went rigid. 'What?'

'Killer Kaiju's latest sensational review is about Den footage, including me being here. The world has a right to know what's going on, don't you think?'

He saw Martin's fingers clench into tight fists – then he forced himself to calm down.

'Mr Baxter, for the last time. Where are your friends? *And where is my daughter?*'

Chapter Forty-One

Clemmie pinched the bridge of her nose, bumping against the side window as they took a turn at speed. A peculiar tingling sensation had developed around her lips and down the left side of her body. She thought back to Clarion and wondered if this was how it had all started for her.

She had transferred the pheromone tracking data to Milton and Blackeyes, and they could now all see a fine cloud of coloured particles suspended in the air around the car, putting her in mind of standing in the midst of a 3-D scatter graph. The dots were mostly pale blue, but they cycled through the spectrum as they looked around, finding a vein of pink particles that flowed from the same direction. And at the end of which would be Ella.

'Theo? Where are you?' Milton sounded desperate now. Since Clemmie's arrival back he had been trying to raise him. 'Clive?'

The car took a right, Blackeyes keeping pheromones in front of them. As they accelerated the pink shades became denser and darker, shifting towards red. The motion made her feel terrible – or was it the revelation about her father that was a stake through her heart?

Since returning from university, she had seen how wrapped up he had been in his work. He spoke about the Dens furtively and his casual racism towards the Slifs had increased exponentially since she was last home. For whatever reason, he had chosen to side with Lewinsky's plans for monopolising SPACE. What is more, he knew Ella. Knew how her foibles could be played to manipulate her. It took ingrained callousness to be involved with the Dens, paxes and other shit Lewinsky had been purveying. She saw how 'Mirri' had watched her suffer the cardiac arrest with a doctor's air of detachment. She rubbed her chest. Every breath hurt. Second-skins changed appearance, but they didn't · mask intention. How could he have stood by and watched that happen to his daughter?

Xif's voice suddenly pulled her back from self-torture to physical sickness.

'Xif here,' barked the Slif, sounding distracted. 'I've found them. Patching through a stream from Nu London.'

A window popped up in Clemmie's and Milton's rigs of the crashed police cruiser. The vantage point was from Clive's personal drone, unblocked as it was streaming through SPACE. The massive circle of vPolice was increasing by the moment, the sky black with cruisers.

'Oh my God,' sighed Milton. 'They must have every vCrime cop in the country right there.'

Milton looked puzzled. 'What's Theo doing?'

Theo's right arm was half-raised and wobbling erratically.

His index and middle finger were defiantly extended. Clemmie shook her head in disbelief.

'It could be Lag. But it looks like he's sticking up two fingers at the drone. What a moron.' Clemmie threw a look at Milton. 'He gets that from you.'

It slowly dawned on Milton what his friend was doing.

'He's signalling for help.'

Clemmie rolled her eyes as she recalled flicking the Vs was Killer Kaiju's adolescent signature move when he hated a game.

'How can *you* help ...?'

'Xif, the retention fields mean you can't eject. But do they stop you from *ascending*?'

After a brief pause, she answered. 'No. And we may be thinking the same thing.'

'Can it be done?'

Milton was distracted as he accessed his personal streaming studio.

The pain in Clemmie's head increased. Following the conversation was proving to be impossible. She tried to ask what was happening, but her mouth refused to co-operate.

Xif answered Milton. 'From here I can temporarily adjust ascension parameters before the System resets it. There will be a small window.'

'Good enough.'

Before Clemmie could summon the energy to speak, Milton's streaming channel suddenly appeared on her rig. Killer Kaiju with a toothy white smile, round shades and a 1980s red suit with winged shoulder pads that could take out somebody's eye. He was livestreaming the message, so she heard Milton's usual voice in one ear; his virtual alter ego's heavily digitised showbiz accent came through the other. Both were speaking slightly out of phase – or was that more Lag?

'Hey, folks, it's me. Big soz for being off the streams for so long, but you've seen my loops on those Dens. They've gone viral!'

Clemmie glanced at Milton on the back seat next to her. He was really getting into his role, and she found it difficult to reconcile the two Miltons, with massively contrasting personalities. Watching him perform was like seeing him become possessed.

'I got some breaking news – one Killer Kaiju can't get into the details of right now. But believe me when I say, it's a matter of life or death. There's a plot to subvert SPACE – to abuse it so we all suffer. And there is one man risking his neck to save it. And he really needs your help *right now*.'

Milton streamed Xif's drone footage of Theo – still in his superhero second-skin – surrounded by vPolice. He sent out a virtual-Echo, pinpointing Theo's location.

'This is Alan ... Aardvark.' Both Clemmie and Milton winced at the rubbish alias. Milton might be good at pandering to his audience, but he was useless at improvisation. 'And he's about to get arrested by the very people I'm talking about. I want to see my millions of subscribers zeroing in on Aardvark's location right now. Bring on the biggest DoS Mobbing SPACE has ever seen!'

He logged out with a sharp exhalation of breath.

'What will happen?' Clemmie asked uncertainly.

Milton shrugged. 'I have no idea.'

*

It started with a low rumble that everybody in the street felt.

Theo's headache was unbearable, and the bass tones merely aggravated it. Avatars, Slifs and vCops looked around in alarm. Police warnings sounded, presumably aimed at Clive and Theo, but were unintelligible. The background chords of panic from the crowd increased as audio throbbed in and out.

The buildings around them began to vibrate. Not the slow lolloping sways of an earthquake, but short sparky move-ments, as if they were deciding whether to exist or not.

Theo managed a grin. 'Milton came through!'

Then, quite suddenly, three million, eight hundred and forty-six people suddenly descended into a single square yard. While the System could easily render a million or more people standing side by side, squeezing them together caused major processing problems. Quantum processors simply short-circuited under the strain.

Audio was the first to crash. The moment Milton's fan base descended, it was as if millions of voices suddenly cried out as one ... then utter silence.

The sky tessellated into a network of triangles. Buildings were next, colours bleaching as the structures rapidly broke down from solid renders to shaded three-dimensional forms, then to vector lines.

Then nothing.

The ground, traffic, and every detail with them glitched and melted into darkness as the System's emo and Physics Engines went offline. Gone was any simulation of touch, smell, gravity or mass. Avatars were next, breaking down into basic stick figure forms like some kind of bad Eastern European animation.

Only Slifs were unaffected, as their entire ecosystem had been migrated on to backup servers when independence was declared. From their point of view, the DoS was ridding them of an invasive species.

Clive hooked Theo's deteriorating avatar around the waist and effortlessly hoisted him off his feet and ran. With physics, time and distance screwed up, it seemed to Clive that he had only taken a few strides and then he was suddenly a mile further down the street, back into fully rendered SPACE.

He dropped the suddenly heavy Theo to his feet, now fully reformed as his usual avatar. Theo had experienced the entire event in a sort of virtual coma, unable to interact or move. But now out of the DoS impact zone, normality was returning, and he turned to see the black hole punctured in the heart of Nu London.

A tsunami of noise suddenly battered Theo's ears as he reconnected with The Real and Milton yelling at the top of his lungs.

'I see them! I see them!'

It took Theo several attempts to access Milton's live stream. The Lag was now severely impairing his mental calibration, not just his physical synchronisation.

Milton's Land Rover was hurtling down a wide A-road, jumping red traffic lights and swerving around keep left signs. Ahead, Lewinsky's quadcopter thundered low over the street.

'We can't bring it down without endangering the oc-
cupants,' said Milton. His view panned behind him as he
focused on four police quads swooping down, sirens blazing. 'Ah shit, the fuzz is on our tail!'

Before Milton looked away, Theo noticed their insignia
wasn't Met.

'City cops!'

Clemmie pinged her Echo. They were beyond hiding now.

'Theo, do you have geo-lock?' Her voice trembled from
the effort of speaking.

Theo's rig matched Clemmie's Echo with his own position.
They were in the same damned street.

His slushy thinking connected his crashed police cruiser
with the quad Milton was chasing. Had the cruiser been the
quadcopter's avatar? Theo wasn't sure if physical objects
could have their own avatars, but couldn't see why not.

'Xif, do you have a lock?' asked Clive, peering into the
middle distance. 'Shoot it down.'

Theo wasn't thinking fast enough to argue.

Events were moving too quickly for Baxter to keep up.

One moment he was being interrogated by Martin, the
bastard's nefarious plan fracturing before his very eyes.
Then the superintendent was called from the room, and
dashed back moments later, hauling a cuffed Baxter ahead
of him.

Baxter had tried to make a scene, but his claims that he
was being kidnapped merely generated bemused smiles
from the corrupt cops around him. He was hustled into the
back of a police quad and was a little surprised when Martin

strapped Baxter's rig on him before sitting shotgun with the pilot. Baxter attempted to raise his friends, but the police had set the rig to *receive only*, leaving him mute to the outside world.

Within minutes they were soaring over London, sirens blazing. It didn't take long to locate Milton's Land Rover recklessly weaving through traffic on the A13, pursuing Lewinsky's quad flying just over the street lights. A download icon suddenly flashed in his visor and a small hand grenade icon formed, just as Theo had described it. He reached out, plucking the augmented object into the palm of his hand.

His eyes narrowed as he chose between orchestrating his own escape or freeing Ella. He focused on the 'copter in front. With one hand he unclipped his seat belt, then using all his strength he hurled the grenade overhead with both cuffed hands. It passed effortlessly through their quad's windshield.

'What the hell are you doing?' shouted Martin, who could only see Baxter's actions before he slumped back into his seat.

The grenade clipped the tail of Lewinsky's quad and splattered across the hull. Black tendrils searched for the engines and sensitive electronics. Seconds later black smoke poured from the rear props and the quad wildly rotated to the road below.

Theo watched it all on Milton's stream. Lewinsky's quadcopter corkscrewed down, narrowly missing a cluster of swerving black cabs, before belly-flopping through roadworks in a burst of orange traffic cones.

But his attention snapped to the virtual street before him as two avatars suddenly ascended, geo-locked to the crash site. One was Ella, who immediately dropped to the floor. The other was Mirri, who hadn't yet noticed him or Clive. She stooped and dragged Ella upright by her hair with one hand. The other held a curved *Avasta* machete.

'No!' Theo screamed as he stopped, unsure what to do next.

Mirri turned, a look of shock passing across her face. She pressed the blade close to Ella's throat. He could see tiny pulses of data speeding along grooves within the modified blade; it was a Killer.

'Don't come any closer, Theo, or she dies.'

Theo extended his hands to show he was unarmed.

'You're out of moves. It's over.'

Mirri's gaze darted to Clive, who was slowly edging forwards.

'If that Virt comes any closer, I'll kill him too.'

Clive stopped.

Theo muted the volume on Milton's point-of-view livestream. The window was becoming too much of a distraction as he watched Milton and Blackeyes dash from their Land Rover, towards the smoking quadcopter wreckage. The aircraft's gull-wing doors opened and Haugen staggered out. Blood pumped from a deep gash across his disfigured face. His eyes were wide and crazy as he hauled an automatic rifle from the aircraft and opened fire.

Milton hit the deck as bullets sprayed around him. Something caught his attention as he glanced back to see the lead police quads landing. Martin quickly exited before the skids touched the road, joining in the firefight with his service automatic.

Haugen was silently shot multiple times in the chest and toppled, dead, into the trench workers had been excavating in the road. Frowning, Theo switched focus between the drama on the livestream and Mirri threatening his mother right in front of him. The mere presence of Martin in The Real had dashed his *Mirri/Martin* conspiracy apart.

'Who the hell are you?' he shouted.

Mirri looked at him in surprise.

'Don't you know?' She yanked Ella's hair to expose more throat, the knife never wavering. 'You didn't find the last packet from her?'

Theo kicked himself – with time against them he hadn't looked for any further clues. What had he missed? He tried to remain poker-faced, but wasn't sure he pulled it off.

Mirri traced the tip of the blade down Ella's throat for emphasis. A fine incision appeared, weeping blood.

'When this ungrateful bitch came to me to plead and beg for help, everything changed, Theodore. She had no idea about the scope of our operation. But we gave her a chance. Let her prove herself. Then she came back and tried to *blackmail* me.'

On the muted video stream, Milton was back on his feet and cowering behind Martin, who was closing in on the quadcopter, holding his pistol in a Weaver stance. Dominic Lewinsky crawled from the wreckage, attempting to hold his hands up, but a broken leg caused him to fall flat on the road. From Mirri's reaction, Theo was pretty sure she wasn't receiving any such feed from The Real.

'You've kept her ascended for far too long,' Theo said, aware that his own speech was slurring. It was difficult to maintain focus, but he pressed on. 'She's not a threat any more. The cat's out of the bag.'

'She's my bargaining chip. There are people out there – famous people, rich people. All of them used the Dens, they all buy paxes. They all got hooked on emotional thrills. If they see me arrested, they'll turn a blind eye, hiding behind their second-skins. But this one ...' She yanked Ella's hair again. 'This one found out their identities, all of them. Even the ones I didn't want to know. And you're going to help me find them. They're my get out of jail free card.'

Theo shook his head. 'I'm so Lagged, I couldn't help you if I wanted to.'

His focus shifted back to the video stream as Martin planted his boot in Lewinsky's back and roughly cuffed his wrists together. The other police quads had landed, more officers running to assist him.

Milton stepped away, carefully peering into the crashed aircraft's open door. He saw a leg, speckled with Haugen's blood. A few steps closer improved his view ...

It was Ella, slouched in the back, her body twisted from the impact. He moved closer, slowing when he noticed the *second* passenger strapped in a seat next to Ella ...

'I don't care how you feel, Theo,' Mirri continued with confidence. 'You and your Virt need to start finding that last packet she was hoarding. I'm not going to eject until you do, and neither is she.'

Milton's stream panned up, following his gaze across the body, which was definitely female ... up to her *face*. Theo wanted to gasp. Instead an icy grip encompassed him and he felt suddenly drained.

He focused on Mirri and held his hands higher and bowed his head in defeat. His Lag was so disjointed that his words were now coming marginally faster than his actions.

'I already have the list.'

The woman's eyes widened. Theo glanced at Clive. At the same time he instructed his body to leap into action. As expected, it Lagged ...

'Clive, show *Augusta* the list.'

He anticipated the Slif would hesitate; he was an awful liar and the plan required an element of improvisation which Slifs were not known for. Mirri turned expectantly to Clive – before the greedy look on her face melted away as she turned back to Theo.

'What did you call me?'

She was too late.

Theo's Lagged reactions kicked in and he sailed through the air towards her. He'd pitched all his weight into the arm wielding the blade. The machete jerked away from Ella's throat and spun in the air. Mirri lost her grip on Ella as she fought to keep her balance.

Theo reached for the still-spinning knife. It was a dangerous gamble while Lagged. His fingers passed through the blade in a searing flash of pain and the digital tips of his fingers puffed into pixels, but there was still enough of his digits left to wrap around the handle as it slipped into his palm. Without hesitation, Theo slashed the blade across Mirri's arm.

It wasn't a killing stroke – but it inflicted maximum pain.

*

Clemmie pushed Milton aside and gawped at the woman strapped in the quadcopter's passenger seat.

'Augusta ...' said Clemmie faintly as she joined Milton.

Her stepmother was the last person she'd expected to see, but the huge relief that her father wasn't implicated in the mess numbed any feelings of pity she had for the woman. A combination of Lag and shock rooted her to the spot.

Martin pushed past her and snatched the rig off his wife. For a moment she was motionless ... then her eyes flickered open and she gazed at Martin with a faint smile.

'Hello, love ...'

Martin's gaze hardened at the woman he loved, unable to find the words. Instead he motioned to remove Ella's rig.

'Dad, wait!' Clemmie pulled him back. 'She's Locked in. Theo's with her.'

Theo ignored the particles of ejected Augusta that twinkled around him. He sat at his mother's side, cradling her head in his lap.

'Ella? Ella?' She didn't respond. 'Mum?'

He blinked. Was that a twitch of the cheek? An attempt to smile? Or just wishful thinking?

Clive kneeled down and ran a hand over her forehead.

'You must take her out, now.'

Marshalling his rapidly fogging thoughts, he activated Xif's Lock-in app and transferred it to Ella's rig. Theo heard a chime as his own rig synced. He squeezed his mum's hand.

'Here it goes ...'

He remotely initiated her eject command. A tiny pressure

wave clapped across his ears, amplifying his migraine as he absorbed her biofeedback. His head threatened to explode – then she exploded in millions of tiny points of light.

Theo strained to watch Milton's feed to see if Ella responded in The Real, but flashes of jagged light tore through his vision. Both worlds went black, the pain vanished and he felt nothing.

Chapter Forty-Two

It took two weeks to rouse Theo from the medically induced coma neurosurgeons used to control the swelling in his brain, brought on by the overload of chemicals and stimulants his extended immersion had triggered.

It had worked, saving him from severe brain damage, although his right hand still trembled every time he held it level. In SPACE, the machete may have been a killer blade, but it wasn't actually capable of slicing apart real flesh. However, the pain it transmitted had permanently damaged the nerves in his fingers.

He had also developed a slight lisp which the doctors thought would be permanent. Theo found it annoying, embarrassing even, but it was a small price to pay for being alive. The specialist treating him suspected that the migraines he had endured since childhood had helped fend off the Lag effects. Anybody else should have been a vegetable by now.

Clemmie had undergone a similar induced coma, but had come out the other side physically intact. Just not emotionally. He had tried to visit her, but the doctors attending her had refused. The news that her family had been shattered was taking its toll.

He was allowed to visit his mother, who had also been placed unconscious and was attached to an army of drips, sensors and monitors. CAT scans revealed lesions on her brain, the effects of which would only be known when she awoke.

He sat by her side when he could, but found it difficult to look at her gaunt face. She seemed to have aged over the week. To while away the hours, he talked about whatever pointless rubbish he could in the hope that his voice would register at some level. Inevitably he would run out of things to say and launch into a series of questions: why had she quit her police training? Was it because of him? Was she disappointed he had followed in her failed footsteps?

It was a catharsis for him, especially as he didn't want to hear the answers. He was pretty sure he knew them already.

Days ticked by and he felt stronger each morning, but by the early evening he was just as exhausted. Time in between was spent in intensive physiotherapy to combat the effects of Lag, although he was acutely aware that the throng of doctors were eager to study such a rare case of prolonged immersion.

While struggling to stay awake in the evening, Theo was then exposed to relentless questions from a police officer. Detective Chief Superintendent Clarke was a young black woman who had such a melodious voice it did little to keep him awake. She specialised in traumatic cases and dutifully drilled through all the details, often circling back on a question to tease out details. With nothing to hide, Theo was frank and open, although the only time he hesitated was when asked to describe Clive and Xif and their location. He knew vCrimes had no jurisdiction over them, but felt obliged to keep their details as muddy as possible. Who knew what retaliation they may face in the virtual?

Without the benefit of a rig, Theo remained isolated from the rest of the world. After four days, Baxter and Milton began to make regular visits. Baxter smiled when he first saw his friend, but remained uncharacteristically taciturn. Milton, however, was effusive and unable to sit down for long. He would pace around Theo's bed, gesticulating when he spoke.

They had been subjected to intense police interviews about the whole terrible affair and only allowed to see their immediate families. Milton was particularly pleased with the five-star hotel they had been put up in during the process, and had tallied up an epic room service bill.

They too had been isolated from the news, and only when leaving the hotel had they been subjected to the media storm that was happening. News crews smothered them with a barrage of questions.

With Baxter sitting back, his hands clasped together, it was up to Milton to fill in the details.

Clive had forcibly ejected Theo, giving him precious seconds that may have saved his life. Their Slif allies had faded into obscurity, despite being heralded as heroes as the truth behind Dominic Lewinsky unfolded. Likewise, Blackeyes had slipped away while the police surrounded the fallen quadcopter, and the rest of the Children of Ellul had disappeared despite a worldwide manhunt and a promise of immunity if they testified.

The spotlight had focused on the twenty-nine women liberated from Lewinsky's basement. Using Xif's app, they had all been located in Joy Divisions across Nu London and safely ejected. Despite their care, three had died from Lag, causing ripples in the international community. Half were still in comas; those that came round suffered a range of physical after-effects, including three unable to walk, two no longer able to speak and one blinded. Their plights touched the world and caused further public arguments about using SPACE.

Theo tried not to act hurt when they said they'd briefly seen Clemmie. Baxter reported that she looked fine, but clearly hadn't slept properly for days. The doctors said she'd only survived the pax-induced heart attack because of Lag. She hadn't even had chance to talk to her father, who had been placed on leave as the investigation into his wife's activities unfolded.

When the news came in, it was Baxter who told him of Rex's murder. As the body count increased, with Sergeant Jones, Clarion and now Rex, Theo felt guilty for involving them. It was evident from Baxter's face that he felt the same.

Augusta had squarely placed the blame on Dominic Lewinsky. The two had met during a Mayoral political fund raiser and it had resulted in an affair. One thing led to another, and Augusta's hatred for Slifs had chimed well with Lewinsky's desire to reclaim his father's legacy. The first step in this was to become the pre-eminent owner of the Den network, taking them out of the hands of the petty crooks who originally established them. The more they controlled, the tighter their grip became on the emotional streams into SPACE.

Diligent journalists dissected every aspect of the unfolding story and, when they discovered Augusta had used Martin's police access to orchestrate the plan, she was reframed as the mastermind, using a weak and vulnerable Lewinsky, while her husband provided a handy scapegoat if it all went wrong.

Baxter shied away from the press attention, but Milton took to it like a politician to a bribe. Now his alter ego was exposed, he was enjoying more fame than ever, and Killer Kaiju's subscription base had exploded. He had finally broken the geek-branded shackles he'd always been bound by and it had given him a new lease of life.

Baxter, on the other hand, had become more subdued. The sight of the women in the Den had made him question everything and he'd decided to quit uni. He didn't know what he wanted to do, but a radical shake-up of his life was required.

Finally, Theo was discharged and with trepidation he returned to his flat alone. It was exactly as he'd left it, which was dispiriting as the door had been left open. Clearly no thief thought they had anything worth stealing.

Still broke, he'd been forced to shop at a local food bank, ignoring the wide-eyed stares of almost everybody he passed. Without his rig on he was easily identifiable. Unlike the movies, he wasn't subjected to a rapturous round of applause or cheering. Nobody dare approach or speak to him and he left the food bank in silence.

The first night home he took his mother's certificate off the wall and lay on the creaking sofa, examining it. The paper had yellowed over the years, but he noticed how clean the glass was. Unlike the rest of the flat, it was the one possession Ella had regularly taken pride in.

Unable to sleep, he eventually succumbed to using his rig to access media streams. His social media sites were crammed with comments and friend requests, all of which he ignored. With no taste for venturing into SPACE even for a quick game, he cycled through the news streams, filling in any blanks Milton and Baxter had left.

The arrests had rapidly led to more gangs and Dens being busted across the country. Hundreds of men and women held in conditions of slavery were freed, while the body count of those who had been killed for a quick pax fix began to climb to disturbing levels.

The London arrests were the breakthrough needed, and enabled authorities around the world to crack down on the problem. Lewinsky's global network crumbled within the week. The number of those indentured climbed into the thousands. The number of those murdered was astronomically higher.

A week after being discharged, Theo returned to hospital to watch the doctors bring Ella out of her coma. The entire time he held her hand as the cocktail of drugs took hold and she eventually woke up with a long drawn-out gasp.

'Hi, Mum,' said Theo, gently kissing her forehead.

It took almost a minute for her to focus on him; her voice was barely audible.

'What kept you?'

A wicked smile crossed her face, and she squeezed his hand. Her grip may have been barely perceptible, but it was there.

Theo wept with relief.

'She'll be in for another month at least,' said a specialist, taking him aside. 'She's lost the use of her legs for now. Whether she'll be wheelchair bound for life, we can't tell. Her short-term memory is patchy. That could fix itself, but ...'

Theo tuned out the rest. It was a long list of ailments and woes. He was just thankful to have her back, and he was certain she'd make a full recovery. If anybody could spoil a doctor's carefully considered prognosis, it would be Ella.

It was the end of the summer and Theo still hadn't spoken to Clemmie. Throughout subsequent interviews, debriefs, cross-examinations and snooping press ambushes, they had seen one another but hadn't the opportunity to talk. Neither of them had dared ascend, or use social channels. Theo began to wonder how his parents had ever met without social media to guide them.

The moment finally came when he visited his mother and found Clemmie already there, having delivered a bouquet of flowers and apparently talking for over an hour. For the first time in weeks they were finally alone in the hospital corridor outside Ella's room.

'Sorry ...'

It was the first word that spewed from Theo's mouth. It was the beginning of a heartfelt apology he had replayed over the last few weeks. But that's as far as he got before drying up.

'No need to be sorry.' Clemmie slipped her hands into her jeans pockets and managed to look both coy and defensive. 'I saw my dad last week for the first time. Do you know what we did?'

Theo dared not ask. The blame he was experiencing from tearing her family apart kept him awake at night. He was surprised to see a flicker of a smile on her face, but noticed a subtle paralysis too – not as severe as Clarion's, but a permanent hallmark of her experience.

'He hugged me. It was the first time I can remember since I was a kid. Since Mum left us. He hugged me and cried.' Tears moistened her eyes, but she drew in a sharp breath and was suddenly the fighter Theo had fallen in love with. 'So yeah, we're actually getting on better than ever.'

Theo stared at his feet.

'You risked everything to help me save her –' he gave a small nod towards his mother's room – 'and all I did was accuse your dad—'

Clemmie thumped a palm into his chest to cut him off. He winced; the broken ribs still hurt.

'Pause right there, moron. I thought the *exact* same thing. I didn't expect it would be Bitchy McBitch face.' She glowered at her feet. 'I don't know what is worse. That she was a criminal mobster, abusing all those people, or that she cheated on my dad with *Lewinsky*.' She caught Theo's look and rolled her eyes. 'Of course I know which was worse ...'

Theo shifted his weight from one foot to the other.

'It's going to be quiet without you here,' he managed. 'Well, not quiet. Just fewer guns and running around almost getting killed. I'll miss our crazy bike rides down by the river.' Clemmie's laugh made him smile. 'There's talk of the government paying for Mum's care costs. So at least I get to go back to *Synger*. Yay ...'

He sarcastically punched the air.

Clemmie looked thoughtfully up at the ceiling.

'I was thinking of maybe hanging around a little longer. I asked for a year out of my course. I may even transfer – there's a decent one here.' Their eyes met. 'And I thought it would be irresponsible to leave you on your own.'

Theo took hold of her hands and was relieved when she didn't recoil.

'And here I was thinking you were the one who needed supervision.'

Clemmie gave a dismissive laugh. 'Well, you've kind of grown on me. Like a mould or a fungus.'

Theo pulled her closer, their foreheads resting together.

'Fungus, huh?'

'Yeah.' She slipped her arms around his neck. 'That lisp of yours ... you know it's kind of cute?'

Then she pulled him in for a long kiss.

It was unquestionably better than the virtual one. Maybe The Real had something going for it after all.

Acknowledgements

Jumping into a new adventure always requires support and backup, and people are often unaware of the inspiration they provide. So special thanks go to Tom Witcomb for his unwavering support and seeking out new lands of opportunity. Ben Willis, who didn't mind his vision taken to unforeseen destinations and provided ample cheerleading the whole way. Sabrina for all those nudges in the right direction. Pete, who pelted me with all those awesome books when we were kids. And my parents, especially my dad, who put me on the right track without ever knowing it.

Credits

Victoria Laws
Rachael Hum
Ellie Kyrke-Smith
Frances Doyle
Georgina Cutler

Operations
Jo Jacobs
Sharon Willis
Lisa Pryde
Lucy Brem